THE
SAFE
PLACE

D1477878

L.A. LARKIN

THE SAFE PLACE

bookouture

Published by Bookouture in 2021

An imprint of Storyfire Ltd.
Carmelite House
50 Victoria Embankment
London EC4Y 0DZ

www.bookouture.com

ISBN: 978-1-80019-709-1
eBook ISBN: 978-1-80019-708-4

To all firefighters, everywhere

CHAPTER ONE

Monday, September 3, 2018

The night sky burned a livid orange.

The intruder stood on the back deck that doubled as a toddler's play area and gazed down the mountain, beyond the small town of Eagle Falls, beyond the lake that slithered between the mountain range and the national park, and watched the wildfire wreak a magnificent destruction. The winds fanned the wall of crimson flames that felled Bear Creek National Park's mighty forest, leaving nothing but a blackened wasteland in its wake. Bordering the park, the popular vacation town of Waterford glowed white, as if scorched by a giant blowtorch. In the darkness, the headlights of fleeing vehicles were like a line of white-hot ants, scurrying one way and then the next, navigating the hairpin bends to reach safety.

Why flee from something so beautiful, so cleansing? They should embrace fire's power, something the arsonist had learned to do, and to do well. Of course, the wildfire was inevitable. The hottest summer and longest drought on record had made the forests tinderbox dry. Everyone prayed for rain, even those without a religion, but no rain was forecast for September. People were calling it the heatwave from hell.

The arsonist saw it as an opportunity.

All manner of crimes could be concealed by fire, and house fires were the arsonist's specialty. They were more personal, more targeted, and more gratifying, even if it took detailed planning and the risk of being caught was higher. The result was worth it.

The intruder turned to face the four-bedroom bungalow. At one in the morning, the residents were fast asleep, immune to the smoky night air or any outside noise because of the thrum from the air conditioning units. Most folks around those parts relied on open windows and fans to keep them cool in summer. However, installing air conditioning units was what the house owner did for a living, and he had equipped every room with them. What's more, dense forest hid the bungalow from the road. The family of four would be dead long before anyone had a chance to report the incident to the already overstretched fire service.

The prowler swallowed back a cough. The face mask, which felt like a cardboard igloo over sweaty skin, kept nose and mouth concealed. It was supposed to also seal out smoky air and was failing to do so. Over a black beanie, a headlamp produced a focused point of light, enabling the intruder to see without waking the sleeping occupants. A gust of hot wind whistled through the tall cedars and Douglas fir trees. It shook the stalks of the shriveled camelia bushes that lined the deck, the waxy leaves curled and crisp, the dying pink flowers scattered on the soil beneath. The arsonist spun around, staring one way and then the next, convinced somebody was laughing. It sounded like Naomi, a screechy laugh, like nails down a blackboard. Or was it Paul, a nasal, mocking, *ha ha ha*! The killer's blood boiled.

Don't mock me!

The wind died down and the sound faded.

Stay focused on the job. The pleasure comes later.

In one hand, a small mallet with a rubber head. In the other, a wooden wedge-shaped doorstop, so small it looked as if it might belong to a doll's house. A couple of taps with the mallet and the wedge was jammed tight into the gap between the sash window and its casing. First, the top panel of glass and then the bottom panel was rendered inoperable. That was the last of the windows jammed, bar one, and that one would be the killer's escape route. The little wooden wedges were perfect for the job: they ensured the windows couldn't be opened from the inside and they would also disintegrate in the fire, therefore leaving no evidence behind. Because this was going to be a tragic accident. The gas stove left on, a candle burning. How very sad, they would say.

Now to lock the doors and start the fire.

Carefully coating a square cotton handkerchief with honey, the arsonist stuck the handkerchief to the sash windowpane, just above the latch. One punch and the panel of glass fell into the living room, landing on carpet, the *crack* muffled by the sticky handkerchief. A moment's pause. Had anyone heard? Then sliding a gloved hand through the hole, the sash lock was unfastened, and the lower window lifted. By now the killer's latex-covered palms were slick with sweat. Once inside the house, the killer momentarily enjoyed the cool air conditioning before creeping along the corridor toward the kitchen.

Bedroom doors were closed. Snoring came from the parents' room. Stepping softly to avoid making squeaking noises on the kitchen's hardwood floor, the arsonist headed straight for the wooden rack on the wall where they kept their house keys. The rack had a family of owls carved into the top of it. Distracted by the rack's tasteless quaintness, the arsonist accidentally kicked the leg of a baby's highchair. It scraped across the floor and hit the wall with a *thud*. The killer's hand slid into the belt's holster and touched the reassuring solidity of the pistol, which was an insurance policy.

Nobody stirred.

A big exhalation.

Tugging the mask down, the intruder opened the fridge and took out a carton of milk and drank from it, relishing its cool creaminess. There was no need to worry about leaving behind DNA or fingerprints. There would be nothing left. However, being a careful type, the empty carton was returned to the fridge and the face mask pulled back into position.

There were two sets of house keys on the rack and a spare set in a kitchen drawer. The arsonist took all three sets, locked all exterior doors, then switched on the gas stove's four burners. There was a satisfying hiss. Knowing that gas sinks, a candle was placed on the hardwood floor and lit. No need for accclerant this time. The explosion would blow the kitchen apart. The killer crept back along the hallway, careful to avoid a toddler's blue tricycle.

Running into the nearest tree cover, the arsonist fumbled for a cigarette and used a brushed chrome Zippo to light it, then threw it into the paper-dry leaf litter. The yellow flames grew quickly. Two more cigarettes were lit and flicked away at different points around the bungalow. Lighting up the forest around the home was a precautionary measure: it would make it more difficult for firefighters to reach the house to save the occupants.

The executioner kept a safe distance but was near enough to watch the performance. Ribbons of red flames in the trees. A boom from the kitchen. Black smoke. Screams. *Ah, the screams.* Music to the ears. Eyes shut, right hand raised as if holding a baton to conduct an invisible orchestra, the killer waved a hand back and forth. A shudder of exquisite ecstasy. More screams, their final wails consumed by the jet-engine roar of the conflagration.

CHAPTER TWO

A cold wet nose on her cheek and a good deal of panting woke twenty-six-year-old Jessie Lewis from a fitful night's sleep. She kept her eyes shut, hoping her dog would let her sleep a little longer. It had been an uncomfortably hot night and from the warmth of the breeze blowing through her bedroom window, she guessed it was going to be another searingly hot day. Long dark strands of hair stuck to her temples as if they had been glued there as someone's idea of a joke, and her nightie clung to her sweaty body. Her one and only desk fan, a cheapie from a company she'd never heard of, had died during the night. The single cotton sheet lay in a bundled mess on the speckled brown carpet that still smelled of the previous occupant's feet.

Her one-bedroom wood cabin on a tree-covered slope had been a run-down vacation home when she bought it six months ago. She had needed to move out of the town quickly and the seller was looking for a fast sale. The best thing about the house was its isolation. And even though the land adjacent to the lake was owned by her reclusive neighbor, he never complained about her crossing his property to swim each day. The worst thing about the house was its lack of insulation: the dated pine paneling on the interior walls and vaulted ceiling seemed to absorb the day's heat, then slowly release it at night. One of many reasons, she now realized, why the house was going cheap.

The dog nudged her arm.

Jessie opened one eye. The other was squished shut by the pillow. Her golden retriever's furry face was close to hers. She loved the way the creases on each side of his jowl gave the impression that the two-year-old rescue dog was smiling. She reached out a hand and stroked his head.

"Morning, Bartie."

The dog's feathery plume of a tail thumped enthusiastically against the wall. Jessie remembered a time when Bartie cowered if she tried to touch him. He'd been chained up for the first year of his life by his previous owner and badly beaten if he barked. It took a year for her to win the dog's trust and now they were inseparable.

Jessie reached for her iPhone on the nightstand to check the time, and her fingers brushed her Glock 43 in its concealed-carry holster. Jessie knew she should keep the pistol unloaded and safely stashed in a drawer or a gun safe. But it was at night that she felt the most vulnerable and she wanted it close to hand. Not that she was a good shot. Quite the opposite. But Jessie figured that if she fired enough bullets, one of them would hit the mark. Bartie slept on the floor at the foot of her bed, which she found reassuring. But the man she most feared had a gun and he wouldn't hesitate to kill her dog.

Stretching her arm out a little farther, Jessie found her cell phone and squinted at the time: 6:30 a.m. She smiled. Of course, it was. How did her dog know the time? He was better than an alarm clock. Jessie swung her legs to the floor and sat up, yawning. She squinted at the daylight pouring through her open window. It was an odd color. Gray. Murky. Were they finally going to get some rain? Then she noticed the bitter taste on her tongue, like she'd licked charcoal. Her eyes felt gritty. It was smoke. And not just any smoke. Wildfire smoke with the distinctive scent of pine and sticky sap. The wind must have shifted direction and blown smoke toward Devil Mountain, where she lived. Tiny particles of ash lay on the floor and furniture.

Enjoying the sensation of the living room's cool tiles beneath her feet, she passed her mom's favorite wingback armchair and her dad's solid-oak desk, which he had used at his family medical clinic. She wished now that she had kept more of her parents' furniture, but the cabin was too small to accommodate anything else. When she had sold the family home, she kept the things that meant the most to her: photo albums, her sports awards, the board games they had played as a family, in particular her dad's chess set. On the desk was her dad's stethoscope, which had its own leather-bound case and also his antique Colt Model 1877 Lightning revolver, mounted in a glass display case.

Her mom's landscape paintings were hung on the living room walls. Jessie's college graduation certificate wasn't. It was stashed in a drawer, a relic from another life, of no use to her now. Her mom's diaries were neatly arranged on a bookshelf in chronological order. Sometimes, when Jessie was feeling down, she would take out one of the diaries and read it, imagining her mother's world: Cynthia, a child of the 1960s, a teenager in bell-bottom corduroy pants, a mother at the age of twenty-two, living in a small country town. It had been Cynthia's greatest wish to see Jessie, her only child, settled down with a nice guy and to give her grandchildren who she could dote on. Yet here Jessie was, single, and determined to stay that way.

Jessie opened the front door. Bartie shot outside and chased after a squirrel. The dog would be back: he never left her side for long. Sometimes she wondered if she had rescued Bartie, or whether Bartie had rescued her. There was no doubt that he eased her loneliness and she loved him dearly. She watched him from the makeshift porch, which was little more than a few planks covering the ground and two pillars supporting a sloping roof. Her cabin was surrounded by pine forest on all sides, which meant that even though the lake was only thirty-five yards away, she couldn't see it. She looked up. The sky was a sickly brownish orange, like a bruised peach.

"This looks real bad."

The three years Jessie had spent as a volunteer firefighter had been some of the best years of her life. She itched to throw her firefighting gear in the back of her pickup and help fight the fire raging in Bear Creek National Park, some sixty miles away. But she wouldn't be welcome. Marcus had seen to that.

Jessie ducked into the kitchen and switched on her mom's 1960s-style radio with big round dials and a varnished pine casing. She found the local news station.

"Twenty square miles of national park have been lost since yesterday," the newsreader said. "Gusty winds are hampering efforts to contain what is rapidly turning into a mega fire. The towns of Waterford and Bear Creek have been evacuated."

"Oh no," Jessie said to herself.

Bartie raced into the kitchen and sniffed his empty food bowl, then looked at her.

The newsreader continued, "Yesterday, Eagle Falls recorded the hottest September day on record—a whopping 94.8 degrees Fahrenheit. The heatwave is forecast to continue. This time last year, the average temperature for the month of September was just 58 degrees."

Could the fire jump the lake, Jessie wondered, and take out the town? Maybe even reach Devil Mountain, so named because it had two peaks, much like horns. It was really unlikely the park fire would cross the water, although the lake was narrow and long like a snake and embers could be blown across it.

I've done all I can to protect my home.

She had cleaned the gutters of leaves and maintained a wide firebreak around the cabin. Her hose was primed and ready, although, like most people in the area, her rainwater tank was two-thirds empty. The drought had created huge water shortages.

Her dog nudged her thigh and gave her a big-eyed pleading look.

"Want to go for a swim?" Bartie's head shot up and he spun around, chasing his tail in excitement. "Yeah, I know, buddy. I need a swim too. It's way too hot already. Coffee first, okay?"

Filling the glass percolator with water, she popped a tablespoon-ful of coarsely ground coffee into the basket, added the lid and switched on the gas stovetop. While the coffee brewed, she opened a can of wet dog food, scooped it into a large steel bowl, then told Bartie to sit. He sat, chest out.

"Eat!"

While Bartie wolfed down his meal, Jessie sipped her coffee, thinking about her plan for the day. She had a gardening job at Pat and Rob's place at nine, as she did every Monday. They lived a half-mile down the road, on a sought-after lakeside lot. Jessie was then due to do a quick job in town for an elderly couple who needed help cleaning leaf litter from their gutters. On Monday afternoons, Jessie usually drove to Prairie Ridge to see her friend Georgia Amarillas—her last remaining friend. Georgia had canceled because of a doctor's appointment, which left Jessie with some free time.

Stuck to the fridge door was a flyer announcing a new women's self-defense class starting today. It had been stuck on there for a few weeks now and every time she opened the fridge door she considered enrolling. Self-defense skills would come in useful if she could just muster enough courage to learn them. Each time she was about to sign up, she stopped. It was the thought of the other women attending the class that put her off. These days, she avoided visiting her hometown if she could.

Except it wasn't her home anymore.

She put down her coffee mug and closed her eyes. How had her life gone so off the rails?

Just then, she heard the rumble of tires on her unpaved driveway. She peered out the kitchen window. Jessie didn't have visitors, especially not at seven in the morning. A squall of dust preceded the vehicle. A sheriff's black-and-white Chevy Suburban came to a halt outside her house and a deputy she had never met before got out. He paused and surveyed the house's exterior.

Jessie ducked down, hoping she hadn't been seen. She gripped her dog's snout, willing him not to bark.

CHAPTER THREE

Ruth Sullivan was preparing her sons' lunchboxes with military precision, as she did with most things in her life. Not that she had been in the military. She had served her country another way: as an FBI agent. At forty years old she retired for medical reasons and became a full-time mom. But old habits die hard. Such as getting up at five thirty. She had already been for her daily forty-minute run, despite the pain in her left thigh muscles, which she was determined to conquer. She had taken the same route along the lake's western shore every weekday morning since she and her family had arrived in Eagle Falls eight weeks ago. She had greeted Martha walking her dog and said hi to Drew, her neighbor, who was training for a half marathon.

The ache in Ruth's thigh was fading with time passing, but her lungs were still sensitive to anything other than clean air. Clean air was one of the many reasons Ruth and her husband, Victor, had decided to uproot themselves from the city and move to the sleepy town of Eagle Falls. Ironically, this morning she had had to use her asthma inhaler and walk the last mile home because of the smoke. She had tried not to look across the lake at the park's 1,442 square miles of forests, beaches, and mountain peaks because she didn't want to see the ominous amber glow or the thick dark smoke just above the treeline. It would send her into a panic attack.

While nine-year-old Noah and six-year-old David ate their scrambled eggs at the dining table, Ruth gulped down a banana and almond milk smoothie. Then she continued to neatly fill the compartments of the kids' new lunchboxes with healthy food.

Don't look out the window, Ruth thought. *We're safe. It can't reach us.*

Regardless, there was a nervous flutter in her chest, and she felt hot and claustrophobic, even though the kitchen was spacious and air-conditioned.

Get a grip!

Today was the second day of the new school year and Ruth dearly hoped it would go better than the first day. Starting at a new school was always scary, *especially* when the kids were new to the area. Ruth was particularly nervous for David. On Friday, the first day of school, David was shoved to the ground and his favorite Spider-Man backpack was kicked around the changing rooms. When the teacher had found David alone and crying, hugging his school bag, she had taken him to the principal's office and both sets of parents were asked to come to the school.

Ruth ground her teeth. Her grip on the carving knife tightened and she pushed down too hard. The knife sliced through the rotisserie chicken and into the wooden chopping board with a loud *thwack* that caused both boys to jerk their heads up.

"Knives are dangerous, Mommy," said Noah, repeating a line Ruth had used when he had showed an unnerving interest in the kitchen knife block.

Ruth saw herself in Noah. He had her thick strawberry-blond hair, her small build, and her more serious approach to life. David, on the other hand, had inherited the looks and personality of his easygoing father.

"You're right. I should be more careful," Ruth said, smiling.

Noah's eyes followed her as she took two kids-sized pouches of juice from the fridge. "Why can't we have berry muffins? Daddy always gives us muffins."

"Daddy doesn't do your lunchboxes anymore. He's busy looking for a job."

Victor was indeed job-hunting, but right now he was asleep in bed. Theoretically, they had swapped roles. The day she first started working for the FBI, Victor became the house husband who cared for the kids. When Ruth was forced to retire from the FBI, she became the stay-at-home parent and Victor was free to kick-start his career. Except, so far, the role reversal wasn't quite working out. Before the kids were born, Victor had been a big shot realtor. But that was eleven years ago. Even before they left Seattle, Victor had applied for numerous real estate jobs. All his applications were rejected.

Ruth had thrown herself into her role as full-time mom and soon had the family running like a well-oiled machine. She had everything programmed as alerts in her phone. At 7:45 a.m. Ruth would drive David to Gatewood Elementary, chat to a few moms, then head back home, shower, change. She then would drive Noah to middle school at 8:45 a.m. The problem was that she had seven long hours before the afternoon pickup: once the house was clean and the grocery shopping done, she was searching for something else to do. Which was why she had approached the local gym about running a series of women's self-defense classes. And today, she was due to teach the first class.

"Pleeeeease, Mommy," pleaded David, seemingly unaware he had managed to spit tiny bits of scrambled egg over the table. "Muffins are yummy."

David gave her the kind of smile that melted her heart and would undoubtedly melt girls' hearts in future. It was the same smile that had won Ruth over on her very first date with Victor. David had his dad's wispy brown hair. Like his dad, he was always grinning, always happy-go-lucky. Kids and teachers loved him. Another reason why the bullying had been such a huge shock.

Ruth thought back to the meeting in the principal's office. Eric, a heavyset boy and tall for his age, claimed they were messing about and David slipped and fell. His father had dismissed the whole incident with the flick of a tattooed hand.

"Kids their age like to rumble. It's good for them. How was Eric to know that your boy's a wimp?"

David had started to cry, head bowed, hands clasped in his lap.

"Shoving my son to the ground isn't play. It's bullying." Ruth had said, furious. "Principal Dalglish, I need to know that this school does not tolerate bullying."

Dalglish had squirmed in his seat and mumbled about a "mis-understanding" between the two boys. Eric wasn't reprimanded, simply told to stay away from David. Eric and his father, Paul, had left the office with smug looks on their faces. When Ruth told Victor what had happened, he advised Ruth not to make a fuss.

"It's a small town. We don't want to make enemies."

But she could tell that he was as upset by it as she was.

"Mom?"

David's voice brought her back to the present. He'd asked her a question. Ah, yes. About muffins.

"You've got yummy chocolate raisins instead. And a banana each," Ruth said, closing the lids and making a conscious effort to stop frowning at the boxes as if they had committed a crime. She habitually frowned when concentrating, which was why she had such ugly frown lines between her fair eyebrows.

"And potato chips," said Noah, his blond brows meeting in the middle, just like hers. Ruth wondered if Noah had learned to frown that way by watching her. "Daddy always gives us potato chips."

"On Fridays you get potato chips as a special end-of-week treat. What day is it today, Noah?"

"Mon-day!" David shouted gleefully, before his brother could answer.

Noah rolled his eyes. "I was going to say that."

"I said it first," David giggled. If he was nervous about returning to Gatewood Elementary, he certainly wasn't showing it.

"Can I leave the table?" asked Noah. He had hardly touched his food. He usually cleared his plate and asked for more. Ruth pulled out a chair and sat next to him. "What's up, buddy? Don't like your eggs."

"Not hungry."

Ruth knew she was being overprotective, but she couldn't stop herself. "Everything okay at school?"

"I guess." Noah swung his feet so the back of his sneakers hit the chair legs. He didn't look at her. Okay, something was definitely wrong. "I like my old school." There was a whine in his voice. "I like Mrs. Brown. I like Sam and Emma." His best friends in Redmond, a Seattle suburb where they used to live.

Ruth took him in her arms and inhaled the sweet apple scent of his shampoo. "I know you do. It's natural to miss them. But you're making new friends, right? What about Aiden? He seems nice."

Aiden lived on their street.

"He's okay." Noah sighed. "Why did we come here?"

Ruth felt something lurch in her gut. How many times had she thought that their decision to move to Eagle Falls was made too hastily? But Victor had been adamant. After all, it was the town he had grown up in. And the kids would have a better childhood in the mountains.

"Good morning!" said Victor, a wide smile on his face as he entered the kitchen wearing his bedtime boxer shorts and sleeveless tee. He was in the middle of wiping the lenses of his wire-rimmed glasses with the hem of his tee, then he popped the glasses on. His wispy brown hair stuck up on one side: the side he'd been sleeping on. He opened his arms wide. "Daddy needs a hug."

Both boys ran into his arms. "Love you." He kissed Noah. "Love you." He kissed David. He released them from his embrace and walked up to Ruth. "Ah there's the most beautiful woman in the world." He kissed her.

How is it that he doesn't notice the hideous scar on my face? "Coffee?" she asked.

"You're an angel."

She poured him a mugful and added cream. As she handed it to her husband she couldn't help noticing that his daily workouts at the gym were paying off. He had never looked so fit.

"Big day for you," Ruth said.

"Yep, and I'm ready, all guns blazing." He mimed firing two pistols, which had Noah and David giggling.

Why can't I be playful like that? Ruth thought.

"What time is the interview?" she asked.

"Two. I just need to pick up a reference, then I'm ready. Oh, and I'd like your advice on what to wear. Suit or smart casual?"

Ruth glanced at her Apple watch. "Sure. When I get back, okay?" Then she looked at David. "Ready?"

"I need to pee." David launched himself off the chair and ran to the bathroom.

"Close the bathroom door," Ruth called after him. A few seconds later she heard the click of the latch. She turned to her other son. "Noah, please finish your math homework. Go collect your tablet from your room. Daddy will help you with the sums."

"Sure I will," Victor said. Then he held up his hand to cover his mouth and whispered, "You know I'm bad at math, right?"

Noah frowned.

"Daddy's joking. He's great at math."

Noah headed for his room at a leisurely stroll. When they were gone, Ruth spoke, keeping her voice hushed.

"I'm worried about David. I can't believe the principal didn't punish the boy."

Victor tilted his head to one side. "Oh Ruthie. Things are a bit more relaxed here. And Davy seems okay to me. Why don't we see how today goes?"

Victor always called their youngest Davy, but Ruth liked to stick with the name they had given him.

Ruth washed out her mug and left it on the drainer. "If you don't stand up to bullies, they keep doing it."

Victor took her hand and drew her to him so he could wrap his arms around her waist. "Eric's dad is a jerk. Always has been. But even he knows that his son picked on the wrong kid. You're ex-FBI. Our kids get special status. The teachers won't allow anything bad to happen."

Ruth pulled free of his embrace. "But they already did!"

He stroked her cheek. "My love, we need to get along with people."

Noah and David reappeared, gripping their toothbrushes. Their mouths dripped with toothpaste foam.

"Daddy, can we go see the big waterfall after school?" Noah said, spitting foam down his T-shirt.

"Yeah!" David said. "It roars like a lion." He then roared, spraying toothpaste far and wide.

"Maybe on the weekend," Victor said, herding them back into the bathroom.

CHAPTER FOUR

Jessie had no idea why a deputy would come calling this early in the morning, but it couldn't be good. Crouched down low so that she wouldn't be seen through the kitchen window, she clung to her dog's collar with one hand and gently clasped his muzzle with the other. The last thing Jessie wanted was for Bartie to charge outside and bark at the unwanted visitor. Everybody knew that wherever Jessie went, her dog went too. If she remained hidden, perhaps the man would go away.

The problem was that her front door was wide open. It was a bit too late to slam it shut. Bartie struggled to be free of her grip. His ears were pricked and the fur along his spine was raised. He wanted to protect her and see off the new arrival.

"Hello, there! Anyone home?" the deputy called.

His voice sounded distant, as if he had decided to wait by his vehicle. Sensible man, given she had a big dog. Distracted, Jessie lost her hold on her dog's collar. Bartie ran to the doorway and growled, teeth bared.

This left Jessie with no choice but to show herself.

"He won't hurt you," she shouted.

She got up and stood in the doorway. She was embarrassed to be seen in her goofy nightdress with a cute puppy face on it and the line *I WUV YOU!* beneath.

"Bartie! Heel!" she commanded.

The dog stopped growling and sat next to her. However, his eyes never left the stranger.

"Who are you?" she said to the tall African American with a shaved head.

The deputy's olive and beige uniform looked fresh out of the packaging, but he stood with a relaxed confidence that only came with experience. He might be new to the area, but he was no rookie.

"Sorry to disturb you, ma'am. I'm Deputy Benjamin Kinsley. I'm new in town. Wanted to introduce myself." He looked at Bartie. "Nice dog. Golden retriever, right?"

"That's right. Look, I don't mean to be rude, but it's kind of early to be making house calls."

Kinsley hovered near his vehicle. "Guess it is. I've got an eleven-month-old baby boy. I've been up since four this morning. Thought I'd take a drive around. Familiarize myself with the area. Meet some folks. Apologies if I disturbed you."

His explanation did little to put her at ease. Deputies didn't make friendly calls. There was always a motive. "Did Cuffy send you?"

"The sheriff? No. This is just to say hi there."

Jessie rolled her lips together as she tried to decide what to do next. She didn't like his unexpected arrival one little bit, but given her strained relationship with Sheriff Cuffy, she thought it prudent to be nice to the newcomer. "Like some coffee?"

"Thanks." But Kinsley didn't move. "Is the dog going to be okay with me coming inside?"

"He is if I am."

Jessie led the way into the kitchen and grabbed a work shirt that was draped over the back of a kitchen chair. She put it on, hoping to feel more dressed. Bartie followed her around the room. Jessie poured some coffee into the only clean mug available. On one side of it was an artist's depiction of the town's famous waterfall, and on the other side were the words *I GOT SMASHED IN EAGLE FALLS*. Jessie couldn't even remember where it came from. Probably one of the fire crew gave it to her as a joke, because Jessie didn't touch alcohol. Whereas Marcus... alcohol had brought out the worst in him.

"Sorry about the tacky mug," Jessie said. "Cream?"

"And sugar. I've got a sweet tooth."

"I don't have any sugar."

"Then I'll take it as is," Kinsley said cheerily.

Jessie handed him the mug. She wanted to know the real reason for his visit. He sat at the two-person table. She leaned her butt against the sink and held the edges of her shirt together. "So what's this really about?" she said.

"Oh-kay," Kinsley said, taking a brief sip, then placing the mug on the table. "Marcus Harstad claims you're stalking his girlfriend."

Jessie's jaw dropped. She had moved out of town to get away from him. And his girlfriend, Jude Deleon. "And I suppose you believe him?"

Because that's what they had always done. Marcus, Mr. Popular. Marcus the hero. Marcus who never lies. It felt as if she had a whirlpool of anger and hurt spinning in her stomach. She rested a hand on her tummy and swallowed down the bile rising up her throat.

"I haven't made up my mind," Kinsley said.

That's a first, Jessie thought. Kinsley clearly hadn't been in town long enough to fall under Marcus's spell.

"It's a lie. I don't stalk her. In fact, I do my best to stay out of their way. I'm rarely in town these days."

"But you have spoken to Jude recently, right?"

"I hadn't spoken to her for almost two years. That's God's honest truth. Then..." Jessie's eyes dropped to the floor. She had to be careful what she said. Marcus had a way of twisting things. "Then something happened, and I wanted to warn her of the danger she was in. I... was worried about her." Jessie looked up, saw the man in uniform and the blank expression and knew she was wasting her breath. "What does it matter? You won't believe me."

"Try me. What did you want to warn Jude about?"

Jessie shook her head. "That's between me and Jude."

Kinsley picked up his mug and drank.

Why doesn't he just leave? she thought. *What does he want? A confession? Well, he's not going to get it.*

"With me you have a clean slate, Jessie. No preconceptions. Do you want to tell me what happened two years ago?" Jessie's heart thumped like a drum. Kinsley's voice was almost drowned out by it. Kinsley continued, "I was a cop in Seattle for eight years before I came here. I saw a lot of cases like yours. It takes some guts to do what you did."

Jessie looked into Kinsley's eyes and thought she saw genuine concern. It was probably all an act. Or ghoulish fascination. As far as Jessie was concerned, anyone who worked for Cuffy couldn't be trusted.

"No point going over old ground," she said. "Now if you'll excuse me, I have to get ready for work."

Jessie walked to the front door and waited for him to get up. To the left of the house, her Ford Ranger pickup was parked in the shade of a tall cedar. In it was her gardening equipment. Down the side of the vehicle's six-foot cargo bed was a sign: EMERALD GARDENING. She had deliberately kept her name off the signage. Nobody wanted to employ Jessie Lewis. Emerald Gardening was nice and anonymous.

Kinsley stayed seated. "You mind telling me why you dropped the charges?"

"The sheriff didn't believe me. Nobody believed me. Except my lawyer. But I guess that wasn't enough."

Kinsley rose slowly. "For your own good, stay away from Jude, okay?"

She didn't answer. He walked past her, then turned to face her on the porch.

"Are you friendly with the Troyer family?" asked Kinsley.

Was that a trick question?

She had installed a water feature for them four weeks back and they still hadn't paid her. It was a modern circular piece with a waterspout at its center that looked like expensive granite but in reality was a cheap replica. Jessie was the only gardener in the area happy to do their job cheaply, for cash. No written quote. So, Jessie had gone and forked out five hundred dollars for the base and water pump, which had almost wiped out her bank account. Once the water feature was installed, she asked for payment. He had procrastinated. Weeks went by. She chased him for the payment. At her wit's end, she cornered Paul Troyer in the supermarket parking lot. It turned into a very public shouting match. Had Paul made a complaint against her?

"Installed a water feature for them a month back," Jessie said.

"Do you know about the fire?"

"The wildfire over at the park?"

"No, at the Troyers' house." Kinsley paused. She felt scrutinized. "They're all dead."

Jessie took a step back. "Jesus!" She couldn't believe it. "Not the kids?"

He nodded.

A whole family, gone. Jessie fidgeted from foot to foot. "How did it start?"

"A tragic accident. Gas was left on."

CHAPTER FIVE

Gatewood Elementary had been constructed in the 1980s and recently updated with double-glazed windows and a climbing frame, complete with tubular slide and watchtower. A local fundraiser had helped to cover the cost. It niggled Ruth that such a generous community hadn't yet seen fit to accept her or, it seemed, her sons.

It was easy for Victor, of course; he had been born there. Schooled there. Got his first job there. Then he'd been offered a promotion with a big-name realtor in the city and that was how Ruth and Victor met. Ruth was Seattle Police Department back then. She had been door-knocking in the affluent neighborhood of Laurelhurst, looking for witnesses to an assault. Taking a break, she had been waiting in line for a takeout coffee. She was surprised when a guy behind her started chatting with her. Most people gave police officers a wide berth. Within a year, they were married. Eleven years later, they moved to Eagle Falls. For Victor, it was as if he had never left. They couldn't walk into a store or down the street without people coming over to chat with him. When she was with him, people smiled and asked how she was settling in. But when she was on her own, people acknowledged her, but there was a wariness, a distance. She was an outsider and so were her kids.

On the upside, being former FBI had landed her an offer to speak at the town hall about life in the FBI—what she was legally able to tell them, anyway. And her new self-defense course had ten signups. Ruth hoped this class might break down some barriers between her and the local community. She just had to be patient, she told herself. But patience wasn't her strength.

Ruth parked her silver Buick LaCrosse on the street outside the school and glanced in the rear-view mirror at David, who was talking to himself in the back seat. "You ready, David?" she asked, her nerves jangling.

She wanted to protect him from boys like Eric.

"Yes, Mommy." A big grin.

She smiled back. Having helped her son out of the back seat, she carried his Spider-Man backpack over one shoulder.

"If any boy hurts you or makes you feel anxious, you go tell a teacher at once, okay?"

"Yes, Mommy."

Taking his warm hand, she headed for the school entrance. Something was different this morning. Too many moms were gathered outside the school gates. Stricken faces. Subdued murmurs. Kids were still with their parents. Ruth felt a rush of panic. She'd seen that look on people's faces before: shock and grief.

Not another child. Please, God, not another.

She sped up, unwittingly dragging David behind her.

"Mommy, slow down."

"Sorry, David."

Bending down, Ruth swooped him up in her arms. She set off at a jog, heading for the teacher at the gate, Ms. Kinsley.

"I'm not a baby," David moaned. "Put me down."

"Just till we get closer," she soothed, upping the pace.

The teacher was dabbing her teary eyes with a tissue. The mom with her was shaking her head. Through the crowd, Ruth could make out that bunches of flowers, tied in colorful ribbons, were propped against the wire-mesh fence. Cream candles in glass jars were lit and lined the fence.

Ruth halted, mouth suddenly dry. *Oh God! Someone is dead.* She hardly noticed that David was struggling to be free until he kicked her thigh hard. She put him down and tried to hold his hand, but he was already homing in on Aiden. She raced after him and caught hold of his arm. David squealed. Heads turned.

"I'm sorry, darling."

"Let me go. I want to find Aiden," he complained.

"I have to speak to Ms. Kinsley, then I'll take you to Aiden, I promise."

Weaving a path through the crowd, Ruth had the unnerving sensation that she was being stared at, while at the same time she was being sucked back into the past, to a time that she had tried so hard to forget. It was as if they were happening in real time. She was back inside Lakes Jewish Elementary School in Seattle, where the white supremacist Graham Baillie had barricaded himself in a classroom, threatening to detonate a bomb that he wore under his coat. Ruth and her partner, FBI agent Doug Fernandez, were on the scene. They were helping kids to evacuate the building when there was a sharp and ear-splitting *boom.*

The blast of hot energy lifted her off her feet and hurled her out of a ground-floor school window. She landed hard on her back in a load of shattered glass, literally stunned and unable to get up. Ruth was suddenly deaf and her vision blurred by smoke and falling debris. She lay on her back, struggling to breathe, as if there were a huge weight on her chest. She tried moving. Her deafness turned into a high-pitched buzzing and excruciating pain, as if a knitting needle were stabbing at her eardrum. She cried out and instantly regretted doing it. The sound of her own voice was unbearably loud. She pressed her gashed and burned hands to both ears. Her balance was gone. It was as if the asphalt were dipping and rising like a boat on a rough sea. Yellow flames filled window frames. Choking black smoke. Children screaming, trapped in the classroom. Her partner, nowhere to be seen. Wailing sirens that sounded muffled because of her damaged ear—she knew backup would arrive too late. She had to act now.

She turned onto her side. The ground swayed, dipped, and rolled. It was too much. She vomited. Ignoring the rocking sensation, Ruth got onto her knees, glass cutting her skin through her torn pants. A uniformed officer helped her up, his voice grating like sandpaper to her brain. On wobbly legs like a drunkard, Ruth staggered back into the burning building.

The heat was searing; it was like walking into a furnace. Her lungs barely worked. Every time she took a deep breath she coughed. She found her partner, Doug, or rather what was left of him, partly buried in a pile of ceiling rubble. His bulletproof vest was embedded with shrapnel from the bomb. He had lost a leg and his face was a mass of gore, his skull oozing blood. She felt his neck for a pulse. Nothing. She vomited again, this time frothy bile. She wanted to stay with him and weep. But he was gone and there were kids in need of help. She followed the screaming and sobbing up a badly damaged staircase, hands over her ears to reduce the volume of their cries for help. Her eyes streamed, stung by the acrid smoke. Through a blazing doorway, she saw two boys and three girls cowering under tables. Desperate faces. Trembling bodies. Filthy clothes. The doorway was ablaze. Ruth hesitated. Could she make it through the flames? On the floor was a kid's coat, which she used to cover her head, and she ran through the flaming doorway. Safely through, she tried to calm the kids, but their pleading voices sent her reeling backward. The doorway's fire worsened. Ruth looked out the shattered window. It was their only means of escape.

One by one she picked up the surviving children and dropped them out of the window and into the arms of bystanders, parents, police, anyone who was on the scene. The heat was so intense she could have sworn her pants and jacket and her skin were melting. Where were the firefighters? She coughed so hard she thought her lungs would burst out of her mouth. The last child landed in the arms of a cop. Fire swept across the ceiling in pulsing waves of red and orange. She was dizzy with lack of oxygen. She fell forward onto the window frame. Someone yelled at her to jump. With a final effort, she tumbled out of the first-floor window, not expecting to be caught, not expecting to survive.

"You're shaking, Mommy," David said, his arms around her neck.

Back in the present, Ruth found herself kneeling on the sidewalk, clutching David to her like she was a protective shield. She trembled from head to foot. Doug's death was her fault. When the call had gone out, they had been only a block away from the school, following a lead about a suspected terrorist attack. Baillie, with the bomb under his coat, had already shot three teachers and was holding a classroom of kids hostage. Ruth had insisted they go in. Doug had wanted to wait for backup. They went in without backup and now Doug was dead.

"I'm okay," Ruth said, staring into the worried eyes of her son. People were watching them. "I just needed a hug." She let go of her son's little body and brushed down his crumpled clothes. "Let's go find Ms. Kinsley." The new teacher was married to Deputy Kinsley.

Ruth pushed into a group of moms surrounding Ms. Kinsley and received some angry glares. Someone was asking the teacher a question, but Ruth couldn't hear her over the noise of conflicting voices. The bomb blast had caused mild hearing loss in Ruth's left ear, which made it difficult to hear in crowds.

Frustrated, Ruth blurted out, "Please tell me what's happened."

The women stared at her.

"You don't know?" a mom said, incredulously.

Ms. Kinsley answered: "Last night a fire killed the Troyer family. Eric and the baby too. It's heartbreaking."

Ruth followed Ms. Kinsley's gaze. A handwritten sign was propped up against the fence by two heavy candleholders. WE LOVE YOU, ERIC TROYER, it said.

Eric? The boy who bullied David? That Eric?

"No," Ruth exhaled, in shock.

Instantly, a wave of guilt washed over her. Only yesterday, Ruth was arguing with Eric's dad in the principal's office. And now they were dead? And only this morning, she had been fuming about Eric. Why hadn't she been more understanding? He was only six years old.

Ruth's mouth was bone dry. "How?"

"An accident. Cigarette. The gas stove was left on."

A mom nodded knowingly. "Paul was a heavy smoker."

Somebody shouted Ruth's name. The woman came up behind her. Ruth turned. "Proud of yourself, are you? Poor kid's dead!"

It was Millie Kemp from the hair salon, who liked to throw her weight around, and she had plenty of weight to play with. Angry eyes in a flat face that was round like a pizza crust.

"I'm devastated," Ruth said. "This is terrible."

Millie stood really close. "It was just a bit of rough and tumble in the playground. That's what kids do. You had to go make a big song and dance about it. In this town we want our boys to grow up like real men."

CHAPTER SIX

The news about the Troyer family's death had upset Jessie more than she imagined it would.

Paul Troyer had been the brawling kind, and truth be told, she had never liked him. He had also been best friends with Marcus, so it was inevitable that as soon as she went to the sheriff to report Marcus, Paul treated her like she didn't exist. Until he needed his water feature installed cheaply, of course. He had probably intended to rip her off all along. It was her word against his, and who would believe Jessie Lewis?

Despite all that, her heart was heavy as she drove her pickup onto the Wilmots' lakeside property—her 9 a.m. appointment—although her spirits lifted when Patricia waved at her from the swing seat on the front porch. Jessie waved back. Pat and her husband, Rob, were her favorite clients. Not only did the recently retired couple tend to their stunning garden with infinite care, they were also friendly to her, which was a rare thing these days. Jessie came to a stop behind their Subaru Outback. The two rear doors and the trunk of their car were open.

"Hi! Can I park here or am I blocking you?" Jessie called out.

Their imposing two-story wooden craftsman, painted in pale green with white trim, was as neat as their garden, which ran right down to the lake's shore. They had uninterrupted views of the lake and, beyond it, the national park. It was Jessie's dream home. *One day*, she thought. *One day.*

Pat got up and leaned her forearms on the wooden porch fence. As usual, her gray hair was pulled back in a doughnut bun. She was an attractive woman with an almost lineless face that belied her sixty-five years.

"You're fine there. Come on up. Bring Bartie. It's stifling hot already."

Jessie let Bartie out, grabbed her battered wide-brimmed hat with a drawstring for under the chin, and took the steps up to the shady porch.

"Homemade lemonade. Would you like some?" Pat offered.

"Thank you."

Jessie hadn't even started work and she was already sweating. The ice-cold lemonade went down easy.

"Take a seat for a moment." Pat pointed at a wicker armchair with a floral-printed cushion. Bartie lay on the cool wooden floor.

Jessie put down her now empty glass and fiddled with the rubber band at the end of her single braid, which was long enough to drape over one shoulder. Sitting down and chatting wasn't their usual routine. Normally Pat would tell her what they wanted her to do and then, after a couple of hours, they would usually offer her something to drink. Jessie took the offered seat, a feeling of trepidation in the pit of her stomach. *Please, don't tell me you don't need me anymore. I really need this job.*

"We're going to stay with my daughter in Oregon for a while." Pat's blue eyes wandered from Jessie's to the lake. Across the water, smoke hung like a fog. "Rob's cough has gotten worse and he's finding it difficult to breath with all the smoke." Rob used to be a heavy smoker until Jessie's father, Dr. Tom Lewis, finally managed to persuade him to quit. However, the damage to his lungs had already been done.

Jessie tried not to look disappointed. She really enjoyed her visits there. "But what about the garden?"

Pat continued, "Your timed irrigation system will keep the flowers watered."

"I can drop by and hose things for you. Clean out gutters. Make sure everything's all right," Jessie volunteered.

"You are a sweetheart, but we were hoping you might come with us."

Jessie sat back in the chair. The wicker base creaked. Had she heard right? "Excuse me?"

"I'm very fond of you. You know that, right?" Pat said. Jessie felt her cheeks redden. She didn't know what to say. "My son works for the weather bureau. He says if the fire jumps the lake, Devil Mountain could go up in flames. You heard about Naomi's house?"

"I thought that was a gas explosion?"

"But it could have easily spread to our homes. Do you know how much forest was lost before the fire service could put it out?"

"No."

"Half a mile in forty minutes. It took out a neighbor's property. Thankfully, they woke in time and escaped." Jessie felt bad that she didn't know this. "Jessie, you live alone, surrounded by trees. Your house is all wood. It's not safe to stay there anymore. My daughter has a granny flat in the backyard. You and Bartie can live there until the danger passes. There's plenty of space for Rob and me in her house."

Jessie blinked rapidly. There had to be a catch. "I don't understand. I'm... well, I'm the gardener. Why would you do this?"

Pat looked away. "I... I feel bad about what happened, you know, when you came clean about Marcus. We kept our mouths shut and by doing so we silently condemned you, like the rest of the town. I don't know what really happened, of course, but you were left friendless, all because the damned sheriff thinks the sun shines out of Marcus's ass."

Jessie was taken aback by this declaration and a little amused that the very proper Mrs. Wilmot had said the *ass* word. Then suspicion set in again. What was really going on? Everybody had an agenda. Since her mom's and dad's deaths, everyone except Georgia had either betrayed her or ostracized her. It was true that Pat and Rob had always been friendly, but they weren't exactly friends. All they had ever shared was a lemonade or a coffee and gardening chatter. Jessie had promised herself to never trust anyone again. She mustn't get sucked in by Pat's kindly smile. And besides, Jessie hadn't been able to pay her house insurance premiums. If her cabin burned down, she would be left with nothing.

"That's very nice of you, but I have to work and I want to be here to protect my house if fire comes."

A man with white hair, mustache and a strip of chin hair that reminded her of Colonel Sanders appeared through the front door carrying a large box, the shape of a picture. He was puffing and wheezing.

Jessie stood. "Rob, let me help you."

"Thank you, Jessie." He put the box down and wiped his sweaty brow with a handkerchief.

"To the car?" she asked.

"That would be great."

Jessie was tall and had the muscular physique of a marathon runner. She knew she wasn't pretty and she lacked womanly curves. But she was strong and she could carry a one-hundred-and-fifty-pound person over her shoulder if need be, as she had been trained to do as a volunteer firefighter. The box she carried to the Subaru wasn't heavy. It was just large and awkward to hang on to.

"Family portrait," said Rob, following her. "We're packing the sentimental stuff first." Once it was loaded into the car he said, "I'm guessing from the way Pat shook her head that you're not coming with us to Oregon?"

"No, but I really appreciate the offer. Thank you."

"You can change your mind at any time."

She nodded. "When are you going?"

"Tomorrow, early."

Jessie felt a pang of loneliness. "I said to Pat I'm happy to keep an eye on the place while you're gone."

"That would be great. If the fire reaches town, maybe hose down the house for us."

The fire was most likely to take out the town first and then burn up Devil Mountain. Jessie would have plenty of warning.

"Sure."

Rob opened his wallet. He pulled out a wad of cash, more than Jessie had seen in a long time. Must be a thousand dollars there, easy. He handed her four hundred. "Take this."

"I couldn't possibly take your money."

Rob plonked the notes into her palm and curled her fingers over them. "Take it. Please. And stay safe, Jessie. Don't risk your life, okay?"

It was twenty minutes past midday and Jessie was seated in her pickup outside the gym and boxing club in the center of town. Jessie usually avoided this area. There were too many people she didn't want to meet. She had the air conditioning on full and Bartie lay on the seat next to her, snoozing. She drank from a water bottle, trying to come to a decision. Should she go in?

She hadn't enrolled in the self-defense class that was due to commence in ten minutes. She was hoping she could simply walk in. It was high time she learned how to protect herself, but, to be fair, there hadn't been a class like this in Eagle Falls until now. The flyer said that a retired FBI agent was running the program. Jessie crinkled her nose. It wasn't that she had a problem with the FBI. It was more about whether the teacher, Ruth Sullivan, was friendly with Sheriff Cuffy. Law enforcement people stuck together, right? Would she go running to Cuffy and tell him that Jessie was learning a few tricks when it came to a fight? Would Cuffy come and visit, just to remind her that he had his eye on her? And it was ninety-five degrees out there. She couldn't leave her dog in the vehicle without the air conditioning running, which meant leaving the car unlocked.

Jessie shook her head as she screwed the cap back on the water bottle.

Why was she taking on all this unnecessary stress? Jessie had much bigger issues to worry about, such as earning enough money to keep herself and Bartie fed and her truck on the road. The cash Rob had insisted on paying her would go straight to the insurance company. She would deposit it at the bank later.

A silver Buick pulled into the parking lot and a fit-looking woman with shoulder-length strawberry-blond hair, in Lycra three-quarter-length pants and a figure-hugging black tank top, got out. The gold cross on a chain around her neck seemed to blink as it reflected the sun. *That has to be the instructor*, Jessie thought. *Maybe I should go talk to her first?*

Leaving the engine running, Jessie left her vehicle and walked toward the blond woman. The asphalt shimmered in the heat.

"Excuse me!" Jessie called out. The woman turned. "Are you running the self-defense class?"

"Yes." She smiled. "I'm Ruth. Please join me."

Now that she was closer, Jessie could see the Y-shaped three-centimeter scar that ran from the outer edge of the woman's left eye and down her cheek.

"I…" Jessi's voice disappeared. It was a nasty scar. Had someone knifed her? "Can I do the class in my work gear?" She gestured to her dusty work shorts, T-shirt, and scuffed steel-toe boots.

"Sure you can. If you don't have sneakers, you can go barefoot. What's your name?"

"Jessie."

A motorcycle pulled up nearby: a black Kawasaki KLR 650s that belonged to Cuffy's eighteen-year-old son, Ford. Jessie felt a prickle of unease. Stocky like his father, Ford had inherited his dad's square forehead and his mom's snub nose. Lord only knew where Ford had inherited his downward-pointing mouth, which gave the boy a sulky look. As usual, Ford flouted the rules and wasn't wearing a helmet.

"Who's that?" Ruth asked.

Only someone new in town would ask that question, Jessie thought.

"Ford Cuffy," Jessie said. "Sheriff's son."

The boy headed straight for them, a swagger in his walk.

"Um, I must go." Jessie backed away and turned on her heels, but she was too late.

"Looking good, Jessie," Ford said, his eyes roaming her body. Jessie bristled. *What a jerk.* "I see you got your motorcycle repaired."

"Yeah, good as new." He shrugged. "Guess I shouldn't speak ill of the dead, but the bike wasn't the only thing he messed up. My phone was totally smashed. Got a new one now. Latest model." He patted his jeans pocket, then turned his gaze to Ruth. "You're the FBI lady, right? You got blown up, right? Must have been a blast!" he laughed raucously.

Is that how Ruth got the scar on her face? Jessie thought.

Ruth didn't bat an eyelid, but Jessie couldn't get over Ford's insensitivity. Or his rudeness.

"And you must be John's son," said Ruth, giving him a tight smile. "Just to be clear, the terrorist bomb you're referring to killed five teachers and sixteen kids under the age of six, as well as an FBI agent and my partner. I now suffer from breathing difficulties, my left leg aches practically all the time, my hands were badly burned,

I lost sixty percent of my hearing in my left ear, and I'm lucky to be alive. So I would appreciate it if you didn't make a joke about bomb victims in future."

That wiped the grin off Ford's face, his dark brown eyes angry. Clearly recognizing Ruth wouldn't take any crap from him, he turned his attention to Jessie.

"Are you doing her class?"

"I… I haven't decided."

"You don't need to do that shit. I'll look after you, babe."

"Ford, leave it, will you?" Jessie said, exasperated. "For the millionth time"—Jessie said the next few words slowly—"I… am… not… interested… in… you."

Ford jerked his chin up. "You'll come around. You'll see."

He then strode into the gym.

"He was rude," Jessie said. "I'm so sorry."

"Water off a duck's back," Ruth said. "Coming in?" Jessie glanced behind her at her vehicle. Bartie was watching her through the windshield.

People around here leave their cars unlocked all the time, Jessie thought.

"I'll be with you in a minute. I'll just check that my dog's got some water."

CHAPTER SEVEN

Parked to one side of the national park road, the arsonist kept the engine ticking over. The hordes of firefighters battling the blaze were focused on the fire front to the north, some twenty miles away, so they were unlikely to travel this way. They had so far failed to contain the mega fire, much to the fire starter's relief. While the mega fire burned, nobody would pay much attention to the house fires. And, besides, it was too beautiful, too majestic, to die away so soon. This section of road afforded a spectacular view of the conflagration and the magnificent devastation it had left in its wake. It was like being in a private box at the movies with surround sound.

To the right, grasses and brush as dry as paper burned and crackled, and beyond them trees snapped and popped as they were consumed in yellow flames. A news bulletin said that almost five thousand hectares had already been destroyed and the fire watcher's heart felt close to bursting with joy. Not even one hundred firefighters could defeat its power, many having been called in from other states. The fire teased them, shifting direction, maintaining its supremacy. It would have been a huge ego boost to claim the mega wildfire, but it wasn't the arsonist's work. It was amusing to watch the news footage, to see the men and women in yellow gear scurry about, dragging heavy hoses with them, their faces grimy, their lungs full of dirt, turning their backs on the TV cameras, knowing they were unable to hold the line.

Fire and wind were a marriage made in heaven. It was a God-given miracle, the show to end all shows. It sang in the wind, a beckoning, seductive song. The fire lover knew it was a risk to be there, but it was worth it. There was nothing better than hearing the roar and the crash as trees tumbled, feeling the singeing heat, and smelling burning pine sap and the occasional waft of dead carcass.

Removing a bag of small wooden wedges from a black daypack, the killer carefully counted out a total of twenty-two wedges, two for each window, and set them aside for that night's activity. Tonight's house fire would be especially challenging but that's what made it interesting. And if the fire didn't take fast enough, there was always accelerant. Of course, it was preferable not to use it because accelerant would alert the authorities that the fire was deliberately lit. If it looked like an accident, the cops wouldn't get involved. Sometimes, however, the fires didn't bloom fast enough and the occupants almost escaped. They were the fast thinkers who broke the glass. It was fascinating how few of the victims were capable of thinking clearly when faced with death. Twice the targets broke the glass and had almost escaped and twice a gun had been used to stop them. As long as the shootings didn't become a pattern, the cops were unlikely to see a link between the current house fires and the previous ones.

The selected wedges were transferred to another transparent zip bag and sealed, then crammed into the outside pocket of the daypack. In the main compartment of the bag was the rubber-headed mallet, a packet of cigarettes, a lighter, a can of lighter fluid. And a pistol. The killer took it out. To the heavenly roar of a forest dying, the murderer loaded the gun, one bullet at a time. Checking the safety was on, he put it back into the daypack's pocket, cushioned by the woolen beanie and a fresh pair of latex gloves.

Out of the corner of an eye there was a sudden flash of red. Farther down the smoky road, a utility pole was enveloped in flames, like red fingers clawing at it. The watcher estimated the time it would take for the pole to fall. Two minutes tops. And the crack and crash would be profound.

Sadly, it was time to leave. The heat was enough to fry an egg on asphalt. Revving the engine, the arsonist drove away, peering into the side mirror for a final look. The utility pole thudded to the ground at the two-minute mark.

God, I'm good!

CHAPTER EIGHT

Eleven women of varying ages were gathered in a semicircle facing Ruth. Ruth had taken over an area at the gym with a padded floor that was usually used for kick-boxing and judo. Down the corridor, a yoga class was taking place. Across the way, an instructor was directing two teenage boys in a boxing ring, while other kids punched bags that swung from chains.

She could teach the class in her sleep, but she felt pressured because she dearly hoped to make new friends today. She had to strike the right balance between instructive and warm and friendly. Sure, she and Victor had been invited to the houses of people Victor knew. Dinners. Barbecues. But it always felt as if they were wary of her as the newcomer. Ruth cleared her throat and smiled, hoping the small group couldn't see the quiver at the edges of her mouth.

"Hi and welcome. I'm Ruth Sullivan. I moved to Eagle Falls two months ago with my husband, Victor, and our two kids. I was previously an FBI agent, based in Seattle. I worked in antiterrorism for ten years. Before that I was an SPD cop. I'm sure you've seen movies about the FBI and how we're always having gun battles with the bad guys. But there are plenty of times when we have to defend ourselves and the public *without* using a firearm. And this is what I'm going to teach you. How to get away from a mugger or rapist or anyone who intends to do you harm. Without the use of a gun."

Eleven eager faces stared back at her. Well, ten eager faces and one suspicious one in the back row, her arms folded across her chest defensively. Jessie.

Eleven attendees was an awkward number because Ruth planned to pair them up. *Never mind*, she thought. *I'll partner up with one of them.* She recognized two moms she had seen but not spoken to outside Noah's school. Sheriff Cuffy's wife, Susie, was a pleasant surprise. In her late forties, Susie had been on Ruth's doorstep the very day they arrived in town, offering freshly baked cookies. An affable, chatty woman, Ruth was soon swept up by her excitement about the forthcoming annual community picnic, and before she knew it, Ruth had volunteered to bake cakes. Susie's hand of friendship had stopped there, despite Ruth suggesting they meet for coffee or take a walk together. Her surprise at Susie's attendance today was because of her husband's reaction to the class. When she had asked "Big John," as he was known, to pin her promotional leaflet to his noticeboard, he had voiced concerns that a little bit of knowledge was a dangerous thing and that women in danger should dial 911 or the local sheriff's office.

"I agree, John," Ruth had said. "But sometimes the danger is too immediate. These classes are about empowering women to get away from an attacker."

The sheriff had suggested she pin her leaflet to a grocery store noticeboard and walked away. What was his problem? Ruth had kept her mouth shut: she had no intention of falling out with him. She chose her battles carefully and alienating the sheriff was a really bad move.

"Okay, ladies, I'm going to teach you some basic but effective Krav Maga moves. The aim is to get away from your attacker. Not to initiate a fight. It's all about speed and surprise."

"Isn't that what the Israeli special forces use?" Susie said.

"That's right." Ruth opened her mouth to continue, but Susie wasn't finished.

"My son told me all about it. Ford's into these things. He's doing the boxing class just over there." Susie basked in the approving looks she got from the other women.

"That's great. Susie, would you be happy to help me demonstrate?"

She willingly stepped forward and stood opposite Ruth, who positioned her a few feet away. "We're going to focus on some very simple counterattacks targeting vulnerable points like the eyes and nose." Ruth pointed to the various body parts. "The throat and the back of the neck. We avoid the solid skull at the top. You hit the skull, it's going to hurt."

A woman in her sixties raised a tentative hand. Ruth had earlier given them sticky labels so they could write their names on them and wear them on their chests.

"Yes, Corrin?"

"Do we wear protective gear?" Corrin asked.

"Not usually. Do you have a medical issue I should know about?"

Corrin shook her head.

"Just let me know if you're finding it too much. Okay, everybody, you will be hitting a padded bag like this one. I call it a melon because of its shape." Ruth held up a padded bag shaped like a watermelon with a grip handle. Corrin nodded. Ruth continued, "The first move we're going to practice is the open-hand strike." Ruth handed Susie the punching bag and directed her to hold it out and in front of her face. "It's a very simple strike. You'll use the heel of your hand to push the bag like this." Ruth demonstrated. "But what gives this movement power is pivoting from the feet." This time the slap with the heel of her hand against the bag was stronger and Susie was forced to step back. "By stepping into this, you drive the energy forward."

Corrin piped up, "How does that stop a big man?"

"You do this to the middle of his throat, and he'll be too busy trying to breathe to attack you."

Corrin winced.

Jessie stood behind Corrin and, because she was tall, Ruth could observe her reaction: a sudden jerk of the head and clenching of her eyes. Jessie then rubbed her own throat absently. Ruth's words were certainly hitting home, but why were they so significant to the young woman?

"Okay, ladies, six of you grab a melon." Ruth nodded at a pile of oval bags on the floor. "And partner up. One of you is with me."

Ruth keenly observed who paired up with whom. It told her about their friendships. It also told her who trusted who, because when you practice self-defense you have to feel comfortable with your partner. Jessie stood there alone with a melon gripped in her hand. Not one person had so much as looked at her. Ruth felt sorry for the woman. And intrigued. Jessie was clearly not welcome. Why was that?

"Jessie, you're with me," Ruth said.

The practice session revealed that Jessie was strong. And angry. Once she'd got into the rhythm, she was smacking the hell out of the melon. "Great work, Jessie."

Jessie smiled at the encouragement. Then slapped her palm against the melon.

"You work out often?"

"No. I'm a gardener and landscaper. Keeps me fit." *Slap!*

"Healthy job. Have you lived here long?"

"I don't live here anymore." *Slap!*

Interesting remark, Ruth thought. It was as if she wanted to disassociate herself from the town.

"So where do you live?"

Jessie stopped punching the bag. Her brown eyes flashed. "Why? You checking up on me or something?"

"No, I'm just curious. I haven't seen you in town before."

"That's because I don't come here much."

Ruth became aware of the other women staring at them. Beneath her tanned complexion, Jessie blushed.

"Great work, everyone. Now we're going to work on something called the three-sixty defense."

The rest of the hour flew by. Afterward, Ruth got some great positive feedback, especially from Susie. Ruth hoped that Susie might encourage her husband to support the program. When Ruth suggested that they might all go to the café next door for a quick coffee, nobody took her up on her idea. Jessie was the last to leave.

"I'll help you," Jessie said as Ruth picked up as many melon bags as she could to take back to the room hosting the boxing class. Jessie carried the rest of the bags and walked with Ruth. "I didn't mean to bite your head off earlier," she said, glancing at Ruth sheepishly.

"You didn't." Ruth smiled at her. Jessie was clearly complex. And vulnerable, and deeply hurt. Ruth would dearly love to know why the other women didn't like Jessie. It surprised her to find that she was drawn to the young woman in a protective kind of way. Ruth guessed there must be fifteen years between them. It was unusual for Ruth to feel motherly to a younger woman, especially one she hardly knew. But she did. Perhaps it was similar to the way she felt about her son being bullied? She didn't like the way the women ostracized Jessie. It felt like a silent form of bullying. "Hey, I'm going for a coffee. Come with me?"

"I, er, I don't do…"

"Please. It's kind of hard being new in town."

Jessie didn't answer immediately. Her eyes danced around the room as she made up her mind. "Sure. I'll go get my dog."

"Great."

They piled the melon bags next to a rack of dumbbells.

"Coming to the next class?" Ruth asked.

"Maybe."

"Can I have your address and email? Anyone who takes the class has to register."

Jessie frowned. "Who sees the data?"

"Just me and gym management."

Jessie pondered this for a moment, then gave Ruth her details. "Don't share it with anyone, okay? I'll meet you in the parking lot."

By the time Ruth left the gym, Jessie was frantically searching the cab of her truck.

"What's up?" Ruth asked.

Jessie turned to face her. "I don't believe it!" She threw her arms up in despair. "My wallet. It's gone."

CHAPTER NINE

Abigail's coffeehouse backed onto the lake. A triangular sail that was strung up between the café and a gift shop next door kept most of the outdoor tables in the shade. Lavender and purple salvia grew in terracotta pots and, despite the heat, the hanging baskets of creeping Charlie, trailing fuchsia, and red geraniums were flourishing and gave the place an abundance of color. The café had no air conditioning, and the single ceiling fan did little to cool the interior, so they opted for the courtyard.

"I can't believe I was so stupid," Jessie said, as she settled her dog in a shady spot under the table. "I thought Bartie would scare them off."

"Unless he knew the thief," Ruth suggested, taking a seat opposite.

"Or he gave the dog food to distract him."

Jessie felt shaky. That wallet contained almost all the money she had. Now she couldn't pay the house insurance premium and she barely had enough in her bank account to cover the cost of groceries.

"He doesn't trust anyone but me." Jessie shook her head. "I don't understand it."

"It would be worth reporting it to the sheriff's office. The sooner they know about it, the more likely it is they'll catch the thief."

"They won't care," Jessie said so quietly that Ruth almost missed it.

"Sure, they'll care. I'll go with you, if you like," Ruth offered.

"It's fine. I'll work something out," Jessie said.

Jessie had a sneaking suspicion that Ford or one of his idiot buddies stole her wallet. Maybe they did it for a laugh. Or to rile her up. Or because Ford could then play hero and return the wallet to her. She didn't want to think about what the creep might want in return. Jessie realized she was tugging angrily at the end of her single braid. She stopped.

"Look, I'm sorry. Can we take a rain check? I don't feel so good," Jessie said.

In truth, she couldn't afford even a coffee right now.

"Let me get these," Ruth said. "You need cheering up. What would you like?"

Jessie's head was spinning. A missing wallet. A former FBI agent offering to treat her to a coffee. The threat of fire. Everything was off-kilter. She longed to return to her quiet isolation. At least she had control over that.

"I… er… okay, thank you. A juice. Orange, apple, and carrot and lots of ice."

"That sounds nice," Ruth said, standing. "I'll have the same."

Jessie watched her enter the café, then she looked around the courtyard. She imagined she heard her mother's voice telling her to enjoy the moment. Forget about your problems, she would say. The lake lapped the shore. Kids squealed with laughter as they paddled in the water. Jessie consciously relaxed her shoulder muscles. This was normal. Jessie was being normal. Maybe Ruth might even become a friend?

Then a little voice in her head mocked her. *Why would an accomplished woman like Ruth befriend a nobody like you?* Ruth had already had a successful career. She had a family. *She* was the normal one. Jessie was the outsider. *She doesn't know, does she?* It wouldn't be long before someone, probably Cuffy, sat Ruth down and told her about Jessie's past. Ruth wouldn't want to have a juice with her in the future, that was for sure. To avoid the inevitable embarrassment, Jessie got up and headed for the parking lot, her dog walking to heel.

An eye-catching European sportscar entered the parking lot. Jessie stopped in her tracks, causing Bartie's lead to jolt tight. There was only one person in town who owned a Fiat Abarth 124 Spider: Marcus's girlfriend, Jude Deleon. Except she wasn't driving. Brittany Fisher was. The two women got out. The same age as Jessie, they had been best friends once. The women hadn't yet noticed her where she stood between two parked cars. Jude was searching for something in her purse. She wore a miniskirt which showed off her smooth tanned legs. The long-sleeved linen shirt was a surprise. Normally Jude wore figure-hugging, strappy tees that showed off her well-endowed cleavage. Jessie hesitated, torn between leaving fast, or talking to Jude, even though Deputy Kinsley had warned her not to.

It wasn't worth the hassle.

Jessie took a couple of steps in the direction of her pickup. Just then, Jude turned around and Jessie saw the fiberglass cast on her arm. Jessie could not help staring. Now she understood why Brittany had been driving Jude's car and why Jude wore a long-sleeved shirt on such a hot day—she didn't want to draw attention to the broken arm.

Hell, Jessie thought, *it's been a shitty day. I might as well cap it off.*

Jessie headed straight for the two women. She put on a big smile, reminding herself that in high school Jessie, Jude, Brittany, and Georgia had been inseparable. Jude had always been the stunning one, her flirtatious smile and curvy figure made her popular with the boys. Shy Brittany, always in Jude's thrall, was now a successful dentist. Jessie was the athletic one who had longed for a career in law enforcement, even though her father had wanted her to be a doctor. And then there was super-clever Georgia. She had gotten into medical school. And then…

Jude gasped at seeing her. Jessie gave a hesitant wave. Jude grabbed Brittany's arm and steered her back to the car. The rejection stung Jessie like a wasp. But what hurt more was the sight of Jude's right arm in a cast. It spurred her on.

"Wait! Jude! Please don't walk away. I just want to talk."

"Don't speak to her," Jude hissed at Brittany. "We're leaving."

Brittany looked behind her and gave Jessie an apologetic smile. She was always the softhearted one.

"Please!" Jessie called. "I want to apologize."

Brittany jolted to a halt. "Come on, Jude, you can do that, can't you? She just wants to say sorry."

"I can't! You know I can't," Jude said.

Jude flicked a look over her shoulder and Jessie saw the fear in her furtive glance. But it wasn't Jessie she was afraid of.

"Jude, please, let me help you."

"Go away!" Jude shouted, refusing to look at Jessie.

Brittany unlocked the car and Jude dived into the passenger seat.

"Drive!" Jude shouted at Brittany, who was fumbling with the ignition.

Anyone would think that Jessie was the devil incarnate from the way Jude was behaving.

"Wait! Please!" Jessie leaned in, one hand on the door so Jude couldn't close it. "He hurt me too, Jude. Dislocated my shoulder. Punched me. Broke my arm. Did he do that to you?" Jessie pointed at the fiberglass cast.

"You're sick, Jessie. Let go of the door or I'm calling the cops."

"Don't do that," said Brittany. "Don't make trouble for her."

Jude's dark eyes were livid. "Stop telling lies about Marcus. He's *my* boyfriend now. Accept it and get over your stupid jealousy."

Jessie's heart almost shot out of her mouth. "Jealous! Jesus! He was the worst thing that's ever happened to me. I'm worried about *you*. What he'll do to *you*."

Jude dialed a number. It was the local sheriff's office. Jessie let go of the door and stepped away. Cuffy would relish the chance to haul her ass into a cell. Jude slammed the door shut and Jessie watched them drive away, then covered her face with her hands.

"Jesus, help me," Jessie mumbled into her palms.

"Jessie? Are you okay?" Ruth was behind her, clutching two juices in tall glasses.

For how long had Ruth been watching them?

"I have to go," Jessie said, flushed red with embarrassment.

"Why?" Ruth looked bewildered.

"Thank you for... being nice to me."

CHAPTER TEN

Tears streamed down Jessie's cheeks as she drove out of town. Why couldn't she leave well enough alone? Jude didn't want her help—she was in denial, just as Jessie had been until Marcus almost killed her. Until that moment, everything he did to Jessie, every bruise, every chunk of hair wrenched from her scalp, every broken bone, Jessie had blamed on herself. She made him angry. He didn't get angry with anyone else, he said. Just with Jessie. So she had to be to blame.

Now Jude was caught in the same cycle of tenderness, then brutality, then apologies as Jessie had been. Marcus had to make sure that Jude didn't betray him to the cops. If she were to claim that he abused her, then Cuffy might finally believe Jessie's claims too. Jude was clearly terrified that if Marcus found out about their chat today in the parking lot, he would fly into a rage. She might tell Marcus about their meeting so that his anger was directed at Jessie rather than herself. And that thought filled Jessie with absolute dread.

Bartie, on the passenger seat, lifted his head and rested it on the crook of her arm. He knew she was upset.

"It's okay, buddy." She stroked the dog's head, keeping one hand on the steering wheel. "We're survivors, you and me. We'll be okay."

Jessie reached a fork in the road.

To the left was Lake View Drive and her house. To the right was Falls Drive, which meandered up the mountain, passing a viewing platform that overlooked the top of the waterfall, known as Eagle Falls, from which the town got its name. Jessie took Falls Drive. The family that had died in the house fire lived on Falls Drive, about three miles beyond the waterfall. The hairpin bends were tight and Jessie slowed to a crawl at each one. There was one particular bend that made her especially nervous: the one known by the locals as Break or Bust Bend. Her pulse quickened and her grip on the steering wheel tightened. Only when she had navigated that bend did the tension in her body begin to dissipate.

The views should have been stunning on a rainless day like this, but the smoke from the national park blurred the view, as if a landscape painting of the valley was covered in centuries of dust. From what Jessie could see in the distance, the wildfire appeared to be getting closer. Black smoke billowed from a gash of burning red. Jessie felt desperately sorry for the wild animals trapped in the forest fire.

When she neared the Troyer family's property she slowed the vehicle. A large chunk of the forest surrounding the house was black and barren. Nothing but the stunted remains of charred tree trunks. No flowers, no ferns, no leaves, no birds, nothing but ash. The Troyers' house had been hidden from the road by the tightly packed pines. Not anymore. It was like a giant excavator had been through the forest, knocking down everything in its path. She pulled over near the entrance to the driveway.

"Stay," she told her dog.

In the cup holder near the handbrake was a water bottle containing a bunch of blue broadleaf lupines and purple fire-weed—wildflowers she had picked earlier and stuck into the lip of the bottle. It didn't look classy but at least the flowers might last a day or two.

Jessie left the vehicle with the air conditioning running. Her thick-soled work boots sank deeply into the still-hot ash. She tied a bandana over her nose and mouth. Even so, the air tasted bitter. She spotted the giant tire tracks of a fire department engine that had churned up soil and ash as it left the property. Propped against a blackened tree trunk someone had left a bunch of flowers wrapped in the local Safeway's distinctive spotted cellophane. Next to the flowers was a foot-tall wooden cross, wedged into the ground, the words *WITH JESUS* painted on it. The driveway was cordoned off with yellow tape: *FIRE LINE DO NOT CROSS*. Beyond the tape, there was almost nothing left of the house except the brick fireplace. The flu, even the chimney pots, were intact, but the walls and roof had been incinerated. Jessie looked around to check that nobody would see her, then she stepped over the fire-line tape.

In among the ground debris were shattered concrete roof tiles. Where one wall had stood, a big AC unit had buckled. The polyethylene rainwater storage tanks had melted and collapsed inward, like a soggy, sunken cake. To the right of what used to be the Troyers' kitchen was the burned-out remains of their Silverado. Jessie had helped put out car fires before. Yet, she hadn't seen a vehicle so completely picked bare as the Silverado. The glass was gone. Tires, gone. Seating, gone. She was looking at the skeleton of a pickup. The heat must have been intense.

"Jesus. They didn't stand a chance."

It was late afternoon. Jessie floated in the lake on her back, gazing mindlessly at the crazy sky. It was a yellowish beige, like chicken broth. She had never seen anything quite like it. She splayed out her arms and legs like a starfish and enjoyed the gentle lapping of the water. It had been an upsetting day and she hoped the gentle rocking would help her to unwind. A whole family had died last night. Her best clients were leaving town tomorrow. She had humiliated herself in front of Jude and Brittany. Her wallet had been stolen: all her cash gone.

She closed her eyes, trying to forget about it all. Nearby, Bartie stood in the lake, still as a statue, the water up to his ribs. He was cooling his paws and watching for fish. Nobody else used this part of the lake, except for the occasional sailboat or waterskier, and they tended to stay far away from the shore. Technically, she had crossed her neighbor's land to reach the water, but she hardly ever saw him, and he never objected. Once or twice, she found him fishing on his pontoon and he had ignored her, which suited Jessie just fine. Sixty-seven-year-old "Weird Bill" Moran hoarded old cars and car parts, which he used to sell to make ends meet. Rumor had it that Bill had as many as seventy cars on his property, dating from the 1950s, but these days he wouldn't allow people on his land, so nobody knew for sure.

Suddenly water splashed over her face. She opened her eyes and sat up. Bartie pulled his head out of the water. Clamped in his jaws was a writhing trout. The fish's tail slapped him in the eye and he almost dropped it but he managed to cling on. She watched Bartie wade to the shore, deposit the fish on the shingle beach and then eat.

"Clever boy!" she called out. He wouldn't need feeding tonight.

Ruth swam a couple of laps to loosen her tight neck and shoulder muscles, then she towel-dried herself and wrapped the towel around her torso. Jessie's long hair dripped down her back as they began to climb the steep tree-covered hill. There was no proper path but she and Bartie always took a particular route through the forest, following the trampled ground cover. Jessie felt so much more relaxed after her swim.

Bartie was a few feet ahead of her when he abruptly stopped, front paw raised, ears pricked. Jessie stopped too. What had he heard? All she could detect was birdsong and the hum of insects. She and her dog were at the edge of the forest. Ahead was the clearing around her cabin. Everything appeared to be as she had left it. But something was wrong. Bartie's fur was raised all along his spine. His nose pointed in the direction of the road and his jowl quivered: he was building up to a growl. She listened again and this time she heard the low rumble of an engine. It grew louder. Then the squeak of a vehicle's suspension. Dust swirled above her unmade drive. Then she saw it. The red Chevrolet Suburban bouncing in and out of potholes, the Eagle Falls Fire Service insignia emblazoned on the car door.

Her vision shrunk to a pinprick. A minuscule light in a world of blackness. No house, no Chevy, no dog, no breath. She was holding it.

Breathe, you have to breathe. He hasn't seen you yet.

She swiveled, intending to run back to the lake and to stay there until he was gone. But her legs were like Jell-O and she lost her balance. She collapsed forward onto all fours. The thick layer of pine needles on the ground cushioned her fall, but her left palm smacked into a pine cone, the seed scales jagged. Her wrist twisted, a shock of pain, but nothing serious. The impact of her fall forced her to gulp in air. She tasted the smoky ash in it.

Don't do this. Get up. Don't let him see you like this.

The Chevy came to a halt next to her Ford Ranger.

Please God, just go away.

Bartie stared fixedly at the Chevy. The dog's lips curled back into a snarl that rumbled deep in his throat. He was ready to attack. *Don't bark, don't make a sound*, she wanted to say, but her tongue was thick and clumsy and Bartie's growl became a ferocious bark all too quickly. Too late she reached out to try to stop him. She held his collar for a second before the dog wriggled free, determined to ward off the intruder. He let rip with a tirade of barking. Two startled magpies shot into the air, their cries piercing.

Jessie froze. She closed her eyes. *This isn't happening. This isn't happening.*

If she kept them closed, she could pretend he wasn't there. It was childish and silly. But she couldn't look.

She heard a creak. She knew that sound. The fire captain's door had opened. A crunch underfoot. She imagined him turning on the heels of his leather boots, peering through the dust haze at the house, at the forest. He must have heard Bartie's bark. When the dust settled he would see her on her hands and knees. And he would enjoy it. This was how he liked to see her. He had made her crawl on all fours like this. He had hit her with his belt like this.

Get up!

She struggled to stand, steadying herself against a tree trunk, her leg muscles as wobbly as a newborn fawn. Pine needles stuck to her perspiring palms, her knees. She straightened her back, but still she couldn't look at him. Bartie stayed in front of her, fangs bared, snarling and snapping.

"Call off your dog or I'll shoot it," Marcus Harstad called out.

No, don't hurt my dog. Not my dog.

She looked at him then. Tall, almost platinum hair, tanned skin, blue eyes. A descendent of a Norwegian pioneer who established Eagle Falls in the 1880s. Marcus worked out in his home gym, and it showed: he had always been the kind of man who turned heads. Women loved him, men wanted to be pals with him. But every cell in Jessie's body reacted with revulsion and fear. She laid a trembling hand on Bartie's head.

"Quiet," she whispered.

Bartie ignored her. He instinctively wanted to protect her. But she had to protect him because Marcus would shoot him in an instant.

"Quiet!" Louder this time, her voice raspy.

The dog ceased barking, but the snarling continued. She managed to grip his collar with fingers that felt frail and useless.

Marcus watched her. His hand rested on the SIG Sauer P365 semiautomatic pistol he always carried on a belt holster. White

T-shirt, jeans, boots. Not in uniform, so this wasn't official business. Which meant only one thing. He was here to warn her to leave Jude alone. Or worse.

"Get…" A croak, barely audible. She tried again. "… out of here."

She wanted to sound strong, but even to her ears her voice was flaky and apologetic.

"That's no way to treat an old friend." He showed his perfect smile.

It wasn't until they had moved in together that she realized that his smile was a smirk. Arrogant and mocking. There was perhaps thirty feet between them but even from that distance he clearly sensed her terror. Or did he smell it on her, like the monster that he was? She cleared her dry throat. *Take back control*, she told herself. *Show him that he can't tell you what to do.*

"What do you want?" she shouted.

"Warning you to be careful."

She shuddered. Did he mean the wildfires or careful of him? "About what?"

"It wouldn't take much for a fire to start. Somebody drops a match by mistake. And *boof!* Your home, this forest, and you *burn*. Paul Troyer dropped a lit cigarette, and somebody left the gas cooktop on. Two errors that cost them their lives." He took a step forward. "Stop messing about and come over here." There was an edge to his voice that she knew too well.

She wanted to turn away. To ignore his order. Of course, it had been fine to order her about when she was a volunteer firefighter. He was the station captain. Everyone did what he said. But he had controlled her in their home too. In the bedroom, where he hurt her the most, always careful to avoid marking her face.

"I said, come here," Marcus snapped.

A trickle of urine escaped her bladder. Her gun was in the house. So was her phone. She looked around. A broken branch on the ground, two feet long. She released Bartie's collar and then used the stick as a prop to keep her upright.

"Heel," she said to her dog.

On rubbery legs she headed out of the trees, using the branch as a walking stick, Bartie at her side, wondering if she could finally find the courage to stand up to him. Ten feet away from Marcus, she stopped.

"Say your piece, Marcus, then go."

During the two years they had lived together, Jessie had learned to read the telltale signs of his mood swings. The tightening of his lips, the hardening of his gaze, the way his right eyelid pulsed, a minuscule movement beneath the skin that few would notice. She saw it now, how his face transformed, a hint of the sadist beneath the Mr. Nice Guy mask.

Bile coated the back of her throat. She wanted to spit it out. Instead, she swallowed.

Marcus looked around him. "I see you've cleared the dry brush. Good to know you paid attention to your training."

"Yeah, I know how to protect my house. Please go."

Marcus took several steps forward. Bartie bared his fangs and snarled. Marcus stopped in his tracks. He eyed the dog, then her. "Stay away from Jude. She doesn't want to talk to you."

Jessie gripped the stick tightly so he hopefully wouldn't see how much she was trembling. "You mean *you* don't want me talking to her."

He pointed a finger at her. "You listen to what I'm saying, Jez."

"Don't call me that."

"You used to like it."

"No, I hated it," she screamed, unable to control the tumult of fear and anger churning inside her. "Get out of here!"

That smirk again. He had rattled her and he got a kick out of it. He climbed into his car, turned the ignition, then said through the open window. "You've got to stop this, Jessie. The whole town thinks you're crazy."

CHAPTER ELEVEN

Jessie woke with a bad feeling.

It was pitch black in her bedroom. There were no streetlights in the mountains and no moon peeping through the gap in her drapes. She reached out a hand and felt around her nightstand until she found the rectangular hard surface of her phone. It was 1:09 a.m. She lay the phone quietly back on her nightstand and listened. What had woken her?

Bartie was making *yip yip* noises in his sleep, probably dreaming, which meant that whatever had woken her hadn't been loud enough to disturb the dog. Her lungs were irritated by the wildfire smoke that blew through her open window like a smoker's breath. She tried to clear her throat, but a tickle made her cough. Was it her imagination or was the air thicker than last night? The harrowing memory of the Troyers' burned-out house spurred her to sit bolt upright and kick off the sheet. What if lightning or the careless flick of a cigarette had started a fire nearby? It would spread fast. She switched on the bedside lamp and blinked away the uncomfortable brightness.

Then she heard it.

It sounded like furniture scraping across tiles. Was somebody in her house? A prickling sensation traveled up her spine. Her lungs ached to cough. Jessie held her breath until the feeling passed.

Bartie lifted his head. He had heard it too. Grabbing her pistol from the nightstand, she flicked off the slim carry holster's clip with her thumbnail and drew her Glock 43, sliding her finger close to, but not on, the trigger. The pressure of her finger on the trigger's tab unlocked the safety, and she didn't want to accidentally fire the fully loaded gun.

Where had the scraping sound come from?

Jessie crept to the bedroom's sliding door. Bartie was up and at her side in an instant. Her heart thudded as she slowly opened the door. The rollers rattled. If there was an intruder, they would know she was awake. Jessie held the Glock out in front and released the tab on the trigger, ready to fire. With her left hand she felt for the light switch. Found it. In the harsh ceiling lighting, the open-plan living-dining-kitchen room was clearly empty. She threw back the door to the bathroom. Nobody in there either.

Bartie sniffed under the front door and barked, then looked at her.

Crash!

Jessie jumped. Something had fallen over outside. *What the hell?*

"Probably a raccoon," she whispered to herself. Then, just in case she was wrong, she shouted, "I have a gun. You get out of here!"

She had purchased the gun to protect herself from Marcus. One day he would come for her. A man with an ego that big would never forgive her for daring to reveal the monster that he was. Was this the day of reckoning?

Switching on the exterior light, she could see out for twenty feet or so. Unlocking the main door, gun pointing forward, she stepped into the night. On the porch was a simple wooden bench and a basic barbecue. A squirrel dashed out from under the barbecue's cover, leapt to the ground, and scampered through the grass. Bartie charged after it.

"Bartie! Here!"

He reluctantly gave up the chase and ran back to sit in front of her. Jessie coughed. *Damn the smoke!* She peered into the forest. It was like a filthy fog, black and toxic. It smelled foul. She knew the smell. Plastic burning. Synthetic materials. It wasn't a forest fire. It was a house fire.

She rushed back into the house and was about to call the fire service when she stopped. Would they even believe her? Worse, would they come out to find she was mistaken? Thanks to Marcus making out she was a consummate liar, the fire crew on tonight would probably think that she was making it up. What did Marcus call her? Attention-seeking. Ironic really, coming from the man who craved adulation all of the time.

Jessie made a snap decision. She would locate the house fire and then call the fire service.

She threw open her closet and over her tank top and boxers she donned her firefighting gear. First, a protective coat and trousers, both in matching yellow with reflector strips on the back and arms. She figured she had paid for them, so they were hers to keep. And now they might come in handy. She then pulled on the heavy-duty fire-resistant boots and pocketed the thick gloves. She had forgotten how clumsy the seven-pound boots made her when she walked. Of course, she lacked the face mask, hood, helmet, and oxygen tank. Those were the property of the Eagle Falls Fire Service. When she was ready, she stared at her dog. She hesitated about taking him with her, but she figured he was safer with her. What if the fire reached her house and Bartie was trapped inside? She would never forgive herself. She took with her a one-gallon container of water and some old towels. If she wet a towel she could use it to protect her head and face from flames.

By the time she was in her pickup, her skin was clammy. The hot night and the heavy, waterproof-fireproof clothing wasn't a good mix. She switched on the air conditioning. Once she was on Lake View Drive, she followed the smoke. The nearer to the lake she got, the poorer the visibility. At the bottom of the hill an orange glow through the trees caused her stomach to backflip.

"Oh God, no."

The smoke was coming from Pat and Rob's place.

As soon as she headed along their driveway, she saw a backdrop of flames like a red silk drape behind the house. The roof was intact. So were the exterior walls. So was the porch and the garage. But through the downstairs windows, Jessie could see the bright yellow of fire rolling like a burning wave through the lower level. The living room drapes burned and curled, deteriorating into black and gold embers. If Pat and Rob were upstairs, they were trapped.

Jessie drove past the perfectly manicured lawn and skidded to a halt on the gravel drive. She made sure her vehicle was far enough away from the fire to ensure she could escape, and her dog would be okay, and she kept the engine idling. She dialed emergency services.

"Hurry! They're trapped upstairs."

She heard screams. Saw a figure move across an upstairs window.

For a second or two Jessie hesitated. She had never fought a fire alone. There had always been a team with her. Firefighters watched each other's backs.

Remember your training. You can do this.

"Bartie, stay!"

The dog cowered on the passenger seat. Animals instinctively knew to fear fire. When Jessie threw open her car door, the heat hit her. Burning trees cracked and popped. A flaming branch snapped, crashing onto the house roof. Tiles shattered.

Jessie jogged as fast as she was able in her heavy boots to where she knew there was a hose reel. But the hose was gone. Just a tap. *What the...?* Pat and Rob would never remove the hose, so where had it gone? There was a second hose reel in the backyard.

Above her, glass exploded. A woman screamed. Jessie stepped back so she could see the upper level. Framed in a window was Pat in a pale nightie. She slammed a chair into the glass. The chair tumbled down the porch roof and crashed to the ground.

"Help!" Pat yelled, then she choked. Her face was contorted as she gagged on the noxious black smoke. "Rob's…! Help!"

The fire crackled and growled. Jessie only heard some of Pat's words.

"I'll get a ladder!" Jessie shouted. "I'm coming to get you!"

The Wilmots kept their ladder inside the double garage. The doors were controlled electronically. Jessie couldn't get inside without the remote. In the back of Jessie's pickup was a tall stepladder that she used when trimming hedges. It would have to do. She turned and ran to her pickup. Bartie was barking in distress, pacing inside the cab, panting furiously. She was a fool to bring the poor dog. Jessie yanked off her protective gloves so she could untie the rope that held her stepladder inside the bed.

Bang!

There was a sound like gunshot. It must have been a tree collapsing. Jessie flicked a look at the Wilmots' bedroom window and Pat was gone. Had the smoke inhalation got to her? Was she already dead?

No! I can save them.

With sticky, sweaty fingers, Jessie struggled to untie the knotted rope.

Out of the corner of her eye she saw someone running at her. His face was covered. For a second, she thought it was Rob. But Rob couldn't run like that. The man was fast. He raised something ball-shaped and swiped the air with it. There was a searing pain as it hit the side of her skull. It was like her head had exploded. Her knees buckled. She tried to grab the rim of the pickup's bed, but she couldn't get a hold. Bartie barked, fast and desperate. Jessie slid to the ground, her hands, knees, then face hitting the rough gravel. She thought she smelled the gaseous stink of lighter fluid.

Her eyes closed.

She felt nothing.

CHAPTER TWELVE

"Don't argue with me and don't bleed on my seats," growled Sheriff Cuffy, taking his eyes off the road for a moment.

In the passenger seat of the sheriff's black-and-white Dodge Charger, Jessie pressed a scrunched-up towel to her bleeding head. Her skull felt as if it had been hit with a sledgehammer. She wasn't sure for how long she had been unconscious. She remembered Clyde Hudson's voice calling her name. He had removed his oxygen mask to talk to her. He told her there was an ambulance on its way. Then he disappeared into the black smoke.

Jessie squinted at the digital clock on the dashboard, but her eyes refused to focus. A searing pain behind her eyeballs made her retch. She covered her mouth with a hand.

"And don't spew in here either," Cuffy said.

Jessie swallowed hard. No way was she going to spew. No way.

"What time is it?" she asked, her voice a hoarse whisper.

"Three in the morning, why? Got some place you have to be?"

She was trying to get her bearings. Piece together what had happened.

"I don't need to go to hospital," she said.

This wasn't strictly true. She probably did need to see a doctor. If it wasn't for the seatbelt the sheriff had insisted she wear, she would probably have collapsed by now. But she didn't want to spend any time with Cuffy. She didn't trust him as far as she could spit.

"Stop your whining," Cuffy said.

Behind her, on the rear seat, her dog lay quietly, calmer now that he was with Jessie and away from the conflagration. At least Bartie wasn't hurt. Leaving him inside the air-conditioned car may have saved his life.

Jessie closed her eyes. She saw it all again. Waking to see Clyde's rugged face. Seeing the gravel strobed with the red light of the fire department's ladder truck. Then came the alternating blue and red of the sheriff's office cars: Cuffy's Dodge and Deputy Kinsley's Chevy Suburban. Beyond them, the black smoke, the yellow flames. Shouting. The fire roaring. Glass exploding. Two blackened bodies carried from the house. Her own sobbing. Then a sound that she would never forget for the rest of her life. The sound of a house dying. The *chug, chug, chug* like a steam train. Every room in the house on fire as if the fire was the only thing holding it up. Then the final moment. A crash as the roof collapsed, then the strangest sound of all. A sigh, as if the house knew that all was lost. Or had it been her sigh? She was so confused.

"Clyde's dead," Cuffy said, his tone accusatory.

Her lids sprung open. "I know."

Clyde had worked for the fire service sixteen years and had been kind to her when she was a volunteer. He had a wife who was carrying their third child. Jessie felt terrible. Was it her fault? Would he have died if she had dialed 911 earlier? Her eyes filled with tears. She used the edge of the towel to wipe them away, then she stared out of the passenger window, trying to ground herself. The night sky was thick like black tar. Nothing but the winding road in Cuffy's headlights.

"Got any water?" she asked.

He handed her a bottle.

She hadn't realized how filthy her hands were or how much she was trembling until she took the bottle. It must be shock, she guessed. Or had the bastard who hit her head done some real damage? She couldn't afford surgery. In fact, she couldn't afford an ER bill, period. She'd be looking at a bill for $500, easy, just for a basic examination. There was no way she could pay that. Twisting the bottle top, some water sploshed onto the seat between her legs.

"Be careful, will you! This car's new and I'd like to keep it that way for a while longer."

Jessie wanted to scream at Cuffy. To tell him to forget his car seats. Good people had died tonight. She had failed to save Pat and Rob and her failure had led to Clyde's death. She wanted to go find a hole and hide in it. But her thirst needed to be quenched and she lifted the bottle to her mouth. Sipped. A trickle ran down her chin. Jessie tried turning her head to look behind her. "Can I give my dog some?"

"No, you can't. Jeez, Jessie."

They were on the main road into town now. Warehouses and small factories and a lumberyard.

"What about my truck? It's got all my gardening gear in it." Somebody drove it away from the fire and left it on the road, but Jessie had been in no fit state to drive. "Oh shit!"

"What?"

"There's a can of gas in the back. For the mower."

"Gas? Why didn't you…" Cuffy shook his head, then radioed Kinsley. He told Kinsley about the gas. "And one of you drive Jessie's pickup to her house, you got that?" The two deputies still at the fire scene were Kinsley and Lee. Grant Lee was a fresh-faced rookie deputy.

"Sir, what's the ETA on the ambulance?" Kinsley asked over the two-way radio.

"It got diverted to a highway collision." Cuffy paused. "Pat, Rob, and Clyde are dead, God rest their souls. A few more minutes won't matter."

"Yes, sir."

Jessie gasped midway through taking a gulp of water. It went down the wrong way and she coughed and spluttered. Cuffy glared at her as if her choking fit was just a means of wasting his time.

"You mind telling me what the hell you were doing there?" he asked. He looked her up and down, pointing out her protective clothing in a flattering mustard yellow.

"I was trying to save them. What do you think I was doing?" she snapped.

"Don't use that tone with me." He flicked her a warning look. "How did you know about the fire?"

"Excuse me?" She screwed her face up in disbelief.

"Answer the question, Jessie."

She tried to think straight but it was kind of hard with a pounding headache.

"I woke up coughing. The air's been bad, what with the wildfires and all. But this smoke was something different. It had a chemical smell, like melting plastic and burning rubber. I knew it was a house fire. I put on my gear and followed my nose."

They were on a straight stretch of road. Cuffy stared at her for a few seconds then focused back on the road. His side profile flashed in and out of silhouette as they sped past streetlights that briefly filled the vehicle with light. Double chin, mustache, small eyes, shaved head, the dark regrowth of his receding hairline just evident. Dark khaki shirt. Light khaki pants. Above his chest pocket on the left was his badge. It glinted in the passing glare from a twenty-four-hour gas station. His gut protruded over his belt and, at six feet three inches, he seemed to fill the whole vehicle. Cuffy might have put on a bit of weight in the last ten years but she knew never to underestimate him. He was as wily as a coyote.

"So what happened?" he asked.

They were now passing houses on the outskirts of town.

"When I drove in, the lower level was on fire. Pat broke the bedroom window upstairs. Shouted for help." Jessie frowned, then rolled her lips together, thinking. "No, that's wrong. I was going to use the hose, but it wasn't there. It's always in the same spot, but it was… gone. Then Pat broke the bedroom window. Their ladder was in the garage. I couldn't get to it, so I went to get my stepladder. I thought if I could get onto the porch roof, I could help her down from the bedroom window."

"And Rob?"

"I don't know. I didn't see him." Was she remembering this right?

They passed the Walmart parking lot. There were a few cars in it. The store was open, although it looked pretty empty. A couple was leaving with a trolley full of what appeared to be groceries. Shift workers, Jessie guessed.

"Then what?" Cuffy prompted.

"A man ran at me when I was untying my stepladder. He hit me on the side of my skull." She raised a hand and pointed. "I fell. I must have been unconscious. The next thing I remember is Clyde leaning over me."

Cuffy's grip on the steering wheel tightened. Jessie didn't envy him the task of informing Clyde's family of his death. Or having to contact Pat and Rob's daughter in Oregon.

"Uh-huh. You want to tell me about the Glock?"

Jessie had completely forgotten about it. Where had she left it? Must be in the glove box. "I have a license."

"I know you do, but why take it to the scene of a fire?"

She swiveled in her seat so she could see his face better. Her head throbbed like hell. Cuffy went in and out of focus. For a second, she thought she might actually spew. "I was afraid, okay? I'm a woman, alone at night. I wanted my pistol with me. What's wrong with that?"

Cuffy just nodded, whatever that meant.

Jessie saw the high school through the windshield. *Her* high school. She had been a straight-A student for a while. Popular even. Her dad had wanted her to go into medicine. Her mom just wanted her to follow her dream. So she had studied criminal justice at the University of Washington and achieved a first-class honors degree. And yet here she was, gardening for a living.

"Why would someone hit you?"

Jessie couldn't help doing a double-take. The last time Cuffy had used a similar phrase he had been questioning her about Marcus. *Why would Marcus hit you?* he had asked, incredulous.

Jessie eventually answered. "I'm guessing he didn't want me to save them."

"What makes you so sure he was a guy?"

She looked down into her lap and tried to remember. The person was little more than a dark blur. She didn't see his face. "At first I thought it was Rob. I don't know why. Man's body, I guess. No curves like a woman. He wore pants."

"A heavy branch was found right next to you. Looks like it has blood on it. Could've hit you on the head when it fell."

"No. I tell you, I saw someone. He ran and hit me. A rock or something." She was too loud. Agitated.

"Calm down, Jessie."

Her intestines felt as if they were writhing. It was her fear at not being believed, yet again.

"You don't believe me, do you? Just like last time."

"Maybe that's got something to do with you being a liar."

"I'm not!"

Jessie's head felt as if it were about to burst open. Shut up, she wanted to yell at him.

"You accused Marcus of domestic violence. You nearly ruined a good man's career—"

"He abused me for two years," she said, through gritted teeth.

"Jude saw you fall and break your arm. Marcus didn't do it."

"She's a lying bitch!" It was out of her mouth, vicious and bitter, before she realized she'd spoken.

Cuffy wagged a pudgy finger at her. "That temper of yours is part of the problem." *He was right there*, she thought. "Did you have a falling out with Pat and Rob?" The question was offered casually, as if it were a passing thought. But Jessie saw now that he had been leading to this question the whole time.

"We got on just fine. I liked them and they liked me. They even asked me to go with them to Oregon. They were leaving this morning to go stay with their daughter. Pat talked about a granny flat I could have. At her daughter's house. She was worried about me." Jessie stared at Cuffy. Did he think she started the fire? "I would never hurt them."

"Did you accept their invitation?"

"No. I have to be here to defend my property."

Cuffy glanced at her. "You're telling me Pat offered her daughter's granny flat to you?" There was disbelief in his voice.

"That's correct. You can't seriously believe I would…" She couldn't complete the sentence. She suddenly felt drained, like she'd run out of adrenaline and she felt a desperate urge to sleep.

Cuffy drove into the hospital entrance and pulled up right outside some sliding glass doors, above which was a sign that said EMERGENCY, lit up in red. That about summed up Jessie's life. One fricking emergency after another. First her dad dies in a car accident, then her mom dies of breast cancer, then Marcus almost kills her, and now it seemed Cuffy was trying to fit her up for Pat's and Rob's deaths.

"Do I need a lawyer?" she asked.

"That depends, Jessie. This is now a criminal investigation. Forensics will go over the place with a fine-tooth comb. Footprints. Tire marks. The blood on the branch. If you're hiding something, Jessie, you better tell me now. Two house fires within a five-mile radius is too much of a coincidence."

"You think someone lit both fires?" Jessie was still struggling to come to terms with the idea.

"That's one line of investigation."

"But Marcus said…"

Cuffy's head flicked around fast. "I thought we agreed you'd stay away from him."

"He came to my place. Ask him. He just turned up. Said Paul started the fire. A cigarette butt." She closed her eyes. There was something she needed to remember. That was it. "Where is Marcus? I didn't see him at the Wilmots' place."

"He was there. Came in on his day off to help out. As I said, he's a good man." He glanced at her, his eyes narrowing. "Why do you ask me that? You want to go around to his house and make a scene? Frighten Jude? Don't make me place a restraining order on you."

Frighten Jude? He really had no idea. Jude was afraid, yes, but not of her. "Everything I told you about tonight is true. I swear. Somebody started that fire and he didn't want me messing with his plans."

"We'll see."

Cuffy drove away. Jessie and Bartie stood outside the emergency department and watched him leave. Then she sat on a wrought-iron bench to one side of the ER's sliding doors. It was sheltered from the weather by an overhang and was lit so brightly it caused her to squint. It was very quiet. Nobody came and nobody went. She guessed Pat and Rob were somewhere inside the hospital or maybe at the Medical Examiner's Office. She tried to clean away the blood spots and dirt on her face with an unbloodied corner of the towel Cuffy had let her keep. In her firefighter gear she must look like a refugee from a costume party, a zombie firefighter perhaps? Bartie lay at her feet wearily. She stroked his back.

"Good boy."

She really should get her head wound checked out. How many times had she been there? Too many. She imagined the gossip. Guess who rolled in here at three in the morning? What was she doing at the fire? You should have seen the state of her. It was bad enough the sheriff suspected her. She was sure he did. Maybe a few painkillers would do the trick? There was a twenty-four-hour pharmacy across the road.

A paramedic walked out the door and lit a cigarette. He didn't bother looking her way, just strolled around the corner. Her head continued to throb. She might have a concussion. But the nurses wouldn't let her take Bartie in there and she didn't like leaving him tied up outside after such a traumatic night. And she didn't want him stolen. Sunrise was in two hours. She'd buy some painkillers and wait for the first bus going to Lake View Drive.

CHAPTER THIRTEEN

The blue-and-white bus turned onto the street at 5:55 a.m. The dawn sky was yet again a sickly yellowish brown and everything beneath it was dark and gloomy. It felt as if she were in some kind of parallel world. As messed up as her real one, but the colors were all wrong.

Jessie ached all over, despite taking pain relief. She had fallen asleep briefly on the bench outside ER and woke with a cricked neck to add to the throbbing skull. By the time she and Bartie reached the bus stop, there was only a forty-minute wait until the first bus of the day arrived. She longed to get home and take a shower, to clean the grime from her skin and the stink of smoke from her hair. She hoped it might also help to wash away Pat's terrified screams from inside her head. How could she ever forget the image of the woman framed by flames?

Jessie held Bartie's leash tightly as she waited for the bus to come to a stop, hoping the driver wouldn't kick up a fuss about her dog. She stared into the bus's windshield, trying to see who was driving, but the light was poor and the bus's headlights blinded her. She signaled to the driver and the bus came to a halt, the compression breaks hissing as the front door swung open. She recognized the man behind the wheel: red short-cropped hair, thin lips. Recently divorced Marty Spaan had been in the year above Jessie at high school. Looking at him now, slouched over the steering wheel, it was hard to believe that he'd once been regarded as quite a catch.

"Look who it is. Jessie Lewis. Ain't seen you around in a while." Marty rolled some gum around his mouth. "What you doing in town this early?"

"This and that. How are you, Marty?"

"Good. You volunteering again?" He eyed her yellow and fluorescent-striped clothing.

"Nope." She stepped onto the bus. Bartie hopped on too.

"He needs a muzzle."

She kept coming up the steps. "Since when?"

"Since forever. No muzzle, no ride." He leaned back into his seat.

Jessie had reached the platform level with Marty. She looked down the length of the bus's interior. There was just one guy seated right at the back.

Jessie tried another angle. "He's a therapy dog."

"Sure he is, and I'm Barack Obama."

"Oh come on, Marty. There's one passenger. He doesn't care about the dog. I gotta get home and I don't have my pickup."

Marty folded his arms across his gray fleece. "Why would I do *you* a favor?" he said with a sneer. This was about Marcus. Marcus had stirred up the men in the town, making out that he was the nice-guy victim and she was queen bitch. She swallowed down a scream and tried to keep her voice level. She was near breaking point.

"Marty, please, give me a break. It's been a long night. I'll pay for the dog."

Marty tapped the top pocket of his fleece. She saw the outline of his phone. "You want me to call the cops?"

She felt like strangling him. The last thing she needed right now was Cuffy or any of his deputies. She turned in the tight space and walked down the steps. "Say hi to Stacy for me," she called out, referring to Marty's ex-wife. "I hear she's getting married."

It was no secret that as soon as their divorce was finalized, Stacy announced she was marrying a pilot who lived in Seattle. Jessie's comment was bitchy, but her nerves were as frayed as the Wilmots' burned drapes and it felt good to bite back.

From the sidewalk she glanced behind her to see Marty's eyes giving her a hard stare.

"Why would I care?" Marty said. "I'm having a fine time being single. More women than I can handle."

As the bus doors closed, Marty gave her the finger.

Jessie wanted to curl up on the sidewalk and sleep. Totally deflated, she sat at the side of the road, her feet in the gutter, and draped an arm around Bartie's shoulders. Coming down the street was a sheriff's Chevy Suburban. The driver flashed the headlights and slowed. Seriously? Had Marty gone and called the cops? Jessie dropped her forehead onto her knees. She wanted to cry but she'd be damned if she would.

A car door opened. Footsteps scuffing the asphalt.

"Jessie, are you okay?"

Jessie looked up into Deputy Kinsley's eyes, which had puffy skin beneath them. He looked tired. His uniform and boots were smudged with gray dirt. He must have only just left the fire scene. "I thought the sheriff took you to the hospital?"

"He did."

"And?"

"And I didn't go in, okay! And I can't get a bus home because of the dog." It was like a water valve was opening behind her eyes and she couldn't stop it. Her eyes filled with tears. "They burned to death," she sobbed. "The worst way to die. And I couldn't… I didn't…" Her voice sounded whiny. She hated whiny people and here she was whining at Kinsley, a guy she barely knew.

Kinsley sat on the edge of the sidewalk next to her. "Jessie, you're in shock. You're injured. I don't think it's a good idea if you go home alone. Is there anyone you could stay with?"

Jessie peered at the deputy through a watery blur. No, was the simple answer. Jessie sniffed hard. She didn't have a tissue to wipe her runny nose. "I have my dog. He's all I need."

"You really should get that head injury looked at. How about I come with you?"

"And look like I'm under arrest? No way."

Kinsley didn't bat an eyelid at her rebuff. "Okay then, how about a ride home?"

Jessie blinked, then used her hand to wipe a tear from the end of her nose. "You mean it?"

"Sure."

"Thanks."

"Here," said the deputy, standing and offering a hand. Jessie hesitated then grasped it.

She got in the back of the vehicle and Bartie lay across her lap. Kinsley drove out of town, windows down, his arm on the door.

"Second house fire in two days." He tutted. "Looks to me like we've got ourselves an arsonist. What do you think, Jessie?"

He eyed her in the rear-view mirror.

"That's what Cuffy thinks. All I know is somebody didn't want me to save Pat and Rob." Her eyelids felt heavy. She longed for sleep.

"Know anyone with a grudge against them?"

Please stop asking questions, she thought. *I'm too tired to think.* "They were good people. I can't think of anyone who'd want to hurt them."

"Talk me through everything from the moment you arrived at the house."

"I already did that with Cuffy."

"Humor me."

Jessie rubbed her forehead and began to recount what she could remember, but she didn't get far before Kinsley interrupted her. "Did anyone see you leave your house or arrive at the Wilmots' place?"

"Of course not. It was one in the morning. I live alone," she snapped. "Why is it so hard to believe I followed the smoke? I tried to save them. I didn't start the fire."

"I'm trying to help you, Jessie," Kinsley said.

Jessie didn't believe him. She'd been a fool to let her guard down. He had seemed kindly. Nothing in life was free, this ride included. "It's dense forest where I live. I could host an all-night party and my neighbors wouldn't have a clue who came and went. We like to keep ourselves to ourselves."

Jessie watched the back of Kinsley's head nod a few times. "Your neighbor, down by the lake. Bill Moran. Said he heard a vehicle on Lake View Drive at around midnight."

Jessie was surprised that Weird Bill would talk to a cop. He had a history of annoying the local sheriff's office.

"So?"

"So maybe you're mistaken about the time you went to the Wilmots' place."

"No, I'm not. I checked my cell when I woke up. It was 1:09 a.m. I left the house ten or so minutes later." Jessie stared out the window and gnawed at a hangnail. Kinsley stayed quiet. Jessie went on, "I'd take what Bill says with a pinch of salt. You know people around here call him Weird Bill?"

"I heard. You want to tell me why?"

Jessie had never ventured onto his property. She only ever saw him from a distance. Word was he would shoot anyone who turned up at his house uninvited. Seems Kinsley had the luck of the devil.

"I've known Bill since I was a kid. Back then he was the only lawyer in town. Did real well for himself. Had a big house, fancy car. Then he lost everything in some kind of scam. I don't remember the details. His wife left him. Took the kid. He lost the house and his business. He had a breakdown. Disappeared for a while. Some say he was in a mental hospital. When he came back, he was a different man. Railing against the government, the banks, police. Everything was a conspiracy. He once walked into a bank on Center Street and dropped his pants and pissed on the floor."

"Oh-kay," said Kinsley, quiet for a moment. "Moran also said he heard a motorcycle go by at around 1:30 a.m." He let the statement hang for a while. "You got a neighbor with a motorcycle?"

"Nope." There was one particular guy who had a motorcycle but there was no way she was going to suggest Kinsley should talk to Cuffy's son. "And I don't own a motorcycle. Can barely afford my pickup."

"I'll need a written statement. We'll do it when we get to your place. While it's still fresh."

Yup, thought Jessie, *nothing in life was for free.*

CHAPTER FOURTEEN

It had been a good morning for Ruth Sullivan.

She was on her way home from Marymere where she had run a two-hour learn-to-shoot and pistol-safety class at an outdoor rifle range. It was well attended and the owner of the range had asked her to take another class in two weeks' time. It felt good to use her skills to help other people, and perhaps this and her self-defense class were the start of a small business she could run from home. Her only problem with the outdoor range had been the poor air quality due to the forest fires. Ruth had battled a tickly cough and had needed to use her inhaler. But the fires would pass soon, she assured herself.

Ruth pulled into the Safeway parking lot on the outskirts of Eagle Falls. She headed into the grocery store and went straight for the bakery-deli section. Popping a freshly baked loaf and some cheese into her basket, Ruth then strolled to the sushi counter. Victor loved sushi, especially the Shoreline Combo with tuna, so she picked up a tray for him and a couple of other options to share. He needed cheering up. Yesterday's interview had gone badly.

"Coo-ee! Ruth!" Susie Cuffy called from the in-store café.

Because the café had only a few tables, most people ordered coffee and meals to go. "Over here!" Susie beckoned.

Ruth joined her.

"I'm ordering coffee," said Susie. "What would you like? I have so much to tell you." Susie's green eyes twinkled.

"A small latte, please, no sugar." Ruth looked down at her shopping basket. "I'll pay for this, then I'll come on over."

"Perfect," Susie said.

Ruth went and paid at the checkout for her groceries and then returned to the café where Susie was seated at a table for two and the coffees had arrived.

Susie patted the seat of an empty chair. Ruth sat. "So how are you settling in?"

"Good. Everyone's been lovely, although I find the park fire worrying."

"Yes, we all do. Never seen anything like it and I've lived here my whole life. You know they've called in firefighters from other states? And then there's the house fires." Had Ruth heard her right? Did Susie say *fires*? Susie continued, "I've known Pat and Rob forever. I still can't believe they're gone."

"There's been *another* house fire?" Ruth asked.

"Yes, last night. Haven't you heard?" There was a hint of criticism in her tone.

"No, I had a course to teach in Marymere this morning. Tell me what happened."

Susie leaned across the small table. "Pat and Rob Wilmot. Couldn't meet a nicer couple. Lived on Devil Mountain. The fires took the whole house and they couldn't get out." Susie shuddered. "And one of our brave firefighters died fighting the fire. Did you meet Clyde Hudson?" Ruth shook her head. "His poor widow's pregnant. It's terrible." Susie pulled a tissue from her purse and blew her nose loudly.

Two house fires, Ruth thought. She felt shaky all of a sudden.

Ruth hadn't met the victims, so their deaths didn't affect Ruth in the same way as Susie. Ruth's overriding concern was for herself and her family. *House fires on consecutive nights. That can't be a coincidence.* A trickle of sweat ran down the back of her neck. The thought of being trapped inside a burning house terrified her. She stared at her untouched cup of coffee. The little fern shape in the froth at the top of her latte had begun to disintegrate.

"Are you all right?" Susie asked, her eyes roaming Ruth's flushed face and clammy skin.

"I've been rushing about. Just need to cool down a bit."

Ruth was short of breath. *No, not now. Not in front of Susie.* To be trapped inside a burning house was Ruth's worst nightmare. She had terrible dreams in which Noah and David would scream for her help and she couldn't reach them. Ruth tried to brush the images from her mind. *Snap out of it*, she told herself. *Ask questions. Knowledge is power. You can control your fear.*

"Do you know what caused last night's fire?" Ruth asked.

"Well," Susie looked around, then back to Ruth. "Marcus is looking into it. He's the fire scene investigator." She looked left, then right, then leaned across the table. "He's keeping his cards close to his chest on this one." She lowered her voice a notch more. "John thinks its arson."

"Any suspects?"

"Ruth, you know I couldn't tell you even if I knew, but it's no secret they found someone unconscious at the fire scene last night. Someone dressed in firefighter gear." She paused, milking the moment. "Someone who isn't a firefighter anymore." She gave a single, decisive nod.

"Are you going to tell me who?" Ruth asked.

"You've met her. She was at your self-defense class." Susie was enjoying the game, spinning her story out for as long as she could.

Ruth didn't want to even try to guess. She might offend Susie if she guessed wrong. "I have no idea. Who?"

"Jessie Lewis."

Jessie? The awkward young woman who was rebuffed by two women in the parking lot after the class. "Why her? Has she lit fires before?"

"I don't know, but Jessie has a nasty streak. She's trouble with a capital T. Did you hear what she did to Marcus? It was a crying shame."

"No."

"Have you met Marcus?"

"Not yet. He's fire captain, I believe?"

"He's a wonderful man. Everybody loves him. And"—Susie winked—"very good-looking. Well, we were all surprised when he started dating Jessie. She's not exactly a stunner, if you know what I mean." Ruth really disliked comments like this. A good relationship was about more than good looks. "There's a rumor that she became a volunteer firefighter because she wanted to get her claws into Marcus. I don't know if there's any truth in that, but they started dating soon after. Of course, I knew it wouldn't last. He was way too good for her and she was a funny, quiet thing. She took after her pa that way. Marcus loves people. A real extrovert. If there's a party, he's at the center of it. He's so entertaining. I mean, they couldn't be more different. And he has always loved voluptuous women, and Jessie is not that at all. Anyway, Jessie moved into his house on the lake, and she started her gardening business, and their relationship was okay for a while. I have to admit I was shocked when rumors circulated that they were getting engaged. She ended up in hospital with a broken arm and a couple of broken ribs. She told everyone she'd fallen off a ladder. Then all of a sudden she changed her story. Claimed Marcus beat her. Broke her arm. She said he'd abused her all throughout their relationship. She went to see John and made it official. Forced his hand."

"I'm sorry, Susie, how do you mean forced his hand?" Ruth's neck and cheeks were getting redder by the second. Not from fear. Ruth was growing angry.

"She was lying. But she made a formal accusation of domestic violence and John had to investigate. Marcus, of course, was heartbroken. He obviously loved her, but she has a jealous streak, and she couldn't bear to see him with other women. Marcus went through a terrible time, poor man. It could have ruined his career. Thankfully she withdrew her allegations."

Ruth had her hands tightly clasped together in her lap. Her blood was boiling. "What made you believe Jessie was lying?"

Susie sat back, frowning. "Marcus would never hurt a fly. And besides, Jude caught Jessie out in a lie."

Ruth recalled Jude scuttling away from Jessie in the parking lot. Curvaceous, tanned skin, beautifully dressed. Confident and yet… upset? Ruth couldn't place her finger on it. "What lie?"

"Jessie claimed Jude witnessed him shoving her down the stairs. Jude denied it. Jude said that Jessie slipped and Marcus tried to catch her."

"What about her medical records? Was there a history of bruises, sprains, broken bones?"

"Jessie is accident prone. I have no idea why she chose to be a gardener."

Ruth stared at Susie, speechless. How could Susie be so sure that Marcus was innocent? Ruth had hunted terrorists who, their parents and friends swore, were kind, lovely people. During her time at the Bureau, Ruth learned that people who committed brutal crimes were capable of hiding their actions from loved ones. They were also often capable of heinous acts and yet could also be loving parents or kind to a neighbor. Nothing was ever as black and white as Susie was assuming.

Susie must have read her thoughts because she lifted her chin defensively. "Ruth, I've known Marcus since he was a day old. He's always been a good boy. He'd never strike a woman."

Ruth sensed Susie was affronted. "Forgive me, Susie, I can't help asking questions. It went with the job."

Ruth was saved from further awkwardness by Millie Kemp, who bustled over to chat with Susie. After giving Ruth a curt nod, Millie pulled a chair over. Ruth made her excuses, saying that she had to go to the pharmacy. She handed in a prescription to the middle-aged pharmacist, Emmanuel Gilliam. This was the first time she'd had to get a fresh supply of sleeping pills since leaving Seattle, having ensured she had an ample supply before they left. While Ruth waited, she scrolled through news bulletins on the latest house fire. The details of last night's house fire were sketchy. Cuffy was probably keen to keep them close to his chest. The pharmacist called out her name and showed her a packet of Restoril.

"Have you taken these before?" he asked, peering through black-framed glasses.

Ruth said she had and held out her credit card for payment. She didn't want people to know she took sleeping pills. The sooner the medication was in a paper bag the better.

"Ruth!"

Susie was racing up the aisle toward her, clutching a brown paper bag of groceries. Ruth's groceries. She had forgotten them.

"Can I pay, please?" Ruth said, her tone urgent. But the pharmacist moved at a sloth's pace.

"There you are! I thought I was going to have to drive these to your house." Susie handed Ruth her grocery bag, then fanned her flushed face with her hand.

The packet of sleeping pills was only partway into a bag.

"Sleeping pills, huh?" Susie rested a reassuring hand on Ruth's wrist. "You poor dear. All those long nights at stakeouts. Must mess with your sleeping patterns. I *so* understand. But you know those things are addictive, don't you, Ruth. I'm right, aren't I, Emmanuel?"

"Yes, Mrs. Cuffy, they can be." He finally popped the packet into a bag and handed it to Ruth. It was all Ruth could do to stop herself from snatching it. "I'm sure Mrs. Sullivan has gone through all that with her doctor."

Susie opened her mouth to speak. Was she really about to ask Ruth if she had discussed this with her doctor? Ruth wanted the conversation over with, so she jumped in first. "Very sorry, but I have to dash. Thank you so much for these."

And dash she did, clutching her grocery bag to her. Victor had warned Ruth to be careful about what she said to Susie, who liked to spread gossip. Soon the whole town would know that Ruth took sleeping pills. It shouldn't matter, but it niggled Ruth. She doubted anyone could fully comprehend the insomnia she suffered as a result of the bomb blast. Every time she closed her eyes, she relived the horror of it. Without sleeping pills, she wouldn't get any rest.

CHAPTER FIFTEEN

Prairie Ridge was much like Eagle Falls. Quiet. Lots of trees. Tight-knit community. But it was flatter and bigger than Eagle Falls, with a river flowing through the town. It was lunchtime and Jessie sat across a Formica table from Georgia Amarillas. Jessie was eating peach and mango frozen yogurt, doing her best to ignore her bone-aching tiredness. Georgia tucked into her cookies'n'cream frozen yogurt, head down, eyes fixed on the waxed cardboard tub.

"I like this one best," Georgia said.

Jessie smiled at the woman she had known since they were two years old. Georgia said the same thing every time they visited Menchie's, even though each time it was a different flavor. Last week she liked the creamy peanut butter one. The week before it was the pomegranate razz sorbet. Jessie took another mouthful of her frozen yogurt and relished the iciness sliding down her raw throat. Her lungs felt sore too from inhaling so much bad smoke last night, as if someone had dragged a rake over them. She felt a cough coming on and she held a paper napkin over her mouth. She was still coughing up filthy black stuff. She scrunched the napkin into a ball and pocketed it to dispose of later.

Jessie had almost canceled her visit to Georgia, but now she was there, she was glad she hadn't. She had only gotten four hours' sleep and she had a lump above her ear the size of a cherry that was so tender she hadn't dared brush her hair. Despite a couple of painkillers, there was a dull throb in her temples and sunlight gave her a piercing pain at the back of her eyes. Which is why she was wearing her shades inside the store.

"You look like a movie star, Jessie."

"Thanks. I've got a headache."

Jessie had left her dog with Irene, Georgia's mom; Georgia lived with her mom and had done so ever since the overdose that had almost killed her. Irene and Georgia had moved from Eagle Falls to Prairie Ridge, some ten miles away, to avoid the scowls from townsfolk who condemned Georgia for being an addict.

"Do you remember Pat and Rob Wilmot?" Jessie asked.

Georgia shook her head of short, dark curls. When she, Jessie, Jude, and Brittany had been best buddies at school, Georgia had long black hair that spiraled and curled like a princess from a fairy tale. Jessie had been envious of her beautiful hair; Jessie's hair had always been straight. Now, even though she was the same age as Jessie, Georgia's hair had turned salt and pepper. Georgia was also painfully thin, which gave her a haggard look.

"Who?"

Georgia suffered from Toxic Brain Injury as a result of the heroin overdose that happened during her second year at medical school. It left her with diminished mental capacity and epilepsy. She also had difficulty remembering people if she didn't mix with them often.

"Pat and Rob lived in the mountains," Jessie clarified. "She was beautiful and glamorous when she was young." Georgia didn't respond. She kept eating. A blob of yogurt slipped down Georgia's chin but she didn't seem to notice. "There was a house fire last night. They died." Georgia kept eating. "I tried to save them." Jessie's voice cracked.

Georgia looked up and frowned. "What's wrong, Jessie?"

"Everything," Jessie said, then immediately felt guilty. At least she had her health. At least her mind functioned properly. It wasn't fair for Jessie to moan like this. "Sorry, Georgie, I'm just being silly. Would you like to see a movie later?"

"Maybe." Georgia stretched out a hand and squeezed Jessie's. "What's up, my friend? You look sad."

"Friends died in a fire last night." Jessie realized that she considered Rob and Pat as friends, not just clients. "They were nice people. That makes me sad."

"Yes, that is sad."

"I tried to put out the fire and somebody hit my head with a rock or something. And now the sheriff thinks I started the fire. He doesn't believe there was anyone else there."

"Big John? He always had it in for you. I don't like him, but Mom says he's a good sheriff." Georgia continued to hold Jessie's hand.

A teenage couple walked past them on their way to place their order and snickered. Jessie heard the boy whisper to the girl, "Lesbians."

Jessie ignored them. The boy was young and stupid. "Marcus came to my house. He warned me to stay away from Jude." The cold yogurt felt heavy in her stomach.

"To your house! Oh my God, you must have been so scared."

Georgia was clearly unaware her fingernails were digging into Jessie's palm. Jessie had to unravel Georgia's fingers. "I was very scared. I hate the way that I can't stand up for myself. I can't even speak. I… freeze and I don't know how to get over it. I'm pathetic."

"I'm pathetic. You're not. Look at me. I live with my mom." She suddenly shifted from glum to excited. "I know what to do. Come and live here!" she said, voice raised with enthusiasm. Jessie momentarily freed her hand from Georgia's strong grip, but Georgia grasped it again. "It would be such fun. Like teenagers again." Her face glowed.

"We have fun anyway, don't we?" Jessie said. "Besides, I won't run from him. I won't give him the satisfaction of thinking he scared me away."

"Jessie, please!" Georgia pleaded like a child. "Come and live here. We could see each other every day. Oh!" she said, eyes wide. "You could meet all the dogs I look after at the pound. Wouldn't that be awesome?" Georgia volunteered at the dog pound three mornings a week. "Wait." Georgia's brow creased and she released Jessie's hand. This often happened. She would go quiet as she tried to clutch onto the thread of a new idea. "Who did you say died?"

"Pat and Rob Wilmot."

"Pat… Wilmot." Georgia pondered the name. "Blonde, pretty lady," Georgia said. "She had an affair with Marty?"

"Yes, that's her." Of all the things for Georgia to remember!

"I remember!" She high-fived Jessie. "Woohoo!" Georgia's recollection of an affair that happened when they were seventeen years old was a good sign. Jessie couldn't wait to tell Irene.

Jessie high-fived Georgia.

Georgia continued, "Marty was quite good-looking back then, wasn't he? Geeky, but tall. Even so, I don't understand why Pat did it. He was half her age."

"I didn't get it either. Do you remember the scandal? Marty bragged about their affair and Rob got wind of it. It almost destroyed their marriage and their business." Jessie thought about the bitter man she met earlier that morning driving a bus. "Marty's still a prick."

Georgia exclaimed, in fake shock, "Oh Jessie!" Then she burst out laughing.

Jessie joined in. It was good to laugh. She was enjoying herself. "There's a new family in town. Well, Ruth is new, so are the kids, but her husband was born in Eagle Falls. You remember Victor Sullivan?"

"Victor?" Georgia licked her spoon. "Fat kid, got pushed around?"

"Back then, yes. Not anymore. He's married to a nice lady called Ruth, and guess what Ruth used to do as a job?"

Georgia shook her head. "You have to give me a clue."

"She arrests very dangerous people."

"A cop!"

"No."

"A deputy?"

"No."

"There's nothing else she could be."

"She's FBI. Retired. Doesn't look much older than forty."

"FBI!" Georgia squealed. Heads turned. "Can I meet her? I've always wanted to meet an agent."

"I don't know her, not really."

"Pleeeeease."

"Okay, I'll ask."

"Tell me everything about her!"

Jessie told Georgia about the women's self-defense class and the moves that Ruth had taught her. Georgia hung on her every word. Then Jessie mentioned that she had tried to speak to Jude after the class and Georgia went very quiet. Her lower lip stuck out giving her a childlike sad look.

"What's up?" Jessie asked.

"Jude never visits me." She shook her head. "Marcus made her mean."

On the way home from meeting Georgia, Jessie took a planned detour. She headed back to the hairpin turn known as Break or Bust Bend. The closer she got to it, the greater the pressure she felt inside her chest. It was as if a giant hand were crushing her heart. She slowed to a crawl as she got near. Between the edge of the road and a precipice was a sturdy metal guardrail. It didn't give Jessie much comfort.

This was where her father died.

In 2007, when her father's car went over the edge and he plummeted to his death, there was no guardrail. Nor had the eight-vehicle parking lot that had been cut out of the mountainside existed back then. That, and the guardrail, had been installed a year after Poppy died. Tourists could now walk the trail from the top of the waterfall down to where it plunged one hundred and eighty-six feet into a deep pool of granite rock which then flowed into Devil's Lake. At the waterfall's base was a much larger parking lot, for visitors who chose to walk up the steep trail to the top and then return downhill.

Jessie couldn't bear to think of her poppy's terror as his Jeep skidded over the cliff edge, bouncing over jagged rocks, knocking over saplings, finally coming to a halt at the bottom of the valley, a twisted lump of metal and shattered glass. The coroner concluded that Dr. Tom Lewis's death was an accident. Her mom, Cynthia, thought otherwise. She had let something slip one day that implied that she didn't agree with the coroner. Jessie had overheard her mom talking to Sheriff Cuffy on the landline.

"I saw the skid marks, John. There were two cars. Somebody drove into him. Why didn't he stop and help Tom?" Cynthia had said.

But the matter was already settled and Cuffy wouldn't hear a bar of it.

Jessie pulled into the parking lot, dust and grit swirling around her pickup. She was the only one there. Not surprising, given the extreme fire-danger warnings. She killed the engine and took a few calming breaths. When she was ready, she clipped a leash to Bartie's collar and they set off. The narrow trail to the lookout platform was a ten-minute hike. Even from the start of the trail Jessie heard the waterfall's splashing and grinding, as rocks, branches, anything that had the misfortune to be caught in the white water, was hurled over the steep cliffs. The viewing platform was shrouded in mist. Water droplets were thrown into the air by the force and speed of the waterfall's descent. The mist was cool and it felt good on Jessie's overheated skin. She sat on a wooden bench and Bartie lay on the wet floor.

Today was the anniversary of her father's death. Tom Angus Lewis, as her father was christened, had always loved thistles, particularly the cobweb thistle that grew in the area. She had picked some of the prickly flowers for him.

"Hey, Poppy," she began, "I miss you loads. I've brought you some cobweb thistles." Bartie snapped at a fly, which buzzed away. "Bartie's come to say *hi* too. He's a great dog. You'd like him." She paused. "Things aren't so good, Poppy." A lump formed in her throat. "To be honest, it's pretty bad. I so wish you were here to guide me." She smiled. "Yes, I know. Ironic, huh? I didn't want your advice when you were alive, and now you're gone, I'm asking you for it. Maybe I'm as crazy as folks say?"

Jessie sniffed back a tear.

"I visit your grave often. And Mom's. Keep them tidy. Always make sure you have flowers. But I feel closest to you here. I know it's weird. You died here. But that's the way it is. And I can talk out loud, like you're sitting with me and there's nobody around to see me doing it. So how are you doing? What's it like up there? It's good you and Mom are together. Sometimes I wish I was... no, that's not true. I just miss you both so much." Jessie rubbed her watery eyes. "I know. I was a bitch as a teenager. I always wanted to be out. I wish I'd spent more time with you. I wish I had listened. Maybe things would be different now if I had."

She imagined her father dipping his chin and looking at her over his bifocals, asking her whether she was happy.

"I'm happy enough. I like being on my own. I stay away from town as much as I can, although I occasionally drive by your old medical practice for old times' sake. My new house is great. It's small, deep in the forest but near enough to take swims in the lake. This summer is the hottest on record. I'm so lucky to have the lake to cool off in." Jessie looked off into the distance. "I hope you're not mad at me for selling your house. I couldn't live in town. It was unbearable. The glares, the threats, and... Marcus.

But I've kept lots of your things. All the family photos." A sob. She clenched her eyes shut but tears leaked. "I'm sorry I wasn't nicer to you. I was all teenage hormones. I thought I knew it all. It turns out that I know very little." She sniffed. "I wish I'd told you that I loved you."

Jessie's eyes stung. Rubbing them with the back of her hand just made the stinging worse. It wasn't just her grief causing it. It was the smoke-filled air. She waited a few seconds for the stinging to subside. "I still hear that man's voice. The 911 caller. The sheriff played it to Mom and me. Asked us if we recognized it, but we didn't know who it was. The 911 man was never found, you know. I still don't understand why he didn't try and help you, why he drove all the way into town before he reported it."

For a while, Jessie listened to the roar of the waterfall. It had shrunk in width over the summer because of the drought. But it was still an amazing force of nature.

"You loved this waterfall, didn't you, Poppy? And the cave behind it. You used to take me in there, remember? I was scared of it at first. So slimy and cold and the noise of the pounding water. But you showed me the unique mosses and flowers that grow there. Thanks to you I saw how clever nature was."

One by one she tossed the flowering thistles over the viewing platform's rail and watched them tumble into the mist.

CHAPTER SIXTEEN

It was four in the afternoon and Jessie sat on her porch listening to the buzz and chirrup of insects. The air was so still and hot it was cloying. The heat rose in a haze above the patch of dirt outside her house. On the washing line, her fire-protection clothing was already bone dry; she had only hosed it off thirty minutes ago.

She tore at a fingernail with her teeth. She was stressing. Her afternoon appointments had canceled, no doubt because the gossip-mongers were spreading rumors that Jessie was found at a crime scene. At this rate, she wouldn't be able to buy food, let alone pay her mortgage.

It would be dark in a couple of hours. And a little cooler. When it was dark and the Wilmots' property was no longer crawling with investigators, Jessie planned to do some investigating of her own. Maybe it was because of the blow to her head but she was no longer sure about what she remembered that night. However, there was one thing that she was sure of: Cuffy regarded her as his prime suspect. She had been found at the crime scene. She understood how to start a fire. And he was too damn lazy to explore other suspects. On top of that, Marcus was in charge of the fire scene investigation. If it came down to his word against hers, she was in no doubt who would be believed.

Jessie had to help herself, because Cuffy and his deputies sure as hell weren't going to. She needed to find proof that somebody else was there that night. Her eyelids started to feel heavy. Maybe she should catch up on sleep for an hour or two before she left the house?

The rumble of a vehicle turning onto her driveway had her instantly wide awake. Had Cuffy come to arrest her? Or was it Marcus, back to wreak his revenge because of Clyde's death? He would surely blame her. Marcus would know that Cuffy suspected Jessie started the house fire. He would be livid, and when he was livid, he was violent.

She had to hide. Jessie grabbed Bartie's collar and steered him into the house and shut the door, locking it. Then she raced to shut the windows. She wanted to make it appear as if she wasn't home. Of course, the cabin was already like an oven. Shutting windows and doors would make it even more unbearable, but she couldn't help it. She then drew the stripy kitchen drapes and watched the approaching vehicle through a tiny gap in them. The setting sun was in her eyes. Regardless, she did her best to spot the vehicle's make and color. It would help her identify the new arrival. It wasn't red, which meant it wasn't a fire station vehicle, and it wasn't a black Hummer, which was Marcus's personal car. The vehicle also wasn't black and white, so that ruled out Cuffy or his deputies. Her shoulders had been drawn up to her ears with tension. She relaxed a little.

A silver Buick LaCrosse materialized from the dusty haze and came to a halt in front of her house. A petite blond woman left the vehicle, then she studied the house from a distance. *What is Ruth Sullivan doing here?* Jessie thought.

"Hello?" Ruth called. "Anyone home?" Her cough was deep and harsh. She took from her skirt pocket an inhaler and took a couple of quick bursts into her mouth.

Jessie hesitated, then unlocked the front door and went out onto the porch. Bartie stood next to her, eyeing the visitor suspiciously.

"Need some water?" Jessie offered.

Ruth nodded and then coughed again. "It's way smokier up here," she said huskily.

"Take a seat here." Jessie pointed at the bench on the porch.

In the kitchen, Jessie poured them both glasses of water. From the road came the growly throttling of a motorcycle engine. *Probably Ford spying on me*, she thought, but by the time she joined Ruth outside, the engine noise was gone.

"How do you know where I live?" Jessie asked, handing Ruth a glass. She stayed standing.

Ruth took a sip. "When you enrolled in my class, you gave your address."

Jessie's skin prickled. She didn't like people turning up uninvited. "Okay, so how can I help you?"

Ruth removed her sunglasses. "I heard you'd been knocked unconscious at the fire last night. I was worried about you."

"I've got the mother of all headaches, but I'm alive."

"What you did was very brave, Jessie."

"It was plain dumb, that's what it was. I tried to save them and all I get in return is accusations." She was gabbling. Why was she telling this to a woman she hardly knew?

"Innocent people have nothing to fear."

Jessie snorted derisively. "Yeah, right." She hadn't meant to be rude. She sat next to Ruth on the bench. "That came out wrong, I'm sorry, but you don't understand how it works around here. How could you?"

"Try me."

There was no way Jessie was going to trust a former FBI agent. For all she knew, Cuffy could have sent Ruth to quiz her. Jessie stared out at the forest as she chose her words carefully. "Pat and Rob were good to me. They asked me to leave town with them and stay at their daughter's place. How nice was that? And I failed them."

Jessie didn't look at Ruth. She didn't want the woman to see how upset she was.

"From what I hear, you did your best to save them. That's what counts," Ruth said. "Try not to dwell on what you didn't do. I've made that same mistake. I'm sure you heard about the Lakes Jewish Elementary School bombing. I survived. My partner didn't. Believe me when I say I know all about survivor's guilt."

Ruth put her glass down on the bench and held out her hands, palms upward. They were covered in raised scars, like barnacles on the underside of boats. "My body got beaten up pretty bad and I'm partially deaf in my left ear and…" She tapped her forehead. "I'm still dealing with what goes on up here. Guilt, fear, all of it." Ruth dipped a hand into a pocket and handed her a piece of paper with a phone number on it. "If you need someone to talk to, call me."

Jessie took it and tucked it into her shorts pocket. "Why are you helping me?"

Ruth shrugged. "We all need friends."

Jessie was about to blurt out that she didn't need friends because friends only let you down, but she held her tongue. She still couldn't fathom why Ruth would want to befriend her. Ruth had to be up to something.

Ruth finished her glass of water. "Do you live here alone?"

"No, I have my dog. Why?" Jessie said warily.

"Someone is deliberately lighting fires. I'm concerned for your safety, that's all."

Jessie's eyes dropped to her bare feet, ashamed at being snappy. When she looked up, Ruth was dabbing her damp forehead with a tissue. "Boy, the air's so still up here."

There was a crack of a twig snapping. It came from the direction of her driveway. Bartie raced forward, barking. Jessie rolled her eyes. Of course. Ford must have parked his motorcycle on the road and walked down.

"Bartie, quiet!" Her dog obeyed but stayed alert, his nose pointing in the road's direction.

"Is that you, Ford?" Jessie hollered. "Do you want me to set my dog on you?"

"Ford?" Ruth asked, following Jessie's line of sight.

"Yes, he's probably filming us, the little creep."

A rattle followed by a *vroom* that shattered the still air. The motorcycle rider revved the engine a couple of times them zoomed off.

"That boy's going to get into big trouble one day," Jessie said.

"What kind of trouble?" Ruth asked.

"I caught him filming me through the bathroom window once."

"What!"

"Yeah. I was in the shower. He didn't think I'd chase him, being naked and all that, but I sure did. I took his phone off him and deleted it. Prick!"

"Does his father know?"

"Cuffy's not going to do anything."

"Has he videoed other naked women?"

Jessie eyed Ruth. Was this all going to be relayed to Cuffy? What the hell, Cuffy already hated her and what she was about to say was public knowledge anyway. "Sure. Pat Wilmot for one. Nobody has access to the foreshore where she lived, so she swam naked. Rob caught Ford filming her and dragged him into the sheriff's office. And nothing happened."

"Nothing?"

"Rob and Pat agreed not to press charges."

Ruth stared in the direction of the road, a V-shaped frown on her forehead. Seconds ticked by.

"Can I ask a favor?" Jessie asked.

"Sure."

"I have a friend. She suffers from Toxic Brain Injury. Lives in Prairie Ridge. Anyway, I told her about you and she was real excited. She wanted to meet you." Jessie looked down at her feet. She was getting tongue-tied. "We go for ice cream every week. Georgia loves ice cream, you see. Maybe you could join us?" Jessie looked up. "If you like ice cream."

"I love ice cream and I'd love to come."

"Really?" Jessie felt a burst of excitement.

"Sure. Text me when and where." Ruth got up off the bench. "I must be going. Kids need feeding."

Jessie watched the former FBI agent head for her car. The words were on the tip of her tongue. *Help me*, Jessie wanted to say. *I don't know what to do. I'm going to get blamed for the fires.* But she kept her mouth shut and watched Ruth drive away.

CHAPTER SEVENTEEN

Ruth was helping Noah with his homework when Victor arrived home from a job interview. He parked his pride and joy—a black Ford Mustang GT Premium—in the garage, then entered the kitchen through the adjoining door, his navy-blue suit jacket thrown over his shoulder, his shirtsleeves rolled up his arms. He had lost quite a few kilos since joining the local gym and his forearms were well toned. He had never looked better. The boys ran into his arms and he knelt, taking them both in a group hug.

"How did it go?" Ruth asked.

"Not so good." He looked up at her briefly, then hurriedly back down at the kids who were begging him to take them to the lake for a swim.

"Their loss," Ruth said, trying to sound positive, although she was getting concerned at how many rejections he had had so far.

"Daddy, Daddy! I've got something to tell you!" Noah said.

His brother tried to talk over him.

"Okay, okay," Victor said. "One at a time. Noah, you go first."

Ruth watched the three of them. Victor was like a big kid with them, cracking jokes, playing games. As Victor hugged Noah, congratulating him for being picked for the middle school baseball team, he mouthed *Love you* to her over the boy's shoulder. Then he looked down at his sons. "Get into your swim trunks and we'll play with water pistols in the paddling pool? How does that sound?"

Noah and David ran to their rooms having completely forgotten they had wanted to swim at the lake.

Ruth took Victor in an embrace. "You want to talk about the interview?"

"Not really." He rested his chin over her shoulder, and she felt his body grow limper. He always tried to be upbeat; it was rare for him to drop the façade. "Maybe I'm too old." He sighed.

"At forty-three? No way."

He clung to her. "I don't want to let you down."

"You'll never let me down." She held him tighter. "Is there anything I can do to help?"

He let go of her. "You could get friendly with Susie."

"Sure, I can do that. But why Susie?"

"She's married to the most influential man in the county. Big John knows everybody. One word from him, and doors will open."

"Okay, I'll invite them to dinner. Saturday?"

"Thanks, beautiful," he said, kissing her.

His tongue parted her lips and she felt the eagerness in his body. How could he think her beautiful with a scarred face and body? Their sex life had been nonexistent since the explosion. She felt broken and ugly. She backed away.

"I'm just not ready."

Victor looked hurt but he recovered quickly. He lifted her left palm to his lips and kissed the ribbed scars there. "You're beautiful and never forget it."

"Mommy!" David called from the bedroom, "Where are my trunks?"

"Coming!" she called out and headed for David's room.

Soon, Victor was in his board shorts and chasing the boys around the backyard with a water pistol while in the kitchen Ruth poured some homemade lemonade into plastic tumblers. David and Noah squealed with delight as they retaliated, spraying water at their dad. The inflatable paddling pool in vibrant turquoise was in the middle of the lawn. It was decorated with cute tropical fish. The water in it was low: with the water restrictions, they weren't allowed to refill it. But it was perfect for paddling and for refilling water pistols.

Ruth carried the tumblers of lemonade outside on a tray and then sat at the patio table.

"Mommy!" cried David, aiming his water pistol at her and firing.

Laughing, she chased David around the pool. Noah took the opportunity to use his water pistol on her too, so she changed direction and began chasing him. Soaked through, she ran inside and put on her one-piece swimsuit and sat in the pool while the boys pretended to be sharks. She was self-conscious about the scarred gash on her thigh and the red and shiny burn scars on her arms but neither Victor nor her sons seemed to notice them anymore, so she relaxed and enjoyed watching their innocent play.

Later on, Victor and Ruth sat at the garden table watching the boys chuck inflatable rings over an inflated pole in the pool. So far only Noah had managed to throw the ring in the right place.

"I hate to spoil the mood, but we need to prepare for evacuation, Ruthie," Victor asked.

Ruth put down her glass of lemonade. "Jesus," she muttered. "Is nowhere safe?"

"We pack the car. That's all. It's just a precaution."

Her whole body tensed. "Why now? What's changed?"

"A cold front is heading this way and it could cause the fires to change direction."

Ruth stared at David and Noah, so carefree and so oblivious of the fire danger. Sometimes she wished she were a kid again and somebody else made all the hard decisions. "When?"

"Could be Thursday."

In two days! It made her nauseous just thinking about it.

When she didn't say anything, Victor added, "The cold front may not happen and they'll probably have the wildfire under control by then. Please stop worrying, Ruthie."

"We have to keep the kids safe. I'll take them to your sister's first thing tomorrow."

"No need for that," Victor said. "They've only just started school, and besides, Kelly's got a lot on her plate." His sister lived ten miles away in Marymere.

Ruth stood slowly. She suddenly felt old and very, very weary. She had the strange sensation that the fire in her nightmares was coming true. "I guess we should get packing."

CHAPTER EIGHTEEN

Daylight was fading to a sliver of smoky-pink on the horizon by the time Jessie and Bartie pulled up at what remained of the Wilmots' home. Hers was the only vehicle parked at the drive's entrance. Crime scene tape in yellow hung limply from the blackened remains of two tree trunks, blocking access to the drive. She killed the engine and listened for voices. The last person in the world she wanted to bump into was Marcus or Cuffy's crew.

She fitted a headlamp over her scalp and, switching it on, she then pulled on latex gloves, which stuck to her perspiring skin. Tucked into her shorts waistband was her concealed-carry holster and her Glock 43, which sat snugly in the small of her back. This time, she wasn't taking any chances. Somebody knocked her out cold last night and she wasn't going to let it happen again. In her pocket she had a couple of transparent zip bags should she find evidence of the real arsonist. She wasn't going to have Cuffy pin Rob's and Pat's murders on her. Or hold her responsible for Clyde's death. No way.

The forest surrounding the lakeside property was so black and lifeless it felt surreal, almost as if she were walking into a fantasy world. Pockets of smoke floated above the ash on the forest floor like ghosts weaving between charred and distorted pieces of debris. Except for the distant lapping of lake water, the area was eerily quiet. Animals and birds had fled the area. Not even insects thrummed and buzzed. Jessie had Bartie on a tight leash as they walked along the drive to where the lawn had once been a magnificent green, and the colorful flowers had grown in abundance. It was now just black dirt.

The house might as well have been bulldozed. All that remained was the rear stone wall, some melted blobs of blue glass, and layer upon layer of ash. It felt as if the house, and not just the owners, had died. Everywhere there was a bitter, chemical smell. Jessie's firefighter training had taught her that in a modern home, most of the furnishings were made from petrochemicals, like the stuffing in sofa cushions and mattresses, plastic toys, and furniture. She recalled watching a video in which a boy's bedroom was replicated inside a shipping container, within the safe confines of a fire service training center. No accelerants or petrol were used, just a lighter. The kid's room became a deadly concoction of flames and black smoke within two minutes. Trapped inside such an enclosed space, she prayed that Pat and Rob died from inhaling the toxins before their flesh burned.

The car, which Rob had loaded with their most prized possessions, was nothing more than a skeleton of bent, blackened metal. Every photo album, every painting, every item of clothing, every memento of their lives had been consumed by the flames. The fire had not only killed them. It had also obliterated their history.

If only they had left one day earlier, they would be alive and in Oregon with their daughter.

Beep.

Jessie jumped and drew her pistol. She turned a full circle searching for the source of the sound in the darkness. At the rear of the property, in the part of the original house that used to be a guest bedroom, a flashlight beam bounced one way and then the other. A person, little more than a silhouette, was bent forward as if inspecting something, then he disappeared behind what remained of a brick wall. Was she watching a killer? Jessie froze, her heart in her mouth. A voice in her head screamed at her to get the hell out of there and dial 911. But she couldn't do that. The sheriff's office would want to know what she was doing at a crime scene, especially as she was already a suspect. If she crept closer, she might be able to identify the person. Perhaps even take a photo.

Switching off her headlamp so that the intruder wouldn't see her approach, Jessie waited for her eyes to adjust to the night. Once she could see well enough to advance, she crept along the exterior side passage. It was impossible to do it quietly. Rubble crunched beneath her boots. But the figure didn't appear to be aware of her approach.

"Useless!" the man said so suddenly that Jessie stumbled.

There was barely twelve feet separating them. Now she could see why he hadn't heard her. He had headphones on and was holding a metal detector. He flung an object aside. *Crash!*

In the man's wide flashlight beam, she saw long bony legs, a baggy collared shirt, and a wide-brimmed straw sunhat.

Beep!

He stumbled. "Damn it! I'll break my leg, and then where will I be?"

Jessie knew the voice. She dropped Bartie's lead, trusting that he would stay close. Then she raised her Glock and with the other hand, she switched on her headlamp.

"What are you doing here?" Jessie shouted.

The man looked up and blinked, blinded by her headlamp. His beard was long and unkempt. One arm of his glasses sat higher than the other on his hooked nose. With his beady eyes, jerky movements, and scrawny neck, he reminded her of an old rooster. "Who the hell…"

"Bill?" Jessie said.

"Who wants to know?" he growled, squinting at her. Her headlamp was directed forward, which meant her facial features were in shadow. "And get that darned light out of my eyes."

"It's Jessie, your neighbor."

"Jessie? Well, why didn't you say so in the first place?" He tutted. "And put down that gun, you silly girl."

Bill was not known for his politeness. She lowered her weapon, tucking it in her holster, and then adjusted the angle of her headlamp so it wasn't pointing in his eyes.

"What are you doing here?" Jessie said again.

"I might ask you the same. But I ain't nosy." For a few heartbeats they eyed each other in silence. "Clear off and leave me alone."

"This is a crime scene, Bill."

He jabbed a crooked finger at her. "And don't I know it. Two deputies came knocking this morning asking a whole lot of questions about *you*."

Her stomach churned. "And what did you say?"

"Told them what I knew. Said you were quiet. Kept yourself to yourself."

"Did they ask about vehicles heading toward this place last night?"

"Yep, and I told 'em what I heard." His focus shifted to Bartie, who was at her side and snarling. "That dog going to attack?"

"Not unless I tell him to."

"Good. I have work to do. Now clear off!"

He began to use his metal detector again, swinging it across the ashy floor from side to side.

"What are you looking for?" she asked.

"Useful objects. Anything I can sell." His lips peeled back into a smirk. "Don't look at me like that, Jessie Lewis. Pat and Rob ain't going to need them."

"You're scavenging? Jesus! Show some respect."

Weird Bill laughed so hard his bony shoulders bobbed. His grating guffaws soon became a coughing fit. He spat phlegm onto the ground. "You ask me, they got what they deserved."

"You take that back. They were nice people." Jessie moved close and shoved Bill in his chest. He staggered backward.

"They were liars and cheats," Bill snarled. "They did deals with developers that should never have happened. How do you think they got so rich, huh? By being nice? By helping folks find affordable housing. No, ma'am. They swindled people like me who trusted them." He spat on the ground again.

"What are you talking about? They never hurt anybody."

"Yes, they did. They took my life away!" He panted. He was worked up into a fury. "Get out of here, Jessie, and let me be."

Jessie didn't want him stealing from Pat and Rob. And he might ruin any chance she had of proving her innocence. In truth, neither of them should be there. For a few seconds, Jessie watched the old man poke and prod in the dirt, unsure what to do about it. Her disgust morphed into sympathy. How desperate must he be to rummage through the filthy stinking remains of a fire? Years ago, he had lost his house to the bank and his wife had left him. She wasn't sure why he blamed Pat and Rob, but it was well known he barely had a cent to his name.

More beeping from the metal detector, but this time the sound was deeper.

Bill's knees cracked as he bent down and ran a bony hand over some ash. "Still warm," he muttered. "What's this?" He held in his hand a tiny metal box that was charred and melted. He pried it open with a penknife. Inside were two blackened rings that looked as if there were a layer of burned sugar crystals baked onto them. "Well, looky here. That'll be gold."

"How can you tell?"

"By the sound my detector makes. Lower pitched for gold."

He spat on one of the rings and tried to rub it clear. The ring stayed black and knobbly. "I never seen gold melt like that before. Maybe I'll sell it as a gimmick." He pocketed the box.

"Seriously, Bill, you can't take it. That could be evidence."

He gave her a dismissive jerk of his chin. "How do you think I survive, huh? Nobody will give me work. So I take what I need." He moved on, head down, searching.

She turned her back on him and walked away. She would pretend she hadn't seen him. Instead of worrying about what Bill was doing, she should focus on finding something that would eliminate her from the sheriff's investigation. She certainly wasn't going to trust Marcus to do that.

Jessie found picking through the rubble depressing work. She imagined how devastated their daughter must be at their loss and her horror when she saw what was left of the house. By tomorrow the place would be beset with more than law enforcement and fire inspectors. There would be the insurance company, contractors, real estate agents keen to sell the land, and, of course, looters. Bill was the first looter. Jessie found herself standing next to the one remaining wall and an aluminum window frame. The glass had shattered but the frame, although tarnished, hadn't melted. How it had survived, she had no idea. Perhaps the wall it was part of had protected the metal. It was a myth that aluminum didn't melt. Jessie knew that aluminum could melt in a prolonged fire, as long as the aluminum's temperature passed melting point.

Beyond the window was the backyard tap. A hose had been attached to that tap. But just like the tap at the front, the hose had been removed. The arsonist must have taken them away. Just to be sure, she searched for a hose. Nothing. At the back door was a stone ornament of a duck with her chick. Pat used to leave a spare key under it. Was that how the fire raiser got into the house? She lifted the ornament and peaked underneath: no key. Had it been taken by forensics or the fire investigators? Or did the killer have it? She lowered the ornament back into position.

Jessie called out, "Bill, did you take the key that was under the stone duck by the back door?"

Bill called out. "No use to me!"

Jessie was about to walk away when something caught her attention in the bright beam of her flashlight. It was black and crisp and jammed between the window and the frame. Jessie gently touched it. Burned wood. How did a piece of wood end up wedged between two sash window frames?

"Bill! Come take a look at this," she shouted.

The agitation in her voice must have penetrated Bill's headphone because he pulled them off and growled, "What do you want?"

"Over here. Look!"

He shuffled over to her, complaining. She pointed.

"That's strange," Bill said. "That had to be put there on purpose."

"Why?"

"How should I know? Maybe it rattled. Maybe it was a security thing."

"You think the window wouldn't open?"

"Sure I do."

Bill wandered away. She took a couple of photos, sensing it was important but not certain why, then went to the front yard and some more for the remains of a discarded hose. She was almost at the entrance to the property when she saw a strip of something metal near a burned tree. Jessie knelt down and picked it up. It was a polished metal pen with a bank's logo down the barrel. She studied it closely.

"Commerce Bank," she said to herself.

The Commerce Bank of Washington operated across eleven Western states. The nearest branch to Eagle Falls was in Marymere. She knew for a fact that the Wilmots' everyday account was with Verity Credit Union. They had usually paid her cash, but occasionally, when the job was big, they asked to pay her via a bank transfer and the payment came from Verity Credit Union.

She supposed it was possible that they banked with more than one bank. Regardless, she found it strange that a pen should have fallen from their pocket, or purse, or even their car, some forty feet from their house and garage.

Unless the pen belonged to Bill?

Jessie located Bill in what used to be Rob's study. "Are you with Commerce Bank?" she asked.

"I don't bank with anyone. They're all crooks." His gaze fell on the pen in her hand. "What have you got there?"

She told him. "Do you think I should put it back and hope the forensics people find it?"

He studied her for a moment. "Tell me honestly. What are you doing here, Jessie?"

Bill, like her, was an outcast. He very rarely left his property. Who was he going to tell?

"Marcus is in charge of the fire investigation and I'm a suspect. You get what I'm saying, right? I'm screwed."

Bill nodded. "Marcus, huh? I see." He rubbed a filthy finger across the top of his lip. "Put it back where you found it and take a photo. Then get out of here." He began to turn away, then changed his mind. "You never saw me here, right?"

"Right. And you never saw me neither."

"Yep. You might want to check for boot and paw prints before you leave."

"Thanks, Bill."

Jessie used a broom to conceal her footprints and the dog's paw marks in the ash, then she headed for her pickup.

Bill called after her, "The only people I know using Commerce Bank are John and Susie. Oh, and their asshole of a son, Ford."

CHAPTER NINETEEN

It was Wednesday morning and Jessie had four voicemails. In the first message, a man called her a murdering bitch and hung up. That left her in no doubt that everybody knew she was the main suspect. The next three calls were cancelations. Each client blamed the fires, but she knew otherwise. She opened her wallet. Forty dollars and fifty cents.

"Looks like we're going on diets," she said to Bartie, who sat on the kitchen floor snoozing.

Jessie's gaze shifted to the bills stuck to the fridge door with magnets painted to look like bees. One was a reminder that her home insurance payments were overdue and from September 6 her house would no longer be covered. Tomorrow was September 6. Next to it was a bill from the power company, threatening to disconnect her if she didn't pay up. Jessie scratched her head. She needed money fast, and if gardening wasn't going to pay the bills, then she'd have to find another job. She'd heard the new Safeway was recruiting shelf stackers, but she doubted they would employ her, given the rumors circulating about her. She would have to look farther afield, where people didn't know her.

Lake View Drive had been unusually busy that morning, the rumble of vehicles coming and going amplified in the still morning heat. She guessed they were heading for the Wilmots' place. Had they found the pen on the driveway? Had somebody noticed the burned chunk of wood in the window frame? Had she adequately smoothed out the foot and paw prints? She had been foolish to go there in the first place. What if she had now left more of her DNA behind?

Jessie smacked her forehead. "Idiot!"

Every decision she made seemed to make things worse. Despairing, Jessie headed outside to check the water level in her rainwater tank. Just twenty-nine percent left and no sign of rain. On the radio that morning, there was a warning from the fire commissioner that a cold front was heading their way. Jessie knew from firsthand experience that when the wind changed with the passage of a cold front, the long side of the fire could suddenly become the fire front. That long side was currently parallel to the lake. The fire commissioner had asked the residents of Eagle Falls and Devil Mountain to prepare for evacuation.

But Jessie wasn't leaving. She was going to fight the fire if it came and to do that she would need to preserve tank water. She planned to collect lake water. She would boil it for drinking and cooking and use it to wash herself and her clothes. She and her dog started down the hill clutching two big buckets, enjoying the relative coolness beneath the thick forest canopy. She hadn't gotten far when she heard a car coming down her drive. She turned around. A Dodge Charger skidded to a rapid halt outside her house. Sheriff Cuffy got out, swatting the swirling dust from his face like flies.

He banged on her house door. "Jessie? Come on out."

Jessie wanted to slink away into the forest and pretend she hadn't seen him. She wanted to feel the cool water on her feet as she scooped it into buckets. She wanted to enjoy watching Bartie hunting for fish. Above all, she wanted to pretend everything was all right. But it was obvious from Cuffy's speed and aggressive movements that something was up. Her stomach plunged, like a stone hitting water.

Cuffy tried the door handle. It was unlocked. He walked into her house. "Jessie? It's the sheriff."

She took a couple of steps toward the lake. It was happening all over again. All those hours of questioning. Disbelieving sighs. Shaking of heads. But if she ran, she would look guilty. If only her mom and dad were alive, they would stand by her. They would know what to do. She halted. Cuffy would find her, one way or the other. Bartie had raced ahead and was already standing in the water, having a hearty drink. She whistled and he reluctantly left the lake and ran up the slope to her. As Jessie had expected, Cuffy heard the whistle and by the time she and Bartie reached the house, he had his eyes glued to her.

"I need you to come with me," Cuffy said.

"Why?" She put down the empty buckets.

"For Christ's sake. Get in the car."

At least the claustrophobic interview room had air conditioning, which was a godsend, given that Jessie's shirt clung to her sweaty back. She hadn't been told why she was there but she guessed last night's escapade had been discovered. Cuffy and Kinsley entered the room and sat opposite her. She knew she was in trouble when Kinsley leaned across the table to switch on the audio recording equipment and went through the preamble of announcing the names of each person present.

"Tell us what you were doing at the Wilmots' house last night?" Cuffy began.

How did they know? Had they seen paw prints and footprints? Had Bill reported her? But why would he? Doing so would be an admission that he had been there too. She decided there was no point denying it.

"A man knocked me out so I couldn't stop the fire. But you don't believe me, so I went looking for proof."

"You think you know better than a forensics team? Better than Marcus, an experienced fire investigator?"

Jessie snorted. "You think I trust Marcus after what he did to me?"

Cuffy rolled his eyes. Kinsley looked on, observing both her and his new boss.

"Looks to me like you deliberately contaminated a crime scene," Cuffy said. "What did you take from there?"

"Nothing."

"We're searching your house now. Might as well tell me."

Jessie sat up straight.

"I didn't take anything, I swear." She paused. "I did find something that could be important."

"And what might that be?" Cuffy said.

"A pen, on the drive, about forty feet from the house. A Commerce Bank pen."

"So?"

"Pat and Rob didn't bank there. They were with Verity Credit Union."

Cuffy pursed his lips, which wasn't flattering. It made him look like a pig with a snout. "You just don't see the problem, do you? For all we know you put the pen there with the intent of incriminating someone else."

"But I didn't, I swear."

"Did you touch the pen?"

She hesitated. "Yes, I picked it up so I could read what was written on it, then put it back where I found it."

"Can anyone confirm that?" Cuffy asked.

Cuffy folded his arms across his barrel chest. There was a look in his eye, almost like a glint of satisfaction. He knew more than he was letting on. Jessie had promised Bill that she wouldn't tell on him. But what if Bill had already told Cuffy he had seen her at the Wilmots' house, just to save his scrawny ass?

But Jessie was a woman of her word. A promise was a promise. She just had to be smart about how she answered the question. "I don't think anyone saw me picking it up." That was the truth. Bill was busy with his metal detector.

Kinsley spoke up for the first time. "Jessie, we have to know how contaminated the crime scene is, which is why we have to know if someone was with you last night. I must remind you to answer our questions truthfully." Kinsley's eyebrows were raised. He stared at her, as if he were trying to tell her something.

Jessie was now convinced they already knew about Bill Moran because Bill had ratted on her. But still she held back. He was old. He'd had a tough life. She didn't want to make it worse.

"I found something weird. I took a photo. Can I show you?"

"Where's your phone?" Cuffy asked.

"Back pocket."

"Take it out nice and slow."

She found the images on her phone. They weren't the best photos. The flash had blown the detail. She pointed. "Ask the investigators to look at the only remaining window. There's a burned bit of wood wedged between the two frames."

"And?" Cuffy said dismissively.

"The sash window couldn't open. Not with a piece of wood wedged there. What if the killer did it to stop Pat and Rob escaping?"

Cuffy yawned. "Did you touch the window or the bit of wood you claim you saw?"

"No." She looked from Cuffy to Kinsley and back to Cuffy. "I think I need a lawyer."

"Why? Because you're lying?" Cuffy asked.

"No, I…"

"Shame about your poor dog tied up at home in the heat," Cuffy said.

"You can't do that!" she shouted.

"Oh yes I can."

Kinsley's head snapped around and he stared at Cuffy hard, but Cuffy ignored him.

"Bill was there," Jessie blurted out, desperate to get home to her dog. "He can vouch for me."

"Bill? Bill Moran?" Cuffy's eyes were popping out of his head.

Shit! It had been a bluff and she'd fallen for it. She had betrayed Bill for no good reason. "Yes," she muttered, feeling ashamed.

"That scavenging old coot!" Cuffy slapped his palms on the desk. "You stay here," he ordered Jessie, pushing his chair back.

"You going to talk to Bill?" she asked.

Cuffy nodded. "You better hope he corroborates your story."

"How did you know I was there last night?" Jessie asked.

"Anonymous tip."

"It wasn't Bill?"

"No."

"I don't understand. We were the only ones there. Just me and Bill."

"That's where you're wrong," Cuffy said, looking smug.

"Someone was watching us?" The fine hairs on her arms stood up and she felt a tingle of fear run down her spine. "Jesus! It was him, wasn't it?" She stood, her breath coming in short urgent gasps.

"Sit down, Jessie," Kinsley said. "Getting upset won't help."

Jessie's hands were balled into fists, her arms rigid at her side. "Don't you see? It has to be the guy who started the fire. He's framing me."

In a loud voice, Cuffy said, "Sit the hell down!"

Jessie gripped the table edge. She needed to hang on to something. Her world was spinning out of control and she clung desperately to it. "I'm not saying another word until I have a lawyer."

"Take her to a cell," Cuffy ordered.

"I want Sharnice Manning!" Jessie yelled, as she was dragged away.

CHAPTER TWENTY

It was midmorning and the kids were at school. Ruth had paid some bills online and checked her emails. She sipped her coffee, then put the mug down precisely in the middle of the coaster next to the keyboard. Victor's desk was a mess of discarded files, other people's business cards, pens, and notebooks. Her fingers itched to tidy them, but she and Victor had agreed that this room, and his workshop in the garage, were his domain: she couldn't put items away, throw things out, or try to sort his papers. His filing system made no sense to her and she hated items left out to gather dust. Being a self-professed neat freak, Ruth found it aggravating that Victor liked to leave his regularly used objects on top of desks, tables, and countertops, but life was too short to argue about it.

Earlier that morning, Victor had been quiet and withdrawn as he dressed for his next interview. He had put on a brave face when he left the house, but she knew him well enough to hear the self-doubt in his voice. In an effort to cheer him up, Ruth had prepared his favorite dish for dinner—ribs with her special homemade sauce—hoping that he'd have some encouraging news when he got home.

Ruth toyed with her wedding ring, moving it around her finger, wondering what more she could do to help Victor secure a job. She had invited Susie and John to dinner on Saturday night and they had accepted. She planned to cook a three-course meal. If there was a possibility that John could help secure a good job for Victor, then she would go all out to impress them. She considered if there were other well-connected people whom she should invite to dinner, and she made a mental note to talk to Victor about it tonight. Ruth had never liked networking. In fact, she hated it, but she would do anything to see Victor happy. Were there any people at her classes who might know someone influential in real estate, she wondered.

Her thoughts moved to one specific person in her self-defense class: Jessie Lewis. Ruth was drawn to this ostracized young woman, and she wasn't quite sure why. There was a sizable age gap between them. Their careers and lives were very different. But Ruth found herself feeling protective of the younger woman. Jessie gave out all the signs of being a domestic violence victim. She was riddled with self-doubt. She mistrusted people. She was afraid of men. It was time Ruth met Marcus. Everything she had heard about him led her to believe he was charming and handsome, and people tended to believe charming, handsome people. Abusers were often narcissists and sadists, and very controlling, although their public façade was very different. But first, she wanted to know more about Jessie.

If Ruth were still with the FBI, she would have had access to Jessie's life history in the blink of an eye. Now she had to rely on Google. The *Eagle Falls News* proved to be a good source. Jessie's father, Tom Lewis, a well-respected doctor, died in a car accident when she was fifteen. That would have been devastating for Jessie and her mom. Then her mom, Cynthia Lewis, died of breast cancer when Jessie was twenty-one. Cynthia was too sick to attend her daughter's college graduation ceremony and died in a hospice the following day. Ruth's eyes widened when she noticed the degree Jessie had completed at Washington State University.

"A first-class Bachelor of Arts in criminal justice and criminology," Ruth said out loud. "Clever girl. Then you set up a gardening business. Why did you do that?"

Not that Ruth had a problem with gardening as a job. It was the fact that with a first-class vocational degree like that, Jessie could have applied for a wide range of law enforcement roles, including FBI. Why didn't she do that? Was it because Jessie returned to Eagle Falls after her mom died and got stuck in a rut? Ruth made another interesting discovery: Jessie became a volunteer firefighter the same year. It made sense now. Marcus was the reason she stayed in Eagle Falls. And an abuser wouldn't want her enrolling in law enforcement.

Ruth searched online some more. Marcus was fire captain at the time Jessie became a volunteer and he was still in that role today. She found a photo taken March 12, 2013, for an article in the *Eagle Falls News* about local firefighters saving three children from a warehouse fire the kids had accidentally started when playing with matches. Ruth studied the photograph and the names listed beneath it: Marcus Harstad, Clyde Hudson, Jamie Rodriguez, Jessie Lewis. They were in their yellow gear with a red fire truck behind them. Ruth enlarged the image and homed in on Jessie, who had one arm resting on the shoulder of Rodriguez in a manner that suggested comradery. She had a broad smile and her body language was relaxed and confident, a far cry from the self-effacing and distrustful woman Ruth had met.

So, Jessie knows how to put out fires. Does that mean she knows how to start them too?

Ruth came across another photo of Jessie, this time from the July 2016 community summer picnic. It showed a crowd of townsfolk at the lake's shore seated on blankets and picnic tables. In the foreground was a large group—she counted ten. Marcus was easy to recognize: his platinum-blond hair and big frame really stood out. Next to him was Jessie, her arm in a sling. Marcus had his arm around her waist. Her head was tilted away from him and her smile was close-lipped. Her eyes looked, what? Scared? Ruth was also struck by the way that Jude Deleon, who sat close to a young man Ruth didn't know, was staring across the picnic blanket at Marcus. Perhaps she had designs on him? A little bit more research revealed that Marcus and Jude started dating a month later, after Jessie dropped the domestic violence charges against Marcus.

For a fire captain to be accused of such a crime was big news. The story was covered by the *Seattle Times* with the headline FIRE CAPTAIN ACCUSED OF DOMESTIC VIOLENCE. The photo showed Jessie leaving the Eagle Falls Sheriff's Office, head down, arm in a sling, and swamped by reporters. With her was a Black woman in a cherry-red suit, her arm raised, clearly shooing reporters out of the way. The woman had to be Jessie's lawyer and her face was familiar. Where did Ruth know her from? About midway through the article, she found the lawyer's name: Sharnice Manning, of Manning and McCarthy. Ruth had crossed paths with Manning a while ago when she was tracking down a suspected terrorist's missing wife, who sadly was already dead. Murdered by her husband.

Ruth picked up her phone and dialed.

"Ruth! Good to hear from you." The larger-than-life attorney spoke only at full volume. Today her voice was echoey as if she were surrounded by hard surfaces. Ruth could also just hear the *tap, tap, tap* of Manning's famously high-heeled shoes on a solid floor. Perhaps marble? "You have two minutes. I'm due in court."

"Jessie Lewis. What can you tell me about her?"

"Depends why you're asking."

"It's personal."

"Personal! What's going on, Ruth? Did that low-life son of a bitch finally kill her?"

"Who do you mean?" Ruth didn't want to jump to conclusions.

There was the sound of a tap running. It sounded as if Manning was in the courthouse washroom.

"Marcus Harstad, of course. Who else?" Manning said. A scratching noise, like paper towel yanked from a dispenser.

"No, she's alive. But she's implicated in two arson attacks."

"Uh-huh." Wariness had entered her voice. "You're still working terrorism, right?"

"I retired a few months back. Moved to the same town where Jessie lives. As I said, it's a personal interest."

"So who's paying for my time, huh?"

"I just want to know why Jessie dropped the domestic abuse charges against Marcus."

Manning was on the move again. *Tap, tap, tap.* She sighed. "I like you, Ruth. You did right by Yasmeen Hassan." Yasmeen died trying to stop her husband committing a terrorist act. Ruth had tried to save her. "So, I'll tell you why Jessie dropped the charges. One word. *Intimidation.* Jessie was spat at, trolled on social media. The sheriff made it abundantly clear that he didn't believe her, although he never came right out and said so. The whole town blacklisted her. Her tires were slashed. Of course, the problem with cases like this is that it's her word against his. The catalog of injuries she'd sustained should have been enough to convict him. We had a good chance of getting a conviction, but Jessie was too afraid to go through with it."

"You believe Marcus Harstad abused Jessie?"

"Hell yeah!"

"Do you think she's capable of arson?"

"Jessie? I doubt it. Hold on, will you?" Then Manning shouted to somebody. "Get in there, hun. I'm right behind you." Then she lowered her voice. "Has Jessie been charged?"

"Not that I know of."

"Tell Jessie, if she needs a lawyer, I'll do what I can. Gotta go."

CHAPTER TWENTY-ONE

After two hours in a hot cell, without so much as a cup of water to drink, Jessie was feeling lightheaded. The bump on the side of her skull throbbed too, which didn't help. She sat on a steel bench screwed to the wall. It was best to stay still and to keep her breathing slow. Initially the stink of bleach, mixed with a hint of human excrement, had made her gag, but after a while she stopped noticing it.

There were three cells at the rear of the sheriff's office, separated by bars. The other cells were empty. The building had air conditioning throughout, but somehow they had forgotten to switch it on where she was held. She guessed this was one of the techniques Cuffy used to get people to confess. Make them sweat. Jessie lifted an arm and sniffed her armpit. Yup, she was rank and her mouth tasted bad too. But that didn't concern her. What had her worried was her dog. Was Bartie still tethered? Did he have enough shade and a water bowl? Bartie would be so afraid, wearing himself ragged barking for her to return.

Kinsley unlocked a steel door that separated the holding cells from the rest of the station. "Man, it's hot in here," he mumbled.

"Are you trying to cook me?" she said.

"You're coming with me. The sheriff wants to see you. Put your arms through the bars, wrists together."

He was going to cuff her. She didn't budge from the bench at the back of the cell. "Where's my lawyer? Where's Sharnice?"

"We're trying to get a lawyer for you. It takes time."

"I asked for Sharnice Manning two hours ago. Have you contacted her?"

Kinsley looked beyond her to the cell wall, in a guilty kind of way. "I don't know."

Jessie ground her teeth. Her frustration was building, and she had to find a way to channel it into getting what she wanted. If she didn't, she would probably say something that would make the situation worse. "I'm not saying another word until I have my lawyer."

"How do you know Manning?" Kinsley asked. "She's a Seattle attorney, right?"

"Right. She's helped me before."

"With Marcus Harstad?"

Jessie's grip on the bench tightened to the point that her finger and arm muscles burned. "Yes."

"Look, Jessie, if you come with me now, I'll do what I can to get in touch with Manning. What do you say?"

"I'm not saying a word."

"That's okay. The sheriff will do the talking. Now put your hands through the bars, wrists together." Jessie stayed put. "This isn't going to end well. You don't want me coming in there and forcibly cuffing you, do you?"

She considered her options for a moment then she stood and pushed her hands between the bars. When he had cuffed her, Kinsley unlocked the cell door and led her to the same interview room she had been in earlier. It was nice and cool in there. Cuffy watched her, arms folded across his chest, his face a crimson color. Was he just hot, or angry, or both?

"Sit!" said Cuffy.

Cuffy then beckoned into the room a woman who wasn't from Eagle Falls. From a plastic box she took out cotton swabs and small plastic test tubes with lids. She used cotton swabs on Jessie's palms and fingers and on her face.

"What are you doing?" Jessie asked the woman.

"Collecting gunshot residue."

"Why?" Jessie asked.

The woman packed up the samples. "On my way to your house now. I'm swabbing your firefighting clothing and boots and anything you might have worn the night of the house fire."

"Don't take them away. That gear cost me a lot of money." Jessie called after the departing figure. The interview room door closed. "What's going on?" Jessie asked. What did Cuffy now know that he clearly hadn't known two hours earlier?

Kinsley switched on the audio equipment and announced who was in the room. Jessie stared down at her hands in her lap. *Don't say anything. Just don't speak.*

"You claim that last night you found a pen on the Wilmots' driveway?"

Silence, except for the sound of a car door slamming outside.

"Don't play games with me, Jessie."

Kinsley piped up. "Sheriff Cuffy is just asking you to confirm what you have already said earlier."

Jessie sighed. "Two hours ago I asked for my lawyer, Sharnice Manning. She's not here, so I'm not saying anything." Her confidence was all bluff. Inside she was shaking like a leaf.

Jessie noticed a vein in Cuffy's neck was extended like a blue snake.

"Have it your way, Jessie, but remember, your refusal to cooperate makes you look guilty." He paused. She squeezed her lips together, just as she did as a child when her parents were trying to extract information from her that she was reluctant to give up. *Not another word.* Cuffy continued, "There's no pen on the Wilmots' driveway. You sent us on a wild goose chase. Why?"

"Who searched for it?" It just came out of her mouth. She couldn't stop herself.

"What does it matter?" Cuffy snapped.

Jessie screwed her eyes tightly shut. It had to be Marcus! Just perfect. She wouldn't be surprised if he had hidden the pen just to make her look like the liar he had always claimed her to be. It would suit him very well if she were charged with the Wilmots' murder. Then again, Bill could have removed the pen last night. She left the scene before he did. But would Bill do that?

"It was Marcus, wasn't it?" Jessie said.

"Bill Moran says he wasn't at the Wilmots' house the night after the fire. He says you're a liar," Cuffy said.

It felt as if the strands of her life were unraveling—again. But this time the price she would pay was far worse than isolation and loneliness. She would go to prison. A surge of adrenaline coursed through her veins, making every muscle tense with a desire to run. She tried to calm herself by thinking of the lake's water, the ripples on the surface and the pebbles beneath, and her body caressed by it as she floated. She opened her eyes.

"I want my lawyer, Sharnice Manning."

"She's in court," Cuffy said.

"I'll wait for her."

"You own a Glock 43?" Cuffy asked.

Jessie again forgot her resolution not to speak. She had to know what Cuffy was up to. "You know I do and if you've searched my house, you'll have found it on my nightstand. It hasn't been fired in a long time."

"What ammunition do you use?"

"Nine by nineteen millimeter. Where are you going with this?"

"The medical examiner found a nine-by-nineteen-millimeter bullet inside Patricia Wilmots' chest. The bullet killed her before the fire did. Why did you shoot her?"

Jessie was lost for words. Pat was shot? Did the man who knocked Jessie unconscious fear Pat might escape and, to ensure he couldn't be recognized, he fired his gun? "I... didn't."

"You hear what I'm saying, Jessie. This is a murder investigation and you're the prime suspect."

Jessie felt starved of breath. This wasn't really happening. It couldn't be real. Cuffy was on a roll.

"Lighter fluid was used at the Wilmots' house to accelerate the fire, which means it was deliberately lit by someone who knew what they were doing. A professional. Someone who understands fire."

"Not by me. I tried to save them."

"Why did you kill Paul, Naomi, Eric, and Luna Troyer?" Cuffy said.

Jessie gasped, eyes wide, jaw open. "How can you... think that?"

"Stop wasting my time, Jessie. With your fire training, you know how to start fires and how to feed them."

"What! No, you've got it all wrong. I put fires out. I'd never ever start one. And I'd never kill anyone."

"You have a temper, Jessie. You lash out at people. Paul was a bit of a knucklehead. Did he say something that made you mad?"

"No!"

"You did some work for him, right?"

"Yes, I installed a water feature."

"You were heard arguing with him in the supermarket parking lot. You wanted payment. But he never paid you. Was that it? He wouldn't pay up, so you killed his whole family?"

"No!" she yelled, unable to maintain composure. She saw how it looked for her. Bad.

"What did you do, Jessie?" Cuffy goaded. "Did you go to their house? Did he refuse to speak to you? So you went back at night and lit a fire, meaning to scare them but it got out of hand?"

"No, that's wrong. I didn't do it."

"Jessie, you're the only person with motive for both murders. Just tell me the truth for once in your life!"

She swore she heard the sound of her self-control snapping, like a small bone breaking. *I am not a liar!*

She was beyond talking. Her wrists were cuffed but her legs were not. She bolted for the door. She was athletic and fast. Cuffy was taken by surprise and took a few seconds to react. Kinsley, however, acted fast. As Jessie reached for the door handle, he kicked her in the back of her knees. Her legs bent but there was fire in her blood and she didn't buckle. She was familiar with physical pain and had learned to accept it. Just as the door opened a few inches and she saw a glimpse of the brightly lit corridor, her head was slammed into the door. Her legs gave way then. She was dazed. She had the odd perception that Kinsley had his arms around her waist and was holding her up. It was Cuffy who had his pudgy hands in her hair and had used it to slam her forehead into the door.

Her vision shrunk to a pinprick.

CHAPTER TWENTY-TWO

Ruth asked a harried-looking nurse for Jessie Lewis and was directed to the far end of the Emergency department. Eight of the twelve cubicles, separated by beige curtains, were occupied. From the sound of the wheezing and coughing, most of the people seeking medical attention had breathing problems. It had to be due to the smoke-filled air. Doctors and nurses appeared and disappeared behind the curtains in a whirlwind of energy. Voices drifted through the space and merged into blank noise.

The last time Ruth had been in ER she had been on a gurney in a critical condition and barely conscious. She had hoped never to enter ER again. She hesitated at the nurses' desk, giving herself time to dismiss such painful memories, before she followed the narrow corridor between the cubicles. Deputy Kinsley had called her earlier: Ruth was the only person Jessie would agree to see. Kinsley had been vague about Jessie's injuries. All he said was that Jessie had tried to flee the interview room and in the ensuing scuffle, she had sustained a bang to her head.

Her poor head, Ruth thought. This was the second blow in as many days.

Kinsley was seated on a chair outside Jessie's cubicle, the curtain behind him drawn. His presence meant that either Jessie had been charged or he was worried that she would try to run. He saw Ruth approach and stood. Ruth put out her hand and Kinsley shook it. His palms were soft and dry.

"My wife told me all about you," Kinsley said. "Former FBI, right?"

"That's right. I hear you were Seattle PD. What brought you here?"

"Amelia-Jane got a job here. We discussed it. Thought we'd give it a go and see how it worked out." He smiled. "Things work differently here. So far so good."

A male voice shouted for help. "My wife can't breathe. Somebody help her."

"What happened to Jessie?" Ruth asked.

A male nurse in blue overalls dragged an oxygen cylinder on a trolley into the next-door cubicle where the man had called for help.

Kinsley rubbed a finger under his nose before he answered, which was often a sign that a person was lying or deeply uncomfortable. Kinsley said, "She tried to flee the interview room. We had to restrain her. In the struggle she sustained a bang to her forehead." His words sounded rehearsed.

"That's a second head injury. Has she had a CT scan?" Ruth asked.

"Yes. The doc reckons she has a mild concussion."

"From which injury? She has had two blows to the head. One yesterday and one today."

"He wasn't sure."

"Was she under arrest?"

"No. She got agitated and needed restraining."

"Who restrained her? You?"

"The sheriff and I."

"It took two big men to restrain one skinny female?"

"Look, if you want to know more, talk to the sheriff."

Ruth was fond of Kinsley's wife. She was kind and decent. Benjamin came across as the same as his wife. He didn't seem like the kind of deputy who would use unnecessary force. And yet, Jessie's forehead had collided with a door with such force that she now suffered from a concussion. "Why were you questioning Jessie?" Ruth asked.

"We're interviewing lots of people."

Ruth cocked her head. "Give me some credit. Do you have anything on her?"

"I can't go into that, Ruth."

She took a breath. She wasn't used to being on the outside of a criminal case and it didn't feel good to be excluded. "What is she still doing here if it's a mild concussion?"

"When she tried to get up, she was dizzy. Nearly fell over. Doc insisted she has someone with her tonight to keep an eye on her. She asked for you."

How sad, Ruth thought, *that in the town she grew up in, I'm the one she asks for—a relative stranger.*

"I'd like to speak to her alone." She hoped Kinsley would leave ER for a moment.

Kinsley nodded. "I'll be here," he said, taking his seat.

"Benjamin, if she's not under arrest, there's no need for you to be here. I'll look after her now."

"The sheriff wants to question her some more."

"She's in no condition to be questioned. Maybe tomorrow, okay?"

"That's not my decision to make."

"Can you at least give us some space, please?" Kinsley didn't move. "Jessie is a vulnerable young woman with a head injury and right now she needs somebody to take care of her. You can trust me."

He took a deep breath in, then exhaled loudly. "Okay, I'll get a drink. Be back in five. Make sure she's here when I get back." Kinsley ambled down the corridor.

Jessie lay propped up on a gurney, her eyes closed. She was in her work top and shorts. Her boots were on a tray beneath the gurney. There was a red lump above her right eyebrow.

"Jessie?" Ruth said.

She dragged the chair Kinsley had been using into the cubicle and sat. The chair scraped across the floor.

Jessie opened her eyes and stared blankly at Ruth. A second or two ticked by and Ruth was afraid that Jessie didn't recognize her. Then Jessie smiled. "You came."

Jessie struggled to push herself more upright. She winced.

"Sure. How are you feeling?"

"I'm good now." Jessie checked the gap in the drapes. "Has he gone?"

"For a drink. He'll be back."

"I want to go home. I'm worried about my dog. They tied him up."

"You have a concussion, Jessie. You need to take it easy."

"What I need is my lawyer. I kept asking for Manning but they said she was busy. I don't believe them."

"Sharnice Manning?" Jessie nodded. "She was in court this morning. Maybe she's finished. Do you want to call her?"

"They've got my phone and wallet, oh, and my keys."

"Use my phone. Her number's in my contacts." Ruth offered her phone.

Jessie was about to take it, then stopped. "Not here. I want to get out of here. Can you drive me to the station to pick up my stuff. I'll phone Manning on the way?"

"We have to let Kinsley know."

"They have no right to stop me leaving," Jessie said.

Jessie swung her legs off the bed, then paused, her fingers gripping the sheet. "Lightheaded, just give me a minute."

There was no way that Jessie should be at home alone in her state. She was a young woman who needed help and Ruth had a guest room.

"Jessie, I'd like you to stay the night at my house. Your dog too."

"I want to go home," Jessie repeated.

"I get that, but with a concussion it isn't safe. You should have somebody with you, just in case you need medical attention."

Jessie reluctantly agreed.

"Here." Ruth picked up Jessie's boots. "Let me help you."

By the time Jessie had talked to the doctor about her departure, Kinsley had returned with an iced coffee. He followed Ruth's car all the way to the station. Jessie collected her personal possessions. Cuffy was not there, which was a relief.

Kinsley walked them out of the station. "Don't leave town, Jessie. The boss wants you back here tomorrow at ten."

"I'll bring her to you," Ruth said.

She drove away.

"I have to pick up Bartie," Jessie said. "He's at my house."

As Ruth headed for Devil Mountain, Jessie dialed Manning. There was no need for Jessie to place the call on loudspeaker. With Manning's penetrating voice, Ruth caught the gist of their conversation. Manning wanted to see Jessie in her office that afternoon, which meant a trip to Seattle.

"Can't we do this over the phone?" Jessie asked.

"If you can get to my office, it's better."

Ruth understood. It was much easier to build rapport with someone face to face. Even Zoom or Teams wasn't the same as sitting opposite a person.

Jessie insisted she was well enough to drive herself to meet Manning, even though her doctor had made it clear that he didn't want Jessie driving for the next few days. Ruth called Victor, but he didn't pick up: she had hoped he might be able to do the afternoon school run. Instead, she asked Aiden's mom if she could pick up both her kids and look after them for an hour. Aiden was Noah's new buddy, and his mom was more than happy to oblige.

They found Bartie tethered to the porch. He was in the shade but he had no water and he was crying pitifully when they arrived. The dog gulped down a bowlful of fresh water and happily jumped into the back of Ruth's air-conditioned car next to Jessie. As Ruth drove to Seattle, she took a quick look in the rear-view mirror. Both the girl and her dog were fast asleep.

CHAPTER TWENTY-THREE

Seattle had become an eerie otherworldly place. Smoke from the wildfires filled the city streets, carried on the wind. No building over two stories was visible. The sidewalks were almost deserted and those who ventured out kept their heads down and moved indoors as soon as they could. On the car radio there had been a news story about the sudden increase in asthma attacks.

Safely inside Manning's office, Jessie ran a finger across the gold-embossed lettering of the leather-bound law books behind the attorney's desk. Jessie had always wanted to be a detective. How different might her life have been if she had gone from graduation straight into a Seattle PD role or maybe even applied for Quantico? She would never have dated Marcus. She wouldn't be a suspect in an arson investigation. But when her mom passed away so soon after her poppy, she lost all her ambition and drive. She felt like she had been cut loose and was drifting aimlessly at sea. The only place she had ever called home was Eagle Falls, so she had given up the idea of a career in law enforcement and headed home.

That decision was proving to be a big mistake.

Jessie almost jumped out of her skin when the office door flew open and Sharnice Manning, in a cream turban and Michael Kors cream blazar with scrunched half sleeves and cream silk pants, strode into the expansive room in heels so high they must have added four inches to the attorney's height.

Manning was on the phone. "Lord above!" she boomed. "The answer is no! N-O!"

The call finished, the attorney came to a halt and eyeballed Jessie, who was standing frozen to the spot behind the attorney's desk. Then Manning opened her arms wide.

"Sweetheart! How are you?" Manning charged forward and gave Jessie a kiss on each cheek. Then she looked down at Bartie and pointed with a long red fingernail. "Is that a dog?"

"He comes with me everywhere."

"Hmmm. Okay, he looks like a good dog and he doesn't smell too bad, so he can stay."

Manning's gaze moved on to Ruth. "Ruth Sullivan. Good to see you again. You're looking great, by the way!"

She shook Ruth's hand. Jessie imagined the attorney's painted talons scratching Ruth's palm but Ruth appeared not to be in any way uncomfortable. Manning then sat behind her desk and kicked off her stilettoes. "Okay, Jessie. Tell me everything. Start with the first house fire."

Jessie cleared her throat. Her headache was back with a vengeance and she felt a little nauseous. It had to be the concussion. "Someone's framing me," she began. She flicked a look at Ruth, who gave her a nod of encouragement.

"Do you need some water, hun?" Manning asked.

"Yes, please."

"I'll get it," Ruth said. "Just direct me to the kitchen."

Manning did just that and Ruth left the room, shutting the door behind her.

"You okay with Ruth hearing what you have to say?"

"I… don't know. I don't understand why she's being nice to me."

"Honey! People *should* be nice to you." Manning leaned her head to one side. "If you want her to leave us alone to talk, that's not a problem, but right now I think you should take all the help you can get."

Jessie nodded. Ruth returned with three glasses of water and Jessie began to tell her story. She started with the house fire that killed Paul, Naomi, Eric, and Luna Troyer, her relationship to them, and her argument with Paul Troyer outside the supermarket a few days before he died. Manning made notes on her Apple tablet, her long fingernails making clicking sounds each time her fingers hit the keyboard.

Jessie moved on to Pat and Rob Wilmot and how they invited her to stay at their daughter's house to escape the approaching park fires, how she had promised to look after their house while they were gone, how she had been woken by smoke and gone to their house to try and save them.

"Brave girl."

Jessie explained how somebody knocked her out and then he shot Pat with a pistol that used the same ammo as Jessie; how Cuffy had tested her for gunshot residue and told her about the lighter fluid; how somebody made a video of her returning to the Wilmots' burned-out house the following night. She had gone there to find proof of the real killer, she said, but in doing so it looked as if she were tampering with evidence.

"Who shot the video?" Manning asked.

"No idea. Cuffy won't tell me."

"Hell, he's going to tell me. And I'll demand a copy."

Jessie ended her tale with her interrogation and her dumb attempt to flee, which led to Cuffy and Kinsley restraining her and her head slamming into a door.

"Would you describe it as unnecessary force?"

"I don't know. I'm not clear about what happened."

By the time Jessie had finished, she could barely hang on to the glass of water, she was so wrung out.

"Jessie, you're looking pale, hun. I want you to lie down on the sofa before you fall down," Manning said.

The sofa was soft white leather with velvet red cushions where she could rest her head. It looked very inviting. "Maybe I'll just put my feet up for a little while." Jessie moved to the sofa, but she kept her back propped up. "So, will you be my lawyer?"

"Sure thing. Pro bono, like we did last time. From now on, you don't talk to law enforcement unless I'm with you, you got that?"

"Yes. I got that. Thank you." Jessie chewed her lip. "There's something I should tell you. It could make things… complicated." Her voice trailed away.

"As your lawyer, you have to tell me everything."

"Marcus is the fire scene investigator for both house fires."

"Well, ain't that just swell! Now let me guess, you think he'll try to use the fires to land you in jail. How am I doing?"

"He wants me to stop talking to Jude, his new girlfriend. She has a broken arm, Sharnice. I know what he's doing to her."

"I get it," Manning said. "Go on."

"I think Marcus is afraid that if Jude goes to the sheriff and says that Marcus is beating her, then Cuffy would have to take my complaint seriously. If I'm charged with murder, I'm not a threat to him anymore."

Ruth, who had stayed quiet the whole time, looked at Jessie and said, "You think Marcus broke Jude's arm?"

"I don't know for sure. But Marcus broke my arm once. It was punishment."

"Would you feel comfortable telling me what he did to you?" Ruth asked.

Jessie looked at Manning for guidance. "Up to you, hun," said Manning.

Jessie was reluctant to relive even a second of her hell with Marcus. Yet, Jessie needed Ruth to understand what kind of a monster lurked beneath Marcus's good looks and winning smile.

"It started soon after I had moved into his house on the lake. I was sharing a joke with another volunteer firefighter, a good-looking guy who's long since moved on. When we got home, Marcus called me a bitch for flirting with the guy. He was so upset that I began to doubt myself. Had I been flirting and not realized it? That night, the sex was rougher, he pinched my thighs and my breast. There were livid bruises in the morning, but not where anybody would see. It got worse gradually, and each time he blamed me. I made him angry, he said. Nobody else made him angry." Jessie paused and took a deep breath.

"Abusers always blame their victims," Manning said. "I've said so before, and I'll say so again, it was never your fault, Jessie."

"I know that now. Back then, he was so clever at making me feel I was the bad girlfriend. The abuse escalated. He kicked me in the small of the back so hard my face collided with a corner cabinet. It turned into a black eye. I told everyone that I'd walked into a low-hanging branch. He was always sorry afterward. He promised to control his temper. The sex became more brutal. It was all about hurting me, making me feel powerless."

Memories went off in her head like muzzle flashes, of one night in particular. Marcus had been at a bar with his buddies all evening. She had spent the evening alone because he didn't like her seeing friends without him. When Marcus stumbled home, his breath was rank with beer and bourbon and his eyes were bloodshot.

"Don't look at me like that," he had said.

She was hunched on the sofa, her hands between her knees, making herself look small. She tried to give him a welcoming smile, but her pupils were black disks of fear. She didn't know if she should look away or hold his gaze. Life was complicated. She walked on eggshells every day.

"I'm pleased to see you, that's all." She had gone to hug him, ignoring the ball of acid in her gut. Her scalp tingled from the last time he gripped her hair too tightly and made her eyes water.

"I saw it, you lying bitch." Head jutted forward, finger stabbing at her cheek. "Who are you to criticize me?"

"I didn't mean…" She looked down at his hands. Clenched. She only knew of one way to defuse his anger. She touched the front of his shirt and tried for a playful smile. "Come to bed."

"Now that's more like it."

His stare softened. He kissed her, undid her belt. Tore down her jeans. This wasn't what she had meant. She wanted to lie in bed and make tender love as they had done in the beginning. He tugged her panties down, then turned her around. Gripping her hair tight, he forced her to bend over the table. With his knee pressing down hard on the small of her back, he ripped her right arm from its socket, dislocating her shoulder. She almost passed out with the pain. But she dared not scream.

"This is your fault," he had said, "but you have to learn."

A month later, Marcus broke the same arm.

It took Jessie a while to hear Manning call her name. "Jessie, honey, don't cry."

She was crying? Jessie lifted her hand and found her cheeks were wet and Ruth was offering her a tissue.

"You don't need to say any more," Ruth said.

"Yes, I do," Jessie said. She dabbed away the tears. "I want you to know what he's capable of." She wiped her nose. "I fell pregnant in January 2016. It was an accident but I stupidly thought it might change him. You know, the idea of being a dad." She shook her head. "He was furious. He said I was trying to trap him, and he wouldn't let me do it. He stamped on my stomach." Ruth gasped. "I lost the baby."

"Oh my God! Did you report him then?" Ruth asked.

"No, to my eternal shame. Marcus told the hospital I fell down the stairs and I said nothing. I was afraid he would kill me. To this day I don't know why what happened next finally broke his hold over me. It was a photograph that appeared in the *Seattle*

Times. Four of us. We had saved three kids from a house fire, and a journalist wrote a story about it. I made the mistake of draping an arm over a colleague's shoulder. When we got home, Marcus used a fire extinguisher to break my fibular. He said that would teach me not to throw my arm around another man. That's when I decided I couldn't take it anymore. When Marcus was at work, I packed my things, then went to Sheriff Cuffy and told him everything. I knew at once that he didn't believe me."

"Just like he doesn't believe you now," Manning said. "So, here's what you do, Jessie. You go home with Ruth and get a good night's rest. I'll talk to the sheriff. If he wants to interview you some more, I'll be with you. Okay, hun?"

Jessie nodded, then regretted the wave of dizziness that followed from the sudden movement of her head.

Manning picked up her cell phone. "Okay folks, this meeting's over. Off you go." Jessie and Ruth stood. "I'm going to break the bad news to the sheriff."

"Bad news?" asked Jessie.

"He's got me to deal with now." Manning winked and gave Jessie a wicked smile.

CHAPTER TWENTY-FOUR

Ruth's sons adored Bartie from the moment they laid eyes on him.

While the boys played with the dog in the backyard, Ruth checked in on Jessie in the guest room. She was sound asleep, despite her noisy kids and the daylight sneaking in through the gap in the drapes. Curled up on her side, with her long hair loose, Jessie looked much younger than her twenty-six years. When Ruth thought about the abuse the young woman had suffered, a fury raged through her veins. She believed Jessie. Ruth had listened to her tell the story of the violence she suffered, and both her head and her heart told her that Jessie was speaking the truth.

Ruth had investigated brutal crimes. She had learned to cope. The secret was not to get emotionally involved. But Ruth was already emotionally involved in Jessie's suffering. She wanted to do something to help her. Okay, it was great that Manning had agreed to represent Jessie pro bono. But Manning's role was to defend Jessie legally. Who was going to discover the truth? The truth about Marcus. The truth about the house fires she was accused of deliberately starting. Why was Cuffy so prejudiced against Jessie?

She wandered onto the back deck to watch Noah and David playing with the dog. She was greeted with squeals and whoops as Bartie suddenly jumped into the inflated paddling pool, water splashing over the boys, soaking their clothes. Ruth laughed. The dog shouldn't be in the pool, she knew that. But what the hell…

"Can I swim with the doggie? Please, Mom," David begged.

"Me too!" said Noah.

Why not, she thought. Wet dog, wet kids. The pool had very little water left in it anyway, and they might as well enjoy it while they could. "Sure. Give me your wet clothes and go put your swim trunks on."

"Yeaaah!" they roared as they ran to her and started to tear off their clothes.

The dog watched them from the pool.

"Bartie stays outside, okay? No wet dog in the house."

Ruth dropped the wet school clothes into the laundry sink and then helped David to change into his swimming gear. Noah, who was quicker than his brother, flashed past the doorway, all blue rash guard and swimming trunks.

"Wait for your brother!" Ruth called. Noah backed up the hallway. "And you don't get in the pool without an adult watching, okay?"

"Hurry up!" Noah complained, fidgeting on the spot.

When Ruth and the kids returned to the backyard, Bartie was still in the pool. Noah and David piled in, scooping up water in their cupped hands and chucking it at the dog. The dog snapped at the water drops as if they were treats. Noah and David giggled.

"He loves water, Mommy!" David said.

"He sure does," said Ruth, seated under a shade cloth.

Ruth relaxed into her seat and watched them play for a while, then she checked her phone to see if Victor had replied to her text message. She had wanted to let him know about their house guests before he walked in. There was no response from him. Surely his interview would be finished by now. He was probably driving home and hadn't noticed her message. Ruth tapped her fingers on the garden table's surface. She was beginning to worry that Victor might not be happy about the arrangement. But he was a big-hearted man and Ruth was certain that once she had explained Jessie's predicament he would be sympathetic. She wasn't so sure about the dog though. Victor didn't like dogs.

"Time to get out of the sun," Ruth called. The sun still had real heat in it.

The boys ignored her, too busy with their game.

She stood up. "Come get something to eat!"

Laughter at the dog. No response to her call.

"Who wants to feed Bartie?"

Now that got their attention. Both boys put their hands up. "Me! Me!"

She beckoned them into the kitchen, shutting the door on the dog so he could dry off before entering the house. She towel-dried the kids and helped them change into T-shirts and shorts.

"Now we have to work out what we're going to feed him," Ruth said, opening the pantry, with Noah on one side of her and David on the other. She hadn't thought to ask Jessie to bring dog food with her.

"Meat!" said Noah, giving her his serious look. "He's a dog."

"Peanut butter!" exclaimed David. "I bet he loves peanut butter."

"Hmm, I got a big pack of ground beef in the fridge. Maybe he can have some? With the rest of it I can make a spaghetti bolognese. What do you think?"

David smiled up at her. "Can I give him peanut butter too?"

"I'm not sure dogs are supposed to eat peanut butter. And anyway, this lucky dog is getting ground beef for his dinner. It's a special treat."

"Can we keep him, Mom?" asked David.

"Bartie belongs to Jessie and she's going home tomorrow."

"Can we have a dog?" David said.

"Maybe when you're older."

David and Noah went onto the back deck and watched Bartie devour the ground beef. In the distance, she heard the purr of

Victor's car engine as he pulled into their drive. She left the boys and the dog in the backyard and went to greet Victor in the garage.

"How did it go today?" she asked, her fingers crossed behind her back.

"One, not so good. The other was good. Belle Property. They want to see me again next week to meet the directors." He took her in his arms. It was so good to hear him laughing.

Ruth gave a whoop. "Babe, that's great news."

Raucous laughter could be heard from the kitchen, which meant the kids must have let Bartie into the house. And Bartie was soaking wet. *Oh no*, Ruth thought.

"Sounds like they're having fun," Victor said, opening a car door to retrieve his jacket, then shutting it. It was really hot in the garage and Victor's forehead was dappled with sweat.

"Ah yes, I have to tell you about that."

"Sounds good. I need a beer. Big day."

She placed a hand on his chest. "They're excited about a dog we're looking after, just for tonight."

Victor blanched. "You know I hate dogs."

"I know, but it's just one night."

Victor looked apprehensively at the door to the kitchen. "Please tell me it isn't in the house."

Ruth grimaced. "I think the kids might have let him in. And there's another thing."

Victor frowned. "What's going on, Ruthie?"

"His owner is staying the night too. She's suffering from a concussion and the doctor didn't want her to be alone, so I offered to have her here."

He lowered his voice. "Who is it?"

"Jessie Lewis."

Victor stepped back. "You're kidding?"

"She lives alone and she needs our help so. It's just one night."

Victor used a handkerchief to wipe away the sweat on his brow. "Oh Ruthie, that's a really bad idea. Big John will think you've sided with her. *We've* sided with her."

"It'll be just fine. I promised to drive her to the sheriff's office tomorrow morning. If anything, I'm helping him by making sure she turns up."

He ran his fingers through his hair. "Ruthie, she is the main suspect in a murder inquiry and we're having her stay at our house. Just think about it for a minute. The sheriff suspects her of *murder*. It's not safe to have her here. What about our kids?"

Ruth had been so focused on Jessie's tale of domestic violence that she hadn't really thought through the ramifications of harboring a murder suspect. "Okay, I'm sorry. I haven't thought this through, but it's just one night and the doctor said that she mustn't be alone."

Victor took her hands in his. "I'm sorry to sound cruel, but that's not our problem. And I need Big John on my side. He can open doors for me. For us. I don't think you understand the power he has in this town."

"I'm beginning to. What do you want me to do? Throw her out? I can't do that, Victor. She doesn't have anyone."

Ruth turned her back on Victor and headed into the kitchen where it was cooler.

"Ruthie," Victor pleaded. "Gossip will ruin my chance of getting a job. Don't you see?"

Ruth stopped short. Victor came up behind her.

"What on earth…?" he began.

David had a dessert spoon inside a peanut butter jar and was busy feeding the wet dog peanut butter. The dog sat at his feet with the sticky peanut butter all over his muzzle, licking his lips. David had managed to get peanut butter on his rash guard and all over his hands.

Noah attempted to grab the spoon from his brother. "My turn!"

David snatched the spoon away. Ruth overtook Victor, saw the mess and the disgust on Victor's face, and raced to take the peanut butter away from David.

But she was too slow. Noah tried to wrench the jar out of David's hands and in the struggle, David dropped it. It was plastic so it didn't break but Bartie seized the opportunity to lick the jar, which rolled across the floor. The dog chased it.

Noah turned on David. "That's your fault."

"Enough already!" shouted Victor.

"Daddy!" David ran at his father, hugging him, pressing his sticky rash guard against Victor's dress shirt. "Can we keep the doggie? Pleeeeease."

Victor gently pushed David back. "David, Noah, go outside and take the dog with you. Jessie is going to have to leave us. The dog too."

The boys wailed.

"Do as Daddy says," Ruth said. She picked up the peanut butter jar and dropped it in the trash can. Then she gripped the dog's collar and led him outside. The boys followed, their shoulders slouched.

Victor ducked into the bedroom and reappeared with his gym bag. "I need some space. I can't deal with this right now."

Ruth listened to the sound of his car leaving the garage. *What am I going to do?*

"It's okay." The voice came from behind her.

Ruth turned. Jessie stood in a nightie that Ruth had lent to her. "I'll go. I feel much better now."

"Oh Jessie, did you hear us? I'm so sorry."

"I heard enough. I don't want to cause trouble." Jessie glanced through the glass sliding doors to the backyard, where Noah and David were patting her dog. "Can I beg one last favor? I need a ride."

"Sure. Where to?"

Jessie paused, as if she were considering someone.

Ruth said, "What about your friend in Prairie Ridge? What was her name?"

"Georgia. Her mom already has enough to deal with. I'll be fine. Honestly. Please, just take me home."

CHAPTER TWENTY-FIVE

Noah and David were down in the dumps after they had dropped Jessie and Bartie home. To cheer them up Ruth gave them a bowl each of double fudge "moose tracks" ice cream and let them watch TV. Victor was at the gym.

Ruth drank some water and gazed through the kitchen window, thinking about her afternoon in Manning's office with Jessie. Victor was unaware that she had met with Jessie's attorney and she knew he wouldn't be happy about that.

"Do I tell him?" she muttered.

Was an omission as bad as a lie? She didn't want secrets in their marriage. However, nor did she want conflict and Jessie was clearly a source of conflict between her and Victor. They needed to keep Cuffy happy so that the influential sheriff would see fit to help Victor get a job. Yet, Ruth couldn't abandon Jessie when she most needed support.

Ruth had a network of contacts in law enforcement who had access to records that the sheriff's office didn't. She could call in favors and keep everything off the record. If she could uncover the identity of the arsonist—and she prayed it wasn't Jessie—then Cuffy might leave the young woman alone. To achieve her plan, Ruth would need an ally in the sheriff's office, someone who would keep her name out of it. Deputy Kinsley was the obvious choice. He seemed a fair man. He was new in town and therefore wasn't entrenched in what Ruth saw as a town-wide prejudice against Jessie. Even so, Ruth knew she was skating on thin ice. She would have to broach Kinsley carefully. Test the waters. Perhaps through his wife? Ruth had been meaning to ask her to join her for a morning jog. Ruth could then casually slip a hint of what she'd like to do into their conversation.

Now that Ruth had the beginnings of a plan she felt restless to get on with it.

The first person Ruth wanted to talk to was Callan Bolt from Seattle's Fire Investigation Unit. If anyone knew about arsonists and how they might use fire to cover up murder, it was Bolt. With a degree in criminal psychology, he had assisted the FBI on several cases that Ruth had worked on. She checked the time: ten past five. He would still be at work. She found a notebook and pen, sat at the breakfast bar, and called him.

"Hey, Ruth, this is a pleasant surprise. How's life in Eagle Falls?" He was a heavy smoker and his voice reflected this: deep and throaty. It still amazed Ruth how many firefighters were smokers.

"Not as chill as I had thought it would be," she replied.

"The mega fire is pretty near you, right?"

The term *mega fire* made Ruth shudder. "Close enough. We've prepared for evacuation. I'm just hoping it doesn't head our way."

She heard him tapping on his keyboard. "There's a red alert for tomorrow. A cold front could send the fire straight for Eagle Falls. I hate to be the bearer of bad news, but I'd urge you to evacuate as soon as you can. Better to be safe than sorry."

This wasn't the conversation that she wanted to have. It made her jittery. She took a sip of water to calm herself.

"Thanks for the heads-up. But that's not why I've called. I'd like to pick your brains about serial arsonists. Specifically, arsonists who use fire to cover up murder."

"Ah, the real nasty ones. I'm guessing your sleepy old town ain't so sleepy after all?"

"You guessed right."

"What's your interest in this, Ruth? Are you assisting the sheriff's office?"

"No, I guess you could say it's personal and off the record."

Silence. Ruth waited. "In that case, I should step outside my office. Give me a moment," Bolt said.

A few seconds later Ruth heard a door creak open, then slam, and then the tap of hard soles on concrete steps. When he spoke, his voice had the distinctive echoey sound of someone in a fire escape stairwell. "Tell me what's going on."

Ruth began: "Two families living in the Devil Mountain have died in house fires within twenty-four hours. The first one was apparently a gas explosion. In the second one, I believe lighter fluid was used, and one of the victims was shot. Both fire scenes are now being treated as crime scenes by Sheriff Cuffy."

"Two suspicious fires doesn't mean you have a serial arsonist on your hands," Bolt said. "Who's the fire investigator?"

"Captain Marcus Harstad."

"Okay, go on."

Did Bolt know Harstad? Was it possible they were buddies? Just like the FBI, the fire service was a close-knit group and they tended to protect each other. "Before I go on, I need to know this conversation won't get back to Marcus."

"I don't know Marcus personally. Occasionally our paths cross professionally. He hasn't asked for my assistance, but he may do so. If he does, I won't be able to help you."

"I understand," Ruth said.

"I get a feeling there's more going on than you're telling me."

"There's a witness to the second house fire who claims she went there to put out the fire. She used to be a volunteer firefighter. She says a man knocked her out with a blow to the head so that she couldn't save Patricia and her husband, Robert. She is the only witness. The sheriff doesn't believe her story. He thinks she's the arsonist and she shot Patricia."

"Why does he think that?"

"Jessie Lewis, twenty-six, is a domestic violence victim, although she withdrew the allegations. According to Jessie, the sheriff believed the man accused of the abuse. The same sheriff thinks Jessie is lying about the house fires. Jessie owns a Glock 43 and she uses the same nine-millimeter ammo that was used to kill Patricia."

"Oh boy. So you're saying you think the sheriff is pursuing the wrong suspect."

"It's possible his bias is blinding him to other suspects."

"Were any of the house-fire victims involved in her abuse?"

"No. And here's my problem. The man she says abused her for two years is Marcus Harstad."

Bolt whistled through his teeth. "That makes life complicated. In the light of what you've told me, I find Marcus as the choice for fire scene investigator an unwise one. If he is personally involved with the prime suspect, he should be replaced."

"I agree, but Marcus and Cuffy go way back. Jessie fears that Marcus will deliberately incriminate her. His testimony could put Jessie behind bars for life."

"You've lost me. If Jessie didn't press charges against Marcus, why would Marcus feel threatened by her?"

"Because she suspects Marcus is beating his new girlfriend and Jessie has encouraged this woman to report it to Cuffy."

"Is there a chance Jessie is making this up?"

"It's possible, yes," Ruth said. "I've met some exceptional liars in my time, and I don't believe she's one of them. The problem is that the whole town appears to believe Marcus. He's a popular man."

"Do you happen to know if he has a history of violence against women?"

"I don't."

"With your contacts, you could find out, right?"

"I could." She had already thought about contacting Special Agent T.J. Samson. He was an old friend.

"Jessie sounds like she's an outcast. Would you say that's correct?"

"It looks that way. She lives alone, except for her dog, in the mountains. Her parents are dead. The townsfolk avoid her."

"Arsonists are often people who have been rejected by their community and live isolated lives, which sounds very much like Jessie." He took a deep breath. "Okay, I'd like to take a step back and look at what motivates arsonists." Ruth picked up a pen to make notes. "There are six broad categories. The first motivator is vandalism, and the offenders are typically juveniles. At least one of the two house fires you described involved murder *before* the fire took its hold, so I think we can rule this one out. The second motivator is thrill-seeking. This includes hero fantasies and satisfying sexual fetishes. Firefighters who are also arsonists fall into this category." For a fleeting moment Ruth considered whether Marcus might be the arsonist. Bolt continued, "A well-known example of the thrill-seeker is John Orr of California's Glendale Fire Department. In the late 1980s and early '90s he started dozens of fires for sexual thrills."

"Wait up," Ruth said. "Jessie used to be a volunteer firefighter, although she doesn't strike me as someone seeking to be a hero. In fact quite the opposite. She is self-effacing in the extreme. She wants to be invisible."

"Arsonist firefighters who want to play hero are narcissists. Is Jessie a narcissist?"

"That's not the woman I've met," Ruth said.

"Let's move on then. The third motivator is arson for profit, and this includes fraudulent insurance claims. Do you know if Jessie benefits financially from the victims' deaths?"

"I doubt it, but I can look into that." The victims' wills, if they had them, would be read soon. Rumors would spread fast about who inherited what.

"The next motive is revenge. These people feel aggrieved over the smallest slight. Even an offhand comment can do it. These arsonists plan their attacks carefully. They enjoy watching their victims suffer. Does Jessie believe that any of the victims have done her wrong?"

"I believe one of them, Paul Troyer, owed her money. She's a gardener and she installed a water feature."

"I should add that the arsonists in this group are usually adult males in blue-collar jobs, so she's not a good fit. I suggest you try to find out if any of the arson victims were friends with Marcus. Did they taunt her? That might be a reason for Jessie to exact revenge on her tormentors. Oh, wait up. I have a call coming in. I'll get rid of them." The pause gave Ruth time to scribble notes. Soon Bolt was back. "The fifth motive is concealing the evidence of another crime. And this is where we move into the use of fire to conceal murder, theft, etcetera. You said that Patricia was shot. The fire may have been started in an effort to conceal this. Was any other arson victim shot, strangled?"

"Not that I know of. That could be hard for me to find out. What's the last category?"

"Extremists. They want to make a political, religious, or social statement. They're angry at society. When they start fires, they like to watch them burn." He paused. "You know what I mean." She most certainly did. In Ruth's case, it was a bomb that started the fire that almost killed her, but the terrorist's motivation was to make an anti-Semitic statement. "I should make it clear that arsonists can fit into more than one category."

Ruth again considered Jessie. She was found at the Wilmots' fire. She was certainly angry with Cuffy for ignoring her pleas for help with Marcus. But why kill Patricia and Robert? Surely the fact Paul Troyer owed her money wasn't a good enough reason to kill him and his whole family?

"What are the age and sex ratios for convicted arsonists?" she asked.

"Females tend to be in their thirties or forties, but there are exceptions of course. Males can be any age, but serial arsonists, who avoid capture for a long time, tend to be in their fifties. The one thing all arsonists have in common is they crave the power that lighting a fire gives them."

Ruth tapped her pen on the notepad. "Are you working on any suspicious house fires at the moment?"

"I have one. Wife died in the fire. Husband lived. I'm pretty sure he did it. She had life insurance. Why?"

"Any others?"

"Last year we had a number of them, scattered all over Seattle. Lighter fuel was the common denominator."

"Did you find the arsonist?"

"We did not."

"Might there be a reason for you to reopen those cases and contact Marcus about the Devil Mountain fires?"

Bolt chuckled. "Yes, there might be a reason. I'll contact him and see what I can find out."

"I owe you, my friend."

As soon as Ruth finished the call with Bolt, she dialed Special Agent T.J. Samson. If anyone knew about serial killers, it was Samson. When he picked up, she explained the reason for her call, and they agreed to meet the next day. She knew Samson well enough to know he would be discreet. At all costs, Cuffy mustn't find out what she was doing.

CHAPTER TWENTY-SIX

Jessie's dog normally slept on the floor. Tonight, he slept on her bed. She needed him close. She felt so lonely that she wanted to cry.

At Manning's office, she had begun to hope that there was a way out of the mess she was in. The brief time Jessie had spent at Ruth's house had meant the world to her because she was treated like an ordinary person. A friend, even. Jessie had dropped her guard then. She wasn't being judged. She was part of a normal family. Then Victor arrived and spoiled it all. Jessie's hope had evaporated and her trust in Ruth had wavered.

Jessie lay on top of the sheet in a loose cotton nightie listening to Bartie's doggie snores. The room was pitch black. Her skin was hot and clammy and despite downing two painkillers before bed, her head felt as if it were being compressed in a vice. She turned over and stroked his soft fur. Bartie must have felt her touch because he lifted his head and looked at her.

Outside the bedroom window there was a snap, loud enough to cause both Jessie and her dog to look up. There were plenty of nocturnal animals that roamed the forest, like skunks, raccoons, and foxes. But it sounded like a branch breaking in two and that took a larger creature. Immediately, Jessie wondered if the arsonist had come for her. She had, after all, partially seen him. Bartie stood on the bed and launched into ferocious barking. Jessie sat up too fast and the room tilted for a second, then leveled. With a shaking hand, she slammed the window shut, then drew the curtains. Then she grabbed her phone, holding it to her chest. She thought about dialing 911 and then just as quickly dropped the idea. What if it was just a raccoon?

Bartie leapt off the bed and charged into the living room. *Dear God!* Was there someone inside the house? Jessie fumbled for the lamp switch and flicked it on. Then she followed her dog to the front door, switching on the lights as she went. Bartie was gnashing and barking so hard his whole body jerked. Jessie didn't have a gun. It was being tested by forensics. She raced to latch all the windows shut. Then she took the biggest knife from the knife block.

"Get off my property," she yelled through the door. "I've got a gun," she lied. "I'm calling the cops."

Whether an intruder would even hear her above Bartie's growls she didn't know but it made her feel braver to shout. Most people would think twice before accosting a big snarling dog, she told herself. But her biggest fear was that somebody would set fire to her cabin. It was all wood and given how dry it was at the moment, her house would light up in seconds. Jessie waited and listened. Bartie's barking subsided. Whoever, or whatever, it was had gone. Jessie sat on the floor and waited, listening intently. Perhaps it had been a raccoon after all. Finally, she plucked up enough courage to put on some sneakers and with a flashlight in hand, she went outside. From the edge of the forest a pair of round eyes shone like white disks. It was a raccoon.

"You scared me," she said to the raccoon.

She did a loop around the house, passing the water tank at the rear. Something was different. She swung the torch over the tank again. Jessie had two hoses, one attached to a tap near the water tank and another at the front of the house. Each one was neatly coiled. What she didn't have was a retractable hose reel in a white plastic capsule and a neat green hose head with an expensive-looking trigger. But that was exactly what was leaning against her water tank. It looked brand new. The only people she knew who had this brand of retractable hose were Pat and Rob Wilmot.

Somebody had put it there.

Her heart almost burst through her rib cage. She stumbled back and swung her flashlight around. Was the killer somewhere in the darkness watching her?

"Bartie! Come!"

Jessie ran into the house, followed by her dog and she slammed and locked the door. Panting, she started to dial the sheriff's office. Then she stopped. Was she out of her mind? She was about to tell them that a crucial piece of evidence was at her place. It would make her look guilty.

She leaned against the sink, trying to think. Even if the killer had come and gone, he could return any night and burn her house down. And what was she supposed to do with the Wilmots' hose reel? The sheriff wasn't going to believe her story that somebody had put it there to frame her. He would say that she took it away to hamper efforts to put out the fire.

Was this the time to run?

Perhaps she could head south, far away from the danger of wildfires. Sleep in her truck at night. She could pretend it was a road trip. A vacation. Briefly, it sounded fun. She just had to stay away until the real killer was caught. She pondered how much of her stuff she could strap onto the back of her pickup. Camping gear, food, water bottles, dog food, photo albums and paintings, her father's stethoscope, his silver whiskey flask, her laptop and power cables, flashlights, a suitcase of clothes, maybe even her mother's red leather wingback armchair. It broke her heart to admit that her father's wooden desk just wouldn't fit, and besides, it was very heavy. Jessie was strong, but a desk like that would take two people to lift onto the back of the truck. Once everything was loaded, she would cover it in a big tarpaulin and tie it down with bungee cords, more to conceal what was underneath than to protect it from rain. Rain wasn't coming anytime soon.

She went to the bedroom and dragged a battered suitcase from under her bed. The last time she had used it was to leave Marcus. It had been packed then in a frenzy of terror. Jessie brushed away a layer of dust on the outer surface, then opened it. And stopped. What would her lawyer advise her to do? Manning had promised to go with her to the sheriff's office later that morning. Before Jessie took the drastic, and very final step, of running away, she should at least talk to her lawyer. If Jessie drank lots of coffee, she could stay awake until dawn and watch out for any intruders. That was a much better idea than running.

Her rapid heart rate began to calm. *It's all good. Manning will know what to do.*

She went to the kitchen and made percolator coffee. Her phone beeped. That was odd. Who would send her a text at two thirty in the morning? There was an image attached to the message. She opened it and stumbled backward. It was a photo of her, taken earlier that night through the bedroom window. In it, she was in the middle of pulling a nightie over her head. The nightie covered just her head and shoulders. Her back and legs were bare. Jessie wanted to scream. The killer had been watching her.

Then she saw the words:

You are next.

Jessie ran to the bathroom and threw up.
She had to get out of there fast.

CHAPTER TWENTY-SEVEN

Jessie's skin felt gritty, and her lower back ached from all the lifting she had done. She had the tarpaulin tied down tight over the mound of possessions she had crammed onto her pickup's bed. Bartie stood next to her, ever vigilant.

"Not bad, huh?" she said, glancing at her dog.

Beyond the forest, the sun was peeking over the horizon and the dawn sky was indigo. She gulped down a bottle of water, then went back into the house and took one last look around. Was there anything important she had left behind? It irritated her that she could find only one of her fire-resistant gloves. Had the forensics lady who had swabbed her fire gear taken one of the gloves away for further testing? Never mind. One glove was better than none, and she had already packed the fire-retardant boots, pants, and jacket. It had almost killed her to heave her mom's armchair onto the truck, but it was done. The room looked unloved without it. Jessie gave one last longing glance at her father's desk. She clung to the hope that the arsonist would lose interest in her house once word spread that Jessie had skipped town. The national park fire still burned, but the expected cold front hadn't materialized. At least not yet. So Jessie was hopeful that her home would be standing when she returned.

She closed the windows and checked there was nothing remaining in the fridge that would rot, then she took the bag of trash with her. She would find a public bin to dump it in. She didn't lock the house door. She reasoned that she had nothing of monetary value to steal and locking her door told folks that she had left for good.

Wearing leather gardening gloves so as not to leave finger-prints, Jessie picked up the Wilmots' retractable hose reel, and called Bartie to heel. With a flashlight in the other hand, she and her dog made their way through the forest to the lake's shore, taking care not to step on snakes or walk through spiders' webs. Bartie was about to charge into the water when she called him back. She really didn't want a sodden dog in the truck. She swung her arm back and then threw the hose reel as far into the lake as possible. The splash shattered the silence. She looked around and squealed when she saw the unmistakable silhouette of Weird Bill a few yards away. Nobody else had such a bent bony body or such a long frazzled beard. He was leaning on his stick and staring straight at her.

"That's illegal dumping," Bill called.

He hobbled over to her.

"You mind your own business and I'll mind mine," she snapped.

"Yikes. What's gotten you into such a foul mood, missy?"

"You, you lying old goat. You told Cuffy that you weren't at Pat and Rob's place the night after the fire. You made me look like a liar."

"Well now, you've got quite a temper, haven't you?"

"Why are you spying on me?" Jessie said.

"Spying! I heard a boat's engine. It woke me, see," Bill said. "Only an idiot goes out in a boat in the dark with no lights, unless he's up to no good. So I came down here to take a look. Found a small motorboat tied to my pontoon. Saw someone running down the hill from your place. I never seen you with a motorboat, so I stay in the trees and watch. He gets in the boat and off he goes."

Jessie suddenly felt very cold. "You have to tell the sheriff. Please, Bill. That could be the man who killed Pat and Rob."

"I want to stay out of it."

Jessie charged up to him, a flash of anger making her bold. "Did you plant Pat's hose reel at my place? It was you, wasn't it, not some guy in a boat?"

"You're talking gibberish, Jessie, my girl."

"Am I? I didn't hear a boat engine. I think you stole the hose reel, then you tried to use it to frame me. Why are you doing this, Bill?" She knew she was screaming, but she was incensed.

"That what you threw in the lake?" Bill asked.

Why couldn't she keep her big mouth shut? "Answer me. Did you steal a hose reel from Pat?"

"No, and I swear, there was a boat here earlier."

"You've been here, what? Three hours? That's a long time for an old man to hang around. I don't believe you."

"Now you're being foolish. I went home. Couldn't sleep. Came back to take another look."

Jessie screamed in exasperation. All she knew for sure was that Bill was a liar. Could he also be the killer? He appeared so fragile, but he was wily and more than capable of starting a fire. She should stick to her plan. Leave it all behind her.

"To hell with you and everyone in this rotten town," Jessie said.

She called Bartie to her and started the trek up the steep slope.

"If you run now, they'll come after you, all guns blazing," Bill yelled.

Jessie strode back to where he stood. "Goddamn it! You *have* been spying on me!"

Bill wiggled his head from side to side. "Maybe a little. Saw you packing up your truck."

"You tell a soul about this and I swear to God I will make your life hell."

"No need to threaten me."

"Don't you get it? I'm being set up for Pat's and Rob's deaths and you have made it ten times worse. Why don't you tell Cuffy the truth?"

"Then I look like a liar."

"That's because you *are* a liar," she bawled. "And now I'm scared the person who killed Pat and Rob is going to kill me." Her words caught in her throat. She was a child again, trying to hold back tears and failing at it. "What if he burns my house down in the night? What if he kills my dog? Don't you see? I have to run."

A tear trickled down her cheek. There was enough light in the rising sun for Bill to see it.

"Oh Jessie, don't cry. I hate it when people cry." He took off his wonky glasses and rubbed his eyes, then put them back on again. "I ain't a bad person, Jessie."

"Then tell Cuffy you were with me last night and about the man in the boat."

"I can't go telling Big John I lied to him! No, ma'am."

She turned away.

"Don't run, Jessie. They'll put out an APB. They'll hunt you down."

"I don't have a choice. I'm not going to jail for something I didn't do."

"You get on the open road, they'll find you. Best thing you can do is hide. With me. It's the last place they'll think of."

That stopped her in her tracks. She swiveled to face him. "With you?"

"Not exactly with me. Hate having people in my house. I mean in the forest. I collect old cars, see? Have seventy-three of 'em. Anyways, I have a 1980s motorhome. She's a beauty. It's at the far end of my property. I can give you a gas bottle. Nobody will know you're there."

"Except you."

"Except me."

"I'll take my chances on the open road."

CHAPTER TWENTY-EIGHT

Jessie avoided roads with tolls, hoping this would mean she was less likely to be picked up on CCTV. She was heading for Park Street, Prairie Ridge. She had called Georgia's mom, Irene, and asked if she could stay with them for a few nights. Irene, who was an early riser, was delighted that Georgia would have company. This arrangement gave Jessie the chance to lie low, talk to her attorney, and work out a plan.

The radio was tuned to local news. If Bill had snitched on her and gone to Cuffy, there would likely be a news bulletin about it. So far nothing, at least not on the channel she was tuned in to, but it was only 7:30 a.m. and she wasn't due to meet with Cuffy until ten. The news focused on a new wildfire in the North Cascades, ten miles away, and nearby towns were being evacuated. The fire service was now fighting two big wildfires. More firefighters from other states had been called in and a contingent from the Australian Fire Service had arrived to assist. If the Bear Creek mega fire joined up with the North Cascades fire, there would be no stopping it. Jessie broke out in a sweat just thinking about it.

She drove into Georgia's street. To her left was Georgia's red brick bungalow. To her right, a large park that sloped uphill. She drove past the house and came to a stop in the park's parking lot. She would wait a little longer before she knocked on their door, and besides, she wanted to call her attorney and talk to her without fear of being overheard. To reach Eagle Falls by 10 a.m. Manning would need to leave her neighborhood by 9 a.m., latest. Jessie needed to speak to her before she left.

She dialed Manning's cell phone. It went to voicemail.

"Sharnice, this is Jessie Lewis. I… I've left town. Call me."

Jessie rubbed her tired eyes, then opened a flask of coffee and drank from the cup. In her haste to leave, she hadn't eaten breakfast and her stomach rumbled. In a cooler box, she had ice and drinks and some perishables, like yogurt, butter, milk. She had thrown together a ham sandwich. She munched on it now. She absentmindedly watched a mom push her little girl on a swing. A man walked his dog up the slope to where the river bisected the town. Ten minutes had passed since she left a message for Manning. She tried again.

"It's me again. Jessie. I've been threatened. I don't want to meet the sheriff today. Please call me."

Her dog sat up and nudged her arm. He did that when he wanted to pee. Jessie pulled her baseball cap low over her face, then got out, followed by her dog. Jessie raised her arms and had a good stretch. Her back was a little store from the heavy lifting she'd done but her headache was subsiding. From her vantage point at the top of the park, Jessie had a clear line of sight down the hill to Georgia's house. Her mom's Honda Civic was parked in the drive. Through a side passage, Jessie caught a glimpse of washing hung on an umbrella clothesline at the back.

The front door flew open and Georgia appeared. Her movements were jerky. Angry. She slammed the door and stomped down a paved path to the sidewalk. The front door opened and Georgia's mom yelled something at her daughter, beckoning her back home. Georgia ignored her. She crossed the road and headed into the park.

Georgia was about a hundred yards away from Jessie. She appeared to be heading for the playground. Jessie put Bartie on the leash and walked toward her friend. She didn't understand why Irene hadn't accompanied her daughter. Georgia could have an epileptic fit at any time. Sometimes they were so bad an ambulance had to be called.

Jessie reached the playground first. She tied Bartie's leash to the railings and waited. When her friend reached the playground's gate, Jessie spoke.

"Hello, Georgie, it's Jessie."

Georgia looked up, her thick dark brows in a deep frown. When she saw Jessie standing before her, she gasped, "Oh Jessie! You're early."

"Yeah, roads weren't busy. Did your mom tell you I was coming?"

"You shouldn't be here, Jessie." Georgia shook her head vehemently. "Run! You have to run!"

"Why? What's happened?"

"Marcus! He's here."

It was as if somebody had run ice-cold fingers down her spine. She snapped her head around and saw Marcus running up the hill: fit, muscular, and fast. A shot of adrenaline had Jessie dive for her dog's leash and then run like the wind to her pickup.

"Stop!" Marcus shouted.

She didn't dare look back. She threw the driver's door open.

"In!" she yelled at Bartie, who obeyed instantly.

Seated at the steering wheel, the doors locked, Jessie's hands shook so badly that she couldn't slip the key in the ignition.

"Come on," she said to herself through gritted teeth.

A palm slammed against the driver's window and she shrieked and dropped the key. Marcus's cold blue eyes peered at her through the glass.

"Get out of the car!" He tugged at the door handle. It sent Jessie's heart into what felt like a spasm. "I've called the cops."

Slam! His palm hit the glass again. She jumped in her seat. Whimpered. She had to find the key. She leaned away from the door and peered at the floor. It was near her right foot.

"Open the fucking door!"

He tore off his shirt and wrapped it around one hand. Jesus! He was going to punch the glass!

She kicked the key to the right and leaned down. Grasped it in both hands to keep it steady and this time it went in the ignition. She reversed out of the parking space so fast the vehicle leapfrogged. Marcus leapt out of the way.

"No!" he raged.

She burned rubber as she accelerated out of the park and hurtled down the road. In the rear-view mirror, she saw Georgia standing in the playground, waving goodbye, an amused smile on her face. Marcus was already sprinting back down the hill, presumably to his car. In the distance, a police siren wailed.

How did Marcus know where to find her?

CHAPTER TWENTY-NINE

Special Agent T.J. Samson had suggested they meet for breakfast and Ruth was looking forward to it. Ostensibly they were meeting because she wanted his help to identify the arsonist. There was also a more personal reason. Ruth missed her pals at the FBI. Six years ago, Samson had worked in counterterrorism and that's how they met. Now he headed up the Puget Sound Regional Violent Crime Task Force, which meant he investigated complex crimes and serial killer cases outside the city limits. He had access to the Evidence Response Team that specialized in challenging crime scenes. The ERT's equipment was way more advanced than standard forensics gear.

Ruth walked down Spring Street enjoying the view of the rejuvenated piers at the bottom of the hill and the glassy waters of Puget Sound. There was a flutter in her chest as she turned onto First Avenue and saw in the distance the red outdoor umbrellas of Fonte Coffee Roasters where they had agreed to meet. It was 8:30 a.m. and it was already too hot to sit outside. The café had air conditioning and she chose a seat at an indoor table by the window.

Ruth faced north so she could see Samson coming. When had she last seen him? It must have been at Doug's funeral at the Uniting Methodist Church, before his body was flown to the Quantico National Cemetery in Virginia for burial. Just thinking about it made her tearful.

Pull yourself together.

Samson was easy to spot. A snappy dresser with a neat mustache, he always walked with a purpose. He had his phone to his ear. Ruth had often wondered, with the grueling hours Samson worked, and his busy home life with four kids, how he managed to always look immaculate. Although such thoughts were not to belittle the special agent's achievements. He had recently tracked down a serial killer who had beaten women to death for over a decade. He had once confided in her that he had his heart set on becoming Seattle's first African American special agent in charge and she had no doubt he would achieve his ambition.

Samson put his phone away and greeted her with the lopsided smile she fondly remembered. He unbuttoned his jacket before he sat, and Ruth caught a glimpse of his firearm tucked neatly under his arm. It felt strange that Ruth did not carry a gun anymore. She owned one, of course, in a gun safe at home. It was a Smith & Wesson M&P semiautomatic. But she made the decision that when she walked away from the FBI, she walked away from carrying a gun every day too.

"Good to see you again, Ruth. I'll order. What would you like?" No messing about. He had assumed she had looked at the menu. And he was right.

"I'll get this," Ruth said, standing. "What would you like?"

"Thank you. I'll have a Turkish latte and the breakfast sandwich with arugula."

Ruth went to the counter and placed their order. She had chosen the biscuit with gravy and an egg.

Back at their table, Samson said, "You're looking great, Ruth. Being a full-time mom suits you."

"The kids keep me busy." As soon as she said it, she realized it wasn't true. If anything, she had too much time on her hands. Did that make her a bad mom?

"And how is Victor? He must be happy, living back in his hometown?"

"Yes, he is. The kids love it too, although they're missing friends, and the park fires are a worry."

"Yes, I heard they're close to Eagle Falls."

"Too close. Although it looks like they're going to bypass the town, thank goodness."

Samson scrutinized her face. He knew about the physical injuries she suffered as a result of the bomb. He didn't know, at least officially anyway, about her anxiety attacks or her chronic fear of fire. Maybe he had guessed? "So, why don't you tell me what this is about. It sounded urgent."

She pulled up on her phone the *Seattle Times* photo of Jessie and Manning leaving the sheriff's office in 2016 surrounded by reporters, just after she had withdrawn her allegations against Marcus. Jessie had the look of a woman who had lost everything. Ruth handed her phone to Samson. "The woman on the right is twenty-six-year-old Jessie Lewis. She lives in Devil Mountain. She is suspected of being a serial arsonist who used fire to cover up the murder of two families." Ruth filled Samson in on Jessie's background, her claims of domestic violence, her ostracism from the town, and why Jessie was Sheriff Cuffy's prime suspect.

Samson listened and occasionally nodded. Their coffees and meals arrived, and they tucked in.

"I'm sure you are aware that two suspicious house fires does not make this the work of a serial arsonist. You need at least three fires with similar MOs to form a pattern."

"I know. I have a friend looking into similar house fires over the last few years within a hundred-mile radius of Eagle Falls."

"And you've contacted me because?" Samson asked.

"I think Sheriff Cuffy has formed a particular opinion of Jessie, which leads to bias." Samson winced. Accusing a sheriff of bias was a big deal. Ruth continued, "He's pally with Marcus Harstad, the man Jessie accused of beating and torturing her for nearly two years. When she finally reported the abuse, she says Cuffy did all in his power to encourage her to withdraw the allegations."

"Why are you getting involved?" Samson asked.

Ruth considered her answer. "Jessie deserves a fair chance to prove her innocence. It looks to me that Cuffy wants these arson attacks pinned on her, no matter what. I can't sit back and watch a miscarriage of justice. I want you to help me uncover the real arsonist."

Samson sipped his coffee in silence. Ruth was used to the way Samson liked to mull things over in his head. He would speak when he was ready. "What if you discover Jessie *is* the arsonist?"

"Then she will be tried for murder."

He nodded. "You miss it, don't you?"

"Work, you mean? Yes. I loved what I did. But the bomb shook me. I'm not the person I once was, T.J. Taking the disability pension was the right thing to do."

The tilt of his head told her that he didn't believe her. "How can I help you?"

"I'd like the Evidence Response Team to visit both crime scenes and review the evidence already collected."

"Are you saying this is a particularly complex crime scene?" he said, clearly coaxing her.

"It is, for many reasons, not least of which is that the fire scene investigator is Marcus Harstad. Her abuser. He has every reason to incriminate Jessie. If she's convicted of murder, her claims of domestic abuse will never be taken seriously."

"The charges were dropped, so he may not be an abuser, Ruth. You seem to have made up your mind that Jessie is telling the truth. Be very cautious about leaping to conclusions. I sense you are emotionally invested in this case. Does Jessie mean a lot to you?"

"I don't know." Ruth looked down. She noticed a crumb hidden behind the salt and pepper shakers. It irritated her that the café

staff hadn't cleaned the table properly. "I feel sorry for her, and...
I guess I like her."

Samson chewed a mouthful of food, then asked, "And how
would I involve ERT? Under what pretext? As you know, we are
usually invited by the most senior law enforcement officer to
assist. That would be Sheriff Cuffy and we haven't been invited."

"There's been media coverage. Could you contact him and
offer your services?"

"Sure. But if he's helping Marcus to frame Jessie, then he won't
want us anywhere near the crime scene evidence."

"I take your point. The lab they're using is in Seattle. ERT
could request access to that evidence. Perhaps pull a few strings
so the lab keeps that information to itself."

Samson put his knife and fork down. "I'll see what I can do
without setting off alarm bells. I can't guarantee that news of my
actions won't reach Cuffy."

"Thank you."

"Which lab?"

She gave him the details and he finished his coffee. "Could you
check to see if Marcus has a criminal record?"

Samson nodded. "In return, I would like you to do something
for me."

Ruth nodded.

"I want you back at the Bureau and working in my team."

Ruth's face flushed with excitement. Working unusual crime
scenes and hunting serial killers would be a whole new learning
curve for her. But she couldn't accept. Not just because of her
anxiety attacks. It was Victor's chance to pursue a career he loved,
and this was her opportunity to enjoy her kids while they were
still kids.

"I'm honored. And a year ago, I would have jumped at the
chance. But I have to decline. I've moved on, T.J., started a new
life. I want to be around to see my kids grow up."

"I understand. But promise me you'll think about it."

Their breakfast came to an abrupt end when Samson was called back to the office. Ruth walked to the underground parking garage where she'd left her car. She got into her Buick and centrally locked the doors. She held the steering wheel, then leaned forward to rest her forehead on the top of the wheel. It felt cool against her brow.

She closed her eyes and immediately smelled burning hair. She knew it wasn't real, but it seemed so. The air was thick with toxic smoke. She was a crumpled body on a classroom floor. Ruth opened her eyes and lifted her head. Beyond the windshield was a dank wall. She was in a parking lot. There was no bomb. Ruth found her asthma inhaler and used it. She had done Samson a favor rejecting his offer, and she would have to reject it again.

As Ruth drove home, she came to the decision not to tell Victor about Samson's job offer. She wasn't going to take the job, so what was the point of upsetting him?

CHAPTER THIRTY

In her past life with the Bureau, Ruth had searched some strange and disturbing locations. "Weird Bill" Moran's twenty-hectare forest property had to be one of the strangest.

For a start, the driveway wasn't a driveway. There was nothing straight or permanent about it. It was as if she was driving off-road, dodging pine trees and rusting cars. The cars had been there so long they were covered in a thick blanket of pine needles, camouflaging them. Moss and plants grew from the cars' nooks and crannies. It was a graveyard of old Fords, big-finned Cadillacs, and even a couple of 1980s Ford LTD Seattle police cars. Ruth thought she passed a 1970 Chevrolet Chevelle SS, just like her dad used to have in red with a black stripe running up the center of the hood. She couldn't be certain because everything except the hood was engulfed by brambles as if the car was being swallowed by nature run rampant. Bill had nailed hubcaps to tree trunks as if they might ward off evil spirits.

Ruth's meeting with Samson had spurred her into doing some investigating of her own. Bill's property was a minor detour on the way home from Seattle. According to Jessie, Bill had denied to the sheriff that he was with her on Wednesday night at the Wilmots' burned-out house. Someone was lying. If it was Bill, she wanted to know why. Perhaps she could persuade him to tell the truth.

The single-level wooden shack, much like the cars, had been partially claimed by the forest. The roof was gently sloping and covered in grasses and weeds, and the porch was wild with creepers. Scattered around the house were rusty mechanical parts, old refrigerators and air conditioning units. He was living in a junkyard. Bill's vehicle, however, shone like a beacon in the morning sun that penetrated the clearing around the shack. A cream 1950s big-finned Cadillac. Even the hubcaps shone like they had been polished that day.

Ruth left her vehicle slowly and made sure her hands could be clearly seen. She had heard Bill didn't like strangers. She had also heard that he had a mental breakdown when he lost his home and business in a scam some years ago. She stayed close to her car and called out a hello.

"What do you want?" shouted the man pointing a wooden stock deer rifle at her from the open doorway.

Ruth raised her hands above her head. Adrenaline coursed through her veins. Okay, so he *really* didn't like strangers. "My name's Ruth. I'm not armed. I just want to talk about Jessie."

"Big John send you, did he?"

"No, he doesn't know I'm here." Had she really just told a crazy man with a gun that the police didn't know where she was? "I'm worried about Jessie and thought you could help me." He was still pointing the rifle at her. "Do you mind lowering that. I don't have a gun."

Bill didn't lower the rifle, but he took a couple of steps forward so she could see him more clearly. He was little more than skin and bones. His shirt and pants hung off him and his long gray beard was straggly. The thin white hair on his scalp had receded and the exposed skin was covered in sunspots and peeling skin, no doubt from sunburn. His glasses sat crookedly on his emaciated face and were broken, an arm held together by blue tape. He looked like he didn't have a dime to rub together.

"You're FBI. You here to spy on me?"

He probably believed in UFOs too. "I'm retired. I'm a mom, with two kids, and I teach Jessie self-defense."

"What a crock of shit! Once FBI, always FBI."

"Can I call you Bill?"

"Call me what you like. Get in your fancy car and go."

Ruth knew not to argue with a man with a gun, but she would give it one more shot. "Jessie's in trouble. She's blamed for the fire that killed Pat and Rob Wilmot and been accused of tampering with evidence. You were there too, weren't you?"

"Not me. Now get!"

Ruth tried to find common ground. She opted for the conspiracy theory angle, hoping it would appeal to the recluse. "Someone wants her to go to jail for a crime she didn't commit. I want to know who's behind the conspiracy."

He stared at her through his crooked glasses for a few more seconds, then lowered the barrel of his rifle so it pointed at the ground. "You're not much of a Fed if you can't see what's staring you in the face. There are two people in this town up to no good. But I ain't making it easy for you. That's your job."

"Help me out here. I'm new in town. I don't know people like you do. Who should I look out for?"

"Marcus for one." Finally, she had found someone who didn't like Marcus.

"Why him?"

"I never liked that boy. A bully. He was real mean to Jessie." He sucked on his teeth. "Good luck proving it. Marcus is untouchable."

Ruth was beginning to get the same feeling. "And the other?"

"I ain't going there. I don't want no trouble."

Ruth changed tack. "Did you see a pen on the driveway at the Wilmots' place?"

"I told you, I wasn't there."

"Jessie told me she found a pen. She thought it important. But forensics couldn't find it. Let's say the pen happened to come your way, maybe you could mail it to the sheriff's office anonymously?"

Bill sucked his teeth again. "Are you recording this conversation?"

"No, sir. Do you want to see my phone?"

"Yep."

"It's in my car. Can I get it?"

He raised the rifle. Nodded. Ruth leaned into her car, then held up her cell phone so he could clearly see it. He drew closer and peered at it. Then took a step back. "Okay. Between you and me, Jessie didn't take anything from that burned-out hulk."

"Then tell the sheriff."

"Can't do that. Can't go through that again."

"What again?"

"People hating me. Coming here and tormenting me."

"Is that why you lied to Cuffy?"

"I was saving my skin. Had no choice."

"Have you any idea who filmed Jessie while she was there?"

"Yeah, I saw him, but I ain't telling you who he is."

Ruth felt a surge of hope. "Arsonists often return to the scene of their crime to gloat," Ruth said. "They get a thrill out of it. Whoever videoed Jessie could be the killer. Please tell me who shot the video."

"Even if I told you, it wouldn't make a blinding bit of difference. Cuffy would hush it up."

"Why would he do that?"

"Lord above, woman! Because he's protecting him."

"Who is he protecting?"

"This didn't come from me and if you tell Cuffy, I'll say you're a lying bitch."

Ruth wanted to tell him to watch his mouth, but she kept her eye on the prize. "Okay, got it. Who filmed Jessie?"

"His no-good son Ford, that's who." Bill gave her a grin, revealing grayed front teeth and reddened unhealthy gums. No wonder his breath was bad. "John has been covering up that boy's crimes for years. I wouldn't be surprised if Ford started the damn fires."

CHAPTER THIRTY-ONE

Jessie careened out of the parking lot, her heart pounding. Marcus sprinted across the park in the direction of Irene's house. Irene raced across the street and into the park, yelling at Georgia, who was seated in the playground whooping with joy, fist raised in the air. Jessie's tires screeched as she turned left onto Park Street too fast. She had to get onto Main Street before Marcus could reach his Hummer and give chase. One thing was for sure, her ancient pickup, piled high with furniture, suitcases, and boxes, could not compete with the speed and maneuverability of the latest-model Hummer.

She winced at the wail of police sirens drawing closer. Too close. Any moment now, she would see patrol cars barreling down upon her. She ducked into a side street and pulled in between two cars and waited for the patrol car to pass. She was trembling all over. As soon as the black-and-white cars had flown by, she hit Main Street. She kept to the speed limit so as not to draw attention to herself, her eyes flitting to the rear-view mirror every few seconds to check for Marcus or the cops. Marcus was sure to anticipate her route out of Marymere. But she knew the streets of Prairie Ridge way better than him, including the back roads. She took a country lane that followed the river, hoping that Marcus would use the highway where he would hope to outrun her.

Jessie used the underside of her arm to wipe the perspiration from her forehead. Her phone, lying in the cup holder, rang. She saw Marcus's name light up on the screen. She leaned over and rejected the call with a trembling hand. When her eyes returned to the road, she saw she was racing toward a brick wall. She had veered off course and was about to crash. She yanked the steering wheel around, swerving dangerously to get back on the road. She made it only just in time. Her dog whined from the floor where he had fallen. Her phone rang again. It had to be Marcus.

Through gritted teeth she muttered to herself, "Leave me alone!"

A quick glance at her phone told her that she was wrong. It was her attorney, Sharnice Manning. Jessie let the phone automatically accept the call.

"What's going on?" Manning said, loud and vexed. "Here I am, on my way to Eagle Falls, and I get a call from Sheriff Cuffy. Says you're on the run. Please tell me he's wrong!"

Fat tears pooled in Jessie's eyes and dripped down her cheeks. All her fear, frustration, and disappointment manifested in guttural sobs. "Everything's wrong and I don't know how to fix it," she wailed.

"Oh Lordy," Manning said. "Whatever has happened?" Jessie had to pull over. She couldn't see the road through the blur of tears. "Hun, you still there?"

"Yes," she sobbed.

"Just tell me, do I keep going or turn back?"

"I… I don't know."

"Okay, I'm pulling into a roadside diner. Hang on, that's it… all righty. Talk to me."

Between sobs and sniffs, Jessie told Manning about the noise that woke her in the night and how Rob and Pat's hose reel was dumped at her place, concealed behind the water tank. "It was him. He was trying to make it look like I stole their hose so they couldn't extinguish the fire."

"Calm down, Jessie. That ain't such a bad thing. The hose reel could be covered in fingerprints. The killer's fingerprints. Please tell me you left it where he put it?"

"I…" Jessie sniffed.

Manning asked again, "Where is the hose reel?"

"In the lake."

"The lake!" shrieked Manning. "What you go and do that for?"

"I'm sorry," Jessie keened. She wiped her runny nose with the back of her wrist.

"You know, forget about that. What's done is done. Tell me where you are, because Cuffy says you're not home and it looks like you've gone for good."

Stuffed down the side of the seat was a rag she used to clean the inside of the windshield. She wiped her nose with it and dabbed her eyes. "He sent me a text. It said… It said that I was next."

"Who?"

"The killer. It came with a photo. He'd taken it outside my bedroom window. I was half-naked. He was there. Watching me. I couldn't hang around and wait for him to burn my house and me in it. You get that, don't you?"

"Please tell me you still have the text?"

"I kept it."

"Good. Here's what you're going to do," Manning said. "You're going to forward me that text, then we're going to meet at a safe place so we can talk and work out what to do next. This highway diner is as good as any."

Jessie squeezed her eyes tightly shut and willed herself to stop being such a crybaby. "Okay. But I'm not going anywhere near Cuffy. If I set foot in town, he'll have me convicted for murder."

"I'll stall him for an hour or two. Hon, you have got to start trusting me."

That was the problem. Trust.

Jessie wasn't sure if she would trust anyone again. Not totally anyway. Everyone, except for Mom and Dad, had let her down. Manning meant well. So did Ruth and Georgia. It wasn't Georgia's fault that her mom betrayed her to Marcus, nor was it Ruth's fault that her husband didn't want her to stay at their house. But at what point would they turn on her? Because, sooner or later, they would. Even Manning had her limits.

"Where are you?" Jessie asked.

"Rosie's Diner on US 101, just before the turn off to Shelton. I drive a red Mercedes."

"I know that diner. I can be there in fifteen."

Twelve minutes later, Jessie parked at the back of Rosie's Diner so that her pickup and license plate couldn't be seen from the highway. She killed the engine and paused for a minute, listening to the rumble of traffic and the ticking of her engine as it began to cool. Her arm muscles ached from gripping the steering wheel so tightly. She hadn't realized how much adrenaline had been racing around her body until now. Her heart was still hammering and she had a pounding headache, not just because of the blows she'd received, but because of the tension in her neck. She tilted her head left and then right, forward then back, trying to stretch out the ache. Bartie sat up on the seat next to her, ready to get out. She put him on a leash and the dog jumped out with her.

She was parked next to Manning's red soft-top Mercedes SL Roadster with cream leather seats. The car was empty. However, Manning's business cards sat in a slot between the two front seats that was designed for a phone. The lawyer was probably in the diner, but Jessie was twitchy about entering a public place. If there was an APB out for her arrest, she might be recognized. She phoned Manning.

"I'm parked next to your Mercedes," Jessie said. "Can we talk out here?"

Manning sighed in a loud and dramatic manner. "I guess so. But I'm not standing around in the heat. You and me, we're going to sit in my car with the air conditioning on full blast, okay?"

"Sure."

"Oh, and no dog. I don't want him scratching my leather seats."

Jessie wasn't in a position to argue. While she waited, she gave Bartie some water, tied him to a tree in the shade. She patted his head. "It's only for a little while, I promise."

Manning strutted around the corner in her high heels, carrying two takeout coffees and four glazed doughnuts in a cardboard box.

"Breakfast," she said. "And man! Do you look like you need it."

Once they were seated in Manning's car, the attorney urged her to eat. "You need a sugar hit."

She was right. The coffee and the doughnut were just what she needed.

"I want to talk about the creepy message," Manning said, having wiped her sticky fingers on a napkin. "I totally get why you were so freaked. This could also be our lucky break. He's never shown his hand before. We have to share this with the sheriff."

"You share it. I told you already, if I go back, he'll arrest me."

"He can't arrest you unless he can prove you shot Pat Wilmot or lit the house fires, or both. As far as I can tell, everything he has is circumstantial. And who doesn't use nine-millimeter cartridges? He would have to prove beyond any doubt that the bullet that killed Pat came from your gun and that you fired that gun."

Jessie shook her head. "Cuffy and Marcus are working together, I'm convinced of it. They'll find a way to have me sent to jail." She looked at Manning, her shiny red lipstick leaving a red smudge on her takeout coffee cup as she drank. "Marcus was waiting for me in Prairie Ridge. He must have guessed where I'd run to. He chased me."

"I'll have a word with the sheriff about that. He must put a stop to vigilantism." Manning returned her gaze. "What if it wasn't a lucky guess? My psycho ex-boyfriend stuck a tracker on my car once. He wanted to know everywhere I went. He was convinced I was having an affair. Anyway, my point is Marcus could have stuck a tracker to your vehicle. You want to take a look. Best place to conceal them is under your car. They're magnetic."

The thought of Marcus knowing her every move made her shudder. "What do trackers look like?"

"Usually small, flat and black. Smaller than your phone."

Jessie left the Mercedes. Before she shut the door, Manning shouted, "If you find one, use a handkerchief or something so you don't mess up any fingerprints."

Jessie picked up the rag she had used earlier, then lay on the ground so she could see under her pickup. She used her phone's flashlight. The undercarriage was filthy. There was nothing unusual under the front suspension. She inspected the hood and the wheel arches. Nothing again. Then she stuck her head beneath the rear of the pickup. She found a tracker beneath the truck bed floor. It stood out because it was shiny, whereas the rest of the chassis was coated in dry mud and dust.

"You bastard."

Even now, Jessie's abuser had a hold on her. The tracker's magnet was strong and it proved difficult to remove it using a cloth, but after a few tugs it came free. She handed the device to her attorney.

"Brush that dirt off your ass before you get in my car," ordered Manning.

Jessie did so, then closed the door behind her once she was inside.

"Yup. A 3G GPS tracker," Manning said, switching it off and wrapping it in the rag and popping it in her glove compartment. Then she gave Jessie a penetrating stare. "Listen to me carefully,

Jessie. You have my word I'll get to the bottom of whatever the hell is going on. But you have to meet with the sheriff. I'll come with you. You've been threatened and illegally tracked. This says loud and clear that you are the victim here."

Jessie shook her head.

"Handing yourself in is your only option, hun."

"Will they put me in a cell?"

"It's possible."

"I have to find someone to take my dog. Otherwise, he'll end up at the pound."

"Don't look at me," Manning said.

The only people she would have trusted to look after Bartie were now dead: Pat and Rob. She briefly considered Ruth. Her kids had loved him, but Victor wouldn't want her dog. Would Bill take him in, or would he sell her dog to anyone who would have him? "I'll follow you to Eagle Falls and make some calls on the way."

Jessie untied her dog and they hopped into her horribly hot pickup. Manning reversed out of her parking spot. Jessie did the same and followed the Mercedes around the corner of the diner. A black Hummer tore into the parking lot. It was Marcus. Jessie couldn't breathe. The tracker had led him to them. Her truck was partially hidden by Manning's sports car. But the gleaming red Mercedes was hard to miss. Jessie watched as Marcus stared at it, then he clocked Jessie in her truck behind her. His Hummer's wheels screeched as he slammed on the brakes.

Driven by primal fear, Jessie accelerated around Manning's car. She shot out onto the highway, ignoring the infuriated drivers honking their horns. Before Marcus could do a three-sixty and follow Jessie, Manning's Mercedes lurched in front of the Hummer, forcing Marcus to stop. He was penned in.

Marcus could no longer locate her. The tracker was with her attorney. But what was Jessie to do now?

CHAPTER THIRTY-TWO

Ruth was busy filling the washing machine when Manning called her. She pounced on her phone and answered breathlessly.

"Please tell me you've found Jessie," Ruth said.

"I had, until Marcus scared her away." Manning relayed the details of her brief rendezvous with Jessie. The lawyer had then met with Cuffy. She gave him a copy of the threatening text and photograph, and the tracking device found on Jessie's pickup. Manning also made it clear that she expected Cuffy to come down hard on Marcus's aggressive vigilantism.

"How did he react to that?" Ruth asked.

"Not so good. He didn't come right out and say it, but I had the feeling he approved of Marcus's actions. I don't like where this is going. I don't like it at all."

Ruth poured laundry detergent into the dispenser, her phone cradled to her ear. Ruth didn't like it either. "Can I see the video clip?"

"I don't see why not. You on WhatsApp?"

"Sure."

Ruth's phone pinged: she had received the video. She looked at it. It disgusted her. "That's stalking. And trespassing."

"I hear you."

Ruth told Manning about her chat with Bill Moran and his guess that Cuffy's son, Ford, was behind the stalker's video. "How can I help?" Ruth asked.

"Find her. As far as I can tell, she's all out of friends."

This was all Ruth's fault. If Jessie had stayed the night at their house, this wouldn't have happened.

"I'll see what I can do. I don't know if she'll listen to me," Ruth said.

"Try hard," Manning said. "And keep an eye out for Marcus. If she doesn't die evading arrest, I wouldn't be surprised if she dies at his hand. He's a twisted son of a bitch. When I stopped him from pursuing Jessie this morning, I swear to God I thought he was going to kill me."

The first thing Ruth did was dial Jessie and leave a voicemail.

"Hey, Jessie. I'm really worried about you, and so's Manning. I can meet you wherever you want. I'll accompany you to the sheriff's office. Running isn't the answer. It'll end badly. Please, Jessie, just call me."

That afternoon, she and Victor were going to Clyde Hudson's funeral. Ruth had already laid her black dress on the bed. She had plenty of time to visit Marcus and make it to the funeral. If Cuffy wasn't prepared to stop Marcus from chasing Jessie, perhaps Ruth could. A quick call to the local fire station and Ruth was on her way to Marcus's house; he had called in sick, so his house was as good a place as any to start.

Marcus and Jude lived in a converted boathouse with a balcony overlooking the lake. It was on an acre lot on the edge of town surrounded by mature elm trees. As Ruth came to a halt in the street outside his house, she was surprised at how nervous she felt. Would Marcus respond aggressively to her? She sat in the car for a moment, wondering if this visit was a mistake. She had a tendency to charge in. At the Lakes Jewish Elementary School she had made the wrong decision to go in when she should have waited for backup.

There was no black Hummer in the driveway, although a convertible red sportscar was. Ruth recognized it as Jude's car. If Marcus wasn't home, perhaps Ruth could find out where he was from Jude. She would have to be subtle about it and find an excuse for popping in.

Music was coming from the upper level of the house. She rang the doorbell and waited, then she heard the *slap, slap* of slip-on shoes on wooden stairs. The door opened and Jude Deleon stood before her in pink cotton shorts cut high on the leg, and a tank top that revealed her ample bosom. Over the tank top she wore a semitransparent loose-fitting lace blouse that had tiny pink butterflies embroidered on it. Through the lace, Ruth noticed the fiberglass cast. From the blank look on Jude's face she clearly didn't know who Ruth was.

"Can I help you?" Jude asked.

"Oh hi, I'm Ruth Sullivan. I'm new to the area and I wanted to pop around and say hello." It was lame, but it would have to do.

"You're the FBI lady!" Jude's full lips stretched into a smile. "Come in, I've been dying to meet you." She stepped aside then closed the door behind them.

The lower level was dominated by the boat garage and the stairs that led to the living area. The boat garage doors were wide open and a cool breeze filled the hall. A Regal speedboat and a rowing boat bobbed on the water. Ruth followed Jude up the pine stairs to a living area that was directly under an A-frame roof. The bedroom, living room, and kitchen was one open-plan space with only a bathroom as a separate space. It was cramped but the views across the lake were amazing. Jude offered her a juice and Ruth accepted.

"Is Marcus home?"

"No, he'll be so disappointed to miss you."

"Will he be back soon? I'd love to meet him."

"I don't know."

Ruth noted there was no mention of Marcus being unwell. They chatted for a while about why Ruth and Victor had left Seattle. Jude then asked how her self-defense class was going.

"So far the feedback's been really positive."

"Yeah, Susie's told everyone how great you are. I'd love to do it. Guess I'll have to wait until this heals." She looked down at the plaster cast.

"Ouch, that looks painful. How did you do it?"

"Fell down those damn stairs. Marcus put way too much varnish on them. I hit the tiled floor and snapped my right radius in two."

Ruth's eyes went from the cast to the long-sleeved lacy blouse. Was the blouse hiding bruises?

"So how long have you and Marcus been together?" Ruth asked chattily.

"Two years. How time flies." Jude handed her a glass of orange juice and invited Ruth to sit on a leather couch.

It was at the two-year point that Marcus broke Jessie's arm.

"Are you a firefighter too?"

"Me?" Jude laughed. "No way. One hero in the house is enough. I design clothes," she gestured to the lace blouse she wore. "I made this. All my design. I have some samples downstairs. You're welcome to take a look."

"Sure."

Jude led Ruth downstairs to what Ruth had assumed was a built-in closet. Jude opened the double doors to reveal an eight-foot-long square room with a tiny window, a small table, sewing machine, and clothes rack, from which hung a range of boho dresses and floaty blouses in pretty colors. A full-length mirror leaned against one wall.

"Take your time. If there's something you like, I can make it to size." Jude switched on a ceiling fan, although the room was surprisingly cool, perhaps because it never received direct sun.

"I could have sworn this was a closet." Ruth looked across the hall to what appeared to be another built-in closet. "Is that a room too?"

"That's Marcus's man cave. He works out in there."

"Weights?"

"Yeah." Jude turned her attention to a knee-length wrap-around dress in turquoise. "This would really work with your blond hair." She took it off the rack. "Hold it against you and take a look in the mirror. And I'd say it's your size."

Ruth had to admit it was the perfect color. "Could I try some on?"

"Sure. I'll separate the clothes that will fit you." She placed three dresses and two blouses at the far end of the rack. "There's not much room, so I'll leave you to it. I'll be upstairs. Just call me if you need anything."

Ruth watched Jude climb the stairs, then she partially closed the sewing room door and took off her blouse and skirt and tried on the turquoise dress. It looked great on her and the fabric was a thin cotton, which was exactly what she needed in this intense heat. But Ruth couldn't stop thinking about Marcus's man cave. She crept across the hall. The double doors opened outward with a click. Thank goodness Jude was playing music upstairs. The room was identical in size to Jude's sewing room except there was a bench press and a stack of free weights. A red punching bag hung from the ceiling.

Ruth closed the doors, then changed back into her own clothes. She climbed the stairs, carrying the dress she wanted to buy over one arm. Jude was seated on the balcony, messaging on her phone.

"I'll take this one," Ruth said.

Jude looked up, startled and put her phone face down on the table. "Sure. I knew it was perfect for you. Cash or card?"

"Card."

"I'll wrap it for you. The paper is downstairs."

"Can I meet you down there," Ruth said. "I need to use your bathroom."

She heard the slap of Jude's slip-ons as she went downstairs. When she was gone, Ruth nipped onto the balcony and picked up Jude's phone. She read the message that Jude was partway through typing.

Where are you? The FBI lady's come calling. Is this about Jessie?

Ruth scrolled back to her previous message.

Please, Marky. Let the cops deal with it.

CHAPTER THIRTY-THREE

The last place Jessie thought she would end up was at Weird Bill's. Yet here she was, about to turn onto Hilltop Loop Road, on her way to the rear entrance of Bill's property. Very few people knew there was a second entrance to Bill's lot. He didn't put up signs. There was no gate and the vegetation was thoroughly overgrown. The route along the loop road enabled her to avoid Lake View Drive, where she lived. There was bound to be a deputy staking out her house.

Jessie's plan was going well until she hit a roadblock across the loop road of yellow bollards and horizontal posts. She checked her local news app and found that a tree had fallen across the loop road. Jessie took a chance that she could drive around the tree. She shifted the horizontal posts out of the way, drove through, then put the posts back in position. Finding the entrance wouldn't be easy. She drove slowly and very nearly missed it, then reversed. The hubcap nailed to a tree was the giveaway, like a round eye watching her. It made her shudder.

The driveway was overrun with creepers and ferns and within seconds she ran out of track. Jessie relied on the gradient to help her find her way to Bill's shack on the shore. After ten minutes she grew worried. There was no sign of habitation. She switched off the rumbling engine and listened. She hoped to hear a powerboat, or the lapping of water, or even Bill's cranky voice. What she heard was the splutter of an engine that didn't want to start. *Grr ruh ruh. Grr ruh ruh.* She moved her head to try and work out from which direction the noise came. A little to the right, but mostly straight ahead. *Grr ruh ruh. Grr ruh ruh.*

"Start, you son of a bitch!" The reedy voice was Bill's.

As a precaution, Jessie took from her glove compartment her poppy's antique revolver. It wasn't loaded. She didn't even know if it could fire, but it might make Bill think twice about firing at her. Her arrival would be unexpected, and she was unsure how Bill might react. Would he even remember offering her a place to lie low? The guy was so out of touch, he didn't even own a phone. She hadn't been able to call him.

Jessie left Bartie in the shaded pickup and walked down the slope. She found Bill leaning on the hood of what looked to be an old Ford from the 1960s. Jump cables trailed from the Ford's engine to Bill's pride and joy, his 1950s Cadillac. It took a while for him to notice her and by the time he raised his shotgun, she was already aiming the Colt Model 1877 Lightning revolver at him.

"Hey, Bill, you invited me here, remember?" she said.

"What you doing pointing your pappy's gun at me for?"

"Because you're pointing a shotgun at me."

They were at an impasse. Jessie lowered her weapon first. "How do you know this belonged to Poppy?"

Bill lowered his shotgun.

"I used to tease him about it. He'd come to my place once a month and fire off a few rounds, then he would sit with me and clean it until it shone like a diamond."

Jessie had assumed her father had gone to a rifle range. "He came here? Why?"

"Me and your pappy went way back. He was one of the few people who stayed friendly after I lost everything."

This was news to Jessie. "If you were Poppy's friend, why didn't you come to his funeral?"

In all honesty, her father's funeral was a blur. Her mom was unable to function. She could barely stand, let alone speak to anyone. Jessie took on the task of organizing the funeral. On the day, she kept busy. Faces came and went. Words of sympathy. Their home, above her father's medical practice, had been packed with people. Tom had been well liked, and his sudden death had shocked the town. Jessie had been angry with Bill at the time for failing to show at the funeral or the after-party.

"I mourned him here," Bill said. "Your father would've understood."

"Bill, I have to know. Did you tell Cuffy I was leaving town?"

"I didn't tell a soul. I swear." He crossed himself. "The motorhome's yours if you want it."

"You swear you won't tell on me."

"I swear to God." Again, he crossed himself.

Jessie studied Bill for a second. "Just for tonight, okay? Until I work out my next move. You want to show me where it is?"

"I can do one better than that. I'll cook you a meal tonight." He smiled. "Make it up to you. How does deer stew sound?"

"Where did you get deer meat?"

"Shot it."

"Hunting's banned, because of the fires…"

"Oh, stop your whining. You want me to help you or not?"

Jessie gave him a nod.

"Okay then, you got any beer?"

"Yes," she replied. There was a six-pack in her cooler on the truck.

"Then bring beer with you. Come over at six. Now I'll take you to your new home."

CHAPTER THIRTY-FOUR

The funeral service at the little whitewashed church for Clyde Foster Hudson—brave firefighter, father of two, husband to Jean—was well attended. Despite the smoke haze, mourners filled the church and spilled down the steps and along the path to the street. The coffin had a guard of honor—his fellow firefighters were given time out from the fire front to attend.

Marcus, in his fire captain's uniform, did the eulogy, describing Clyde's life and achievements in a voice full of love, accompanied by projected images on the church wall: school photos, family snaps, images of Clyde with his firefighter buddies. Marcus captivated his audience entirely. Like a trained actor, his speech was nuanced, his delivery perfect. He managed just the right tightness around the jaw and a tear at the very end. He was every bit as beautiful as Ruth had been led to believe, a square-jawed Viking of a man with a perfect white smile. While he appeared sad about Clyde's passing, she sensed how much his power over the audience thrilled him. It was more about him winning their adoration than it was about mourning his friend. Ruth hoped he would attend the after-party. Perhaps she could peel back some of his many layers and see something of the real Marcus.

The wake was at the widow's house, a turn-of-the-century four-bedroom home. Friends arrived with plates of food so that Jean didn't have to concern herself with the catering. The widow, who was heavily pregnant, sat on the sofa with a numb expression on her face, surrounded by people offering their condolences. Her kids, Rose and Anne, were in the backyard with other kids, under the shade of a big oak from which a swing hung. Noah and David stuck close to Ruth and Victor, unnerved by the bleak atmosphere and uncomfortable about approaching a group of kids they hadn't gotten to know yet.

"We're so very sorry for your loss, Jean," Victor said. Jean nodded, her lips gripped together, no doubt to hold back tears. The dark circles around her eyes spoke of sleepless nights and the pain of her loss.

Ruth, Victor, and the kids moved away to allow others to speak to the widow. "There's John and Susie over there," Victor pointed out. "How do I look?" He smoothed down his navy blazer.

"You look great. Do you want to go over and say hi?" Ruth asked.

Victor removed his glasses and cleaned them with a lint cloth. He did this when he was nervous. "I need to make a good impression. I was thinking about asking him to be a reference for the Belle Property job. Is now the right time or should I wait? What do you think?"

"Maybe not right now. But we should go chat with them. Coming?"

They wove through the throng of mourners, with Noah and David following. Cuffy was in uniform and was in conversation with a tall red-headed man, who wandered off as they approached. Susie took Ruth in a hug. Victor offered his hand to Cuffy, who shook it. "How's it going, Victor? Settling in after life in the big smoke?"

Ruth didn't hear her husband's reply because of Susie's loud voice. "You must be Noah and David," Susie smiled warmly. "My! What fine-looking boys you are!" The boys mumbled awkward thank yous. Then to Ruth, "This is so, so terrible. Poor Jean is beside herself, as you can imagine. And there's a killer on the loose. It's enough to make you give up on humanity, it really is. Thank goodness we have your dinner party to look forward to on Saturday."

"We're delighted you can come. Is Ford joining us?" Ruth replied.

"Just us two," Susie said. "Ford does his own thing."

Cuffy shoved a small triangular sandwich into his mouth and chewed. "I gotta get going. I'm not leaving a stone unturned until I find the son of a bitch who did this."

"We have total faith in you, John," Victor said. He glanced at Ruth. "Don't we, dear?"

"Of course. We're all very worried about the house fires."

"If there's anything we can do," Victor said. "I'm job-hunting, so I have some free time. Many hands make light work."

"Thank you kindly, but leave it to the professionals, Victor."

"Job-hunting?" Susie said. "Are you going back into real estate?"

Before Victor could answer, Cuffy said, "If you'll excuse me."

Ruth saw the look of disappointment on her husband's face as he watched Cuffy leave.

Someone behind Ruth placed a hand briefly on her shoulder. Ruth hated people doing that. It was an intimate gesture that she only felt comfortable with her husband and close friends doing. Marcus gave Ruth a charming smile, "You must be Ruth. It's a pleasure to meet you." He shook her hand. "Jude mentioned you dropped by earlier. I'm sorry I missed you."

Victor's eyebrows shot up; Ruth hadn't mentioned it to him.

"We had a great time. I had no idea that Jude was such a brilliant designer." She looked at her husband, "I bought a dress."

"Beautiful eulogy, Marcus," said Susie. "It had me in tears."

Marcus gave a little bow. "Clyde was a great man. It was the least I could do."

"Is Jude with you?" Ruth asked, quickly checking the room and not seeing her.

"With her girlfriends on the porch. I hear you're running self-defense classes. It's about time the women of this town learned how to protect themselves, with all the weird things happening around here." He looked her in the eyes as he said it, his gaze earnest. He was either an exceptional liar or he actually meant it.

"When Jude's arm has healed, I hope she'll come along," Ruth said. "Are you feeling better?"

His smile froze for a few seconds. Perhaps he had forgotten that he was supposed to be sick. "Much better."

"I haven't seen you at the gym, Marcus. Where do you work out?" Victor asked. Ruth tried not to notice that Victor was holding in his stomach muscles.

"At home mostly. You're looking in great shape. Whatever you're doing, just keep doing it. There's a group of us guys that go mountain biking. Why don't you join us?"

Victor's eyes shone and he said that he would like that. Marcus then led him away to meet the guy who organized the group's activities.

"You poor dears," Susie said to Noah and David, who looked very bored. "I happen to know where the cupcakes are hidden because I brought them." The boys' faces brightened. "And Ruth, I'll introduce you to some people."

Ruth, Susie, Noah, and David entered the kitchen. "Is Ford okay?" Ruth asked. Ford was conspicuously absent from the funeral and after-party.

"He finds these things difficult. He's a sensitive boy. And besides, he's still recovering."

"From what?"

"The accident. Haven't you heard? It happened a few months back. He was knocked off his motorcycle."

Before Ruth could ask more about the accident, Susie introduced her to a group of women. The only one Ruth knew was Millie Kemp, who had yelled at her outside David's school. Millie was cutting a home-baked quiche into slices. She said hello.

"Sorry about the other day," Millie said. "I was upset about little Eric."

"No problem. Did you bake that? It looks delicious."

"Sure did. Would you like a slice?"

Ruth accepted a slice. She had missed lunch and was really hungry. "This is delicious. Can I ask you for the recipe?"

Millie seemed happy with the compliment and said she would email it to Ruth tomorrow. She even offered to cut Ruth's hair at a ten percent discount because she was new to the salon. Perhaps Millie wasn't as scary as Ruth had first thought.

"I need a smoke. I'll see you later," Millie said, heading for the backyard.

Noah and David tucked into Susie's chocolate cupcakes and Susie told them a story about Clyde rescuing her cat from a tree. Then a portly man with a thick beard entered the kitchen with a box of beer on his shoulder. He introduced himself as Millie's husband, Ray. Putting the box on the kitchen counter, he unpacked some bottles and put them in the fridge, then began drinking one. Susie had moved on to another tale about Clyde, without so much as taking a breath. This time it was about Clyde at the annual community picnic last year and how patient he had been with all the kids who wanted to sit in the cabin of the fire truck.

Out of the corner of her eye, Ruth noticed the red-headed man who had spoken with Cuffy earlier, hovering in the doorway. He surveyed the kitchen as if searching for somebody. His eyes rested on Ray, then he turned on his heels and merged into the crowd in the living room. Intrigued, Ruth asked Susie to keep an eye on her sons while she used the bathroom. This gave her an excuse to wander through the house in search of the young man. On the front porch Marcus was holding forth to a group, and Victor was one of them. The group roared with laughter as Marcus reached his punchline.

Ruth stepped through the French doors and onto a deck that had steps down to a shady backyard. To one side was a garden shed and next to the shed Millie was smoking. And with her was the red-headed man with a lit cigarette. Millie's face had soured. She flicked some ash onto the lawn. The man kept glancing at her. He was doing the talking. Their body language was tense. Ruth grappled with an excuse to join them, but she wasn't a smoker. Then she had an idea. She took a pen from her purse and used an old receipt from the grocery store and wrote her email address on it. Then she strolled toward the two smokers. It wasn't until Ruth was almost upon them that Millie nudged the man in the ribs, causing him to look up. Just before that, Ruth thought she heard Millie say, "I lied for you." Or was it, "I lied to you"?

"Millie, here's my email for the quiche recipe." She handed her the piece of paper. "I have to go, I'm afraid. So nice to have chatted to you."

Millie automatically took the proffered note. "Thanks, and don't forget to book a haircut."

Ruth said she would, then smiled at the man. "I'm Ruth, we haven't met."

"Marty Spaan. You're married to Victor, right?"

"That's right. How do you know him?

"In this town everyone knows everyone. Right, Millie?"

"Yup," Millie concurred. "Victor was quite a celebrity when he was in his twenties. His face was on the TV. You remember, Marty?" Marty nodded. "He was the go-to guy for real estate sales. We were sorry when he moved away."

This was news to Ruth. Victor on TV? Wow!

"Are you in real estate, Marty?" Ruth asked.

Marty laughed. "Bus driver." He took a drag on his cigarette and blew it up to the sky. "I got my own business too, a twenty-passenger luxury mini-coach. Take the old folks into Seattle sometimes. School trips too. And the monthly ladies lunch excursions." He smiled at Millie. "Millie organizes them. A day out shopping in the city, then a lunch somewhere, and I get you back home safely afterward."

"It's the last Saturday of the month," Millie said. "You should come. Get to know people."

"I'd love to. Say, what do you think about the house fires? It's scaring the hell out of me."

"That girl should have been locked up years ago," Millie said, her jawline hardening.

"Who do you mean?" Ruth asked, feigning ignorance.

Marty looked at Ruth as if she were an alien. "Jessie Lewis. Ever since her dad passed, she's not been right. I think the grief sent her a bit screwy in the head."

Millie said, "I don't see it that way. Jessie lost it over Marcus, not her dad. She was insanely jealous of him and who could blame her. He's so good-looking."

Marty gave her a disapproving glance. "Yeah, okay, Jessie went crazy over Marcus, but he wasn't so perfect neither."

Except for Bill, Marty was the first person to make a negative remark about Marcus. "How do you mean?"

"He was banging Jude when he was living with Jessie."

Millie elbowed him in the ribs. "Leave Marcus alone."

Marty rolled his eyes.

"Has Jessie ever lit a fire?" Ruth asked.

Millie and Marty shrugged. "Who knows?" Millie said.

Marty threw his cigarette on the lawn and stamped it out. "I need a drink. See you ladies later."

Millie also stamped out her half-smoked cigarette, then picked up both cigarette butts from the ground. "We don't want to start another fire, now do we?"

Ruth headed home with the two boys, leaving Victor to catch up with old friends. What was going on between Millie and Marty and why, in her bones, did Ruth feel that understanding their relationship mattered? Ruth also pondered Ford's motorcycle accident. She didn't know why, but she felt that it was significant too.

CHAPTER THIRTY-FIVE

The 1980s motorhome was so deep in the forest that Jessie had to leave her pickup a few yards away and walk the rest of the way. The motorhome's tires were flat as pancakes and the windows were so caked in filth that when Bill opened the van's door, the interior was as dark as a cave. Bill sniffed.

"Can't smell damp. A good sign." He looked behind him at Jessie. "Get me the gas bottle. I'll set it up for you. Water is up to you. Collect it from the lake and boil it to kill any nasties. You got water containers?"

"Yeah. Is there a fridge?"

"Yep. No idea if it works. I guess you'll find out."

Jessie went back to her truck and grabbed the gas bottle. In the other hand she carried her cooler containing her perishable food. Soon Bill had the gas set up. Only one light fitting worked, but the bar-sized fridge hummed into life, and when she tested the two burners, they ignited just fine.

Bill nodded with approval. "She's a beauty, ain't she? They don't build things to last these days. Not like this old girl."

The interior was in a poor state. Bartie barked at a cabinet under the sink. When she opened it, there were mice droppings. The mice were the least of her worries. The chipboard cabinetry was falling apart. Two of the windows were boarded up. At least there were drapes, neatly held back with ties. The mattresses on the benches on either side of the central aisle were stained but were luckily dry to the touch.

"Had a leak. Long time ago," was Bill's explanation.

It didn't matter. Jessie planned to sleep in her clothes.

"Keep the noise down. Sound travels easy," Bill said, "And only collect water at sunset and sunrise." He stepped out of the motorhome, then looked back. "Don't forget the beer tonight."

Noah and David bickered all the way home. They were on a sugar-induced high after eating Susie's cupcakes. Ruth sent them into the backyard to let off steam while she used her laptop on the deck. She scrolled through Ford's social media. He was on Instagram, Snapchat, and TikTok. On TikTok, Ford had four thousand follow-ers, the majority of whom were Ford's age or younger. There were plenty of clips of motorcyclists and skateboarders. She recognized the skatepark by Devil's Lake. The rest were shot to humiliate people or were voyeuristic and unsettling. That included several of Jessie. Jessie leaving the gym with Ruth after the self-defense class. Jessie on her front porch drinking beer alone looking hot and sweaty. Ruth found one in which Jessie and Paul Troyer were arguing in a supermarket parking lot. It was apparent that Ford wasn't interested in the argu-ment. He had zoomed in on a gap in Jessie's work shirt where a button had been lost, revealing the hint of a bra underneath. Ruth found them distasteful, but it didn't make him an arsonist or a killer.

After ten minutes of watching his videos, Ruth found a ten-second clip about the motorcycle accident Susie had mentioned, dated three weeks ago. In it his dented Kawasaki lay on the road. "He totally wrecked it and the jerk tried to blame me," Ford said. "No way, man. It was Paul's fault. And he's going to pay up. I got witnesses."

Paul? Paul Troyer? How many Pauls lived in Eagle Falls? It couldn't be many.

What struck Ruth was that the style of Ford's video clips on TikTok were similar to the photo Jessie received with the threatening text: *You are next.* Had Ford meant it as a sick joke, or, God forbid, was he serious?

Ruth needed to find a way to talk to Ford without his mom and dad around. But how?

She scrolled through the local skatepark videos again: they were all shot between six and seven in the evening. It was almost six now and Ford had been a no-show at the funeral. He might be hanging out at the skatepark. Ruth would need to take the kids with her, but that was okay because the skatepark was right next to the playground.

"Who wants to come to the playground?" she called.

Noah and David raced inside and after she had managed to get them into T-shirts, shorts, and sneakers, they set off for Lakeside Park. As she came to a halt in a shady spot and switched off the car engine she looked around for Ford's Kawasaki. It was a distinctive black bike and she spotted it immediately. She got out of the car and, clutching her sons' hands, followed the grinding sound of skateboard wheels on concrete.

The mega bowl was empty, which was not surprising, given the heat haze trapped in the cup-shaped concrete. It would be like skateboarding into a pizza oven. Several teenagers had congregated to one side of the undulating section of the skatepark: a long track where there were ledges the kids could jump onto, ride along, and then hop off. She spotted Ford in a baseball cap and a black Stüssy-branded tee. He was watching a younger skater kick the board into a spin before landing back on it. The kid made it look so easy.

"Look, Mommy," said Noah. "That's so cool!"

"Shall we watch for a bit, then we'll go to the playground?"

Their interest waned fast. Noah complained that he wanted a skateboard and David wanted to play on the swings. Ruth took them to the gated playground. From inside the play area, she said,

"I'm going to stand over there"—she pointed to the edge of the skatepark, just twenty feet away—"and watch you. Do not leave the playground, okay. Just call out if you want to go."

Both boys promised.

Ruth wandered back to where Ford and two teenagers stood, all the time keeping an eye on her kids.

"Nice kickflip," Ruth said. Ford and his buddies turned their heads. "Great skatepark."

Ford folded his arms defensively. "What do you know about skateboarding?"

"Had a skateboard as a kid," Ruth said. Ford raised a disbelieving eyebrow. It was the truth. Ruth had been good at it too. "I want to get a board for my son. He's almost ten. What do you recommend?"

Ford unfolded his arms and seemed to think about his answer. "My first board was a Santa Cruz, 7.75 wide."

That board was pricey. She had looked online. "What do you think of the Powell Peralta Golden Dragon?"

"A really cool board."

Ford's two friends went to practice a flip trick.

"I saw your TikTok skateboarding clips. You have a talent for filming action."

"Thanks." He took his phone from the back pocket of his knee-length shorts and scrolled through his TikTok video clips. He pressed play and turned the screen to face Ruth. A guy in his twenties was doing a 540-degree turn performed on a ramp.

"A McTwist," she said. Ruth saw he was impressed. She glanced at her kids to check they were okay, then she got down to business. "I hear you have footage of Jessie at the Wilmot crime scene." Ruth kept her voice light and chatty. "However did you manage that?"

Ford reared back, clearly shocked. But he recovered fast. "Not me."

"Really? It's your style."

"Bullshit." By now his eyes were looking everywhere but at Ruth.

"You have a lot of footage on Jessie. Are you sweet on her?"

"Are you crazy?" He walked away.

Ruth knew she should stop. But there was a question she was dying to ask. A quick glance at her kids told her they were okay. They had moved on to the climbing frame. They waved at her. She waved back.

"What kind of a mom are you?" Ford's mouth was a sneer. "Leaving your kids alone."

"They're not alone. I'm right here." Ruth saw red. The question burst from her lips. "Did you photograph Jessie seminude last night?"

Ford swung around to face her. "Fuck off!"

An aggressive response but not a denial. "Did you send her a threatening text?"

"No, now fuck off!"

Ford's friends must have heard him yelling. They stopped their practice and stared. Ruth felt her blood pressure rising.

"Tell me about your motorcycle accident."

"What? Why?"

"Was it Paul Troyer?"

"If you don't get out of my face, I'll get my dad to arrest you."

"I don't think so, Ford. We're just shooting the breeze." Ruth had already gone too far. Where had her usual self-control gone? "Nice chatting with you," she said.

Ruth made a beeline for the playground. She heard footsteps behind her. It was Ford. "My dad's in charge around here, not you." He stabbed a finger at her.

"I know that, Ford. I just want to know who knocked you off your motorcycle."

"Why? So you can fix me up for the fires? I don't light fires, lady, and I don't kill people."

He stormed off.

Ruth collected the kids and went home. Teenage boys like Ford tended not to confide in their parents. Or so she hoped. If she had read Ford's reactions right, Ford probably did shoot the video of Jessie trawling through the Wilmot fire scene. Why he was there in the first place was an interesting question.

She wasn't able to gauge if he sent Jessie the threatening text and the seminaked photo. Although she was now almost certain that Paul Troyer knocked Ford off his motorcycle. Given Paul's poor track record of paying money owed—he didn't pay Jessie for installing his water feature—Ruth hazarded a guess that he objected to paying for a new motorcycle. That would make someone like Ford very angry.

Was it enough motive for murder?

CHAPTER THIRTY-SIX

It was past seven in the evening when Ruth, Noah, and David sat at the dining table eating sausage and cheese pasta. Victor wasn't home yet.

A car stopped outside their house, then there were footsteps on the drive and a key turned in the front door's lock. When Victor entered the room, he had a pinched look, as if somebody had broken bad news. Both boys leapt up and gave their dad a hug. He reciprocated but his jaw was set tight and he looked angrily at Ruth.

Oh no, she thought, *Ford went running to Mommy and Daddy about our chat.*

"Hey boys," Ruth said, keeping her voice light, "Dad and I have to talk. Sit down at the table and eat your pasta and we'll be right back."

Victor followed her onto the deck, and she closed the patio door. She could smell the beer on Victor's breath.

"Something's wrong," Ruth said. She tried to take his hand, but he pulled it away. "Tell me."

He stared off into their yard. "I know it's difficult for you to let go of your job. I know you miss the FBI. But interrogating Cuffy's son about the arson attacks? What in God's name were you thinking?"

"I didn't interrogate him, Victor. I can explain." She gestured to a couple of rattan chairs.

"I'm good as I am."

"All right. I took the kids to the playground in Lakeside Park." A little white lie. She didn't want to explain her ulterior motive. "Ford was skateboarding. I asked him about a board he would recommend for Noah, you know, as a birthday present." Noah was turning ten in two weeks. "Then I asked him about the video of Jessie at the Wilmots' house, the night after it burned down."

"Why? That's none of your business."

Ruth lifted her chin a fraction. "I'm making it my business."

"But why? If you interfere with the case, you'll turn him into an enemy."

"I don't want that. Of course, I don't. But I can't sit idly by while a young woman takes the rap for a crime I don't believe she's committed."

His jaw hung open. His voice, when he spoke, was high-pitched with astonishment. "You're doing this for Jessie Lewis?"

"Yes. I hate the way everyone in this place treats her like a pariah. I think it likely she was a domestic violence victim."

Victor shook his head. "Marcus wouldn't do that."

"Do you have any idea how difficult it is for women in abusive relationships to report their abuser? They are terrified, isolated. They often risk their lives to do it."

"She withdrew the allegations. Why are you raking over old ground?"

"Because now she's being made a scapegoat for someone else's crimes."

Victor threw his arms up. "How do you even know what Jessie is like? You've spoken to her, what... once?"

"More than that."

He dragged his fingers through his hair. "Why didn't you discuss this with me first? You know I must keep Cuffy on my side. Don't you see what you're doing? You're jeopardizing my chances of getting a job."

Ruth stared at him. Had she gone too far? Was she doing this for Jessie or because she longed for her old job? Ruth needed a challenge. A cause. And Jessie had become that cause, when Ruth knew she should be championing her husband's cause. Ruth sat heavily. "I'm sorry. I didn't mean…" She looked up. "What can I do to make things right?"

He sat on a chair next to her. "Apologize to Cuffy."

"I'd rather cuddle a porcupine."

"You think this is funny? If you mess this up, we'll have to move to a new town."

She sighed. "Maybe that's not such a bad idea."

"You can't be serious."

"Maybe I am? I can't live in a town that's at the mercy of a sheriff who is judge, jury, and executioner."

"We can't afford to go back to Seattle."

"We can," Ruth said, "I could always go back to the Bureau."

"Damn it, Ruth!" he said. "I don't want you going back there. I want you to be my *wife*."

CHAPTER THIRTY-SEVEN

It was almost dark by the time Jessie had settled into the motorhome and then made her way through the forest to Bill's cabin. She had a flashlight for the return trip in one hand and the six-pack of beer in the other. Bartie trotted along beside her, sniffing tree trunks and following scents, happy to be back in the forest environment. Jessie was feeling more hopeful too. Perhaps it was due to the refreshing swim she had taken in the lake. Or was it that she was simply having dinner with another person? It had been a long time since anyone had invited her to dine with them.

The evening was hot and sticky and by the time she arrived at Bill's shack she was perspiring again. At least she didn't smell bad, which was more than could be said for Bill. Good as his word, though, he served a tasty venison stew with potatoes, carrots, and beans, and they ate it on his front porch. Bill sat on a swing seat that hung from the porch roof by chains. Jessie took the rocking chair. They ate mostly in silence and Jessie was fine with that. When the meal was done, Bill started on his second beer.

"The fires are heading this way."

"So the wind's turned?" she asked.

"It's turned. Don't go getting too comfortable because we could be running for our lives soon."

"Are they that close?"

"Take a look."

Bill's knees cracked as he stood. He led her beyond the woodpile at the side of the house. The night had closed in, but the interior lights gave her the sense of where the walls and roof were situated. There was a steel ladder propped against the back wall. He started to climb.

"Where you going?" Jessie asked, downing the remainder of her first beer.

"Where do you think I'm going?" Bill chortled. "You get the best views from up here."

Given the dilapidated state of Bill's property, Jessie wasn't sure if the roof was safe to walk on, but if it could take Bill's weight, it should be able to take hers.

"Stay!" she told Bartie, who cocked his head to one side as if to question the wisdom of what she was about to do.

She climbed. The grassy roof slanted toward the rear but only marginally, which made it easy to walk across. She found Bill cross-legged, as if he were meditating, his gaze set on the distant blaze. She sat next to him. He pulled two fresh beers from the pockets of his shirt, popped off the lids and offered her one.

"Welcome to Bill's movie theater!" He gestured to the scene ahead.

They clinked bottles.

The air was smoky but the moon still reflected off the lake. On the western edge of the shore, the streetlights of Eagle Falls created a yellow glow above the town. Beyond the lake was the solid black silhouette of the national park, marred by a brilliant red gash.

"See," Bill said. "It's real close."

Jessie felt a breeze on her face. The wind had changed direction. It was blowing the mega fire right at them.

"I reckon it'll hit the town tomorrow," Bill said. "Serve them right, the damn lot of them."

She stared at him. "How do you know so much about fires?"

"I watch and learn. Been coming up here every night since the fires started. It has its own kind of beauty."

Jessie didn't agree. She knew from firsthand experience that fire was terrifying. It was the very worst way to die.

"You got any idea who started it?" She tilted her beer bottle in the national park's direction.

He sipped his beer. "Some idiot lit a campfire and, boom, everything burned. I mean, it's that hot—trees are just bursting into flames on their own. The house fires, now that's a different story. Someone is going around lighting them."

"The sheriff thinks I did it."

She felt Bill's gaze on her. "Nah, you didn't do it. You don't have it in you." He took another gulp. "I have my theories, but I ain't sharing them."

"Come on, Bill, why not? I'm on the run, remember? Who am I going to tell?"

Her eyes had adjusted enough to the darkness for her to notice Bill picking the label off the bottle, using a fingernail that was too long. "Your friend, the FBI lady, she came by asking about you."

Jessie tensed. "When?"

"This morning. I didn't tell her I'd seen you, okay?"

"Okay, so what did you tell her?"

He picked the last bit of label off the bottle and rolled it into a tight ball. "I told her who was videoing you that night."

"Hell, Bill. You telling me you knew all along?"

"Quit your moaning. You want to know who was watching us or not?"

"Tell me."

"Ford."

"Ford!" No wonder Big John wouldn't tell her who had supplied the footage. What in God's name was Ford doing there in the first place?

"How can you be sure?"

"I know the boy's motorcycle, see. I used to be into motorcycles when I was in my twenties. Before I got into cars. Know the sound of the Kawasaki engine like the back of my hand."

She rubbed a finger across her forehead. "That's just perfect. What if Ford is the arsonist?"

Bill pulled out a packet of cigarettes and offered her one. She declined. He lit his cigarette with a lighter that looked expensive, perhaps from the time when he was the town's lawyer. Bill inhaled, then threw his head back and exhaled at the sky. "This will all be over soon."

"What do you mean?"

"The fire," he pointed at the national park, "It'll cleanse that cesspit of a town."

Jessie tried not to betray how freaked out she was. She was on a roof with a crazy guy, and nobody knew she was there.

"Why does the town need cleansing?" she asked.

He blew some more nicotine at the sky and didn't answer.

"Back when I was a kid, you wore fancy suits and had a fancy house," Jessie said. "How did you end up here?"

"You would have been twelve when my Abigail was fifteen. As pretty as a picture she was." He turned his head to look at Jessie. "Do you remember her?"

"I do. Blond hair. Real clever."

"That's right." He looked down and picked at something on the sole of his old sneaker. "I was a bloody fool and lost everything. I lost my beautiful girl."

She waited. He continued to pick at his shoe. "You going to tell me how you lost everything?" she prompted.

"I was sucked into a scam." He looked at her. "Would you believe it? Me, a lawyer, and I didn't see it coming."

"A scam?"

"You know what foreclosure fraud is?" Bill asked.

"Nope."

"I was behind on the mortgage payments. Spent too much money on fancy suits and vacations overseas, and Maggie had to have designer clothes." Maggie was his ex-wife. "Anyway, my business was struggling. I'd gotten too big for my boots and people in town couldn't afford me. They started going to a new young lawyer in Marymere who was way cheaper and faster too. To be truthful, I had gotten fat and lazy. So I got a loan in exchange for upfront fees and an agreement to transfer the property title to the loan company. Turned out, the guy who loaned me the money was a criminal. He kept the payments I made and didn't pay the bills. He ran off with the money, leaving us without the home, but I was still responsible for the debt." He shook his head. "I was totally sucked in."

"I'm so sorry, Bill, I guess I was too young to know what was going on."

"Maggie left me and took Abigail. I lost the house to the bank and my firm collapsed because nobody trusted a lawyer who was dumb enough to fall for a scam. I had a breakdown. Your pappy did his best to help me. He was a good man. Got me onto antidepressants. Got me some counseling. Didn't do no good. I was broken, see?"

"Is it true you pissed on the floor of the bank that took your house?"

Bill chuckled. "Yeah. It was my grand protest and it backfired big time. When they called the cops and I refused to leave, I ended up punching a cop. Got charged with assaulting a police officer. Got put away for a while."

"I thought you went to a mental health hospital. I didn't know you went to jail."

"I got treatment there. In a weird kind of way, prison saved me."

"Did the guy who defrauded you get caught?"

"No, because there was a certain sheriff who made damn sure he never did."

"Cuffy?"

"Sure it was Cuffy, who else? He knew who was behind the scam but he did nothing. I reckon the bastard paid Cuffy to look the other way."

"You're saying Big John took a bribe to make the case go away?"

"That's exactly what I'm saying. He's as crooked as a dog's hind leg."

"Can you prove it?"

"Hell no. Cuffy's too canny. He went through the motions, you know, as if he was investigating. But the will just wasn't there. You see what I'm saying."

"Yes. Same thing that happened to me. He decided Marcus couldn't possibly abuse women. He pretended to look into it, and all the time he did everything he could to get me to withdraw my allegations."

"I'm sorry, Jessie."

"Why are you sorry? It's not your fault."

"I shouldn't have let Cuffy bully you like that. I should have spoken up or something. Your pappy was good to me and I owe him. But I'm not the man I used to be."

Staring at the silhouette of Bill, with his skeletal body and wild beard and crooked glasses, seated on the roof of his junkyard home, she found it hard to imagine him the swanky lawyer he had once been. Life had been cruel to him, or perhaps it was Cuffy who had been cruel. "You're still a good man," she said.

Bill removed his glasses and rubbed both eyes. "I'm afraid, is what I am. Of Cuffy and his crew. That's why I can't get involved in the arson investigation and why I can't admit to being at the Wilmots' house when you turned up. You see what I'm saying, Jessie?"

She sure did. "Bill, do you know who was behind the scam?"

"I know one of them. There were two, see?"

"Give me a name."

"Rob Wilmot."

CHAPTER THIRTY-EIGHT

Ruth was having yet another nightmare. Part of her knew it wasn't real, but she couldn't escape it, however hard she tried.

She was alone with the terrorist; his finger was on the detonator. She pleaded with him not to blow up the school. With every word, she moved a step closer to him. One more step and she could grab his arm and stop him. But he pressed the button. She flew through the air, and the school walls and ceiling flew around her as if she were being swept into a tornado. Then she found herself, inexplicably, in a classroom, the walls and ceiling intact, but everything else was on fire: desks, books, kids' bags, pictures on the walls. Children screamed but she couldn't see them. She coughed so hard she thought she would cough up her lungs. She spun around searching for a way out, but whichever way she looked, there was fire. A sudden crack and the ceiling collapsed.

"Ruth! Wake up!" A man's voice.

Her body was being shaken. Was this part of the dream? A honking cough woke her with a start. Victor stood over her, something white tied over his nose and mouth. He was blurry. Why couldn't she see him clearly?

"Fire!" he yelled, throwing back the sheet and taking her wrist. "Call 911. I'll get the kids!"

What?

He pulled her up to a seated position. "For Christ's sake, move!" Victor screamed.

Victor never screamed. This had to be real.

Ruth threw off the sheets. Her skin was seared by the heat and the room was murky with smoke. Through the open doorway she could see all the way along the hall to the living room. It was filled with flickering yellow flames that spread across the floor and crawled up the drapes, as if it were a living creature. Ruth heard Victor cajoling the kids. She heard their cries of terror. But she couldn't wake up. Those damn sleeping pills! Or was the smoke poisoning her ability to think? Ruth reached out for her phone on the nightstand.

Crash!

The flaming drapes collapsed onto the living room sofa and in seconds black toxic smoke rose from the cushions as the foam stuffing disintegrated.

Boom!

She knew that sound. Windows exploding outward. The air sucked in from outside would fan the conflagration. The roar grew ever louder, like a train heading right at her.

Ruth coughed and gagged for air. Her hands shook as her fingers tapped 911.

"Nine one one, what is your emergency?"

"Fire!" she gasped.

Just saying the word sent her into panic mode. Ruth screamed, a high-pitched shriek. She inhaled too much smoke and she retched and choked. The operator asked for her address. Ruth must have given it, because she was told that the fire service was on its way.

Noah and David!

Ruth stumbled out of the room. The fire in the corridor had almost reached David's room. Her baby boy. She had to save him. She stumbled, weak from lack of oxygen, her eyes streaming from the acrid smoke.

Clinging to the doorframe for support, she found her son's bed was empty.

"Ruth!"

Victor steered her into Noah's room.

"Where are they?" she wheezed.

"Safe."

The window was wide open. He dragged her to it. She resisted.

"My babies!"

"In the street."

She was close to collapse, her body wracked with coughing fits. Victor lifted her in his arms and, feet first, he passed her into the arms of a neighbor and she was carried away from the house, her chest heaving, unable to stop her coughing. He laid her on the sidewalk.

"Mommy!"

It was David's terrified voice. Val Wynkoop, from next door, held David and Noah close, her arms wrapped around them. Mike Wynkoop had his hose switched on and he was doing what he could to save their house. It was bizarre to see their neighbors in nightwear. Her boys ran to her, Val following. Ruth cuddled them, weeping.

"It's okay," she said, kissing them. "You're safe."

"Where's Daddy going?" Noah asked.

Victor ran down their driveway. Dear God! Not the car. Her car! No! It was full of gas. She opened her mouth to call his name and her croaky voice was drowned out by the roar of the fire. Ruth squeezed Noah and David to her, sobbing, "Victor! Don't!"

He got in her car, turned the engine, and drove out of their drive and farther down the street. He had saved their most precious possessions, packed and ready to flee from the park fire. Little had they known that their home might go up in flames.

"Daddy's a hero," she said to her sons.

The fire engine, all flashing yellow lights and wailing siren, sped down the street and came to a halt outside what remained of their home. The fire crew swiftly unrolled their fire hoses and began to douse the flames.

Victor joined Ruth and the boys. "It'll be okay," he said. "We've got insurance."

Firefighters dragged a hose in through the front door. Fire seemed to have engulfed the whole house. More sirens, this time the *boop, boop, boop* and then the howl of an ambulance. Time passed in disconnected chunks, much like Ruth's nightmares. The paramedics wanted them to go to hospital. Ruth didn't want to leave.

A firefighter in breathing mask, helmet, and air pack on his back jogged over to them. He removed his transparent face shield and the breathing apparatus. His face was grubby but even in the semidarkness and strobing lights it was easy to see it was Marcus Harstad because of his sapphire-blue eyes.

"Any idea how this started?" Marcus asked.

Ruth and Victor said they didn't.

"Any naked flames, faulty wiring?"

"No," Victor replied. "The air conditioning was on, but we've had no problems."

"I found this." He held up a small wooden wedge. "Know anything about it?"

"No, why?" Ruth asked.

"It was wedged into a rear window."

Ruth's brain was struggling to keep up. "Why?"

"Don't know yet," Marcus said. "Do either of you have fire-protection gear? Thick leather gloves?"

They both shook their heads.

Marcus held up a slate-gray glove. "Know whose this is?"

They both said they didn't.

"Okay," he said, then he walked over to where Sheriff Cuffy leaned against his vehicle.

Ruth watched the two men in conversation. Marcus dropped the glove and the wooden wedge into transparent evidence bags and handed them to Cuffy.

CHAPTER THIRTY-NINE

Jessie woke suddenly from a deep sleep. Bartie was barking. Distant barking. For a brief moment, she had no idea where she was.

She was flat on her back and the surface beneath her was too hard for a bed. Her lower back ached. Above her, a dirty-brown night sky, no stars. Smoky air tickled her windpipe. She sat up groggily and a blanket slid off her chest and pooled around her legs. She succumbed to a honking cough. When it subsided, she noticed the gentle lapping sound of the lake over pebbles. She was at Bill's cabin. She must have fallen asleep on his roof. In the distance were vast expanses of glowing, rippling orange and yellow, as if a volcano had spilled molten lava over the whole national park. Farther away, the wildfire at the North Cascades crept closer as if drawn to the other fire like a magnet.

She patted her pockets and found her phone, switching on the flashlight. With it she could now see the roof's edges and the upper rungs of the ladder they had used to climb up there. It was 2:36 a.m. Far below, Bartie let rip with another warning bark. She crawled on all fours to the roof's edge. Looking down, she saw her dog standing in a tensed position, his head lowered, his nose pointing in the direction of the rough-shod driveway that connected to Lake View Drive. Someone was out there.

"Bartie!" she whispered. "Quiet!"

The dog looked up at her, his eyes like white balls reflected in her phone's flashlight. He stopped barking, then turned his head to peer into the forest.

A vehicle's engine. The snap of twigs under tires. It was moving slowly through the trees. A flash of headlights arced through the dark forest. Her first thought: the sheriff. Who else would risk navigating Bill's perilous drive in the dark? But how did he know she was there? Panic gripped her. Absolutely nobody else knew her location but Bill. No, he wouldn't betray her. He just wouldn't. Jessie had to get off the damn roof and run to her vehicle. If Bartie made another sound, the visitor would know that she was there. The vehicle's high beams bounced up and down, growing bigger and brighter by the second.

Bartie growled. A light came on inside the house and spilled out onto the dirt outside. Bill was awake.

"Bill!" she shouted. "Someone's coming. Don't tell on me."

She fumbled with her phone, trying to turn off the flashlight. It made her location obvious. The phone slipped through her fingers and hit the roof with a clunk. Slapping the roof's surface, she found it again, pocketed it, and grabbed the top of the ladder. There was just enough light spilling out of Bill's windows for her to see the rungs. Ahead, she saw the outline of the vehicle approaching. Square and wide. Her knees almost gave way. It couldn't be? Spurred on by absolute terror, she climbed clumsily down the ladder, arms and legs trembling. Once she was on the ground, she crouched behind the pile of chopped wood at the side of Bill's shack and pulled Bartie into the shadows, just as the car came to a halt in a cloud of dust, its high beams blindingly bright.

Inside the house, Bill's feet slapped the floors.

Jessie hoped that the woodpile was wide enough to keep her and her dog concealed. She put her hand over Bartie's muzzle, just like bitches do with their mouths to keep their pups quiet. If Bartie barked now, she was done for. A car door opened. Footsteps.

Bill called out, "I got a rifle pointing right at you. You stay where you are."

"Marcus Harstad. Don't shoot."

Jessie gripped her lips together firmly to stop herself from whimpering. Dear God, Marcus! He was relentless. He had hunted her to Prairie Ridge. Now he had found her at Bill's. No tracker this time. How? The venison stew she had enjoyed earlier that night churned in her stomach.

Marcus continued, "We need to talk, Bill. I wouldn't be here at this hour if it wasn't urgent."

She knew that tone well. It was his velvet crocodile voice. Smooth and reasonable, it made him sound safe to be with. He used that tone when he was at his most dangerous. She wanted to yell out, to warn Bill not to drop his guard. But that would mean giving herself away.

Bartie struggled to be free of her grip. He sensed her terror and he naturally wanted to protect her and that would mean charging at Marcus. She kept her hold of his muzzle and hugged him close.

Please leave, she thought. *Leave me alone.*

"Get off my property!"

"Put down that rifle before it goes off in your face. There's been another house fire. Tonight. You know Ruth Sullivan, the FBI agent?"

"Yeah, what about her?"

"The fire was at her house." He paused, like he was teasing Jessie, knowing she was there. "She died. Inhalation injury."

Jessie almost choked. *No, no, it's not true. It can't be.*

"I'm sorry to hear that, Marcus," Bill said. "But there was no need to come all this way to tell me."

"Can we do this inside?"

"No," yelled Bill, "you stay where you are."

"You have Jessie with you, don't you?"

Jessie clenched her eyes tight shut and held her breath.

"There's no one here but me, Marcus. You've said your piece. Now get in your car and drive away."

"You're protecting a killer," Marcus said. "Jessie's fire-retardant glove was found at the scene. She burned down Ruth's house."

Her missing glove? Marcus could have walked into her house at any point and removed it, then planted it at the fire scene. It was just as she had thought. Marcus had set her up.

"Not my problem," Bill said. "Now go!"

"Okay, no need to get upset. The sheriff is on his way. He won't be as polite as me. You're best off talking to me."

Don't fall for it, Jessie willed. *Don't open the door.*

Jessie heard Bill's house door scrape across a raised floorboard. "Come inside and we can talk."

Don't do it!

Fear gripping her throat, Jessie scanned the treeline. Once Marcus was in the house she would run into the forest. She heard the sound of boots on grit then the creak of the porch floorboards taking Marcus's weight.

"You can put the rifle down, Bill." Marcus's voice came from inside the house.

"Like a coffee?" Bill offered.

It was now or never. Jessie took her hand off Bartie's muzzle and leapt up.

"Looks like you had company," said Marcus. "Two dirty plates, two sets of cutlery." The menace in his voice was building. "Where is she?"

The thump of boots, then a loud thud. Bill squealed. "Get off me!" It sounded like he was gagging.

"Drop the rifle or I'll break your scrawny neck," Marcus said. More choking sounds.

Bartie growled. The scuffling sounds in the house stopped.

"What was that?" Marcus said.

Run, she told herself. *Run*. But her legs wouldn't move. He was coming and he would kill her.

Bill said in a throaty voice, "Leave her alone!"

"Shut up!" said Marcus.

There was the meaty sound of a fist punching a body, then a sickening *crack*, like bone snapping, followed by a *thud* as something or someone hit the floor.

He's killed Bill, oh God, oh God!

Without knowing how, her survival instinct bypassed her paralysis. She sprinted for the treeline, her dog close at heel. Marcus had murdered Bill. And she would be next.

CHAPTER FORTY

Marcus was coming for her. Jessie heard his boots thump the deck. Keys jangled in his pocket. She glanced behind her. He was rounding the corner in big powerful strides. Jessie squeaked like a frightened mouse. Another few yards before she reached the treeline. Her legs and arms kept pumping. *This time I'll get away. This time he won't hurt me.* Bartie dived into the forest first.

"Stop!" Marcus hollered.

His heavy breathing sounded too close. He was gaining on her. A sob caught in her throat. She reached the tree cover and kept going. Her lungs burned with toxic air and she spluttered. Inside the forest, it was unbelievably dark. She kicked a root. Stumbled. Her ankle wobbled, but she didn't fall. The tip of a low branch slapped her right cheek. It stung. She narrowly avoided running into a pine's trunk but as she dodged it, her boot snagged on a tangle of creepers and she fell forward, landing hard on her knees. She dragged herself up and sped off again, but she had lost her momentum. She sensed he was close. She didn't dare look around. Something brushed her middle back. Her head was whipped backward, the hair on her scalp almost ripped out. Her neck jarred painfully and she yelped like a beaten dog. He had her braid in his grip and he pulled her to him until the back of her skull collided with his chest.

"Hello, Jessie. Like old times, huh?"

He put a bent arm around her throat and pulled it tight, crushing her windpipe. He was strangling her.

Caaahhhh! Jessie clawed at the crook of his arm, squirming and choking.

"You never learn, Jessie," he said in her ear. "You do what *I* want, when I want, you hear? And I want you in jail."

A rustling in the ferns and Bartie lunged at Marcus's left ankle, sinking his teeth into it. Marcus screamed, and released Jessie from his grip, then he punched the dog in the eyes. Bartie yelped and released his bite. Jessie couldn't catch enough breath. Through tear-filled eyes she saw Marcus grab Bartie's collar and lift him off the ground.

He'll kill my dog.

Marcus twisted the dog's collar. Bartie writhed. He was crushing the dog's windpipe.

Jessie lunged forward and clawed at Marcus's face. He dropped the dog and shoved her hard in the chest. She almost fell over. Bartie lay on the ground making retching noises.

"I'm going to teach you a lesson."

He took out of his pocket some brass knuckles and slid them down the fingers of one hand.

Urine leaked down the inside of her leg. He was going to make her death painful. Her dog staggered in front of Jessie to protect her. She knew then that she had to stand up for herself and her dog. Jessie stepped around Bartie and took up the defensive position that Ruth had taught her: one leg forward and one leg back.

Marcus laughed, a sneering, mocking laugh that triggered a rush of fury through her body, strengthening her muscles and hardening her resolve.

With the heel of her hand toward Marcus, she pivoted forward and then thrust her palm as quickly and forcefully as she could onto his throat. Her hand struck his Adam's apple. He reeled back, gasping.

Jessie was momentarily stunned that the move had worked but it wouldn't deter Marcus for long. She lowered her head and charged at his stomach.

Searing pain shot down her neck upon impact. His abdominal muscles were hard from training and her stunt didn't have the desired effect. He merely took one step back then raised a balled fist. Bartie came to her aid again, this time latching his jaws around his wrist. This was her chance. She wrapped her arms around his waist and felt for the SIG that he carried on his belt. Her slick fingers found it. She ripped it out of the belt just as Marcus kicked Bartie hard in the ribs. The dog fell to the ground with a piercing yelp.

Jessie fired the gun, aiming wide. If she killed Marcus, nobody would believe it was self-defense. The boom woke the sleeping forest. Birds and bats flew skyward. Marcus raised his hands.

"Take it easy." He smiled as if this was just a game. "Cuffy will be here any minute. If they find us like this, they'll shoot to kill."

It was lies! All lies. He had come here alone to kill her.

"What did you do to Bill?" Jessie said, her breathing heavy.

"Knocked him out. He'll be just fine." He lowered his arms. "Put the gun down. You know you could never kill me."

"Keep your arms up and walk to the house. I'm not afraid of you anymore."

"Okay, whatever you say."

He turned to face Bill's cabin and she saw his smirk. "We were good together once, remember?" Marcus said, in his smooth and beguiling voice. "We had such good times. Why did you have to ruin it?"

"Good times! You hurt me, raped me."

"You need help, Jessie. I never did any of those things."

"You killed our baby!"

"It was an accident."

"Accident! You stamped on my stomach." Tears had filled her eyes. "You didn't want me loving anyone but you, you narcissistic piece of crap! Now get moving!"

"That temper of yours will be the death of you."

Bartie lay on his side, whining. "Can you get up, buddy?" Jessie encouraged.

The dog pushed up with his back legs and stood awkwardly but it was clear from the way his tail was tucked under his belly and his slow walk that he was in pain.

"Keep moving," she shouted at Marcus.

They left the forest and passed the woodpile she had hidden behind earlier. As they turned the corner, Bill staggered out of the house door. He cradled an arm. His right shoulder had a hideous peak to it, like a snapped bone was about to break through skin. Marcus had smashed Bill's clavicle.

"You son of a bitch!" Bill said, staggering like a drunk.

Bill tripped and fell to his knees on the porch floor. He screamed.

"Stay where you are, Bill. I'll help you," Jessie called.

Too late, she saw Marcus grab a chunk of chopped wood. He swiveled on his heels and in one fluid motion he slammed it down onto her gun hand. It hurt like hell and Jessie dropped the SIG. Marcus dived for it.

As Marcus leaned over the semiautomatic pistol, Jessie reached for the woodpile and her fingers touched a rectangular chunk of wood. She raised it above Marcus's bent head with both hands and slammed it down on the back of his skull with all her might. His knees gave way and he lay spread-eagled in the dirt. She raised the piece of chopped wood again, ready to hit him a second time. He hadn't moved, he hadn't groaned. She lowered her arms.

"Jesus!" said Bill. "You've gone and killed him."

CHAPTER FORTY-ONE

The chunk of hewn wood fell from Jessie's fingers. It hit the sun-baked ground with a *thunk*.

"No," she whispered. "He can't be."

It had been a blow to stun Marcus. She never meant to kill him. Blood seeped from a gash in his skull. He didn't move a muscle.

"I ain't going near him," Bill said, kneeling on the rickety porch. "You did this!"

"I can't bear to touch him."

"Snap out of it and check for a pulse," Bill said.

Jessie recoiled at the idea. She turned her head just in time and vomited up undigested venison stew.

"Jesus, Mary, and Joseph," Bill complained. "Now I'm going to have to hose that away."

Jessie lifted a shuddering hand to wipe some vomit from her chin. *This has to be a dream. It can't be real. I'll go to jail for life.*

Bill shuffled forward on his knees until he was close enough to Marcus to place two bony fingers on Marcus's wrist. "No pulse."

Jessie's stomach heaved again, and she spewed a second time, more bile than anything else. "What have I done? Oh God, oh God. I just wanted him to stop."

"I know, Jessie. I saw. It was self-defense. Problem is nobody is going to believe us. Now help me up, will you? We need to talk."

Jessie picked up Marcus's SIG and tucked it into the waistband of her shorts. Then she took Bill's one good arm and helped him up, guiding him to the rocking chair. "Goddammit! That hurts."

"What am I going to do?" Jessie said. "I can't go to jail. I just can't!"

"There's only one thing we can do."

"What? Tell me!" Jessie asked.

"We get rid of the body and this never happened. You were never here. Marcus was never here."

"But I killed him!"

"Yes, because he was going to kill you and me. You had no choice."

"Then I should say that. Tell the sheriff what happened. You'll back me up." Bill said nothing. "You'll back me up, won't you? Bill? Say something."

"The truth doesn't matter, Jessie. Marcus is the town hero. Everybody loves him. And they hate you and me. You'll be lucky if you escape lynching."

Jessie paced. "Then I run. Tonight."

"And leave me to clean up your mess? No way. We sort this out together."

"But what can we do?" Jessie said. "He's dead."

"You'll need to do the heavy lifting. My shoulder's busted. You have to get rid of the body." Bill turned his head and stared at the black Hummer. "And his car."

Jessie shook her head. "I can't. It's wrong. Totally wrong."

"Jessie, you're young and healthy and you have a life ahead of you. Don't let that evil brute take that from you. If you own up to this, Marcus will have got exactly what he always wanted. He's controlling you, even from the grave. Don't let him win!"

Jessie's head pounded. What kind of a person had she become? Someone who killed and then hid the body. She spat out the sour taste in her mouth. "What do I have to do?"

"You see the jetty." He pointed toward the lake. "It's wide enough for a car. The water at the end is forty feet deep. You lift Marcus into position behind the wheel. You take off the handbrake and roll the car forward and consign Marcus to a watery grave."

CHAPTER FORTY-TWO

Why was it, mused Sheriff Cuffy, that hospital chairs were designed to be as uncomfortable as the ones he used for suspects?

It was three thirty in the morning and Cuffy longed to be in bed with his wife. Instead, he was at Eagle Falls Hospital waiting for Victor Sullivan to open his eyes. It had been a distressing night for the Sullivans, and a good night for him. Firstly, Ruth wouldn't be capable of undermining his investigation anymore. There was nothing like a near-death experience to put interfering bitches back in their boxes. Secondly, once forensics confirmed that the fire-resistant glove found at the Sullivans' house belonged to Jessie Lewis, he would have enough to charge her with six counts of murder and the attempted murder of Ruth, Victor, Noah, and David Sullivan.

Cuffy shifted his butt cheeks on the rock-hard plastic. He leaned to one side then tugged at his briefs through the fabric of his pants, the seam of which was digging into his sweaty balls. Once he was comfortable, he glanced at the door to check that a nurse wasn't about to enter the room, then he gave Victor's bare arm a rough prod.

"Victor?"

Victor was in a hospital gown with an oxygen mask over his face. He was sleeping. In the next-door room, his wife was in a worse state. Until tonight, Cuffy was unaware that her lungs were already damaged by the bomb blast, and, as a result, the smoke inhalation earlier had caused her severe breathing difficulties. Her prognosis was good but recovery would be slow. Perhaps there was a God after all. Their sons, both unharmed, although very shaken, were staying at a neighbor's house.

It took a second prod to get Victor to open his eyes.

"How are you feeling, pal?" said Cuffy cheerily.

Victor blinked a few times.

"Hey, buddy. It's John."

When Victor spoke from behind the oxygen mask, it was difficult to make out what he said. "What time is it?"

"Three thirty and way past my bedtime, but a sheriff's lot is never done. I need your help, Victor."

Victor shifted his head to one side so he could look at Cuffy. "Sure. How?"

"You saw who did it, right?"

"I wish I had."

"Victor, you need to listen to me very carefully. Jessie's glove was found in your backyard. Marcus also found a wooden wedge, the same as we found at the Wilmots' house after the fire. We think they were used to jam windows shut. There's only one person who could have done this. Jessie Lewis."

"You think she's capable of murder?"

"Sure she is. You saw her out the bedroom window when you looked into the backyard, right? You saw Jessie running away?"

Victor stared at him for a few seconds, then lifted a hand and tugged the mask down so that it rested on his chin. Both his hands were bandaged because of minor burns. "I can't lie, John."

"She's an arsonist and a murderer. She's the only one with means, opportunity, and motive. She tried to kill you, Victor. Tried to kill your kids. If I don't stop her, how many more people will die? Hmm?"

"I take your point but—"

Cuffy counted off his reasons on stubby fingers. "One: Jessie has a history of lying to law enforcement. Two: Jessie had a relationship with all the victims. She fell out with Paul over money. She was found at the second fire scene, once during the fire and once the day after, messing with evidence. And recently she's got chummy with your wife. Who knows what goes on in that sick mind of hers, but I'd hazard a guess that you made her angry when you turfed her out of your house. *And,* she dropped her fire-retardant glove in your backyard."

"Are you sure it's hers?"

"We're having it DNA tested, but Marcus has already confirmed it's the exact same glove she wore when she was a volunteer firefighter. Same size and all."

Victor's eyes wandered to the water jug and paper cup on the nightstand. "Can you pass me some water, John?"

If it would help Cuffy get what he wanted, he would pour Victor a whiskey. Cuffy handed the man the cup with a paper straw in it. When Victor had sipped enough, he gave the cup back to Cuffy, who begrudgingly put it down on the nightstand. Victor started coughing. He pulled the mask back over his mouth.

Annoyed by Victor's intransigence, Cuffy stood up and stretched the cricks out of his sore back and the numbness out of his ass.

"I want to help, John, I really do, but Ruthie wouldn't want me to lie," Victor said from behind the mask.

"Victor, you're a hero, my friend. You saved your family. The whole town's talking about giving you a medal. People will believe whatever you tell them."

Victor smiled. "They are? A hero? Are you serious?"

"Oh yes. And imagine how impressed they'll be to learn that you helped capture Jessie Lewis. She has to be stopped and you're the man to do it!"

Cuffy waited. He was pretty certain that Victor would bite. The loser had such a fragile ego that a bit of flattery was bound to work.

Victor shook his head. "I don't know…"

It was time for Cuffy to use his ace card. "My good pal Henry tells me you were real impressive in your job interview. It's between you and a younger fellow with an active client list. He's veering toward the young guy. One word from me, and the job's yours. What do you say?"

Victor licked his dry lower lip. "I guess I saw Jessie running away."

"Good man! I need it in writing."

Victor pulled his mask away. "You sure the job's mine?"

"You have my word," Cuffy said, producing pen and paper.

CHAPTER FORTY-THREE

Marcus was 155 pounds of dead weight. Because of Bill's broken collarbone, even using his one good arm to help Jessie move the body was agony. They tried to divide the load: Bill took Marcus's feet, and Jessie slid her arms under Marcus's armpits and lifted the heavy torso. She tried not to look at his matted bloody hair where she had struck him, or her blood-soaked tank top and shorts. Even though Jessie took most of the weight, they only managed to shift the body a few inches before Bill dropped Marcus's legs. Jessie laid the rest of his body on the ground.

"Sorry, Jessie," Bill panted, his face screwed up in pain. "I can't do it."

She stared at her palms, which were sticky and red. Her stomach heaved again, but there was nothing left to spew. She gulped a few times and waited for the sensation to pass. The night was so hot, it was like working in a greenhouse in the peak of summer. Her clothes were soaked with perspiration. She blinked her stinging eyes and coughed. "Jeez, this air is filthy."

"When we're done here, we got some cleaning to do," Bill said through gritted teeth.

They sure did.

A few minutes earlier, Jessie had moved Marcus's Hummer right next to his body, taking care to wear her gardening gloves so as not to leave fingerprints inside the vehicle. Those gloves were now in her back pocket: she needed them to be blood-free. All she had to do was lift Marcus up and into the passenger seat. The plan had sounded so simple. She was beginning to doubt that she had the strength to do it.

"I guess I'm doing the fireman's carry," Jessie said.

Bill's forehead was dripping with sweat. "You have to shift him. Got no damn choice."

Jessie took a deep breath and steeled herself. Every cell in her body recoiled at having to touch her abuser. The smell of his sweat made her gag, bringing back memories she would rather forget.

You have to do this. Otherwise, he wins.

She rolled Marcus onto his stomach. Even that simple action took some doing. She then knelt close to his head, one knee up, one on the ground, so that she leaned over his shoulder blades. Next she slid an arm under each of his armpits. Her gut heaved and she thought she might vomit down his back. She took some calming breaths, then continued. "I'm going to slide him toward me and lift him as I stand up. That's the plan, anyway." Getting a body into a vertical position was the hardest part.

Jessie grunted and panted but she was strong and she had practiced this as a volunteer firefighter. Albeit the volunteer had been a woman. Jessie knew she had to use her knees, not her back, to lift Marcus, otherwise she'd probably pop a disk. As she strained and heaved to drag Marcus up, her face purple, teeth gritted, she could hardly believe what she was doing. Not only had she killed Marcus, she was now endeavoring to conceal the body.

After a supreme effort, she had Marcus in an upright position, but her back and knees were complaining.

"Help me keep him steady," she panted, her clothes soaked with sweat.

Bill did as she asked, bearing some of the weight. She ignored Bill's moaning.

Jessie stuck her right leg between Marcus's limp legs. Then she gripped his right hand with her left and draped it over her shoulder. This was the bit she had been dreading. If she got this right, his body would drape over her shoulders, his legs dangling on one side, his head and arms on the other. She inhaled, exhaled deeply hoping to oxygenate her muscles. Then she leaned down and stuck her head under his right armpit and wrapped an arm around his knees. Her bent knees took the strain.

"Help me… get him… balanced."

Once that was done, Jessie held on to Marcus's right hand and attempted to straighten her knees.

She couldn't do it. It was like having a brown bear on her back. He was just too heavy.

"Do it, Jessie!" Bill said. "You have to."

Jessie closed her eyes and tensed every muscle in her body. She thought her back was going to break. Her face was red, the veins distended. Her legs wobbled. She got as straight as she could manage. She stumbled sideways, almost losing her balance, then she took a shaky step forward. She just had to chuck him onto the seat behind the steering wheel. Her calf muscles cramped. She couldn't hang on a second longer. Leaning forward, she let gravity take its course. Marcus slid from her shoulders. He fell into the Hummer, his body straddling the two front seats. At least he was in the Hummer. Jessie collapsed to the ground, breathless, and rested with her back against the car's body. She clutched her cramped calves and tried massaging them.

"Shit! That hurts."

"Stop your groaning," Bill said. "I'm the one with broken bones. You sit him up and I'll get his feet in position. We need this done before sunup."

"Get me some water, will you?" Jessie said, wincing with the pain from the cramps.

Bill tutted but he went into the house and got her a glass of water.

With one last huge effort, Jessie secured Marcus behind the steering wheel. The seatbelt held him in position. Now all they had to do was get the Hummer into the lake. That was no easy task either and Jessie was all out of energy.

"Taking a break," she panted. She found it hard to straighten her aching back.

"I gotta get me something to kill the pain," Bill said, shuffling into the house.

"Get me some too."

Bill reappeared with a bottle of whiskey and a packet of painkillers tucked under his one functioning arm.

He sat in his rocking chair on the porch. Jessie hobbled over to the swing seat. Her leg cramps were subsiding, but the muscles still pulsed with pain. Bill swallowed two painkillers, each time gulping them down with whiskey from the bottle.

"You want some? You come and get it."

Jessie took the bottle and the pills and swallowed two, feeling the whiskey's heat travel down her throat. The pills would dull her physical pain, but they couldn't dull her guilt. In fact, she doubted she would ever feel better. Marcus had beaten and tortured her, but he didn't deserve to die.

"How am I ever going to live with myself?" she said.

"Get over it, Jessie. He was a bad man."

Jessie stared at her dog. She was really worried about him. He lay on his side, his tail tucked under his belly: a sign that he was in pain. Had Marcus broken his ribs or done something worse? She stood on unsteady legs and got Bartie some water to drink in a bowl.

"Best thing you can do is shoot him and put him out of his misery."

"You go near him and I'll kill you." She still had Marcus's SIG in the back of her waistband.

Bill chuckled. "Kind of ironic, don't you think, given you already killed one of us."

Jessie couldn't look at him. "How can you joke at a time like this?" Jessie stroked the dog's head. "I've got to get him to a vet."

"Not until Marcus goes in the lake."

There was a crunch, like a stone crumbling underfoot. She sensed something had changed. She turned her head to look at Bill and saw movement behind his rocking chair.

It can't be.

The sharp blade of an axe came down on the top of Bill's head. There was a grunt, a splitting sound, a squelch. A trickle of blood ran down the center of the old man's scalp and his forehead. Bill's eyes were wide with shock, frozen in that moment. As the axe was yanked out of Bill's skull, his head wobbled as if he were laughing. Then Bill slumped forward in the rocking chair, his shattered head hanging over his knees. Marcus stood behind him, the axe in his hands, a manic grin on his face.

"You're next," Marcus said.

CHAPTER FORTY-FOUR

It felt as if it all happened in slow motion.

Marcus, stance wide, his blond hair stained crimson with blood, an axe in his hands.

Bill in his rocking chair, slumped forward, his skull partly cleaved in two, blood pooling on the porch floor.

Jessie's wounded dog lying in the dirt, struggling to stand, to protect her.

Jessie was crouched down, too stunned to move. Had she gone insane? Marcus was dead and now… he wasn't.

Marcus staggered. He swayed into a porch post and stayed there for a few seconds, blinking, as if trying to see straight. He might be alive, but he had lost a lot of blood and he was weakened.

"You fucking bitch!" he muttered, lunging forward.

In that second, her cramped muscles, pain, and exhaustion were forgotten. It was just her and Marcus. This was all about her survival.

She pulled the semiautomatic pistol from her waistband and aimed it at his chest. This time she wouldn't aim too wide. This time she would kill. She was a poor shot and he knew it. The center of his body mass was her best option.

"You haven't got the guts to do it."

He moved one leg forward. His body shook like a heroin addict going through withdrawal. The blow to his head must have done some brain damage.

"Stay away, Marcus. I'm warning you!"

He stumbled forward, the bloody axe gripped in both hands.

"Not another step," Jessie yelled. "I will shoot you."

He grinned. There was blood in his mouth and on his teeth.

"Let me go, Marcus." She couldn't keep the gun barrel still. "You'll never see me again. Please."

Marcus lifted the axe to take a swing at her and she fired, again and again. She felt the barrel jump each time. His body jerked as the bullets hit. Three in the chest and gut. He fell to his knees. The axe thudded to the floor. Then Marcus collapsed forward, flat on his face. The porch floor shook.

The fingers on his right hand twitched a few times and a leg jumped, then every limb was still. Jessie didn't budge an inch: the gun trained on Marcus. How long she stood like that, she didn't know. Her arm muscles were trembling with the effort to keep the gun raised. When she couldn't hold it up for another second, she lowered the barrel but kept her finger on the trigger. Was he really dead this time?

She crept closer. His eyes were open and his stare was blank. She kicked his hip. The body jerked, then it went still. His ribs didn't expand and contract. Still, she watched him. The bullets had gone through him and blood oozed from the exit wounds. Finally, she plucked up enough courage to place two fingers on his carotid artery. His warm skin freaked her out, but she pressed down hard with her fingers. There was no pulse.

Only when she was certain that Marcus was well and truly gone did she move to where Bill's body lay slumped forward in the rocking chair. His head and neck were covered in blood and the pool on the floor was like someone had knocked over a can of red paint. She took Bill's wrist and felt for his pulse. She owed it to him to be certain. When she was sure, she bowed her head.

"I'm so sorry, Bill. Poppy would be proud of you. You saved my life." She held his emaciated hand against her lips and kissed it, then released it so it hung by his side.

Jessie sat on the floor before her legs gave way beneath her. She felt strangely calm. Her heart rate began to settle. She calculated what to do next, a little disturbed by her own practicality. If she tried to explain to the authorities what happened here, nobody would believe that she shot Marcus in self-defense. She would probably get charged with Bill's murder too. Should she call her attorney? But Jessie already knew what Manning would tell her to do and she wasn't going to hand herself in. Could she hide the bodies? The ground was too hard to bury them, and two dead weights were more than she could shift. As she saw it, she only had one option: get rid of all evidence that she had been there and get the hell out of there. She could stage it so that it looked as if they killed each other. Bartie had waddled over to where she sat and he nudged her arm. He was rightfully uneasy. He smelled death all around.

She made up her mind.

Like a robot, Jessie began to clean up every trace of her presence. First she removed her boots, the soles of which were bloody. She pocketed the pack of painkillers and then, barefooted, she carried the whiskey bottle inside, and wiped down the glass surface with a cloth. She dropped her boots into a large trash bag then washed and dried the pan, plates, and cutlery. She found an old pair of mechanics' gloves under the sink and put them on, then wiped clean every surface she could remember touching and put away the plates and cutlery so that it didn't look as if he'd had company. She found a clean T-shirt of his and a pair of old rubber boots. She tucked the tee into her waistband for later and pulled on the boots. They were too big but she could walk in them. Next, she climbed onto the roof and dumped the empty beer cans into the trash bag. Then she wiped down the ladder to remove her fingerprints. The bloody axe lay close to Marcus's right hand. She hadn't touched it, but she had touched the chunk of hewn wood that she had used to knock him out. She added the wood to the trash bag. She scooped up her vomit using a cup. The vomit and the cup went into the trash bag, then she hosed the ground, including the side of the shack to remove her size-eight footprints. She wiped away the porch's bloody footprints using a cleaner spray and cloth, working around Bill and Marcus, then added the cloth to the trash. She pulled off her bloodstained, filthy T-shirt, put it in the trash bag, then, in her bra, she hosed the blood from her hands, face, and hair. She also gently hosed her dog, making sure there was no blood in his fur, and she emptied the bowl she'd used to give Bartie water and put it in the trash. Then she wiped the blood off the passenger seat and seatbelt of the Hummer. It had taken over an hour to complete the cleanup and Jessie felt nothing but relief when it was over. She finally put on Bill's clean T-shirt.

Jessie surveyed the scene. There was bound to be something of Jessie's DNA left behind, but she had done the best she could. Now all she had to do was clean her fingerprints from the SIG and wrap Bill's fingers around the grip and trigger.

"I'm sorry, Bill."

Once that was done, she left the pistol on the floor right next to Bill's left hand because Bill was left-handed, hoping it looked as if he had dropped it.

The walk through the forest with the trash bag over her shoulder was slow going. Not just because of her dog's slow pace. Even with a flashlight Jessie found it hard to navigate the forest at night. Every tree looked the same. It was the freaky hubcaps on tree trunks that saved her. Their distinctive shape and size guided her to the motorhome, where she lifted her dog onto the passenger seat of her pickup so he could rest, then she cleaned the motorhome's interior surfaces and cleared the fridge. At long last, she left Bill's property the way she had arrived, using the loop road.

She planned to drive to Marymere, where there was a twenty-four-hour vet hospital. She wouldn't let Bartie die. He was all she had left.

CHAPTER FORTY-FIVE

At five in the morning, the loop road was treacherous. The fallen tree was the least of her worries. The road was littered with potholes, which seemed to appear out of nowhere. Jessie had no choice but to use her headlights on high beam. If she broke an axle or punctured a tire she would be in real trouble, given the heavy load on the back of her pickup and the absence of a spare tire, which she hadn't replaced. Her dog lay on his side on the front seat and whimpered whenever the pickup lurched. With the windows down, Jessie found the night air was getting smokier by the second. Where was it coming from? She glanced down the mountain slope. She thought she saw a flicker of red through the dark silhouette of trees. Maybe it was a reflection of the park's fire in the lake's surface?

Then a terrible thought hit her. Had she accidentally caused a fire at Bill's place? But she hadn't gone anywhere near the gas and there were no naked flames when she left. Jessie put her foot on the brake and took a moment to look properly at the distant red glow. It was growing in size rapidly and the smoke was getting thicker. The flames were too far west to be coming from Bill's property. Her cabin was due east.

"Please God, not my home!" she said aloud.

If she was right, what could she do about it? Drive down there and use the hoses? The fire had to be deliberately lit and she wasn't going to go down there and face a killer alone. Jessie thought of

Poppy's desk and the other possessions she hadn't been able to load onto the truck. She thought of the house insurance she hadn't been able to pay. The arsonist was taking everything from her and every cell in her body wanted to stop him. She had her dad's antique pistol in the glove compartment. But these were crazy thoughts. She already had blood on her hands.

It broke her heart that she had to keep moving.

She left the loop road, placing the poles back in position, then took the turn that led to Marymere. As she pulled out onto what she thought was a deserted road, another vehicle sped past her heading for Eagle Falls. The driver was in a real hurry. Who drives at a crazy speed at night down a mountain road?

The vehicle had come from the direction of Lake View Drive, where Jessie lived. Could it have been a sheriff's car? No, she told herself. A deputy wouldn't leave the scene of the fire and, anyway, they would have flashing lights on the roof. It had to be the arsonist, fleeing the scene of his crime. Jessie did a U-turn and gave chase. She knew the stretch of road well, so she could anticipate the tight bends, but the heavy load in the back of her truck slowed her down. She finally caught up with the speeding vehicle on the outskirts of the town.

I shouldn't be here. I'll get caught.

But she had to know who the arsonist was. The car she was pursuing slowed at a junction. They were entering a light industrial area with warehouses and small factories. Farther down the road was a gas station that stayed open all night and a McDonald's opposite. Both would have security cameras. The car turned right. She paused, to create some distance between them, then she followed. The road was empty. She pulled back a bit, aware that it was just her and the other driver.

Suddenly the driver did a U-turn. His headlights were on high beam and she was blinded by them. He must have spotted her tailing him. Her heart lurched when the driver swerved onto her side of the road and drove straight at her. Was he playing chicken, or did he really intend to ram her? It wasn't like she could swerve onto a grassy verge to avoid him. The road was lined with trees. He kept coming at her. Jessie braked and did her best to do a U-turn, but her pickup had a wide turning circle and she almost hit a tree trunk. She slammed the gear stick into reverse, then revved hard, accelerating as fast as her heavily laden vehicle would go. The car behind her was closing in fast.

Her side-view mirror shattered.

Jesus! He's shooting at me!

She instinctively ducked. Her pickup veered dangerously but she managed to get it back on course. He was a few yards behind her now. His window was down and his arm rested on the doorframe. She caught a glint of the gunmetal in a streetlight. Because of the height of the load in the back of her truck, he couldn't get a clear shot at her. Unless he overtook her. Adrenaline zinged through her body. She couldn't outrun him. She slapped the steering wheel, desperate for an idea. If he came alongside of her pickup, she was dead. Then it came to her.

Earlier they had passed a gas station. It had security cameras. At this hour, a solitary soul would be working inside the shop. A witness. She drove like a maniac to reach the gas station, swerving one way and then the other, making it impossible for her pursuer to come up alongside her vehicle. Her wheels squealed as she turned off the road at high speed and hurtled into the gas station. She aimed for the shop, where the cameras had to be. She compressed the foot brake gently at first and then harder. She plowed into a rack of newspapers, tire rubber burning, and came to a screeching halt. Between Jessie and the open road were six gas pumps. One bullet could blow her and the gas station to kingdom come. He wouldn't do that, would he?

The man pursuing her slowed but he didn't stop. Jessie ducked, leaning over her dog to protect him. She waited, panting with fear. All she heard was a vehicle speeding away. By the time she sat up, the car was gone.

Jessie looked up at a security camera pointing her way. Time to get out of there.

CHAPTER FORTY-SIX

Cuffy stood too close to Ruth's hospital bed. She was wearing a flimsy blue hospital gown that barely covered her backside, and even though she had a sheet draped over her lap, she felt exposed. She had had a sleepless night because of breathing difficulties and worry. It didn't matter that Noah and David were unharmed and staying with Aiden's mom. She wanted to be with them. Victor had left the hospital earlier to check on the kids and to get Ruth a clean set of clothes. The doctor had given her the all-clear to leave the hospital. Cuffy's unwanted arrival was delaying her departure.

"We need to talk," Cuffy said, his eggy breath smelling foul.

"John, can this wait? I've only just got off the ventilator and I want to be with my family."

She turned her head to look at Victor, who stood on the other side of the bed, her eyes seeking his support.

Victor gently squeezed Ruth's hand. "John needs our help to find the person who did this. It won't take long."

"I want him caught too," Ruth said. "But I'd like to get dressed first."

Her throat felt rough. Her lungs even rougher. Just talking triggered an agonizing coughing fit. Ruth asked for a tissue and coughed into it. She was still bringing up black stuff from her lungs. She screwed up the tissue into a ball.

"I know who did it," Victor said. The words tumbled out.

"Really? Who is it?" Ruth said.

"You won't like it."

"Just tell me."

"Jessie Lewis."

"Oh come on!" Ruth exclaimed.

"I'm serious," Victor said.

Ruth shook her head. "Jessie wouldn't."

"She was in our backyard. I saw her run away."

Ruth continued to shake her head. "How could you possibly see anything? There was fire everywhere. Smoke everywhere." She started wheezing. "Can you pass the water?"

Ruth sipped from a straw. The cold water felt good on her sore throat.

"I know you wanted to help her," Victor said, taking a seat on the bed. "But I can't lie about what I saw. The flames were bright. I saw a tall woman with a long braid. She ran across our lawn and jumped into Chet's yard." Chet was their elderly neighbor. "Don't you see, Ruthie? She didn't stop to help. She ran."

"And what was she doing there in the first place?" Cuffy added.

Ruth shut her eyes and tried to think back to the moment she woke, smoke everywhere and Victor yelling about fire. She had been more than hopeless and she felt ashamed. Victor had got the kids out of the house, and then her. Could he have seen Jessie through Noah's bedroom window? She remembered people in their backyard. Val and Mike Wynkoop. Was Chet there too? It was a blur.

Cuffy drummed his fingers on the headboard of her bed. "Ruth, think like the agent that you are. Jessie knows I'm onto her. She goes on the run. Your husband sees her in your backyard. Did Jessie come to your aid? No. Did she dial 911? No. I'll tell you what she did. She started the fire and then ran away, leaving you, Victor, and the kids to die."

Could Jessie really do that? Jessie was damaged, certainly. She didn't trust people. But Jessie had never struck her as vengeful or violent.

"Why would she?" Ruth asked. "We got on just fine. I even took her—" Ruth stopped herself just in time. She didn't want Cuffy, or her husband, to know that she had driven Jessie to her attorney's office. "There's no reason for her to hurt us."

"Who knows what goes on in a sick mind," Cuffy said. "Maybe she thought you didn't do enough to help her?" Cuffy shrugged. "Point is, she tried to kill your family. The next family she tries to kill may not be so lucky."

The more agitated Ruth became the more difficult it was to suppress the coughing. Once again the conversation went on hold while she coughed into a tissue.

Victor said to Cuffy, "Can we do this another time? My wife's unwell."

"No can do. She could strike again at any minute. Three fires in one night, Victor. I can't afford to be understanding. I have to catch her before anyone else dies."

Ruth's head jerked up. "Three fires?"

Cuffy explained to her about the fires at Jessie's and Bill's houses. There was nobody in Jessie's house at the time. "Bill's house is another story. Two bodies. Not much left of them, but we're pretty sure that Bill is one of the victims and Marcus is the other. We found a Hummer at the scene."

"When were those fires? Before or after ours?" Ruth asked.

Cuffy tugged at the tip of his narrow mustache. "You don't need to know that."

Ruth bristled at his condescension. Her lungs might not be in the best shape, but her brain was functioning okay. "I'll assume it was during the night. So what was Marcus doing at Bill's place at that time? And why would you think Jessie would burn down her own house? It was all she had in the world."

"Don't you worry about any of that, Ruth."

But she did worry about it. She thought carefully about what she said next.

"John, I want to help. I really do. You must be under so much pressure to get results. This has become a serial killer case and people are afraid. You're dealing with extremely complex crime scenes. I know someone who can help you. His name is Special Agent T.J. Samson. This is his area of expertise."

Cuffy's shoulders pulled back and he straightened.

"No need to bring in the FBI."

"Think about it, John. The Evidence Response Team could save you a whole load of time and money. They have access to equipment and databases other forensic units don't. By tapping into this resource, you could save lives, John. And save your budget."

"I'll think about it," Cuffy said. "But I need you to do something for me."

Cuffy explained the plan to lure Jessie into a trap. If Ruth had been working a case like this one, she might well have tried a similar strategy. Except this time, Ruth was the bait and she believed that the person she was being asked to entrap was innocent. Victor had to be mistaken about seeing Jessie run away. Perhaps he saw another woman? Perhaps the smoke inhalation and terror had muddled him?

"I may be the only person she trusts," said Ruth. "If I betray her, she'll never trust anyone again."

"Not your problem," said Cuffy. "You're the only person who can do this, Ruth."

"She may not take my call."

"You won't know until you try," Cuffy urged. "If she doesn't answer, leave a message. Say that you know she didn't start the fire and ask her to return your call."

"John, if you're right about Jessie, you're putting my life in danger. If she realizes it's a trap, she might respond with violence. I want something in return."

"This isn't a negotiation," Cuffy said.

"I say it is. I will do it if you contact Special Agent Samson and invite his ERT to work on the arson crime scenes. All of them."

Cuffy's face turned purple. "I won't—"

"Then I won't."

Ruth leaned back into her pillow, put the oxygen mask on and closed her eyes.

"Ruth?" she heard Victor say. "What are you doing?"

Ruth kept her eyes shut and focused on breathing the oxygen.

"I don't believe it," blustered Cuffy.

He left her room, slamming the door shut.

Victor took her hand. "Ruthie, please? You have to help him."

She opened her eyes and pulled down the mask. "Why? What aren't you telling me?"

Victor took off his glasses and began cleaning the lenses with the edge of his shirt. "He's going to talk to the owner of Belle Property and tell him to give me the job."

Oh perfect. Now I have no choice.

"And if I don't cooperate? Will he tell Belle Property *not* to hire you?"

Victor hesitated. "I don't know. Maybe."

"And my health? I can barely breathe without coughing. I'm not in a fit state to meet Jessie."

"Please, Ruthie. Just do this and then our lives go back to normal."

Cuffy barged into the room. "I've spoken to Samson. He can be here in two hours. So do we have a deal?"

Knowing that Samson's team was involved made her feel better about cooperating with Cuffy. "We do."

CHAPTER FORTY-SEVEN

Jessie fidgeted nervously, like a kid waiting outside a dentist's room.

She was at Marymere's twenty-four-hour vet hospital. Bartie was being sedated and X-rayed. Jessie had no idea how she was going to pay the bill because she didn't have the money. Fortunately, due to her laziness, her dog was still registered at the rescue center where he came from, rather than her address, and she had given them a fake name. The vet, Dr. Penny Gilkes, had suggested that Jessie might like to pop over the road to the diner while she waited. But Jessie was reluctant to leave, fearful that if she did, something bad would happen to Bartie. It was an irrational fear, but her dog was her world. For the next ten minutes Jessie tried to ignore her growling stomach, and then gave up. She needed to eat. She had some cookies in the truck. Maybe she could treat herself to a coffee and munch on the cookies? It would probably help her to think straight. She gave the receptionist her cell number and asked her to call her the moment that Bartie was ready to be collected.

The diner had a black-and-cream-checkered floor and ceiling. It was an old-style diner that served hearty breakfasts all day. Three roofers laughed loudly as they chowed down on their meals, and at the back of the diner two nurses in uniform gossiped over their cups of coffee. At the other end of the counter two muscular guys shoveled steak and omelet into their mouths as they exchanged stories about their nightshift at a nightclub where they worked as security. Jessie sat on a stool at the far end of the counter. From here she could watch the vet hospital across the street. She ordered coffee and tried not to feel envious of the man next to her eating fried egg, American cheese, and bacon on a fluffy biscuit.

I can't afford it.

The service was fast and the music loud and for a few joyful minutes she forgot her traumatic night and her worries about Bartie. Then her phone rang. It might be the vet, so she took a look and almost dropped her phone on the countertop when she saw the caller was Ruth.

It can't be.

Marcus told her Ruth died in the fire.

She laid her phone face down on the counter and waited for it to stop ringing. Then it pinged. She had a voicemail. Either somebody was using Ruth's phone, or Marcus had lied. If Ruth had survived the fire, why was she calling Jessie? Maybe it was time to speak to Manning. How do you explain to a lawyer that you killed your abuser after he had murdered your neighbor? Jessie didn't know where to begin. So, she sent a brief text.

I'm in trouble. Need to talk. Urgent.

It was a Saturday. Did Manning answer work calls on the weekend? She put the phone down again and stared out the café window. The sidewalk was busy with shoppers. Jessie scanned the cars parked in the street. No police cars. She returned her attention to the mysterious message from a dead woman. What if the voicemail really was from Ruth?

"What the hell," Jessie mumbled.

Jessie listened to the voicemail.

"Hey, Jessie. It's me. Ruth." Her voice was hoarse, but she was most definitely alive. "We've lost our house. There was a fire. Thank

God, we're all okay. Look, I think I know who's doing this. But I need your help. I can't do this alone. Please call me."

Marcus had lied. Why was she surprised?

Forget him. Ruth's alive! And she may know the identity of the killer.

Jessie sat up. Her heart was beating faster. Was she finally going to have some luck? Nobody would question Ruth's truthfulness, as they did Jessie's. But why did she need Jessie's help? All she had to do was give a description of the arsonist to Cuffy.

Just then she got a call from Dr. Gilkes. The X-ray revealed one cracked rib, which would heal slowly. There were no internal injuries, just bruising around the throat. Bartie needed rest and she prescribed some anti-inflammatories for the pain, which were an extra twenty dollars on top of the already hefty bill. How was she going to pay? She stared out the window searching for inspiration and noticed a pawnshop diagonally across the road: Lane's Loans. There was a lanky guy with hair in a ponytail opening up the shop, removing metal security grilles from the display windows. Maybe Jessie could sell something? She needed two hundred and twenty bucks. She thought about selling her gardening equipment. That would get her no more than a hundred dollars if she were lucky. The problem was that without her gardening tools, she couldn't work. It would be foolish to sell them.

Then she thought of her father's antique gun. The Colt Model 1877 Lightning revolver was a collector's item. In good condition. She knew it must be worth a thousand dollars because her poppy used to have it listed as a specified item on the insurance, but the idea of selling one of the few items she had of her father's made her heart sink. She couldn't think of another way to raise the money. On top of which, the pawnbrokers would pay her in cash. She paid for her coffee, then reluctantly collected the revolver in its brown leather case and crossed the road to the shop.

The pawnshop was crammed with big display racks of electrical equipment, including TVs, sound systems, electrical tools, even a big generator. One aisle was full of sports gear. Jessie walked past a big glass display cabinet for watches and jewelry. Hung on the wall behind the counter were classical and electric guitars. The pistols were in a locked glass cabinet, behind which the manager stood. Jessie told him the story of her father's antique revolver. The pawnbroker inspected it, then offered one hundred and fifty dollars.

"No way! The insurer valued it at a thousand dollars. It's an antique, one of a kind, in its original case."

"Then go sell it at an auction." He put it back in the box.

"Give me five hundred. That's a fifty percent discount. You'll sell it for a thousand, easy."

"Two hundred."

"Three."

"Two fifty, and that's my best offer."

They shook on it and he counted out the money in fifty-dollar bills. Jessie knew she had been cheated, but it was no good moping over it. She paid the vet's bill and collected Bartie, who was wobbly on his legs. She lifted him gently onto the vehicle's passenger seat, where he fell asleep almost immediately.

Jessie sat behind the wheel with the windows down. Luckily, the vet hospital's rear parking lot was in the shadow of a tall building, which kept the direct sun from hitting the lot. Should she call Ruth back? Could she trust her? Maybe she should try calling her attorney again? Minutes ticked by and she remained indecisive. She watched Bartie's rhythmic breathing. Maybe she should curl up and have a nap, like her dog. Her lack of sleep was making her eyes drowsy and her limbs heavy. Her lids closed and she fell asleep.

She woke with a start, her chin on her chest. Her neck ached and she had some dribble at the edge of her mouth. She wiped it away with the back of her hand. Her phone was ringing. She saw the time: she had been asleep for almost an hour.

"Jeez!"

It was Ruth calling again. She had been kind to Jessie when nobody else was. If Ruth needed help, Jessie should give it. What could be the harm? She answered.

"Thank God you're okay. I heard about the fire. Was anyone hurt?" Jessie asked.

"We're shaken up. Some smoke inhalation, but we're okay. And you? How are you doing?"

Jessie had watched movies in which a person's location was pinpointed by the cops during a phone call.

"How long before my location can be traced?" Jessie asked.

A pause. "Thirty seconds," Ruth said. "But you're not being traced."

Twelve seconds had already gone by. Jessie counted off the seconds using her watch.

"Tell me who started the fire, Ruth."

"It's complicated. Where can we meet?"

"Meet?" Jessie wracked her brain for a place she knew well that was far away from Eagle Falls. Somewhere she could escape from if this was a trap. Somewhere she would have the advantage over Cuffy and his deputies. "Can you drive?"

"Yes."

There was a campsite that Jessie's family had gone to every summer when she was young. It was in a national park two hours south of Eagle Falls, with a beach called Cathedral Cove, famous for its dramatic rock formations.

"Do you know the Hole in the Wall at Cathedral Cove?" Jessie asked. It was an arch formed by cliff erosion.

"Of course."

"Can you make it by eleven?"

"I think so. Why there?"

The Safe Place   269

The clock was ticking. "Come alone. And don't phone me again."

Jessie ended the call at twenty-nine seconds. She had no idea if Ruth was telling the truth about the thirty seconds it took to discover her location. Just in case, she had to get moving. She switched off her phone and glanced at her injured dog. If the meeting with Ruth went pear-shaped, she had to know that Bartie would be looked after. Jessie hopped out of her vehicle and entered the vet's. She said it was an emergency and she needed Dr. Gilkes to come to her car immediately. Something was wrong with Bartie. Within minutes, the vet was jogging alongside Jessie to her pickup.

"Bartie's good. I needed to get you alone."

Gilkes stopped beside the truck's cabin. She frowned. "What's going on?"

"There's a guy. He's after me. I need you to take Bartie for one night. Keep him safe for me. My dog means the world to me." Everything she had just said was true. A killer was after her. So was the sheriff, but she kept that to herself.

Gilkes looked from Jessie to Bartie asleep on the seat. "This guy wants to hurt you?"

"Yes. I need to sort this out, but I can't do it if I have one eye on Bartie. Please, just one night."

"An overnight stay is expensive."

She pulled out her wallet and offered the vet all the remaining cash she had. "This is all I've got. Seventy dollars. Take it. I'll have the rest tomorrow."

"If this guy's violent, you should report him to the police."

"I did that, they didn't believe me." She pushed the cash into Gilkes's hand.

"Keep your money. I'll make sure Bartie is looked after, okay? But you must get advice. A support group, women's shelter, something."

"I'm meeting a woman who can help me."

"Good."

Jessie then led her drowsy dog back into the vet's and settled him in a large cage in the recovery unit, with a blanket and a bowl of water. She cuddled him and whispered in his ear, "Love you, Bartie." Then to the vet she said, "I'm leaving my pickup behind. That way you know I'm coming back for him."

Jessie thanked Gilkes and walked out of the building. She consoled herself that her dog was better off at the vet hospital. She had a feeling that her meeting with Ruth was going to decide her future, one way or another. She filled a duffel bag with anything she might need for her rendezvous with Ruth, including a flashlight, then she tucked her braid into her baseball cap and wore shades—she didn't want to be recognized. Then she set off to steal a car.

CHAPTER FORTY-EIGHT

Cathedral Cove's campground was just as Jessie remembered it, minus the crowds. Normally in early September it was packed with families on vacation. The current high risk of wildfires had forced the campground to close. The ranger station at the park entrance was manned but Jessie knew of an off-road track that took her on a circuitous route where she wanted to go. She estimated she had a thirty-minute head start on Ruth because Jessie had set off from Marymere. Ruth was driving from Eagle Falls, which was farther away. Jessie parked the stolen 2002 Honda Accord between two towering trees, nudging it as far as possible into the undergrowth of ferns and shrubs to conceal it. Fortunately, it was black and filthy, which made it easier to hide. She had found the car in a shopping mall's parking lot, the key stashed under one of the rear wheel arches.

With a small bag strapped to her back, Jessie set off at a jog along the trail to the cove. Thankfully the trees lining the path gave her shade all the way. The forest abruptly ended, and a steep path led down a rock face to the silvery beach. It was energizing to feel the cool onshore wind and to taste the saltiness on the breeze. Not far from the shore, sea stacks protruded from the water resembling tiny islands. At one end of the long beach was a vast stone arch, six or seven stories high, known as the Hole in the Wall and much loved by photographers and visitors alike. It was low tide and pools had formed on the rocky shore. On vacations with her parents, Jessie had explored those pools and discovered crabs, starfish, and sea anemones in stunning colors. She smiled at the memory.

But she didn't have time to reminisce.

If Ruth was legitimate, Jessie was about to learn the identity of the arsonist who was framing her. But Jessie had to be wary. *Trust no one*, she told herself. She gazed around. If Ruth had betrayed her and brought Cuffy and his deputies too, she guessed they would take up position on the cliffs overlooking the beach. They would regard her as a sitting duck.

She had to be certain that she didn't become just that.

Jessie jogged along the beach until the sand became rock covered in slippery yellow and green seaweed. She trod carefully then. If she slipped and twisted her ankle, she was done for. She made it to the arch and walked through to the other side. Once she was clear of the slimy rock, she jogged across sand to one particular cave in the cliff. About forty feet in, she knew, the cave tapered off to a point that was only four feet high and very dark.

At this point the cave divided into two narrow tunnels, known as Double Jeopardy. When she was twelve years old, two boys had disappeared in the cave. They had taken the right-hand tunnel, which looked promising because the entrance was wider. That was a mistake that had almost cost them their lives. Jessie knew the left-hand tunnel was the way to go. She bent down and, using her flashlight, peered into the left-hand cave. She reckoned she could still crawl through it.

Jessie waited for Ruth in the shadow of the Hole in the Wall. Ruth was easy to spot in a red-and-white loose-fitting dress and red sneakers. She took each step down the steep path to the beach tentatively. Once she reached the beach, Ruth stopped and coughed into a tissue, then she put her hand above her eyebrow to block out the sun and peered in the direction of the arch. Jessie scanned the length of the cliff for signs of company: a glint of metal, a sudden movement, a sound that was out of place. She saw nothing peculiar. Had she done Ruth a disservice imagining that she might betray her?

Ruth approached the rock arch as agreed.

"Jessie?" Ruth called, her voice croaky. She wasn't far away now. "It's Ruth. Are you there?" Ruth coughed.

Jessie stayed silent and hidden. Seconds later, Jessie heard the slap of sneakers on wet rock.

Jessie peaked around the corner. Ruth was facing the other way. "Don't look behind you. Keep facing out," Jessie whispered.

Ruth went rigidly still. "Oh-kay," she replied slowly. "I'm not going to hurt you. I want your help."

"Did you bring company?" Jessie asked, her eyes once again following the length of the clifftop.

"I'm alone. Are you?"

"Sure. I'm always alone."

"Can I turn around? We need to talk."

"We can talk like this. Keep looking straight ahead. You said you knew who started the fires. Tell me who it is."

"Can I look at you? I want to know you're all right."

"Don't turn around."

"Jessie, this isn't necessary. When have I ever given you a reason to distrust me? I drove you to meet your lawyer. I welcomed you into my home. I came all this way because this is where you wanted to meet. Can't we walk along the beach and talk calmly?" Jessie didn't respond. "I'm feeling weak. Can we go sit on one of those big logs near the path?"

That would take Jessie too far away from her escape plan, should she need it. Yet, she felt sorry for Ruth, obviously still suffering from the smoke inhalation. "You can turn around. Come through the arch. There's a rocky outcrop we can sit on."

She watched Ruth do a one-eighty-degree turn.

"Hey," Ruth said, smiling, but the smile was forced. It didn't reach her eyes. Was it because she was sick, or…

"Who's behind the house fires, Ruth?" Jessie asked.

Again, Ruth sidestepped the question. "What happened at Bill's place?"

Jessie blinked several times. "How would I know?"

"Do you know your house is gone? Bill's too. Are you sure you know nothing about that?"

"Why would I destroy my own house? Jeez, Ruth, I thought you were on my side. Now tell me the name of the arsonist."

"A witness saw you running from our house as the fire started." She saw Ruth's green eyes turn hard.

"You think I…" Jessie looked up. Saw a flash of beige uniform behind a clifftop bush. Her face crumpled. "You lured me here to trap me?" She saw the glint of a rifle poking through the treeline. Armed deputies wearing black bulletproof vests scuttled down the track to the beach. "You lied to me!"

She backed away from Ruth, then turned and ran like the wind, legs and arms pumping. As she made a beeline for the cave she heard Ruth cry out, "Don't shoot!"

Someone shouted. There was a loud crack, like a burst of thunder, and a bullet bounced off a rocky outcrop to her left. Jessie sped up.

"She's unarmed! Don't shoot!" Ruth screamed behind her.

At the entrance to the cave Jessie slipped on the wet rocks and fell flat on her butt, landing hard. Bruised, she picked herself up, leaping across rock pools, running as fast as she could to the back of the cave. She didn't dare use the flashlight because this would tell the cops where to aim their weapons. It was very dark in the cave's depths. She fell into a pool of water and cut her left calf. The salt water stung the wound. She crawled out and kept going. She glanced behind her, squinting into the brightness. Neither

Ruth nor the deputies had caught up with her yet, so she risked using the flashlight briefly to locate the two narrow tunnels. She found the one she wanted on the left, switched off the flashlight, shoved it into her back pocket, and crawled on her hands and knees into the tunnel.

Behind her she heard a man shout, "In here! Use the flashlight on your phone." It was Kinsley.

Splashing, stamping, running. Flashlight beams danced as they searched the cave.

"Jesus! She could be hiding anywhere," somebody said.

"She's unarmed," Ruth called out, then was interrupted by a honking cough.

Water dripped on Jessie's exposed skin and her breathing quickened. She felt an ache grow in her chest. She tried to ignore her claustrophobia.

I can do this. I've done this before, Jessie thought. *Just breathe normally.*

Her shoulder smacked into rock wall and she winced. The surface beneath her hands and knees was wet and slippery. The tunnel walls closed in on her. She stubbed her pinkie and repeatedly whacked the top of her head. Soon she had to lie flat on her belly, with her arms out in front of her as if she were about to dive into water. The front of her shirt caught on a sharp edge of rock and it tore. She used her feet to push herself through the constricted space. Ahead, she glimpsed light. She was almost through to the hidden cave. A few more inches and her hips were jammed between solid rock. Jessie wiggled and pulled but she couldn't drag herself free. The last time she had crawled through this tunnel, she had been thirteen years old. Her hips and butt had filled out since then. Panic welled inside her.

I can't go back!

Jessie tried wriggling but that only succeeded in pinching the skin beneath her shorts. Then she realized the problem. The flashlight in her back pocket had snagged on the tunnel's roof. She reversed, which was way harder than going forward. By now her arm and leg muscles were burning and her whole body was slick with sweat.

"Where did she go?" someone said from the main cave.

If they peered down the tunnel, would they catch sight of her?

"Got to be one of those tunnels."

"You're kidding? I'm not going in there. Could get stuck and never come out."

"Use your flashlight."

"Get a ranger down here!"

Jessie turned on her side and pulled one arm to her chest, grazing the skin on the tunnel roof. She almost dislocated her arm as she forced it behind her where she managed to grip the flashlight and free it from the back of her shorts. *Mustn't drop it.* Any noise would draw the deputies' attention to the left-hand tunnel that she was in. She turned back on her belly and with the flashlight gripped firmly in one hand, she slithered forward through the narrowest section. This time her hips squeezed through. She exhaled with relief as she arrived in a vast and echoey cavern. She paused for a moment to catch her breath and to reacquaint herself with the cave's interior.

Dusty sunlight penetrated through the roots of a vast tree spanning the collapsed roof of the cave. It was a Sitka spruce. How it hadn't dropped into the hole beneath was a mystery. Each year more of the roof collapsed and yet the tree still hung on. Some of the roots were as thick as her upper arm. Crisscrossing the chunky roots were slimmer ones. Fifty feet below, chunks of the roof lay where they had fallen. Their surfaces were damp and covered in black pellets that smelled like oil-based decorator's paint. Now that her eyes had adjusted to the light, she studied the cave roof. It was black and writhing. Sleeping bats hung there and the black pellets were their poop. They occasionally shifted position or opened and closed their wings, but they were quiet. At all cost, she must not disturb them. If she did, they would screech and fly away, the noise carrying across the national park. It would be like a great big arrow alerting the deputies to her location.

The voices coming for the beach cave were now muted, but she could hear them discussing where the tunnels might lead. Someone suggested talking to the rangers. Jessie knew that eventually she would be found. But it might take some time. What she needed to do now was find a way to climb the cavern wall and escape through the open roof.

With her flashlight in her back pocket, she began to climb boulders piled against the north wall. Sooner or later a park ranger would guess where she had gone. She had to climb out before that happened. Initially the bat droppings caused her feet to slip. She took each step warily. But the higher she went, the less slippery the boulders. At the fifteen-foot mark she ran out of boulders. Now she had to climb the wall and the many hours that Jessie had spent at the indoor climbing wall with fellow firefighters was going to pay off. It had been part of their fitness training and it now gave her the confidence to climb the vertical rock face. However, this wall was unstable, which meant that she had to test each handhold and foothold before she used it. It was slow going. The higher she went, the nearer to the sleeping bats she got. She could now see the detail of their furry faces poking out of a cocoon of rubbery wings.

Jessie made it to the very top of the rocky wall. Now for the really tricky bit. She would have to let go with one hand. A bead of sweat trickled into her eye. It stung. Jessie didn't dare to look down. *Stay focused on your next handhold.* Adrenaline surged around her body. She stretched out her hand toward a root about the circumference of her wrist. As soon as she had her fingers wrapped around it, she tugged it to test its stability. Sandy soil dropped down to the cave floor fifty feet below, but the root didn't snap or come free from the ground it clung to. She then tested another root, this one a bit wider. It didn't budge or break. Her skin tingled with fear. She planned to use the two parallel roots like a gymnast's parallel bars and swing her legs up and over so she could sit up on them. Then she hoped to crawl across them, like train tracks, to solid ground. If the roots gave way or she slipped, she would fall to certain death.

Jessie gripped one root firmly, then swung her other hand across to the other root. Now to release her footing. She took a deep breath and felt her feet swing through the air.

It's just like a climbing frame, she told herself. *You did this as a kid all the time.*

She swung her legs like a pendulum, gathering momentum. The tree creaked. There was a loud snap.

CHAPTER FORTY-NINE

Ruth was livid. This was not what she had agreed with Cuffy. Jessie was unarmed and had posed no threat. They had no right to shoot at her.

Four deputies, two from Eagle Falls and two local deputies, had been searching the cave's interior for fifteen minutes and they couldn't find her. They had called in reinforcements. Eventually they would catch her. Every misgiving Ruth had had about trapping Jessie had come true.

"Sheriff?" she said, attempting to interrupt Cuffy's conversation with a national park ranger who had unrolled a map of the park. "Can we talk?"

"In a minute, Ruth." Cuffy swatted her away like a fly.

Ruth sat on a boulder near the mouth of the beach cave, suddenly desperately weary. Her chest wheezed and she felt lightheaded.

"What have I done?" Ruth said to herself, staring out at the picture-postcard-perfect white sand and the blue sea.

Was Ruth going to be responsible for Jessie's death? She felt sick at the thought. What if Victor had been mistaken? She glanced at Cuffy, stabbing a finger at the map which lay across a boulder as the ranger shook his head. Had Cuffy pressured Victor into stipulating that it was definitely Jessie that he saw fleeing their house? Her husband was desperate to win Cuffy's support for the

Belle Property role, but she found it hard to believe that he would lie just to secure a job.

"The cave has two tunnels," the ranger explained, "They lead to two different caverns. One tunnel is blocked. The roof collapsed years ago. The other remains open but it's very narrow." The ranger pointed at the map. "It leads to a cavern with a hole in the roof that's home to a rare species of bat. The roof cavity is partly hidden by the roots of an old Sitka spruce."

"Could an adult woman crawl through the tunnel?" Cuffy asked, using a cotton handkerchief to wipe sweat from his forehead.

"She might be able to, yes. It would be a tight squeeze."

"Where does the cave lead?"

"Nowhere. The only way out is through the hole in the roof. And that would be incredibly dangerous. The cave ceiling is highly unstable."

"Can your people rappel into the cave?" Cuffy asked.

"We could, but it would disturb the bats and we really don't want to do that. They're already suffering because of the intense heat and drought. We're finding bat carcasses all over the park. And they sleep during the day."

Cuffy went puce in the face. "I don't give a damn about your bats. Jessie Lewis is a wanted criminal. I need to get into that cave and if you won't do it, I'm calling in a specialist team that will."

"Hold on a moment, sir. They're a protected species. Give me a chance to discuss this with head office."

"You can discuss all you like, son, but we're going in there whether you like it or not. Now take me to this Sitka spruce."

Cuffy directed two of the deputies to stay at the beach cave's entrance, should Jessie materialize there. The other two deputies, Kinsley and Wang, accompanied him and the park ranger. Cuffy walked straight past Ruth as if she didn't exist. She was tired of being treated like a third wheel. She caught up with him.

"Sheriff, I must insist we talk. Jessie is unarmed. Why did your deputies shoot at her?"

"Don't interfere, Ruth."

The sun beat down on her and her lungs weren't responding well to the fast pace she was having to walk. "Sheriff, you *cannot* fire at an unarmed suspect."

"I'll do whatever it takes to arrest Jessie. You should go home now and rest. You're looking mighty peaked."

Ruth bit back the urge to remind Cuffy that she didn't have a home anymore. "Is this about Marcus?"

Earlier, during the cave search, Ruth had overheard Kinsley and Wang discuss the discovery of Marcus's body at Bill's place. Marcus hadn't died as a result of the fire, or so the deputies believed. He had died from gunshot wounds to the chest and abdomen. Bill's skull, they said, had almost been cleaved in two, and he had died before the fire began. Their theory was that Jessie had murdered both men. But from what Ruth could glean, Samson's specialist forensics team hadn't confirmed any of their rash theories.

Cuffy swiveled so fast he kicked sand over her sneakers. "It's about catching a serial killer. You of all people should understand," he shouted, then stomped off across the beach.

Ruth wasn't strong enough to give chase. Her lungs hurt with the exertion and when she began climbing the steep path up the cliff, she had to stop and use her inhaler before she was able to continue. Ruth finally reached the top of the cliff path and paused to catch her breath. There was a deafening screech, like hundreds of fingernails dragged down blackboards. She looked up into the sky. A mass of screaming bats, like a swirling tornado, had risen out of a spot in the forest. Jessie must have disturbed them.

Ruth set off again. Her phone rang. She glanced at the caller ID. Callan Bolt, from Seattle's Fire Investigation Unit.

"Callan?"

"I heard someone tried to burn your house down. I'm so sorry. Are you okay?"

"I'll live. Hey, can I call you back?"

"Sure, I have some information you might find useful."

Now Ruth had to know what it was. "Tell me more."

"There have been two similar arson attacks to the ones on Devil Mountain. Both in Seattle, the first in November 2017 and the second in February this year." Callan paused. "Are you running?"

Ruth was walking as fast as she could and breathing heavily. "Kind of."

"The November fire was attributed to a gas leak from the stove. At the February fire, the husband was shot in the chest before the fire consumed him. Lighter fluid was used to accelerate the fire. The Devil Mountain house fires and the Seattle house fires could have been started by the same person, although this isn't conclusive. I've emailed you the reports."

"Thanks. Have you sent them to Marcus too?"

"I did this morning. He doesn't know that you have a copy."

"He won't ever know, I'm afraid, because he was shot dead in the early hours of this morning. Another man with him died from a blow from an axe. Both bodies were burned in a fire."

"This happened the same night your house was set on fire?"

"Yes," she panted.

"The killer has escalated. Two arson attacks on the same night. He's spooked. What do you and the other two victims have in common?" Bolt asked.

Ruth didn't want to say that the obvious answer was Jessie Lewis.

CHAPTER FIFTY

Jessie wasn't sure how much longer she could cling to the tree root with just one hand. The root acted like a trapeze bar, and it was the only thing stopping her from falling to her death. She was surrounded by screeching, swirling bats. It was terrifying. She shut her eyes and waited for their frenzied evacuation of the cave to die down. They slammed into her body, causing her legs to swing. Her baseball cap was knocked off her head; it tumbled through the darkness to the cave floor fifty feet below.

The fingers of Jessie's right hand were slipping. In just a few seconds she would lose her grip altogether. She swung her left hand up, aiming for a parallel root. Just as she was about to wrap her fingers around it, a bat slammed into her shoulder and she missed her mark.

I refuse to die!

She tried again and this time she kept hold of the second root. She clenched her stomach muscles and swung her legs up. One heel hooked over a root. She then swung the other leg up too. Next, she bent her knees over each root as if it were the bar of a trapeze artist. She wriggled her hips up and over the roots until she was able to sit up. As long as the roots didn't give way, she might make it out of there.

Jessie now slid her thighs forward, as if she were sliding along parallel bars like a gymnast. Her leg and arm muscles shuddered with the strain. It felt as though it took hours to reach solid ground; in reality it took her only a few seconds. Jessie knew not to trust the cavern's roof. It might collapse beneath her. Jessie crawled across pine needles until she reached the safety fence surrounding the Sitka spruce. Exhausted, Jessie gripped a fence post to support her as she stood on shuddering legs.

Gasping back tears of relief, Jessie looked around. She was surrounded by forest. She heard voices. Men shouting. Cuffy's deputies were heading this way. Jessie had escaped the cave. Now she had to evade capture. Which way to the campsite? She was disoriented with no markers to help her find her way back to where she had left her stolen car. Tapping her back pocket, she found the flashlight gone. It must have fallen during her acrobatics. But she still had her phone. Using its flashlight, she aimed the bright beam down into the cavern. If she could see the tunnel entrance that led toward the beach, she knew she had to walk in the opposite direction. The darkness ate up the beam but there was enough for her to locate a circle of subdued light from the tunnel.

She set off, slowly at first, her leg muscles complaining. But as the voices of her pursuers got louder, she sped up. It was tough terrain, overgrown with shrubs and vines. She longed for some water to drink. She materialized from the forest behind the public bathrooms. The campsite had two of these, the only concession to civilization on a site that had no power and no showers. She listened. No voices. Sneaking into the bathroom, Jessie threw cold water over her face and arms, then drank deeply from the tap. She used wet paper towel to clean her grazes.

With her back against the cool bathroom wall, she tried to calm her rapid and panicked breathing. She needed a plan to get out of the national park. The place would be teeming with reinforcements soon, perhaps even police dogs, and the exit roads, including the one she had used to get there, would have roadblocks. She could walk out of there, but the nearest town would take a day's hike to reach. All her choices were bad. In the end she decided that her only course of action was to drive like the wind in the hope that she could outwit her pursuers.

Jessie left the public bathrooms, using the trees to obscure her presence. She made good progress. She was perhaps seven or eight yards from where she left the car when she heard a crackly voice over a two-way radio. She ducked behind tree cover and then poked her head out, enough to see a deputy she recognized heading for his SUV. It was Kinsley. A silver Buick LaCrosse pulled up alongside Kinsley. The driver's window was down; the driver was Ruth. The low rumble of their voices reached Jessie but she couldn't make out what they were discussing. Kinsley's parked SUV was nearer Jessie than the deputy. A crazy plan popped into her head. Jessie snuck behind Kinsley's vehicle, opened the driver's door and slipped inside. The keys were in the ignition. Jessie glanced at Kinsley and Ruth chatting. They hadn't seen her. She started the engine, revved, and tore away. Kinsley looked around as Jessie drove like a maniac out of the campsite. He started to run after her, but must have realized the futility and he used his two-way radio.

The deputy at the campsite entrance had clearly been alerted to the situation and took up position to fire at Jessie. Jessie ducked down as low as she could and went for maximum speed. A bullet hit the bodywork. Jessie kept going. The deputy jumped aside just as Jessie's bull bars rammed the barrier, snapping it in half.

CHAPTER FIFTY-ONE

The road leaving the campsite was long, straight, and tree-lined, and hers was the only vehicle on it. There was no way of blending in. She was a sitting duck. Behind her, the wailing of police sirens set her teeth on edge. Her skin broke out in goosebumps. She stamped on the gas pedal. *Faster!*

In the rear-view mirror she saw a sheriff's patrol car with roof lights flashing, speeding through the park gates some two hundred yards behind her. Jessie wanted to scream. Everything she did to try to prove her innocence only served to make her situation worse. The deputies were going to kill her, there was no doubt about it. They had tried do it on the beach. How had her life turned into such a train wreck?

All Jessie knew right now was that she had to dump Kinsley's SUV and she couldn't wait until she reached the nearest town. It was like a beacon for law enforcement everywhere. Ahead, the road bent to the right and then to the left like a giant capital *S*. The bends were enough for the pursuit vehicle to lose eye contact with her SUV. Few people lived around here but there were some isolated motels and holiday rentals. If she could ditch the SUV and swap it for another car, maybe she stood a chance.

She rocketed down the road as it bent to the right. Before the second bend there was a turnoff. She decelerated and took it. It led to some houses with holiday rental signs in their front yard, and a run-down motel with discarded construction materials in a dumpster out the front. The motel consisted of six rooms in a row with plastic chairs and a table outside each unit, and a separate bungalow to one side that Jessie assumed belonged to the motel owner. The rooms looked like they had seen better days: the exterior sky-blue paint was speckled with black mold and the faded curtains hung unevenly from the rails. Parked in the bungalow's driveway was a Ford Transit cargo van, which looked in better condition than the rooms. There was a parking lot around the back and Jessie pulled into it, hoping the motel would conceal the clearly signed sheriff's vehicle from passing traffic.

Her GPS revealed that she was on a loop road that ended at the town. A Nissan Versa was parked outside room six. There was a cleaning cart on the concrete path outside room one. A woman wearing headphones dragged a vacuum cleaner into the room and switched it on. Jessie left Kinsley's SUV behind a mound of builder's sand that had been there for so long there were grasses and weeds growing from it. She took the keys from the SUV's ignition so the vehicle couldn't be used to pursue her. Then she wandered over to the Nissan, hoping there might be keys in it. There weren't, and the car doors were locked. She didn't have much time.

She jogged to the front of the house. As casually as possible, she looked in the main window and saw a man in a cotton undershirt seated with his feet on a bamboo coffee table watching a football game on TV. Jessie then peeked into the Ford Transit van. The key was in the ignition and a plastic keychain with the insurer's name dangled from the key. Jessie hated having to steal another vehicle, but it was her only chance of escape. With her heart thumping hard, she opened the van door cautiously to avoid a creek, then jumped in. The door clicked shut. The engine growled into life. *Damn!* It was a noisy diesel. It was too late to hope for stealth. She accelerated and drove away as fast as the bulky van would allow. In the rear-view mirror, she saw the owner outside his door yelling.

On the passenger seat was a wide-brimmed straw hat, the kind people often used when gardening, with a string and toggle to secure it under the chin. Keen to disguise herself, she popped it on her head and tucked her braid inside it and continued along the road until she reached the small town of Pine Ridge.

There were no roadblocks as yet. Sheriff's vehicles raced back and forth but none pulled her over and she left the town unnoticed. Her phone rang and it automatically went to speaker. It was Manning.

"Hun, don't say a word, just listen. Meet me soon as you can at the place you lay down on the sofa. Now I want you to turn your cell off and remove the SIM. You got that?"

"Yes."

The office of Manning and McCarthy was so quiet that Jessie thought her attorney had given up on her and gone home. But the main office door was unlocked, so Manning had to be there somewhere.

"Hello?"

Through the frosted glass pane of Manning's door she saw movement. Manning threw the door open. It was her day off and yet the lawyer wore a vibrant amethyst dress that was tailored. Her sandals had a lower heel than Jessie had seen her wear before, which meant that for the first time Jessie, in an old pair of sneakers, was the same height as Manning.

Manning enveloped Jessie in a perfumed embrace. "Thank the heavens you're okay. You had me so worried!" Pulling back, with her hands resting on Jessie's shoulders, she asked, "Were you followed, hun?"

"I don't think so."

Manning locked the main office door. "Water? I only got sparkling."

Sparkling water sounded amazing. Jessie drank greedily from the bottle she was given. "Follow me."

They sat in Manning's office, side by side on the white two-seater sofa.

"My clothes are a bit dirty," Jessie said apologetically.

"Stop your fussing. Now you tell me everything," Manning said. "And I mean everything." She lifted a manicured finger. "But, before you do, I have some news for you." She paused. "Marcus Harstad is dead."

Manning watched her reaction. Jessie probably should look aghast, but she had never been good at faking it. She looked down and interlocked her fingers. Should she tell Manning that she was the one who killed him?

"Whatever you tell me goes no further, hun. Attorney-client privilege." She cocked her head. "Did you know Marcus was dead?"

Jessie raised her eyes and stared out the window to buy herself time. The city was in a heatwave. Everyone dodged the blistering sun. Even the birds were too hot to fly. Or was it the smoky air that made them fearful? "They're going to kill me," Jessie said, her eyes on the window.

"Lord above! Who's going to kill you?"

"Cuffy's mob." Jessie wrung her hands. "They tried to kill me at the beach. I want to make a will and do one of those signed statement things. I want you to keep them locked away until I'm gone from this world."

"Nobody's going to kill you if you hand yourself in."

Jessie snapped her head around and looked Manning square in the eye. "Please, before the police arrive. I want a will."

Manning raised her hands. "Okay, hun, I'll do you a will. I thought you said you weren't followed?"

"I can't be certain."

Manning went and sat behind her computer, a shiny new Apple. "I have a template we can use. You tell me what you want.

Then I print and you sign. We need independent witnesses. I think the graphic designers down the corridor are working today. They'll do it."

Manning asked her questions then typed as Jessie dictated her wishes. It wasn't a complicated will. Anything of value that she possessed was to be sold and the money put in a trust and that trust was to be used to keep her dog fed and healthy and in the care of a kind owner. The trust was to be overseen by Manning, who received a small fee for doing it. Manning rounded up two designers from a neighboring office to witness Jessie's signature and they left immediately afterward.

Manning gestured to her desk chair. "Sit here. I'll leave you to write your statement."

Climbing the cave wall and then hanging from the roots across the ceiling had left her fingers stiff and her palms blistered.

"Can you do it? You'll be quicker."

"Okay, you tell me what you want to say." She sat at her desk. "First up, I need to establish who you are, the date, and so on." Manning typed. Then she waited, her long purple fingernails poised over a keyboard. "Is this about the house fires, cause if it is you have to start with where you were the night the Troyer family died."

"But you know all that."

"This is a statement, Jessie. Start with your relationship with the Troyer family."

Jessie did just that. Manning nodded occasionally; she knew most of the early details.

Jessie moved on to the night she was knocked unconscious by the person she believed started the Wilmots' house fire and shot Pat. She described returning to the scene, finding Bill Moran scavenging there and then her interview by Sheriff Cuffy, at which he accused her of murdering the Troyers and the Wilmots. She went on to the night she heard an intruder outside her house and discovered the Wilmots' hose reel had been dumped on her property to make it look as if she had removed it. Next she spoke about Marcus pursuing her to Georgia's house and then the discovery, with Manning as a witness, that her pickup had been bugged by Marcus. Everything that came after that was news to her attorney. Jessie took a deep breath and looked sheepishly at the lawyer. How would Manning react to what she was about to say?

"You lost your tongue?" Manning asked, leaning back in her chair and flexing her fingers.

"I did something real bad."

"Jessie, it's not my job to judge you. It's my job to defend you."

Jessie described how Bill offered to hide her on his big property. "That night, we ate together and he told me how he lost his house, his business, to foreclosure fraud and the scammer was never charged because Cuffy made sure the investigation went nowhere."

"Are you saying the sheriff misdirected the investigation?"

"That's what Bill told me. He said there were two people in on the scam, and one was Rob Wilmot."

Manning raised a penciled eyebrow and she asked several questions for clarification.

"Okay, what happened next?" Manning said.

Jessie looked at the floor. She cleared her scratchy throat. When she spoke, her voice was tremulous. "Marcus found me. God knows how. He turned up at two in the morning at Bill's place, only a few hours after Ruth's house was set on fire. He wanted Bill to give me up. Bill wouldn't." Her voice trailed away. "The poor guy died because of me."

"Do you need a break?" Manning asked.

"No, I want the truth known." Jessie balled her fists. *Just say it*, she willed herself. "Marcus attacked Bill and broke his clavicle. Then he came for me. I used a chunk of chopped wood to defend myself and hit him on the head. I… I thought I'd killed him…"

Her voice trailed away.

"But he wasn't dead, was he? Marcus was shot. Was that you or Bill?"

Jessie hung her head. "It was me. Marcus attacked Bill with an axe. He was going to kill me, I swear. I shot Marcus with his own pistol. It was self-defense."

"Then what?"

"I ran."

"Did you start the fires that burned their bodies?"

"No way. I saw someone leaving my property. I followed him. He fired at me. There's a Chevron on the road into town. I pulled in there to get away from him. They had CCTV. The cameras might have caught the killer's registration plate."

Manning recorded everything she said.

When Jessie explained about the trap Ruth helped Cuffy lay for her at Cathedral Cove, Manning's only comment was, "Somebody's turned her against you."

"A deputy shot at me. I was unarmed. Ruth told them to stop. But they kept firing. I tell you, Cuffy wants me dead."

"I'm beginning to think you could be right. He's protecting somebody. Any idea who?"

"Ford, his son.

"Why Ford?"

"Ford videoed me at the Wilmots' place the night after the fire and the sheriff used it to accuse me of attempting to cover up my crime. I think Ford is framing me. He had a falling out with Paul Troyer, who damaged his motorcycle and Paul never paid up. Ford is the kind of person to hold grudges."

"You think his daddy knows he's the arsonist and this is all about covering up his son's murders?"

"I don't know, Sharnice, but it might explain why Cuffy wants to pin the arson attacks on me."

"Do you suspect anyone else?"

"I'd like to know who the second person behind the scam is. Maybe someone is eliminating loose ends?"

"Anything more to add?" Jessie shook her head. "Okay, hun, I'll print this out and you can sign it." Manning collected the documents from the printer and gave them and a pen to Jessie, who signed.

Manning checked the documents. "I'll keep these in the safe, along with your will, okay? Now, as your lawyer, I must advise you to turn yourself in." Jessie opened her mouth to object but Manning raised one of her painted fingernails. "Hear me out. Now I've said what I'm supposed to say, here's what we are going to do. You're going to lie low while I talk to the governor."

"The governor?"

"Yep, she's the only person who can rein in a sheriff. Give me time to work on her. With your permission, I'll show her your statement."

Jessie thought about how much her body ached. How she had lost her house. How deputies were pursuing her across the state. She was all out of ideas. "Okay, but I've got no place to stay."

"I can get you into a women's shelter." Jessie nodded. "Before we leave, I have some good news," Manning said. "I learned today that Jude Deleon has come forward accusing Marcus of domestic violence."

"Seriously?" It was as if a star had exploded inside her chest. Maybe now people would believe Jessie?

"Seriously. She's also made a statement that she witnessed Marcus hitting you."

Jessie rested her face in her blistered hands and cried with relief.

CHAPTER FIFTY-TWO

On the drive home from the Cathedral Cove debacle, Ruth kept telling herself to leave well alone. For her husband's sake. For her kids' sake too. Jessie had Manning on her side. Ruth should be looking out for her husband, helping him find a job. She sat at a traffic light. One way took her home. The other took her to what used to be Marcus's house, where Jude would be. She couldn't decide what to do. Then a man in the vehicle directly behind her gave her the finger because she was holding back traffic, and that made up her mind for her. She glared at him in the rear-view mirror and took the turn to Marcus's house.

Ruth knocked on Jude's front door and waited. Jude's Fiat Spider was in the drive, together with a Hyundai Sonata that Ruth hadn't seen around before. When nobody came, she pressed the doorbell. It worked. She heard the tap of shoes on wooden stairs. The house door opened to reveal a man in his late fifties with white hair and the same skin tone and features as Jude.

"I'm Ruth. A neighbor." Ruth said. "I wanted to offer my condolences to Jude."

"Condolences? Pah!" the old man said. "That evil son of a bitch hurt my beautiful girl. If he wasn't dead already, I would kill him myself!"

From upstairs Jude called out, "Show her in, Papa. I want to talk to her."

In the living room, Jude lay in her mother's lap, her legs tucked in tight. She appeared small and fragile, and her eyes were red from crying. Jude sat up. "Mama, I need to talk to Ruth alone. Can you give us a minute?"

"But why?" her mother asked.

"Ruth was FBI, Mama."

Her mother looked at Ruth in awe. "*Si, si*, I understand. We go outside and look at the lake."

Once Jude had closed the balcony doors on her mom and dad, she sat next to Ruth on the sofa and held Ruth's hands as if they were the best of friends. "Can I trust you?"

"Of course, but if you know who the arsonist is, you must tell the sheriff." Jude's eyes stared down at their hands. "Jude, do you know who it is?"

Jude didn't make eye contact. "If I talk, I have to be anonymous. It's bad enough that everybody now knows I lied about Marcus. What he did to me."

"Do you want me to go with you?"

"I don't know, I…" Jude shook her head.

"Was it Marcus?" Ruth said.

"No. He was an abuser, not an arsonist. But Marcus knew that Jessie was at Bill's place on Friday night."

"Why did Marcus go there?"

Jude's eyes flashed with anger. "Why do you think? She was a threat. He wanted her silenced."

"Kill her, you mean?"

"I don't know. Maybe. He had a terrifying temper."

"How did Marcus know that Jessie was with Bill last night?"

"Do you know Marty Spaan?" Jude said.

"I met him briefly at Clyde's funeral."

"You gotta promise me you won't tell anyone I said this, okay? Marty is a psycho and I don't want him coming after me."

Ruth didn't want to commit to such a promise, but after the abuse that Jude had suffered, Ruth sympathized with her reluctance to tangle with another dangerous man. "I promise. When you say psycho, what do you mean exactly?"

"Marty was the weird kid at school. Had a temper too. Rumor has it that he burned down the primary school when he was eight because he hated his teacher."

This was the first Ruth had heard about the primary school burning down. If he could set fire to his school at the age of eight, what was he capable of as an adult?

"Who investigated the school fire?"

"Sheriff Cuffy."

"Was anyone charged with arson?"

"Nope. It had me thinking, you know, about the house fires."

"I see your point."

"There's something else. Marty has a thing about older women," Jude said. "When we were eighteen, he had the hots for Pat Wilmot, who was really beautiful back then. I don't know if this is true, but Marty claimed she took his virginity. He was obsessed with her. When she dumped him, he went and told her husband about their affair. Rob and Marty came to blows."

"So Marty doesn't take rejection well?"

"Not at all." *That gives Marty motive to murder Rob and Pat Wilmot*, Ruth thought, *and a possible history of arson as a minor.*

"But that's not what I'm trying to say," Jude said. She leaned close to Ruth and lowered her voice. "Marty lied about where he was the night the Wilmots died. He told the sheriff he was visiting his mom. He wasn't. He was with Millie Kemp. At least some of that night anyway."

Ruth thought back to the furtive looks that passed between Millie and Marty at the gathering after Clyde's funeral. Millie had to be in her fifties and Marty would be about twenty-six. That was quite an age gap.

"How do you know he was with Millie?" Ruth asked.

"I saw him sneaking into her salon after closing."

"Have you told the sheriff?"

"God, no! It was hard enough to own up to Marcus's abuse."

"I understand. That takes a lot of courage."

"If Marcus were alive, I wouldn't dare tell you any of this."

"I'm glad you did. Is there anything else?"

"Marty was here last night talking to Marcus. Their voices woke me. I heard them talk about Jessie and how she was hiding out at Bill's place."

"Jude, what you've told me could be really important. You have to tell the sheriff."

"You promised not to tell!" Jude raised her voice. Her parents turned and stared through the balcony glass doors.

CHAPTER FIFTY-THREE

Ruth slept badly. She'd been woken several times by heavy bouts of coughing and then she couldn't get back to sleep. But it was more than the coughing that troubled her. John and Susie had a granny flat in their backyard and she, Victor, and the kids were staying there temporarily. Victor had taken them up on their offer without consulting Ruth, and once the invitation had been accepted, they couldn't then go and stay someplace else. Victor saw it as a way of bonding with John and Susie, of making amends. Ruth hated being under the ever-watchful eye of Susie and suspected that John wanted her close so he could keep tabs on her. When John had canceled their dinner arrangement that evening, Victor was clearly devastated. He saw it as a reflection of how angry John was with Ruth for siding with Jessie.

"Why can't you support me, Ruthie?" he had said as they got into the sofa bed that night. The boys were sharing a double bed in the only bedroom. "All you have to do is be friendly. Now John hates me and my job prospects are zero."

By six thirty Ruth gave up trying to sleep. She took a cool shower and got dressed while Victor slept. She found Noah and David in the kitchen searching the fridge for something to eat.

"Hey, guys," she said softly, "Daddy's asleep. What do you say we head out to the lake and swim and then get some breakfast?"

"But I'm hungry," David whined, making no effort to keep his voice down.

Ruth hadn't had time to buy groceries, so the fridge was bare. "Okay. Breakfast first and then maybe we can go for a swim once we've digested our food? How does that sound?"

Both boys cheered. Victor, on the sofa bed, groaned then rolled over.

"Shush," Ruth whispered, "Daddy needs his sleep."

Ruth led them to the bedroom, got them dressed in swim trunks and T-shirts, grabbed some towels, sunscreen, and baseball caps, then left a note for Victor so he knew where they had gone. Ruth and the kids then crept down the side passage of the Cuffy's house to the car.

At Abigail's coffeehouse they sat in the courtyard in the shade of a big umbrella and ate breakfast. Afterward, the boys paddled at the lake's shore. It worried Ruth that it wasn't possible to see across the lake—the shore on the opposite side was enveloped in smoke—although the air quality where she sat right next to the water was okay.

"No swimming for half an hour," she told them.

She nursed a coffee, but she wasn't enjoying it. It tasted bitter or maybe that was because of her bitter mood. She didn't know who to trust. She wanted to confide in Victor but she couldn't. He was already angry with her. After speaking with Jude, Ruth was pretty sure that Cuffy should question Marty Spaan again, but Jude had refused to tell Cuffy what she knew, and Ruth had made a promise not to betray her. Ruth felt very alone. She missed the city. She missed her colleagues at work. It was too early on a Sunday morning to phone them. All except T.J. Samson. He and his team were staying at a local motel so they could continue to work the crime scenes.

She texted him.

Can you talk?

Samson phoned her immediately. "Never a boring moment in your part of the world, is there?"

"That's for sure. I wondered if you would like to meet for a coffee?"

"I'm at Bill Moran's property. We thought we'd start early, to avoid the midday heat."

"There's something you should know," Ruth said. "Do you remember Callan Bolt?"

"Sure do."

Ruth explained what Bolt had told her about two house fires in Seattle with similar MO to the Devil Mountain and Eagle Falls fires.

"Good to know," Samson said. There was an awkward pause.

"Are you alone?" she asked.

"Yes, and before you ask, I don't have anything conclusive yet, and if I did, you know how it works. My report goes to Cuffy."

"I get that. I wanted to give you a heads-up. There are two people I think have motive to light the fires. I don't know if their prints are on file, but you might like to see if you can get them fingerprinted. The first is the sheriff's son, Ford Cuffy."

"Ouch!" said Samson.

Ruth explained why she thought Ford had motive. "The other is Marty Spaan." Again, Ruth explained herself.

"That's helpful, thanks. Interesting that this is the first I've heard mention of these two suspects." Samson went quiet. Ruth waited. She was pretty sure that Samson wanted to tell her something. "I never said this. Okay?"

"Okay."

"Accelerant was used at Jessie's cabin. We found the can. Must have been dropped when the arsonist fled. There are prints on it. We don't yet know whose they are. We do know that they are not Jessie's."

CHAPTER FIFTY-FOUR

Every Sunday morning at eight thirty Cuffy went target shooting. He didn't have to travel to the rifle range at Marymere like
ordinary folk because Cuffy had his own rifle range on a tract of
Devil Mountain land he had leased on behalf of the sheriff's office.
It was a lonely spot, on a rocky granite ridge where the soil was
too shallow for trees to grow but was nicely hidden away by the
forest above and below.

A while back, Cuffy had set up a wooden shelf at chest height
and on it were empty food cans, spaced equally apart. He liked to
hear the ting as the bullet hit the metal target. Since the wildfires,
he couldn't shoot at cans anymore. One spark from a hot bullet
hitting tin might set the dry groundcover on fire. Instead, Cuffy
pinned paper bullseye targets to two trees. The wind today was
strong enough to send a bullet off course. Cuffy would have to
compensate in order to hit the target. It would make the morning's
practice session interesting.

This was Cuffy's R&R time. Alone with nothing but the birds
yabbering in the trees, he could blast the hell out of the bullseye.
Here there were no voters he had to please, no lawbreakers to
throw in jail, no mangy lawyers getting in his face. From his
vantage point on the mountainside, he could see across the valley
to the national park. It looked like a meteorite had hit the middle
of the park and the shockwaves had flattened everything around

it. Smoke hovered like mist above the stunted, blackened remains of thousands of trees. At last, the fire service had managed to get the park's wildfire under control.

But the town wasn't safe. Someone was murdering folks, and he'd be damned if he would let them burn another house. Jessie Lewis had skipped town and disappeared. She made him look a total fool and he wouldn't put up with that. She always had a high opinion of herself. That criminal justice degree wouldn't save her neck, however smart she thought she was. He knew what the gossips were saying. That he wasn't up to the job anymore. Too old, they said. They wouldn't vote for him at the election in the new year. He would be damned if he'd get kicked out of the sheriff's office like an old dog.

No, sir!

Cuffy held up a hand. The tremble was worsening. How long would it take before his Parkinson's disease became obvious? He'd caught Kinsley staring at his hands more than once. Had the new deputy already guessed?

He took his Glock 17 from his belt holster. He removed the magazine, then pulled the slide back. On the hood of his Dodge Charger was a box of nine-millimeter bullets. Cuffy loaded one round at a time, enjoying the feel of the spring pushing back on the increasing number of bullets.

Bill's murder had hit Cuffy harder than he would have imagined, although he had done his best not to show it. Susie knew something was wrong. He had blamed his moodiness on the arson cases. Bill had been a pain in Cuffy's side for almost two decades. But when the autopsy report came back, he had to admit he felt sorry for the old guy. An axe split his skull and entered his brain. His shoulder blade was broken before death, so he would have been in great pain.

Marcus was luckier. Shot through the heart, his death would have been instant. The other two bullets were superfluous. So who wielded the axe? And who pulled the trigger? Was Bill the shooter, as the crime scene suggested. Why kill Marcus? And more to the point, what the hell was Marcus doing there?

There had to be a third person present that night, Cuffy was absolutely certain, although there was no evidence yet to confirm his theory. It was this mysterious third person who caused Cuffy to have a sleepless night. Jessie was most likely that person. But a voice from the past whispered in his ear, mocking him for his cowardliness. *There's another suspect*, the voice said, *and you know it. It's time you challenged him.*

Had Cuffy's moment of weakness all those years ago finally come back to haunt him?

He was so focused on loading the magazine and his own thoughts on the case that he didn't notice someone approach until he felt the prod of a gun barrel in the small of his back.

"Put the gun down on the ground next to you," she said. "Nice and slow."

Jessie knew Cuffy's Sunday morning routine. The mountain didn't keep secrets and everyone living on Lake View Drive heard the gunshots ring out every Sunday at the same time. Not even the churchgoers dared challenge Cuffy for firing a weapon on the Lord's Day. Cuffy was, after all, the boss of Eagle Falls.

Jessie had left the women's shelter in Seattle at dawn and driven to this spot early enough to ensure she was hidden behind a big boulder before Cuffy arrived. Yesterday, her attorney had made a valiant effort to persuade the governor to investigate Sheriff Cuffy for failing to do his job. Manning had asked that another sheriff take over the arson-murder case, a sheriff with no vested interest in its outcome. The governor refused. Right up until that moment, Jessie had been hopeful. When Manning told her that she had no choice but to hand herself in to Cuffy, Jessie made her decision to confront the sheriff. After all, what did she have to lose?

"What are you doing, Jessie? Pulling a gun on a sheriff is a criminal offense." Jessie looked down at the stick she had poked into Cuffy's fleshy back. The circular end of the stick was the same diameter as a Glock.

"Do as I tell you. Put the gun on the ground. Slowly, then step forward."

"Okay, Jessie. Don't do anything stupid."

Cuffy held his hands wide so she could see them. He bent down and left his Glock in the dirt. Then he took a step away from her.

"Keep going."

"Sure thing, Jessie."

He did as she asked. When he was far enough away for her to feel safe about picking up the gun, she swooped down and grabbed it. She then shoved the barrel into Cuffy's back.

"We should talk, you know, face to face," he said.

Jessie didn't want him to turn around. She had always found him intimidating. And besides, it was easier for him to try and grab the gun if he were facing her.

"Stay as you are. I want you to tell me the truth. No more lies."

"I don't lie, Jessie."

"Bullshit!" she yelled. He flinched. "You know who the killer is and you're protecting him. Just like you protected Marcus."

"We'll never know the truth now that Marcus is dead."

"Truth?" Her blood was boiling. "You protected Marcus. He was a violent monster and I want to hear you admit it."

"As I said, we'll never know the truth."

"I came to you for help. You betrayed my trust."

"You always were fixated on Marcus." He shook his head. "You killed him, didn't you?"

Jessie wanted to pistol-whip him. Maybe that would knock some decency into Cuffy's warped mind.

"You know who the arsonist is, don't you? Tell me!"

He chuckled. "It's you."

"I'm the scapegoat. I'm always the scapegoat. But not this time. Who are you protecting?"

"I've had enough of your stupid games. Put the gun down."

"It's your son, isn't it?"

He laughed. "You're seriously cuckoo."

"Bill heard a motorcycle the night Pat and Rob died, driving away from their property. Where was Ford that night?"

"How dare you!"

"Do you know if he was at home? Do you know if his motorcycle was in the garage? He had motive to kill Pat and Rob because Rob told you of his dirty little habit of videoing women naked."

Cuffy shrugged. "Just boyish pranks. He promised not to do it again."

"Why was Ford at Pat and Rob's house the night after the fire, huh?" No response, so she kept going. "I'll tell you what he was doing. He went back for the pen he left behind by mistake when he killed them. The pen I pointed out to you on the driveway. The pen from the same bank that you and your son use, Commerce Bank."

"It doesn't matter why he was there. What matters is that he caught you contaminating a crime scene."

"It was Ford who sent me the threatening message—*You are next*—and the footage of me seminaked. He was outside my bedroom window, John. He was trying to freak me out. And it worked. I was terrified. That's why I ran."

"You ran because you are guilty."

Jessie wanted to scream. "He stole my wallet." She was clutching at straws now. "Search his room, I bet you'll find it there."

"So what if I do? It doesn't prove he's an arsonist."

Jessie kicked the rocky ground. She was wasting her time. Even if Ford turned out to be the next Green River Killer, Cuffy would still cover for him. She had to find leverage somehow. What was the chink in Cuffy's armor?

"Why didn't you find the scammers who took Bill's house from him?"

The muscles in Cuffy's neck tightened like he had clenched his jaw. Jessie took that as a sign that her question made him nervous.

"Scammers? What are you talking about?" Cuffy asked as if he were confused, but his bravado was fake.

"Rob Wilmot was one of the scammers. Who was the other?"

A bead of sweat trickled down the back of Cuffy's neck. "You're talking shit. I don't know who was behind the foreclosure fraud."

"Liar! You know and you looked the other way. What dirt did they have on you, John? Or did they offer you money to bungle the investigation?"

Jessie watched his hands. She had noticed the slight tremor in them when he'd interrogated her. Now they were trembling a lot, and he was sweating. His shirt around the armpits was soaked. Cuffy was scared.

"Bill was a fool."

Jessie pushed the pistol harder into Cuffy's back. "I'm going to prove you're a liar and a cheat."

"You'll prove nothing. Now give me the gun and surrender yourself and I'll put in a good word for you with the judge. If you kill me, you'll get the death penalty."

A shot rang out like a clap of thunder.

Both Cuffy and Jessie instinctively ducked. They knew the sound of a bullet leaving a hunting rifle only too well. The bullet landed a few feet away in dry leaf litter. Jessie ran behind a boulder, then craned her neck and peered up the mountain.

Cuffy stumbled in the opposite direction. Unfit and overweight, he only just reached tree cover when a second bullet was fired. It thudded into a tree trunk just a few inches from his head. Jessie looked up again. What the hell was going on?

"Use the pistol!" Cuffy shouted at Jessie. "Shoot them!"

"I can't see them."

They probably had a telescopic lens and were positioned some distance away. She could make a run for it. But could she be sure the shooter was only aiming at the sheriff?

"Then chuck it to me," shouted Cuffy. "I'm a sitting duck."

As soon as he had the gun, Cuffy would aim it at her. He was using his phone, no doubt calling the sheriff's office for backup. If he wanted to, he could claim that she was the shooter. It was time to get out of there. Jessie sprinted across the open gap between the boulder and some trees. She kept running uphill, legs pumping, muscles burning, praying that she wouldn't come face to face with the shooter. Another shot rang out. Jessie ducked, then ran harder, her lungs hurting, her throat and mouth dry. By the time she reached her vehicle and started the ignition, her eyes stung and she was coughing badly. Her mouth tasted bitter. It was smoke.

No one followed her as she drove up the winding road. A ribbon of yellow and red caught her eye farther down the mountain. It was fire and it was near Cuffy's shooting range. Dear God! Had one of the bullets hit granite and caused a spark? The fire would grow quickly in bone-dry leaves and twigs. Worse still, the strong wind would fan the fire. Had Cuffy called the fire station or was he dead? She patted her pockets and found her phone.

"Damn!"

Jessie had taken the SIM card out yesterday. If she switched it back on, there was a risk that she would be found. Black smoke was already billowing up into the pale blue sky and the wind was blowing it toward Eagle Falls. She pulled over and opened the glove compartment. In it was an envelope that she used to keep her shopping bills. She had left the SIM in the envelope. With trembling fingers, she slotted it back in her phone and switched it on.

Come on!

As soon as she had a signal, she dialed 911.

"What is your emergency?"

"Wildfire, above Lake View Drive on Devil Mountain. It's heading straight for the town of Eagle Falls."

CHAPTER FIFTY-FIVE

"Fire's coming!" It was Susie's voice, squeaky with fear. "Hello? Anybody there? You have to leave!" She thumped on the granny flat's door.

Ruth tensed. Next to her on the sofa bed, Victor paused mid-sentence. They were talking about making a claim against their house insurance and the reams of forms they had to complete.

Not another fire, Ruth thought. *I don't think I can survive another one.*

Victor reacted first. He flung the door open. Noah and David stopped their bickering and came out of the bedroom to see what all the commotion was about. Ruth stood, but her legs were unsteady and she almost tripped over the rug.

Susie was breathing heavily. "There's a fire coming this way. John's evacuating the whole town. You need to go. Now."

Ruth made it to the doorway and used the wall for support.

"But how?" Victor said, sounding incredulous. "The national park fire is under control."

"No, Devil Mountain's on fire and the wind's sending it this way."

"Oh my God!" said Ruth, staring at her husband. Fear prickled her body like stinging nettles.

Ruth looked outside. The mountain was shrouded in smoke.

"How long have we got?" Victor asked.

"An hour at most. There's so much to do, I just don't know where to start. And I can't find Ford." She looked close to tears.

"Is your car packed and ready to go?" Victor asked.

"Not really." She grimaced, embarrassed. "I know. Of all people, we should be ready, but John's been distracted. Will you help me with the heavy things?"

"Victor, you go help Susie," Ruth said, "I'll get the kids ready."

Victor went with Susie.

David wrapped his arms around Ruth's waist. "Mom, I'm scared."

Noah hung back. He chewed his lip, which was a sign that he was uneasy.

"It's going to be okay," Ruth said, doing her best to disguise the fear in her voice. "We'll drive away before the fire gets here. But I need your help packing our things, okay? We have to hurry."

At least their prized possessions, clean clothing, and survival gear were already in the trunk of her car.

Once the boys had gathered the computers and toys that survived the fire, Ruth threw everything into a couple of sports bags and then crammed them into the remaining space in the trunk. The air was getting smokier by the minute. She filled some water bottles, checked that all the power switches were off, and shut the doors and windows. Then she dragged the pillowcases off the pillows and threw them into the kitchen sink, letting the tap run over them so that the cotton was soaked.

"What are you doing, Mommy?" Noah asked.

"It'll keep the fire away."

If necessary, they could throw the sodden pillowcases over their heads to protect them. Dropping the pillowcases into a bucket, she then took her loaded Smith & Wesson M&P semiautomatic from the very top drawer of a kitchen cabinet. There was no gun safe in the granny flat, so she had put the gun out of reach of the kids. She now slotted it into the holster that she fastened around her waist.

"Whoa!" said David, eyes wide. "That's so cool." It had been months since she'd carried a gun.

"Let's go," Ruth said.

They found Victor in the driveway dropping a large suitcase into the trunk of Susie's car. Susie was on her cell phone.

"Have you seen Ford?" she was asking someone. "Call me if you see him. I'm so worried."

"You should leave, Ruth," Victor said, placing his arms around her. "The mountain road is blocked. There's only one route out of town and it's going to get gridlocked."

Susie made another call. "Have you seen Ford?" A pause. "Oh, you left already?"

"Victor, we can't wait for Ford to turn up," said Ruth. She was being selfish. But she wasn't going to lose her husband and kids.

Victor gave her a kiss. "I'll help John evacuate the town. He needs all the help he can get."

Ruth shook her head. "*I* need you. *We* need you. Please don't." She held him tightly in her arms and whispered in his ear. "Think of your sons. They need a father."

"I have to do this, Ruthie. People need my help."

"Daddy," Noah said, "I'm staying too."

Victor knelt down. "You go with your mother, Noah. And you too, David. I want you both to look after her. You have to promise." He opened his arms wide. "Group hug!" They ran at him and he embraced them.

Ruth wanted to keep arguing but her lungs wouldn't allow her to. She coughed so hard it felt as if she were going to pass out.

"I've got my Mustang," Victor said. "She goes like a rocket. Now get going."

"No." She coughed. "We leave here together."

Ruth's phone rang. She saw it was Jessie and moved a few feet away because Susie's voice was growing louder and more hysterical with each phone call she made.

"Get out of town right now," Jessie said. Her voice was muffled, as if she were speaking through a mask. "The fire's too big and too fast."

Susie was now on the phone to Cuffy. "Go and find Ford!" she screamed. "I don't give a damn. He's our son!"

Jessie must have overheard Susie because she asked, "Who's that?"

"It's Susie. Ford's gone missing."

"I saw Ford just a minute ago," Jessie said. "He's shooting video of the fire."

"You saw Ford! Where?" Ruth said.

Both Victor and Susie turned to look at Ruth.

On the other end of the line there was crackling static. "Can you repeat that?" Ruth asked.

Jessie replied, but again there was too much static.

"I'm putting you on speaker," Ruth did just that. "Say that again." Victor and Susie knew the area well. Perhaps they could decipher enough to know where Jessie had last seen Ford.

"Do you trust her?" Victor said.

"Yes," Ruth replied. Then louder, "Jessie?"

Again, just static. If Jessie's name hadn't still appeared on her screen, Ruth might have thought that she had severed the connection.

Ruth shouted, "Where did you see Ford?"

When Jessie spoke, she sounded hoarse. "The Adams…"

"Veronica and Sam Adams? I know their property." Victor shouted so Jessie could hear him. "Jessie, tell Ford to get out of there." More static. "We can't get to him in time. You have to save him."

Suddenly the connection was broken and Susie was dialing her husband.

Victor ushered Ruth and the boys to the Buick. "Go to my sister's," Victor said. Kelly and her husband, Finn, a garage mechanic, lived in Marymere. "I'll join you when I'm done here."

David started to cry. "Don't leave me, Daddy," he wailed.

It took all of Ruth's powers of persuasion to coerce her youngest into the car. She wanted to drag her husband with them, but Victor was stubborn and he wasn't going to change his mind.

The traffic leaving Eagle Falls moved at a snail's pace but at least it moved. Behind them, a wall of fire was creeping ever closer, destroying forest and houses and anything in its way. They passed an SUV with FBI insignia and an Evidence Response Team truck, and Ruth saw that Samson and his team were helping to evacuate the town. A journey that should have taken twenty minutes took two hours. As soon as they arrived at her sister-in-law's house, she phoned Victor to tell him that they were safe.

"Please, Victor, get out of there. It's not your job. We need you."

Her pleading fell on deaf ears and she felt indignant. Shouldn't Victor care first and foremost about his family? She was filled with pent-up frustrations and she needed to do something physical to let off steam. She busied herself with carrying boxes, suitcases, and bags from the car to Kelly's guest room while Kelly gave the kids cookies and milk in the kitchen.

When everything was unloaded, Ruth sat on the edge of the bed and stared at her shaking hands. Was it shock?

Her eyes came to rest on one of the cardboard storage boxes. It had been overfilled and one side of the box had split. It contained passports, birth and marriage certificates, and documents, such as their car and house insurance providers. In their haste to pack, some old childhood photos of Victor had been flung in there too. She had some sticky tape somewhere, but where? Unable to find it, she asked Kelly for some. Then Ruth did her best to mend it. The tape was flimsy and, as she fiddled with the box, the split got even wider.

"Jesus!" she cursed.

Furious at everything, she ripped the box lid off and removed some of the documents inside, transferring them to a section of floor. On top of the pile was a document with the FBI insignia on it and Victor's name. Curious, she scanned it quickly. It was a spousal questionnaire relating to Ruth's enrolment in the FBI in 2008. All spouses and partners were asked to complete a security check. Did he belong to groups that incited civil unrest? Did he have a criminal record? Had he ever been approached to spy for another country? The document in her hand contained Victor's answers to such questions. The one about their marriage caught her eye. She had assumed he would say their marriage was good.

Ruth frowned as she read Victor's comment. He had stated their marriage wasn't going well and they might separate. It was absolutely not true. Why would he say that? Never had they ever discussed separating. Given this answer, she was lucky to have been accepted into Quantico. Unstable marriages were regarded by the FBI as potential security risks. Ruth might never have had a career in the FBI as a result. It must have been her exemplary record at Seattle PD that tipped the balance in her favor.

Ruth stared out the bedroom window. A ginger cat walked along the top of the wooden fence. All these years, Victor had been living a lie. He hadn't wanted her to win a coveted position at Quantico. He had wanted her to stay with Seattle PD. If she had, then they could have managed their kids and both worked. All the time that he had been playing the role of stay-at-home dad he had been mourning the loss of his career in real estate.

The ache in her chest caused her to clutch her sternum, waiting for the pain to pass. It wasn't indigestion though. It was guilt. She had been selfish. She had pursued her career at the expense of her husband's happiness. And now, neither of them had a career, or a house for that matter.

The door swung open and Noah looked in. "Mom, do you want some cookies?"

"I'd love some," Ruth said brightly, dropping the FBI form into the box and securing the lid.

CHAPTER FIFTY-SIX

Seated inside her pickup, Jessie stared at the phone in her hand.

The line had been bad. Not surprising really, given that Devil Mountain was on fire. The fire front was directly ahead of Jessie and it roared like an airplane during takeoff. Did Ruth even hear what Jessie told her about Ford filming the fire front at the Adamses' property?

Her pickup's engine rumbled as the air conditioning churned. Through her windshield she could see up the Adamses' driveway to the two-story home, the wooden fence, the American flag on the porch. Dwarfing the house was a towering, flaming tsunami. Embers danced on the house roof like golden stars. She would have to be out of her mind to leave her vehicle. She should turn tail and leave Ford to his fate. He was probably the murdering bastard behind the arson attacks and now he was caught in the hellfire of his own making.

But she knew in her heart that she couldn't leave another human being, or an animal for that matter, to die if she could help it. If there was one thing Jessie had learned in her twenty-six years, it was how to fight fire. Although this one was the mother of all fires. It was traveling at unprecedented speed, blown by strong winds and heading straight for her. In a minute, maybe two, Ford would be consumed in flames. His precious phone would melt like a chocolate bar in the sun. His hair would ignite and

crackle, his skin would blister and then disintegrate, the stench
like pork crackling.

Jessie was sweating in her firefighter's protective clothing. The
vehicle's interior was already hot enough to cook her. She was
missing a glove, an oxygen tank, a face mask, a protective hard
hat. All she had was a bandana over her nose and mouth. Her
heart was racing as adrenaline coursed through her body. It was
now or never. Rescue Ford or drive away?

She accelerated up the driveway and came to a halt in the front
yard. The asphalt was already melting into black viscous pools.
Ford's Kawasaki lay on its side, crushed by a burning branch.
It was useless. She could barely see more than a few feet ahead.
Movement caught her eye on the front lawn. Ford was crouched
down into a ball. He wasn't moving. Jessie looked up at the wall
of fire that had already torched the house roof.

Damn you!

She left her pickup and the heat almost seared her skin through
her clothing. The smoke was so thick it was like breathing dirt.
Jessie retched. The crackling trees were dying around her. A
window shattered. A roof beam smashed down into the room
below. She had literally a few seconds before she and Ford would
be toast. She struggled to reach him, her gear heavy, the heat and
lack of oxygen exhausting her. Ford was spewing up his guts. In
his hand, his iPhone. The idiot boy was still filming.

He hadn't seen her. There was no point yelling, she wouldn't
be heard. She shoved his shoulder. He flinched, his head snapped
around, his face creased in terror, his cheeks wet with filthy tears.
He reached and gripped her jacket. "Help!"

"Get up!"

Jessie dragged him up. Behind him the flag was on fire, the
house interior too. She put his arm around her shoulder and
started walking. He was weak and she had to take much of his
weight. Her breathing became coughs. *Just a few more steps.* She

yanked open the passenger door. A crash like the whole mountain had collapsed made them both look around. The house had caved in like a sunken cake. The picket fence was lit up like birthday candles. They were out of time. She shoved Ford into the vehicle head first, then pushed his legs in too, slammed the door, then got in herself. He lay on his side unconscious. Jessie did the fastest three-point turn she had ever done, then smashed her foot on the gas. In the side mirror she saw Ford's motorcycle explode.

Jessie drove at breakneck speed down the mountain, only minutes ahead of the raging inferno. She passed a fire truck. She pitied the guys having to fight the impossible. Houses, forest, even the road glistened with fire. All the firefighters could hope to do was hold it back long enough for people to escape. They didn't have a hope in hell of stopping the fire front's progress unless the wind turned. As she cranked up the air conditioning, Jessie's coughing slowly subsided. She prodded Ford.

"Wake up! I've risked my life for you, you son of a bitch. Don't die on me."

Ford moaned, opened his eyes, coughing and coughing. When she reached the outskirts of town the roads were eerily empty. She drove past the gas station at a hundred miles an hour. When that blew, she didn't want to be within a mile of it. She dialed Susie.

"Ford's with me. Where are you?"

Susie hadn't left the town. Her response was euphoric. Soon Jessie skidded to a halt outside Susie's house. With her help, Jessie managed to maneuver Ford into his mom's car. Ford still gripped his phone like a talisman.

"Jessie?" Ford's voice was so rasping she could scarcely hear him. "Sorry."

Susie flung her arms around Jessie's thick fireproof jacket. "Thank you for saving my boy."

"Tell John I saved him. Tell him to stop hunting me."

"Best thing you can do is stay clear of him. He's with Victor in Denny Street. They're evacuating the old people's home. Take Rosemary Avenue instead."

Susie drove away and Jessie was all alone in a deserted street. Windows had been boarded up. Three doors down, a suitcase lay open on the front lawn, left behind in the rush to leave. There were no cars in the driveways, no kids playing, no movement at all, except for black smoke that rolled toward her. An ear-splitting boom. She covered her ears. In the distance, red and blue flames jettisoned skyward. It was a gas station exploding.

She ran to her truck. The tarpaulin across the cargo bed was riddled with burn marks and holes. She was lucky she still had tires. Her radio had lost all reception. The last she had heard, the road leaving Eagle Falls was gridlocked. Fights had broken out as people jockeyed for position. One car had plowed into a ditch and was stuck there.

Jessie took Rosemary Avenue, just as Susie suggested. She passed a few stragglers packing their cars. Jessie slowed and wound down her window and yelled out, "Leave now!" At the T-junction with Denny Street she peeked to the right. The old people's home was down that road. Through the blackened smog she could just make out the red and blue swirling lights of a sheriff's car and a confusion of red and white lights, which had to be the ambulances called in to transport the elderly residents to safety.

So Cuffy was doing his bit to save people. *About time*, she thought. If he wanted to be re-elected as sheriff next year, he needed to earn it. But Ruth's husband, Victor? Why did he stay behind? Was he super nice or did he fancy himself as a bit of a hero? Jessie had an uneasy feeling in her gut. Something just wasn't right. But what? It was something about Victor. His voice. She had heard only bits of it through the phone's static.

It sounded familiar, but how could it? Victor had left Eagle Falls when she was fifteen and she hadn't seen him since. She had *heard* him tell Ruth that Jessie had to leave their house. Nothing triggered alarm bells then, even though he was clearly upset. So why now? What was it about his voice that made her gut writhe like a jar full of worms?

"We can't get to him in time. You have to save him."

Victor had been talking about Ford. Why did that sound familiar? Or had the smoke inhalation muddled her? She shook her head and drove on. She wanted to see her dog. They would cross state lines, start a new life somewhere. She passed by her family home where her poppy had run his medical practice.

"Goodbye."

Soon the house, the clock tower, the street would be decimated. It felt to Jessie as if the last eleven years had all been about good-byes. Her dad, her mom, the friends she had lost. She thought back to when she was fifteen and in her bedroom working on a science project. It was nearing her bedtime. Poppy had been called out to an elderly patient who lived on Devil Mountain. Complaining of chest pains, the old lady wouldn't call an ambulance, unable to pay the fees. So her kindhearted father had agreed to go.

"Won't be long," Jessie heard him say to her mom. "Back within the hour."

She had been in bed when she heard a vehicle stop outside their house. Flashing lights strobed the drapes. She had peeped through a gap in them. A much slimmer John Cuffy with a fuller head of hair stepped out of the vehicle and up their path. His face was solemn. Something was wrong.

Jessie found her mom and Cuffy in their living room. They stood in the middle of the room.

"What are you taking about, John?" her mom said. "He's with Mandie Thomson."

Cuffy looked grim. "Take a seat, Cynthia. Please."

"Mom?" Jessie said from the doorway. "What's going on?"

"Come sit with me, Jessie," her mom said, as she perched on the edge of their pale blue sofa.

Jessie sat next to her mom, so close their hips touched. She shoved her hands between her knees to stop herself from nervously biting her nails.

"I'm very sorry to have to tell you…" he began, and Jessie knew then her poppy was dead.

"What?" said Cynthia, "Tell us what?"

Cuffy told them about the accident. Poppy's Jeep Cherokee had plummeted over the edge of a mountainous cliff and crashed into a ravine below. It was dark and he must have taken the infamous hairpin bend too fast. Her mother made a noise like a dog yelping. Tears began to fall, but her mom didn't say a word.

Jessie leapt up and screamed at the sheriff. "You're lying!" She pummeled Cuffy's chest, tears running down her face, until he grabbed her arms and tried to calm her. She wrenched herself free of his grip. "Poppy never drove fast. Never ever!"

Jessie ran from the room.

The next day, Jessie and her mom were asked to listen to a recording of a 911 call. A man had reported the accident but had refused to give his name or contact details. They discovered later that the call had been made from a phone booth in town, and not at the scene of the accident as the caller had pretended was the case.

"He took the bend too fast," the caller said. "He couldn't stop. It… it skidded over the edge. He's down there somewhere. I can't see a thing. I can't get to him. You have to save him. Hurry!"

Neither Jessie nor her mom recognized the 911 caller's voice.

Even though there were suspicious skid marks on the road that suggested there was a second vehicle involved, the coroner came to the conclusion that Tom Lewis's death was accidental. Jessie never forgave Cuffy for giving up. She never believed it was an accident and she suspected that the 911 caller was responsible. She had been hoping her whole life to find the 911 caller and now she finally had.

It was Victor Sullivan.

CHAPTER FIFTY-SEVEN

Jessie sat in her pickup, the engine idling, blocking the right lane of Rosemary Avenue. It didn't matter because the road was deserted. Jessie rested her chin on the steering wheel. Victor Sullivan. Ruth's husband. It couldn't be, could it? Had he caused the accident that killed Poppy? Was it Victor's voice on the 911 recording as she now believed?

All her adult life she had wanted to know what really happened that night. How had such a careful driver plummeted to his death on a hairpin bend that he knew was dangerous? What about the skid marks that were left behind by a second vehicle? Except it wasn't an *accident*. Jessie had always believed somebody caused her father's death. Now she had a chance to confront the one person who knew what happened that night: Victor.

Jessie peered down the smoke-filled street to where Victor and Cuffy were supposedly evacuating the old folks from the nursing home. If Victor died in the fire, she would never know the truth. She should confront him now. The problem was the sheriff. She doubted that Cuffy would cut her any slack because she saved his son. But the smoke was thick; it might be possible to speak to Victor without Cuffy noticing.

Jessie swiveled in her seat to look behind her at the approaching fire front. Through the dirty rear window, the road and the houses were nothing more than a smudge. She couldn't even see the mountains, just gray smog with an eerie orange glow. She knew how to calculate the speed a forest fire was traveling. A town fire was more difficult to predict because of the range of surfaces and substances, built environment and natural environment, and the varying-sized spaces between buildings. Jessie estimated that she roughly had thirty minutes before her truck and the nursing home were consumed.

Jessie turned into Denny Street and kept to twenty miles per hour. She was driving almost blind. The nursing home materialized out of the smoke as did the three stationary ambulances, their flashing lights strobing the gray air with pulses of color. But no sheriff's vehicle. The bastard had left the old people to die. Nursing staff in surgical masks raced about as old folks sat on the sidewalk in wheelchairs wearing oxygen masks. The doors of one ambulance closed and the paramedics set off, passing her truck, siren wailing.

Jessie was in her firefighter's gear, with a bandana over her nose and mouth and a baseball cap on her head. Nobody was likely to recognize her. And everyone was too busy evacuating to pay her any real attention. She counted nine people, five of whom were in wheelchairs or had walking aids. Was Victor even there? And would she recognize him after all this time? She vaguely recalled him as a friendly man in his twenties with steel-rimmed glasses, average height, brown hair, a wide smile, a little bit tubby around the waist. But that was a long time ago.

She squinted, searching for a car that might belong to a civilian, but it was hopeless. She couldn't see a thing. She would have to leave the pickup and search. She put a hand in her jacket pocket and felt the hard surface of Cuffy's Glock 17. She never wanted to shoot another human being again, but its presence in her pocket comforted her.

Nobody turned a head when she stopped her vehicle near the nursing home and got out.

Act confident, she thought.

It was easy to identify the paramedics in their white shirts with the blue badge on their sleeves. She asked a female paramedic if she knew where Victor was. She shook her head. Two men pushed a bed on wheels out of the main entrance. One man was at the bed head, the other at the foot. In the bed was the wizened form of a person with an oxygen mask over his or her face. She walked up to them and called out, "Victor?"

"Yes," said the shorter one, his back to her.

He looked around at her, saw the firefighter's gear, and kept pulling a patient's bed to an ambulance. She had to get him alone. She tugged at his sleeve. "I need your help. My mom, she's fallen. I can't get her up. Please."

"Can you handle this on your own?" Victor asked the man pushing the bed.

"Sure. You go," the other man said.

"What's up?" Victor asked, following her.

She beckoned him in the direction of her truck. His mask hid his features but he still wore glasses. His hair was now gray and receding and he was more muscular than she remembered.

"This way," she called.

"How far?" he asked, jogging to catch up. "The old folks need my help."

"Just here," she pointed ahead to a random house.

When she was sure that the ambulance crew couldn't see them, she stopped walking. "You're Victor Sullivan?"

"Yeah. Where's your mom? Show me."

"You knew Tom Lewis. He died in a car accident." He stopped dead in his tracks. "I'm Jessie Lewis."

"Jessie, what the hell are you doing? Your mom passed years ago." He shook his head. "Stop wasting my time." He turned his back on her.

"Wait! I know you were the 911 caller. Tell me what really happened to my poppy."

Victor's step faltered. A slight turn of the head. He had heard her all right. Then he continued walking away. Jessie caught up with him. She grabbed his bare arm. He ripped it from her grasp.

"Stay away from me."

"I know it was you. I recognize your voice."

"That's bullshit."

She jogged ahead of him and blocked his path. "Why didn't you come forward?"

He looked beyond her, at the outline of the nursing home in the distance, then he used the heel of his hand to shove her shoulder. It forced her back a few steps. He walked around her, muttering, "Get lost."

The more she listened to his voice, the more convinced she was. She drew the Glock from her pocket. "Stop! I've got a gun. Turn around and keep your hands where I can see them."

Victor did as she had ordered. "Are you out of your mind? I'm trying to save people's lives and you're... what? What is going on?"

Jessie's throat prickled and she could taste ash on her tongue. She swallowed back an urge to cough.

"You're not going anywhere until you tell me how my father died."

"I don't know. I wasn't there."

"Why didn't you help him? Why did you wait until you drove into town to dial 911?"

"Please, Jessie, put the gun away. Ruth likes you a lot. What will she think about this?"

"Answer my question! Why didn't you use your cell to call 911?"

He shouted. "People didn't have cells back then! You dipshit!"

"In 2007? Yeah, they did. You did. Everyone in real estate had a cell phone. Tell me the truth!"

"Truth! You wouldn't know the truth if it hit you between the eyes. Now put down that fricking gun."

"It was you, wasn't it? Those tire marks on the road. He swerved to avoid you and he couldn't stop in time. You killed him," she screamed.

The smoke caught in her throat. She choked. She closed her eyes for only a second. A sudden excruciating pain in her gun hand, like her bones had shattered. The pistol fell from her throbbing fingers. Eyes open, she realized he had kicked it from her hand. His fist collided with her jaw. It was like her brain exploded into millions of stars that were sucked into a black hole.

CHAPTER FIFTY-EIGHT

As Cuffy toured the streets in his Dodge, a tear of relief ran down his cheek. Susie had called. His son was safe. His wife was safe. They were on their way out of this blazing hell. And he had Jessie to thank for that. Who would have thought Jessie would rescue his son? Of course, it didn't excuse the arson and murder, but he had to admit that not many killers would stop to rescue the son of a sheriff. Why had she risked her life like that?

He cleared his throat. "Evacuate now! This is your final warning!" Cuffy's voice boomed out through the vehicle's loud-speaker system.

He had just driven away from a man standing on the roof of his house, the hose running, convinced he could save his property. Cuffy couldn't force him to leave. He had tried everything to persuade the stubborn fool to do so, but the guy wouldn't listen. So Cuffy drove on. Deputies Kinsley and Wang were driving around too, checking for stragglers. Samson's FBI team and state patrol were also helping out.

Cuffy had left the nursing home evacuation to the ambulance crew, the nursing staff and Victor. Then Victor had called him, asking him to get back there. Too many sick old folks and not enough transportation vehicles. As he drove onto Denny Street, his heart sank at the sight of so many people gathered on the sidewalk.

I'm not risking my life for those old coots.

He could transport four passengers out of there. It was the perfect excuse to leave town. The new boy, Kinsley, could take the rest.

He contacted Kinsley. "Get over to Rosieville Nursing Home. We need your help transporting folks."

Cuffy wasn't a religious man, although he pretended to be when it suited him. In his mind, the law was the law and that's how justice was handed out. Today was the first time in his life that he considered there might indeed be a kind of divine justice. Perhaps he, and the town, were being punished. Bad things had happened here. Their secrets had hurt others. Their fears had festered. Guilt weighed heavily. One mistake had not only cost Cuffy his peace of mind, it had ruined Bill Moran and killed Tom Lewis. Cuffy had carried that burden for eleven years. It had made him a bitter and cruel man.

Cuffy should never had fallen for the smooth-talking real estate agents, with their winning smiles and charming anecdotes. Rob Wilmot, supporter of charities, sponsor of town fundraisers, the kind of guy who you would trust with your house keys when you went on vacation. And Victor Sullivan, just twenty-seven years old back then, a popular high-flyer, already christened Young Realtor of the Year and the most eligible bachelor in town. Rob and Victor had known Cuffy was in financial trouble: nothing stayed secret in the small town. Cuffy's salary wasn't enough to buy Susie her dream house and pay for the overseas vacations she loved. Egyptian pyramids, the Taj Mahal, Paris, Vienna, England. Cuffy had bought Susie the house they lived in now with a mortgage he couldn't afford to pay. He had called in a favor from the bank and that favor got Cuffy into crippling debt. Then Rob and Victor offered Cuffy a way out of his financial problems. They had set up a new company, they said. They would loan him the money to cover his expenses and consolidate his loans. In return there would be some upfront fees and an agreement to transfer the property title to their company. Cuffy signed up for the scheme, as did Bill Moran and an elderly lady with no children, who died soon afterward.

To this day, Cuffy couldn't believe their audacity. It took some cheek to commit foreclosure fraud on a sheriff. But they knew he was a proud man and he would keep his mistake a secret. They also knew Cuffy only held on to his position of sheriff because Rob's real estate firm donated thousands of dollars to his election campaign. When Cuffy realized what he had signed up for, and his house was no longer his, he had confronted the pair. They calmly offered to return the ownership of the house to him if he paid them ten thousand dollars cash. Cuffy would still have his debts but they would ensure that he was re-elected as sheriff. In return Cuffy had to keep quiet about their scheme. They had him dangling on the end of a metaphorical leash and there was nothing he could do about it. He had agreed.

So he had watched Bill Moran lose his house, his firm, and his family, and he did nothing to help the poor guy. Five years later, Victor moved to Seattle. It was 2007 and Tom Lewis had died in a car accident. Although it wasn't an accident. To his eternal shame, Cuffy had always known that Tom's death was murder.

Cuffy drove past a pickup piled high with stuff, a tarpaulin over the top. He couldn't see the registration plate but it looked like Jessie's old Ford Ranger. What in God's name would she be doing here? The smoke was as thick as the foul-tasting pea and ham soup his grandma used to make. Even with headlights on high beam, he could see no more than a few feet ahead. His AC was on full bore but the smoke got in somehow and his throat burned. He came to a halt outside the nursing home, the lights on the top of his vehicle flashing red and blue. He peered out through the windshield, reluctant to get out of his car. Where was Victor's car?

Damn that man. Victor would be the death of him.

Sighing, Cuffy put on a face mask and was about the open the car door when an uneasy feeling in his chest caused him to pause.

Had Jessie worked it out? Did she know who murdered her father?

Tom was a clever man and a good friend of Bill's. Tom had painstakingly accumulated enough evidence to prove that Rob and Victor were behind the foreclosure fraud that had destroyed Bill's life. Of course, Tom had no idea that Cuffy had been caught in the same trap as Bill. The day before he died, Tom showed his evidence to Cuffy. Tom had threatened to take it to the governor if Cuffy didn't arrest Rob and Victor.

Cuffy would never forgive himself for what he did next. He contacted Victor and Rob. Warned them about Tom's evidence. The next day, Tom had his tragic accident. Victor claimed he had done it for them. Without Tom, Victor argued, Bill would shut up and Cuffy could rest easy. Victor had engineered the whole situation. Mandie Thomson hadn't needed a doctor that night. Victor had imitated the old woman's raspy, twenty-a-day smoker's voice. All Victor needed was an excuse to ensure Tom took the dangerous mountain road in the dark. He had then rammed Tom's vehicle over the cliff.

Cuffy left his Dodge and asked a nurse where Victor was. She didn't know.

"I can take three in the back and one in the front. Load them up and I'll be back in five."

Cuffy left the engine running and the door unlocked, and he went to inspect the pickup. It was Jessie's but she and her dog were nowhere in sight. His gut squirmed. He had a bad feeling about this. Where had Victor parked that fancy car of his? He heard the *thunk* of a car door slamming. Cuffy followed the sound. A sleek black car seemed to materialize from the smoke. Victor had a rear door wide open, and he looked to be hefting a heavy object onto the seat.

Cuffy called to him.

Victor's back straightened. "John, thank the Lord it's you. Help me get Jessie in the car."

Cuffy was near enough to see Jessie, unconscious, head slumped forward, a bruise on her face. "She knows about Tom. I have to get rid of her."

No more killing, Cuffy thought. *It stops now.*

"It doesn't matter what she thinks," Cuffy said, clearing his throat to suppress a cough. "Nobody will"—cough—"believe her. Let her be."

"It's my voice on the 911 recording. She fucking knows it was me."

Cuffy shook his head. "I'm not doing this anymore, Victor."

A searing pain in his stomach and Cuffy dropped to his knees.

Cuffy was cold. He lay in the street, a hand clutching the bullet wound to his stomach. His eyes fluttered open. Taillights, like angry red eyes. The vroom of an engine. The car vanished. Victor was gone. The pain in his stomach was like fire. The acid was eating his innards. He didn't have long. He dragged his phone from his pocket and dialed Kinsley.

"Victor shot me. He… has Jessie. She… knows." He coughed up blood. "Tell Susie I…"

He dopped the phone. He couldn't feel his fingers or his legs. He was so very cold. There was no stopping the sleep that took him.

CHAPTER FIFTY-NINE

Ruth sat in Kelly's kitchen staring blankly at the cookie in her hand, wondering what other secrets her husband had kept from her. David and Noah were in the living room watching TV. Kelly talked incessantly as she flittered from the countertop to the fridge and back again, fussing over everything and nothing at all.

"I don't understand. Why didn't he come with you?" Ruth didn't know. "Ruth, hello?" Ruth looked up. "I said why didn't Victor leave with you?" She had her hands on both hips.

"He was helping with the evacuation."

"My brother's too nice. Always has been." Kelly shook her head. "Call him, will you?"

She dialed and it went to voicemail. "Victor, where are you? Call me. We want to know you're okay." In the background, Kelly cleared her throat and pointed at herself. Ruth got the message. "Kelly's worried. I'm worried. Just let us know you're okay."

Before Ruth had even ended the call, Kelly urged her to call the sheriff. "He'll know where he is."

Cuffy was the last person she wanted to talk to, but Kelly had a point. Ruth would give it ten more minutes, and if she hadn't heard anything from Victor by then, she would contact Cuffy.

Kelly stared into the freezer compartment. "I have burgers and ice cream." Then she opened the fridge door. "I have cheese, onion, lettuce. No bread rolls. I'll go and get some. And Victor's favorite chili sauce. There's a store around the corner."

Ruth zoned out again. She was terrified that Victor might not escape Eagle Falls alive. She was also upset that he had tried to sabotage her application to join the FBI. Why had he encouraged her to apply if he hadn't wanted her to do it?

"Ruth?" She looked up. "I asked if you wanted me to get you anything while I'm out."

"I'm good, thanks."

Kelly picked up her wallet from the hall table and left the house. It was a relief to have the place to themselves.

"Where's Daddy?" David asked, wandering into the kitchen with a dejected slouch.

"He won't be long, honey."

Ruth's phone rang. It was Deputy Kinsley. *Why would he call me?*

"I just need to take this," she told David and then she ducked into the guestroom.

"Ruth Sullivan?" Kinsley asked.

Ruth shut the door. "Yes?"

"Deputy Kinsley," he said. "Where are you?"

"With my sister-in-law in Marymere."

"Thirty-four Stone Avenue North?"

"Yes." Why did a deputy want to know where she was?

"Is Victor with you?" Kinsley's voice sounded muffled, yet loud. Was he shouting through a mask?

"No, why?"

A pause. Just a second or two. But long enough for Ruth to feel as if the floor had disappeared beneath her feet.

"He left the nursing home suddenly. Has he contacted you?" Kinsley asked.

In the background, a wailing siren. An ambulance, Ruth guessed. "What's wrong?"

He sidestepped the question. "If he calls you, phone me immediately. Is that understood?"

Kinsley's abrupt tone set her teeth on edge. "What aren't you telling me?" Another pause. "Whatever it is you don't want to tell me, I suggest you spit it out."

"The sheriff is dead," Kinsley said.

"Oh my God! How?"

"Shot."

"Shot! Who by?" Ruth's mind raced. Who in their right mind would shoot a sheriff? Surely not Jessie. Was it the arsonist?

A pause. "Your husband."

Ruth snorted derisively. "I'm in no mood for jokes."

"They were the last words the sheriff spoke. He clearly said that Victor shot him."

"It's a mistake. He would never do that." Her voice went up a pitch. "Why would he? He revered Cuffy."

"Ruth, I need you to listen to me, okay? I have put out an APB for Victor's arrest. Marymere deputies are on their way to your address."

Ruth sat heavily on the bed. "I… I don't understand. You can't… you can't do this."

"We believe he has taken Jessie Lewis hostage."

"That's ridiculous," Ruth snapped. "What would Jessie be doing in town?"

"The sheriff said Jessie knew something. Perhaps he meant about Victor. Do you have any idea what he meant?"

"No. Look, leave my husband out of this! He's risked his life to evacuate the town. Just… leave him alone!" Ruth knew she sounded hysterical, but she couldn't keep her emotions reined in.

"If you speak to Victor," Kinsley said, "tell him to hand himself in. You got that?"

Ruth was left staring at a blank phone screen. She wanted to scream. Scream until the walls fell down. How could Kinsley even think that Victor shot a sheriff! Had the world gone totally mad? Victor didn't even have a gun. He was her loving husband. A great dad. He made people laugh. He wouldn't hurt a soul. Ruth knew how a criminal mind worked and Victor just didn't work that way. If anything, he was too easygoing, as Kelly kept reminding her.

Ruth dialed Victor's number. It went to voicemail. "My darling, where are you? Please, please call me. I have to know you're all right. Cuffy is dead. Call me."

She heard a key in the apartment door. "I'm back!" Kelly called out.

Ruth made a split-second decision. She had hidden her Smith & Wesson and its holster high up in the walk-in closet. She now put the holster around her waist and pocketed a box of ammunition. In the kitchen, she filled a water bottle.

"Lordy!" Kelly exclaimed, staring at the pistol on her hip. "Where are you going with that?"

"Can you look after the kids for a few hours?" Before Kelly could respond, she continued, "Does Finn have any cable ties?"

"Maybe, try the garden shed. What for?"

"Mommy, where are you going?" Noah asked, following her into the backyard.

"I'm going to collect Daddy. You stay here with Auntie Kelly. I won't be long."

"Why have you got a gun?"

Ruth pulled open the shed door. A lawn mower and various items of gardening equipment filled most of the floor space. Shelves covered one wall and on one of those shelves was a bag of cable ties. She reasoned that whoever was behind the disappearance of her husband and Jessie might need restraining.

"Don't go, Mommy," Noah begged.

Ruth knelt down and gave him a hug. "I won't be long. I'm going to collect Daddy from Eagle Falls and bring him here. It'll be okay, I promise."

Back in the kitchen, Kelly put a bag of burger buns and a bottle of chili sauce on the counter.

"Has something happened?" Kelly said, sounding worried. "Is Victor hurt?"

"He's fine. Kelly, I need you to listen to me carefully," Ruth said firmly. "Two deputies will be here very soon. They're going to wait for Victor."

Kelly's jaw dropped. "Deputies? Here? Why?"

"I don't have time to explain. I'm taking a couple of your bathroom towels. I'll buy you new ones."

Kelly protested, but Ruth wasn't listening. She took two towels, soaked them, and carried them in a plastic laundry basket. She gave each of her sons a hug and a kiss and left the apartment with Kelly still complaining.

The freeway heading for Eagle Falls was totally clear, save for a fire engine and an emergency response truck that overtook her. The lanes leaving the town were still packed with vehicles. Ruth resolved that whatever it took to find Victor, she would do it. She wanted to find him before Kinsley did. But her resolution wavered the closer she got to the conflagration. A few damp towels and a bandana wouldn't save her from a towering inferno.

CHAPTER SIXTY

Jessie woke to the sound of roaring, as if she were near a railroad track and a train was hurtling toward her. She lay on a rough, rocky surface. Her shirt was wet and clung to her skin. She couldn't breathe through her nose. She tried to open her eyes. One lid wouldn't budge at all. The other peeled open a fraction and sent a shooting pain through every nerve in her face. What had happened?

She was in a dark, damp place. Above her the high ceiling was wet and slimy, and cold water dripped onto her skin. It smelled of moist earth and rotting foliage. She blinked her one open eye to clear her vision. The walls were jagged rock covered in moss and sprouting green plants. What was that thundering sound? She moved her head to the left and the pain caused bile to shoot up her throat. She rolled onto her side and in so doing she realized that her right hand throbbed. Her firefighter's jacket was on the floor, far enough away that she couldn't grab it. How had she removed the jacket if she was unconscious? Nothing made sense.

Now she could see shimmering sheets of water that seemed to go on forever. The water fell past the rocky outcrop she lay on and kept falling. Jessie knew where she was. Her poppy's favorite place: inside the cave behind the waterfall. The drop from top to bottom was one hundred and eighty feet. About thirty feet above the rock pool, a cave had formed through centuries of erosion.

Jessie was in that cave and she had no idea how she had gotten there. The deafening roar was not just due to the millions of tons of water tumbling over the cliff edge. It was the way it pounded the rock pool below, churning stones and smashing granite. She tried to sit up, but the movement sent a zing of pain through her neck and into her skull. She lay back down.

"So you're awake," he said. The voice reverberated in the semi-enclosed space.

She remembered the thick smoke, the nursing home, and confronting Victor. The bastard had punched her in the face.

A shadow passed above her. Victor stood at her feet. Only when Jessie struggled to crawl away from him did she realize that her feet were bound.

"I'm sorry, Jessie, you know too much."

He picked up her legs by the rope that bound her ankles. The rope was thick, the kind you would use to hang a swing for a kid. Jessie kicked out, but his grip on the rope held. He began to drag her across the bumpy surface. Something weighty scraped the rock and tugged at her ankles. She bent at the waist and saw a rectangular piece of stone the size of a shoebox that had been wrapped in rope and tied to her ankles. The stone would hold her under the water even if she succeeded in beating the down-pull of the currents. Panic hit her and she found it hard to catch enough breath. He was going to throw her into the bubbling, swirling rock pool some thirty feet below. It meant certain death. Over time the softer rock at the base of the waterfall had eroded, creating an overhang at surface level. The pool's currents would drag her underwater and jamb her beneath the overhang. Once she was in there, the currents would never let her out.

"I don't know anything!" Jessie screamed, despite the agony of opening her bruised jaw.

Jessie kicked and writhed but the weight around her ankles had to be forty pounds or more. Each time she kicked, the weight restricted her movement. And Victor was strong. He clung fast to the rope.

"I can't have you telling tales," Victor said. "I've got my family to protect."

She tried to dig her fingers into the rock beneath her. Fingernails tore away, but she couldn't get a grip. With each step, he dragged her closer to the edge. The hem of her shirt snagged on a sharp piece of bedrock. She used the pause to try to find a handhold.

"How could you leave my dad to die?" Jessie yelled. *Keep him talking. Distract him.*

"He'd gone to Cuffy with evidence that Rob and I were behind the scam. Your dad was persistent. He just wouldn't stop meddling. He gave me no choice."

She kicked out in violent jerks. She wanted to destroy him. "You rammed him off the road, didn't you? You murdered him!"

Victor struggled to free Jessie's snagged shirt from the jagged bedrock. There was a ripping sound and she slid forward. "You're just like your dad. You don't take the hint."

"You killed my dad and you ruined Bill's life."

"Boohoo," Victor mocked.

The surface beneath her began to slope downward. Falling water hit her face like wasp stings. She coughed and spluttered as the water entered her nose and mouth. *I don't want to die!* She writhed like a snake and when that didn't work she used her stomach muscles to sit up and clawed at Victor's hands. She drew blood.

"Bitch!"

His boot collided with her ribs. She yelped and fell back.

Victor tugged her closer to the waterfall. Jessie screamed and choked and coughed, as water went down her throat. The force of the water was dragging her over the edge. Victor dropped her legs. In desperation, Jessie sat up and wrapped her arms around his knees. *If I go, you go!* With lightning speed, he pulled from his belt Cuffy's Glock 17 and shoved the barrel against her forehead.

"Let go of my legs!" Victor said.

She clung on tighter. It was one thing ramming a car off the road. It was a whole other thing to blow her brains out. Did Victor have the guts to do it?

The sudden blow caused her to let go and slump sideways. He had pistol-whipped her already battered face. She saw glittering lights. The cave tilted from side to side like a seesaw.

He walked around her so that he faced out to the waterfall, then he knelt and shoved her to the edge. The cascading water felt like blows to her body. She turned her head and tried to bite his forearm, but he saw what she was about to do. He reeled back so he was out of reach and then with one final shove she tumbled off the ledge.

CHAPTER SIXTY-ONE

Jessie slammed into the surface of the rock pool and all the air was ripped from her lungs. Water filled her mouth and nose. The churning water swallowed her. Every part of her body was battered, as if she had been hurled into a wall. But she was alive. The water tension had been first broken by the heavy rock roped to her bound ankles. Reeling from the whole-body pain, it took her a few precious seconds to work out which way was up and which was down. She was in a washing machine of swirling white foam. The rock dragged her down and she had to fight it.

Jessie clawed at the bubbling, writhing water. She was a strong swimmer but the forty pounds of rock she carried was too much. She had to free herself of it. The deeper she went, the less turbulent it became. She curled into a ball and tried to find the knot holding the rope in place. Her vision was blurred but she felt the raised ropey surface and picked at it desperately. A fingernail tore away and there was a brief moment of pink as her nailbed bled. Down she went, panic freezing her mind. She needed oxygen. She longed to open her mouth and inhale. That would kill her. She willed her lungs to wait. The knot! It was saturated and swollen, but she kept picking at it. A part of it came loose. She pulled it free and the rest of the knot unraveled. With a jerk, the rock fell away and the rope unwound. Down, down it drifted into the pebbly blackness. She was lighter now and her descent slowed. Her ankles were still tied together but she had her arms free and she could wiggle her legs like a dolphin's tail. She had a fighting chance.

Jessie looked up at the light penetrating the churning water. Any moment now an impulse to take a breath would suck water into her lungs. *No, don't inhale. Wait!* She swam. But the light wasn't getting closer. Her body was getting sucked sideways. She looked in the direction she was being dragged. A black hole: a dark cave beneath the overhang. *Dear God! No!* Last summer, two backpackers had foolishly swum under the waterfall and had been sucked under the overhang. An emergency dive team found their bodies wedged under the rocks.

I won't die. I won't!

Instead of fighting the tumultuous currents, she took a gamble and allowed her exhausted body to be sucked into the underwater cave. It was like she was on an invisible conveyor belt. She watched carefully as the cave drew ever closer. She saw the overhang and she reached out for a handhold. It was slippery, and she missed her grip. She fought the current and this time she managed to hold on to the ledge. Dizzy with lack of oxygen, she bent her knees and felt for a foothold. She found one, and with all her muscles straining, she started to climb. Her head popped through white, bubbling water. She sucked in the smoke-filled air. It was the sweetest breath she had ever taken. With one final effort she clawed her way onto the ledge overhanging the pool and collapsed onto the slippery surface. She gasped and spluttered, retching up water.

When she had coughed up the water in her lungs, she lay still, too weak to move a muscle. Sleep whispered to her and she closed her eyes. But her trials were not over. The mountain was on fire. The town was on fire. And she had no vehicle. Her safest bet was to use the waterfall like a shield and wait out the fire, and that meant returning to the cave that Victor had thrown her out of. The ledge she was on was too exposed. Jessie sluggishly sat up and through her one good eye she looked around. The ledge was no more than a few feet deep. Smoke crept behind the waterfall like a ghost seeking her out. It wasn't deep enough to protect her from flames. Yet Victor would kill her if she went back to the cave.

Sleep beckoned to her once more. Just a little nap, then she could think clearer. Then she thought she heard Poppy whisper to her. *Save yourself!* he said. A rush of fury hit her and with it came adrenaline. Victor murdered her poppy, the kindest, loveliest man in the world. He had tried to help Bill and had died because of it. She couldn't let Victor get away with it.

Jessie tore at the remaining rope that held her ankles together. Once she was free of it, she emptied each sneaker of water, then put them back on. Then she stood on shaky legs.

"I'm going to live," Jessie said through clenched teeth. She thought of Victor. "You're going to pay for what you did."

CHAPTER SIXTY-TWO

Jessie dragged herself onto all fours and crawled across the narrow ledge, ever mindful of the waterfall to her right. Beyond the ledge, water pounded and roared as it cascaded into the rock pool below. The closer she got to the trail, where steps led up to the top of the waterfall or down to the lower-level parking lot, the smokier the air became. And hotter.

Once she stood on the trail steps, she leaned against the handrail to catch her breath. She felt the wind on her damp skin. A hot charred wind that smelled of death. As her body warmed up, the agony of her bruises became acute. It was like she was thawing out and her nerves were working again. She raised a hand tentatively to her beaten face. At least the cold water had reduced some of the swelling around her left eye.

She looked up the mountain. High above her and to the right, the mountain was ablaze. Black smoke belched into the sky as if Devil Mountain were an erupting volcano. Jets of yellow flames shot skyward, dwarfing the fir trees. Then she looked in the opposite direction. In the valley, the smoke was too thick to see the town clearly but from the bursts of orange, she knew that the town was ablaze. Because of the wind direction, the waterfall and its forest to the left were so far unscathed. But for how long? If the wind shifted, it would come straight at her. She must hurry.

Jessie was about the start climbing the steps when she thought she heard a car engine rev. Victor was getting away!

"Oh no you don't!"

As fast as her wobbly legs would allow her, she took the steps down to the parking lot. It was empty, except for one car: a black Ford Mustang. She couldn't make out if Victor was in it and she couldn't hear the engine rumbling. Had she been mistaken? Acutely aware that she had nothing to defend herself with, she stumbled over to the car. There was a smear of blood on the passenger window. Her blood no doubt. The car was empty. She tried the door handle. She hadn't expected it to open, but it did. No keys in the ignition. For a fraction of a second she considered trying to fuse the ignition wires and drive away. But flashy cars like this had all kinds of antitheft tricks and, besides, how would that solve anything? She had to make Victor accountable for what he did to Poppy and Bill.

Victor had Cuffy's Glock 17 and Jessie had no weapon. There had to be something in this car that she could use to defend herself… the jack kit! She opened the trunk. It was empty and perfectly clean. There was a netted section to one side that contained a chamois, window cleaner, and a can of something. Then she lifted up the trunk's carpet and found the jack kit on top of the spare tire, along with a plastic bag of wooden pegs. All she wanted was the lug nut wrench, an L-shaped bar. She threw the peg bag to one side. The wrench was thick and heavy and if used right, it could break a limb. She took it and shut the trunk. She saw her reflection in the shiny black paintwork and winced. Her face was a mess.

Then she stopped dead. A memory of a black speeding car. The driver firing at her. If she hadn't pulled into the Chevron gas station, he might have killed her. Jessie walked around the sleek car inspecting it.

It couldn't be, could it? Was this the car that chased her?

Her head was spinning. She moved farther away so she could look at it from a distance, just as she had done when the driver cruised past the gas station.

The Mustang was black, sleek, and fast, just like the vehicle that pursued her.

It had the same tinted windows.

Another memory exploded in her head. She threw open the trunk and picked up the transparent bag of what she had thought were pegs. She opened it and took out a tiny wooden wedge, like a mini doorstop. Just like the one she had found at the Wilmot fire scene. Her eyes were then drawn to the yellow and red can in the netted pocket. She pulled it out. It was lighter fluid. Who drives around with lighter fluid in their car?

Jessie dropped the can in the trunk as if it had burned her fingers. She staggered back.

Victor was Rob's partner in the scam.

Victor killed her father.

Victor was also… dear God!

He was the serial arsonist. He had left her property just as her cabin burned. He'd fired a gun at her. And who else drives around with a packet of tiny wooden wedges, just the right size to jam windows shut? But why? Why would he do that? Did Ruth know? Was she as bad as Cuffy, prepared to cover for a killer? Was that why Ruth laid a trap for her? Was her hand of friendship all just a big charade to make sure that Jessie was convicted of murder?

Jessie left the bag of wedges where she had found them in the trunk. A dark fury rose inside her. She had been played, and Victor was at the center of all her pain. She resolved to make him tell her the truth, whatever it took. Her hand gripped the lug nut wrench so tightly her finger joints clicked. Jessie had one tiny advantage: he thought that she was dead.

She set off up the steps to the cave. The smoky air would hopefully conceal her arrival and the roar of the waterfall would dull any noise she might make. She had to sneak up on him and get close enough to disarm him before he knew that she was alive. The steps were steep and quickly drained her newfound burst of energy. A bald eagle soared overhead, its call mournful. On a rocky outcrop, a marmot sat up on its hind legs and let rip with a high-pitched wail, then dashed into the undergrowth. A squirrel skittered across her path, its tail flicking anxiously. It knocked over a beetle onto its back. Jessie bent down and flipped it over. It scuttled away.

Only thirteen steps to go.

CHAPTER SIXTY-THREE

Ruth was flagged down by Deputy Wang as she took the slip road into Eagle Falls. Hers was the only vehicle heading into the town. She wound down her window and Wang leaned in, a deep frown on his young face. The white mask over his nose and mouth was speckled with ash, as was his hair and uniform.

"Mrs. Sullivan, you can't go this way. The town's been evacuated."

His eyes were red and sore. His voice was raspy.

"I forgot something," she lied. "I have to go back."

He looked at her as if she were out of her mind, and maybe she was. After all, she was driving into an inferno. Wang stepped away from the car and his hand moved to his gun holster. "Are you meeting your husband?"

The dying sheriff had accused Victor of shooting him. They were wrong. They had to be. Ruth was going to prove it. And she was going to find Jessie.

"No."

Had it come to this? She was lying to a deputy. She wanted to help a fugitive. Two fugitives. Was she now the bad guy?

"I'm sorry, Mrs. Sullivan, you can't enter the town. Get back on the highway and get out of here."

"I just need five minutes. That's all. Please."

Wang craned his neck and touched a button on the two-way radio attached to his lapel. "Kinsley?" Wang was calling in backup. He was rightfully suspicious of her motives.

Ruth stamped her foot on the gas and sped away. She had never run from law enforcement before. Then again, she had never had someone she loved wanted for murder. In the rear-view mirror she saw Wang lift the radio to his mouth and speak. Ruth was banking on the evacuation effort taking precedent over tracking her down. It would buy her time.

Ruth sped along the empty lake road. Eagle Falls was a ghost town. Smoke. Fire. No people. Even with the car windows shut and the air conditioning on, she could feel the singeing heat creep through the gaps in the car's bodywork. She played some soothing classical music with the volume up high. She didn't want to hear the silence of a dead town. Her shirt was glued to her back and her hands on the steering wheel trembled. She turned right, away from the lake and up a hill. In a few hundred yards she would arrive at the falls' parking lot. Victor had taken her and the kids to see the magnificent waterfall the day after they arrived in town. He was so proud of its beauty and he took great delight in pointing out the cave where he and his buddies had played as kids. He had been upset by the fencing and the warning notices that blocked entry to the cave.

"What a shame," Victor had said. "It's incredible in there. And if there's ever a fire, that cave is the safest place to be. The water keeps the air clean and the fire out. Come to think of it, you could probably survive the apocalypse in there. Not that we're going to need to."

David had then asked, "What's a poc-lips, Daddy?"

"Just another word for when something big and bad happens," Victor said. "Once I stayed the night in there with a buddy. I must have been ten. It was a great adventure. The trouble was that we forgot to tell our parents and they were very worried. They called the police and they sent out a search party to look for us. We had no idea about the worry we'd caused. The next morning, we left the cave and walked home. I was grounded for a month after that."

Ruth smiled at the memory as she drove into the parking lot. She hoped that her guess about Victor's whereabouts was right. Otherwise, where else would he go? Her heart lifted when she saw Victor's car parked close to the falls trail. She came to a halt next to it and left the engine running. The mountainside was on fire. Embers floated in the air and landed on the hood of her car.

All she had to do was follow the trail to the cave, find Victor and Jessie, and sort out whatever misunderstanding had happened between them. Her hand lingered over the internal door handle, but she couldn't open the door. And her feet wouldn't move. Her throat was closing over. The more she tried to breathe normally, the less air reached her lungs. It was like her airways had shrunk. She fumbled for her inhaler and once she had it between her lips, she pressed the button and inhaled sharply, waiting for its contents to make breathing easier. Gradually her breathing relaxed and she sipped some water.

Ruth checked that her Smith & Wesson M&P semiautomatic was fully loaded and holstered it. The gun was for her protection. It was also her exit strategy. She would rather kill herself with a bullet than burn to death in a forest inferno. The pain she had experienced when the bomb detonated was something she never wanted to feel again.

"You're wasting time," Ruth told herself.

She grabbed a damp towel from the laundry basket in the footwell and draped it around her shoulders. She would put it over her head if the fire got too close. Finally, she tucked the bag of cable ties in a back pocket and tied a bandana tightly over her nose and mouth. The feeling of the fabric encasing her airways made her claustrophobic. Her body prickled with anxiety.

Ruth stepped out of the car.

*

Jessie had reached the cave's entrance. It was blocked by a wire-mesh fence, fixed into position with bolts. However, somebody had used wire cutters and then peeled the mesh back so there was a space large enough for an adult to crawl through. Jessie ducked low and squeezed through the gap.

As soon as she was inside the dank cave, the smoke receded. Jessie crawled behind a boulder near the entrance and waited for her eyes to adjust to the darkness. In her right hand was the lug nut wrench. There was no sign of Victor, but the very depths of the cave were as black as night. Behind her, she heard a chitter. Then a splash. She saw a raccoon's glistening round eyes. The creature had followed her, no doubt desperate to flee the wildfire. It limped across the cave floor and started to lap water from a shallow pool. A shot rang out. She winced at its deafening sound, amplified by the cave's echo. The raccoon twitched, then lay still. Victor had shot it.

Jessie cowered behind the boulder. She heard the splash of shoes in puddles.

"Damn it!" Victor said, his shadow moving past her hiding place.

She peeked out. Victor stood over the dead raccoon. He raised his pistol and aimed at the cave's entrance.

"Who's there?" he shouted.

All Jessie had to do was sneak up behind Victor and clobber him with the metal wrench, then tie him up. After that, her plan was a little hazy. Perhaps she could record a confession on Victor's phone?

Jessie crept toward Victor, her heart in her mouth, each step gently placed so as not to alert the killer to her presence. She raised the wrench. Two more steps, then she whacked his right shoulder with the bar, intending to break his clavicle and incapacitate him. It was the same injury that Marcus inflicted on Bill. Victor yelped and the Glock fell from his fingers. He swung around to face her.

"You! Why won't you fucking die!"

Between them lay the pistol. Jessie dove for it. And so did Victor. Jessie got there first. She dropped the wrench then scooped the gun out of a puddle and aimed it at Victor.

"You murdered all those people!" she screamed. "And now you're going to pay."

"Jessie! Don't!" shouted a woman from the cave entrance.

CHAPTER SIXTY-FOUR

The darkness of the cave's interior made it difficult for Ruth to see the two figures clearly. But there was no mistaking Jessie's voice or that she had a gun pointing at her unarmed husband. Ruth's heart lurched. Victor had his back to Ruth. She was taken aback by his words. "Why won't you fucking die?" he had yelled. Nothing made sense. Victor was wanted for Cuffy's murder. Jessie was wanted for arson and murder. Who was innocent and who was guilty? Ruth didn't want to believe that either of them had committed the crimes of which they had been accused.

Ruth was trained to diffuse situations like this, but her love for Victor and her compassion for Jessie were making her indecisive. On top of that, the fire raging outside was a terrifying distraction and the smoky air hampered her breathing. *I have to do this*, she thought. *Calm and disarm.* Two guns, three people, and her unarmed husband in the middle. She had to think like an FBI agent, not as a wife or friend.

"Jessie, it's me, Ruth," she said. She felt a cough building in her lungs. She swallowed to suppress it. "I'm here to help you. Please, put down the gun." Jessie leaned to the left, trying to see Ruth around Victor whose position blocked her view. "I'm going to take one step to my right so we can see each other. Is that okay?"

"Ruth? Is that really you?" There was a lift in her voice. She sounded relieved.

Of course, the bandana covered most of Ruth's face, which made it hard for Jessie to identify her.

"Yes, it's me. I need to get away from the smoky entrance, then I'll lower my bandana," Ruth said. "Can I come closer?"

Ruth was unable to suppress the urge to cough and it racked her body.

"Yes, but keep away from Victor," Jessie said.

Ruth stepped forward and around Victor, her pistol out in front of her. She now had a clear line of sight to Jessie and was parallel to her husband. Jessie's skin appeared a silvery color, striated by the light penetrating the tumbling water. The young woman had a black and puffy eye, and her jaw was swollen and bruised. Someone had punched her in the face.

"I'm going to lower the bandana."

As if in slow motion, Ruth tugged the cotton cloth down. The air inside the cave was cool and less smoky and she breathed more easily.

"He tried to kill me." Jessie sounded desperate. "He threw me over the ledge. Had me weighted down with a rock. You've got to help me!"

"Ruthie, listen to me!" Victor said, his voice tremulous. "She's deranged. She forced me here at gunpoint."

"Liar!" Jessie snapped. "Don't believe him! He killed my poppy. He scammed Bill. He's bad, Ruth. I'm sorry. Victor's a bad man."

Her husband wasn't a bad man. He was a good man. He loved her. He loved their kids. He had been the rock she clung to after the bomb blast. Okay, so he had tried to sabotage her application to Quantico, but that was forgivable. Why was Jessie saying these terrible things?

"Jessie, whatever it is you think Victor has done, we can work it out. But not here and not when you're threatening him with a gun," Ruth said. "Lower your weapon, Jessie."

"No way," Jessie said, the Glock 17 twitching in her hand. "Don't you get it? He forced Poppy's car off the road because Poppy knew that he was behind the foreclosure fraud."

Ruth knew that Jessie's father died in a car accident. She also knew that Bill was the victim of foreclosure fraud. There was no way that Victor was involved in any of it.

"Look at me, Ruthie," Victor pleaded. Ruth turned her attention to him for a moment. "She's raving mad. I have no idea what she's talking about. Shoot her, Ruthie. Before she kills me."

"Ruth!" Jessie said. "My face! The bruises. He punched me. Knocked me out. Look at my clothes. I'm saturated. He weighted down my legs with a rock. My ankles. See the rope marks. He tried to drown me."

Ruth looked down. There were red welts around her ankles. And Jessie's clothes were wet. *No, there had to be another explanation.* Victor wasn't a killer. Ruth's top priority was to stop Jessie from shooting her husband. If she could do that, they might all get out of there alive.

"Jessie, we don't have much time," Ruth said, keeping her tone reasonable. "All it takes is a change in wind direction and this part of the mountain becomes an inferno. We have to leave. Now. Calmly. And you have to give me your gun."

"We can survive the fire in here," Jessie said with authority. "Douse ourselves in water. Cover our mouths. Stay at the back of the cave. We're more likely to die in a car."

Victor gave Jessie a sympathetic tilt of the head. "Jessie, please let me go." His voice was as smooth as silk. "I get that it's been hard for you, losing your mom and dad and then all that nasty business with Marcus. But you're wrong about me. I'm not your enemy. And we can't stay here. Ruthie suffers from breathing problems. Please, Jessie, give your gun to Ruth."

Jessie shook her head. "You're unbelievable. That Mr. Nice Guy act won't work anymore. You're a manipulative liar and a killer and, so help me God, you are going to pay."

"Jessie, please calm down," Ruth said. *Victor is a nice guy. He always has been*, she thought. *Maybe Jessie really is unhinged.*

Victor jerked his head around and glared at his wife. "Do something, will you!"

"Victor, please!"

"He's the arsonist, Ruth!" Jessie yelled. "He killed Paul and his family, Rob and Pat, then he tried to kill me. Victor burned your house down. Not me. He's sick in the head."

Ruth's mind was racing. Jessie's accusations were getting wilder by the second. Was Jessie seriously accusing Victor of serial murder, of putting his family in danger? He would never harm his family. He would never harm anyone.

"Jessie, what are you saying?" Ruth asked.

Jessie looked at her as if she had two heads. "How can you live with a serial killer and not know? Or did you know?"

No, Ruth thought. *Jessie has it all wrong. Victor saved me and the kids from the fire. And yet… Victor swore he saw Jessie running from the scene. Was it possible that Victor had lied because Cuffy wanted him to?*

"We can talk about this when we're somewhere safe," Ruth said. "Right now, my number one priority is to get us all out of here alive."

"She's insane." Victor's voice had grown more strident. "Come on, Ruth, you know me. I wouldn't hurt a fly. I'm the stay-at-home dad. I go to mothers' groups. I help people. I don't hurt them. She forced me here at gunpoint. It's all in her crazy mixed-up head. I had nothing to do with her father's death. It was an accident. I wasn't even there."

"You confessed," Jessie shrieked. "You said Poppy could prove that you and Rob were the scammers. Poppy took it to the sheriff and the sheriff warned you. That's why you killed him. You told me!"

Victor shook his head. "Call Cuffy," he said to Ruth. "Ask him. This is all bullshit."

"I can't ask him," Ruth said. "He's dead."

Jessie gasped and her hand holding the Glock sagged. She looked genuinely shocked. "How?"

Ruth glanced at Victor's side profile. His reaction was delayed. Deadpan, then a look of surprise, as if his reaction was… what exactly? A word popped into her head, but she rejected it almost immediately. That word was *calculated*. "All I know is that he was shot." She paused, eyeing the Glock in Jessie's hands. "Is that Cuffy's pistol?"

"I… don't know. I wrestled it from Victor." She jerked her chin at Victor.

"Jesus, Ruthie. You're not believing any of this bullshit, are you? Seriously, this has to stop. Shoot her and be done with it."

"No, no, no!" Jessie cried, straightening her arm and aiming at Victor's chest. "Ruth, I have the 911 recording from the night Poppy died. Listen to the voice. It's Victor. He never came forward. Why, Ruth, why would he do that?"

"If you fell into the pool as you claim," Ruth said, "your phone won't work."

Victor bellowed at his wife, "Shoot her!"

Ruth was jolted by the forcefulness of Victor's voice. *Stay focused*, she told herself. "Let me handle this, Victor."

"Oh, right, yes, I forgot, you always have to be in charge."

Where the hell did that come from? Ruth thought. She kept her eyes on Jessie.

"My phone's in my jacket, over there," Jessie said. "He took it off me before he rolled me over the ledge."

"Don't listen to her!" Victor barked.

Ruth saw the jacket, its reflector stripes visible in the flickering light. She edged over to it. Knelt down and patted the pockets, all the time keeping her gun aimed at Jessie. She felt the rectangular solidity of the cell phone and pulled it out. To play the audio, she would have to look down. This meant taking her eye off Jessie. What should she do?

Ruth glanced at Victor who mouthed the word *Shoot*. Ruth wasn't going to do that unless she absolutely had to. Ruth straightened her legs and moved closer to Victor and Jessie, so she could better keep an eye on them.

"Where is the 911 recording?"

"In the audio folder."

The moment that Ruth looked down at the screen, Victor pounced.

CHAPTER SIXTY-FIVE

Ruth saw Victor lunge at her, and she reacted just in time. She jumped back so that Victor's fingers snatched at nothing but air. All those years as a cop had taught her to react quickly. She didn't even have time to consider why Victor was doing it; it was intuitive.

"No!" Jessie screamed. She fired.

It was like a firework exploding inside the cave. Victor flung himself to the ground and yelped in pain. For a second, Ruth thought her husband had been shot, then he rolled onto his back. There was no blood. The bullet hit the cave ceiling with a *ping*. Jessie was either a lousy shot or she had meant it as a warning.

Ruth kept her Smith & Wesson pistol trained on Jessie.

"Put your gun down, Jessie, before you kill somebody," Ruth said, her finger on the trigger.

Jessie looked as shocked as they did. Her pistol hand shook. "I didn't mean to... he moved... I thought he was going to... I'm sorry."

"She shot at me! For Christ's sake, do something!" Victor yelled.

"She aimed wide. Victor, please!"

"You almost got us killed!" Victor raged.

Jessie was shaking. "Please, just listen to the recording!"

In the commotion, Ruth had forgotten about Jessie's cell phone in her hand. She pressed play and put it on speaker. The voice of the 911 operator was loud and clear.

"Nine one one, what's your emergency?"

"There's been a terrible car accident," a man said. "He didn't make the turn. He… he skidded over the edge. Oh God! There was nothing I could do."

The roar of the waterfall made it difficult to hear the audio.

"Okay, sir, please stay calm. Can I have your name?" asked the operator.

"Hurry, he could be alive. Devil Mountain, Break or Bust Bend… I mean Falls Drive."

Was that Victor? Ruth thought. *Same baritone. Certainly a local person. Only a local would know the nickname Break or Bust Bend.*

"I need your name, sir," said the operator.

The caller hung up.

Jessie stared at Ruth, her eyes pleading with her. "Please tell me you recognize your husband's voice? He caused the accident, then fled. He pretended he was at the accident site when he made the call, but he wasn't. He waited until he was in town before he used a phone booth. Why would he do that? Why wouldn't he give his name?"

Ruth couldn't think. That was the problem. The recording was poor quality. The cave was noisy. Ruth was exhausted. And she didn't want to believe that Victor would lie. She hated to admit that the man on the recording had the same intonations, and made similar word choices, as Victor. She hadn't realized that she was staring at her husband with a deep frown until he started to vehemently deny it was him on the recording.

"Why didn't you…?" The words stuck in Ruth's throat. She coughed to clear the raspiness. "Why didn't you give your name?" she asked.

"For Christ's sake," Victor said, "that isn't me."

In her gut, Ruth knew it was. She told herself that the recording proved nothing. Victor was in shock. He panicked. He forgot to leave his contact details. It didn't prove that Victor killed Jessie's father. And there was no way that Victor was a serial killer. She would know, wouldn't she? She was a cop at heart, not some innocent civilian easily duped. Ruth's main problem right now was that Jessie was pointing a gun at them and the girl was in a highly emotional state.

"Jessie, listen to me," Ruth said. "This isn't the time to debate who made the 911 call. I came here to find both of you and now I've found you, we have to get out of here." She coughed. Was the cave getting smokier? "Please, Jessie, put the gun down. I promise nothing will happen to you." Ruth knew that she sounded scared, because she was. Even though the waterfall drowned out the crackle and roar of the wildfire, she knew it was out there and any minute it could head their way.

"We're going nowhere until you say you believe me," Jessie said. Her finger could so easily squeeze the trigger by mistake.

"Jessie, I can promise you Victor had nothing to do with the arson attacks."

"How do you know what he gets up to when you're asleep?"

"He was with me on the nights of the house fires."

As she said it, it struck Ruth that this wasn't true. She had seen him go to bed. She had seen him first thing in the morning. But ever since the bomb blast, she and Victor had slept in separate rooms. Initially it was so that she could get a good night's sleep to aid her recovery. Victor's snoring was incessant and loud. Then their sleeping arrangement became a routine, and she wasn't interested in sex. The damage to her body and her confidence had an impact on her sex drive. She felt ugly. She was damaged goods. Then there were the nightmares. The only way she could get a decent night's sleep was to take sleeping pills. If Victor had snuck out of the house at night, Ruth wouldn't have a clue. "What were you doing in our backyard when our house burst into flames?"

Jessie blinked several times, the confusion on her face seeming real. "I wasn't anywhere near your house."

"I saw you running away," Victor said. "We have two young boys. What kind of a monster tries to kill kids?"

"I didn't… I would never do that." Jessie took a step closer to Ruth. "I like you. You were kind to me and my dog. Why would I try to hurt the only… friend I have?"

"Christ!" Victor threw his arms up. "Isn't it obvious? Cuffy knew she was the arsonist, that's why she killed him. Paul Troyer wouldn't pay up for the water feature, so she killed him. Pat Wilmot died from a bullet identical to the ammunition Jessie used in her Glock. She torched Bill's place to hide the double murder. She's a frigging serial killer, Ruth!" Jessie mumbled the word *no*, but Victor went on in a booming voice, "Then she came after us, for whatever twisted reason a sick mind like hers fixates on. Do I have to continue?"

Ruth's mind had jumped to the report that Callan Bolt had shared with her. In it, Bolt identified two Seattle fires with the same MO as the recent house fires in Eagle Falls. Fires deliberately lit using accelerant. Doors locked, windows jammed with tiny wedges. At the time, Ruth hadn't recognized the names of the deceased in Seattle. Now one name rang a bell. Florence McKenzie who had lived down the road from them in Redmond.

"What was the name of the lady who didn't want you in the mother's group?" Ruth asked. "When we lived in Redmond." Victor looked at her blankly. "You know, when David was a toddler. All the other moms adored you, but she kicked up a stink about something. What was her name?"

"What's that got to do with anything?" Victor said, sounding exasperated. "We have to leave. Now."

"Humor me. In the end she left the group and started a vindictive campaign against you on Facebook. Who was she?"

"Florence McKenzie. Why?"

Florence, her partner, and their daughter died in a house fire the year before Ruth and Victor moved to Eagle Falls. Ruth began to feel very cold on the inside, as if her innards had frostbite. Was she seeing meaning where there was none? It could be a coincidence. Of course, it could.

"He killed Florence too, didn't he?" Jessie said.

"Okay, I've had enough," said Victor. "I'm leaving. If we leave together, she won't shoot. She likes you, Ruth."

Jessie looked as if she were about to cry. "I'll go with you, Ruth, but I keep the gun and you drive us to the Marymere sheriff's station."

Ruth glanced at the cave's entrance. She couldn't even see the steps outside, let alone the trees. It was like a smoky soup. Was the wildfire edging closer? She swallowed down a whimper of terror. Then she looked at Jessie, who looked equally terrified. But not of the fire—of her husband. "You have to trust me, Jessie. I won't let Victor or anyone hurt you. You have my word. The only way we can make it to Marymere is if you put your gun down and we walk out of here together."

"Trust you?" Jessie said. "Everybody I've trusted has let me down. Even you. You lured me into a trap at Cathedral Cove. You're as bad as him."

"That was wrong of me. I'm sorry. I honestly don't think you're the arsonist. I think you've been set up. Do I think my husband is behind it all? No. I have my suspicions about who is, but that doesn't matter now." Ruth was thinking of Ford and Marty, who were her prime suspects. "What matters is that we all stay alive. Jessie, please, I beg you, put the gun down."

Jessie looked from Ruth to Victor and shook her head. "How can I trust you when you're married to a killer?"

CHAPTER SIXTY-SIX

Jessie's arm muscles ached from holding the Glock up for so long. A bigger problem was the cramp in her trigger finger. At the best of times, Jessie was a lousy shot. Right now, her vision was impeded by the swollen bruise around one eye that throbbed like hell. Her body was battered and all out of energy after her battle to escape drowning. She was emotionally and physically broken. This was the worst time to make a life-or-death decision.

Should she trust Ruth and hand over her weapon? Ruth had lied to her. Lured her into a trap at Cathedral Cove. Someone had shot at her, and Jessie might have died. Now she understood that Ruth did what she did because of Victor's lies. Even so, could Ruth be trusted to keep Victor from killing her?

For days now, Jessie had existed on a knife edge. She had feared for her life, not knowing who, if anyone, she could trust. People she knew had been murdered, her dog was injured, her house gone, and every cop in the state was hunting her. It was all she could do to simply stand up, let alone think clearly. There was one thing she was certain about: Jessie wanted justice. For her poppy. For Pat and Rob. For the Troyer family. For Bill. And, for Cuffy. He had failed Jessie and Bill, but he didn't deserve to die.

It was the adrenaline that was keeping Jessie going. But how much longer would it last? And Victor was so convincing, so manipulative. What more could Jessie say to convince Ruth that her husband was a killer? She didn't blame Ruth for believing Victor. Ruth loved him. He was the father of their two kids. Perhaps he was a loving husband. So had the serial killer John Wayne Gacy been a loving husband, and yet he tortured and murdered thirty-three teen boys. Gacy's wife had refused to believe his guilt, despite the stench of the bodies beneath the crawl space under their house. Love could make people blind. Jessie believed that Ruth was a fair person, but her perception of Jessie was tainted by her husband's lies.

Jessie and Ruth were at a stalemate: Ruth pointed her gun at Jessie, and Jessie pointed hers at Victor. Just the three of them in a cave beneath a waterfall that, ironically, was right near the road where Poppy's car careened off the cliff and crashed into the valley. Maybe this was fate? But what the hell was Jessie going to do next?

"Do you have anything to tie his hands?" Jessie asked Ruth. "Do that and I'll put down my gun."

"I have cable ties. You put the gun on the floor first." Ruth coughed, a honking gritty sound.

Jessie felt a tug of sympathy for Ruth. It was the kind of cough that firefighters with damaged lungs suffered from. Ruth was sick and Jessie wanted to end their ordeal. But she was at a loss how to do it.

Think. What did I learn at college? Evidence. It's all about evidence. But what more proof do I have?

Victor's Mustang.

The wooden wedges. The accelerant.

If Ruth saw the evidence with her own eyes then she would have to believe her husband was a killer. But the car was a means of escape for Victor. Jessie mustn't give up her gun.

"For Christ's sake! Give me that gun," Victor yelled at Ruth. "I'll do it if you won't."

"What?" Ruth sounded flabbergasted.

"You're FBI," Victor said. "Nobody will doubt your word."

"No, Ruth, don't!" Jessie begged. "In the trunk of his car there's accelerant. Wooden wedges. It's what the arsonist used!"

Ruth blinked away some sweat that had trickled into her right eye. She was the only person keeping Jessie and Victor apart. If Ruth collapsed, there would be bloodshed.

"Is this true?" Ruth asked Victor. Ruth's skin had turned ghostly gray.

"No!" Victor said. "I'm your husband, for Christ's sake. I can't believe you'd ask me that."

"Ruth," Jessie shouted. She wanted Ruth's full attention. It was crunch time. There was only one way she could prove to Ruth that she was innocent, and it scared the hell out of her. If it failed, Jessie was as good as dead. "I'm going to trust you, okay? I believe you will do what's right. I'll put down my gun. But you have to give me your word that you won't let Victor have a gun. You cannot arm him. I will go with you to Marymere. But the deal is you keep Victor away from me. Do you promise?"

Ruth seemed to brighten. "I promise."

Jessie hesitated. Victor's expression was unreadable. What was going on in that psychopath's head? "And I drive Victor's car," she said. "He sits in the front with me. You, in the back with the gun."

"Okay," Ruth said, her breathing calming a little.

Jessie grasped the Glock with both hands. She took one hand off the pistol and raised it so that it was level with her shoulder, as a sign that she was surrendering. Her gun hand moved slowly to the ground, her eyes on Victor the whole time. She bent her knees and placed the weapon on the damp rock floor. Her fingers brushed the cold water of a puddle. She barely felt the water's chill because her fingers had gone numb from holding the gun still for so long. Then she straightened her knees until she was standing tall. Slowly she raised both hands above her shoulders.

There was a blur of movement. Jessie instinctively braced. Victor charged, but not at her. He tackled his wife as if he were a defensive back, tackling a rival quarterback. He threw both arms around her and his momentum sent Ruth tumbling sideways. She landed hard on the rock floor, her ankle at an awkward angle. Ruth gave a strangled scream, her Smith & Wesson tumbling from her hand. It rattled across the floor. Victor clawed at the semiautomatic, got a hold of it, and sat up. He aimed it at Jessie.

"Don't move a muscle," Victor said.

"Don't… Victor, don't," Ruth protested, breathless from her fall.

Victor scrambled up. The look he gave Jessie chilled her to her core: a terrifying mix of triumph and hatred. He now had all the power. Ruth and Jessie were unarmed, and Ruth was getting more incapacitated by the second. Near Jessie's feet, her Glock was only a few inches away. Could she grab it before he killed her?

"Don't even think about it," Victor said, anticipating Jessie's next move.

In a few strides Victor was so close that Jessie could smell his rancid sweat. He kicked her Glock out of reach. Jessie watched it skitter across the slippery surface and disappear into the tumult of water falling into the pool below.

The gun was lost. And so was Jessie.

Victor calmly removed his glasses and wiped their outer surface down the front of his shirt, then put them back on. "You lose," he said to Jessie. "I'm going to enjoy this."

Ruth didn't seem to hear. She was struggling to get up, unable to put pressure on her left foot. "What are you doing, Victor? I've twisted my ankle. Help me up, please!"

Victor gazed at her outstretched hand. He didn't take it.

"You don't want my help, Ruth. You never have."

"Of course, I do." Victor didn't budge. Ruth's expression suddenly changed, like she had been dazed and now she saw clearly. She lowered her hand. "Is it true? Do you have accelerant and wedges in your car?"

"It takes courage to do what has to be done," Victor said. "And your affection for this loser has clouded your judgment. It's down to me now. I'll save us because you're too weak to do it."

"Answer my question, God damn you!" Ruth demanded. Despite the anger in her voice, her eyes were watery and her lower lip trembled.

Jessie wanted to go to Ruth. To comfort her. Ruth had finally worked out that her husband was a killer and she looked totally crushed by it.

"Shut up, Ruth, I need to think," said Victor.

"Don't speak to me like that!"

"It was all about revenge, wasn't it, Victor?" Jessie said. "You locked them in and watched them burn."

"You shot Pat Wilmot?" Ruth asked, her eyes pleading with Victor to deny it.

"I don't have a gun, you stupid bitch!" Victor snapped at Ruth.

"Oh my God," Ruth said, "you used *my gun*."

"I said, shut up."

"You lit *all* the house fires?" Ruth asked, incredulous.

Victor stared at the cascading water and didn't answer. He was planning their deaths, Jessie was sure of it.

Ruth continued, "And the house fires in Seattle. You lit those too? You're the common factor. Seattle and Eagle Falls."

"What's the matter, Ruthie?" Victor taunted. "All these years you've played the superhero, the lady with the badge who charges in and saves people. Now you expect me to believe you're the quivering broken-hearted wife? Give me a fucking break."

"Let Ruth go," Jessie begged. "She loves you. She won't tell anyone. Your kids need their mom."

"And what the hell would you know?" Victor said. "Get Ruth up off the floor and both of you stand over there." Victor pointed the gun at the precipice. "Move!" he shouted.

Jessie hurried to Ruth's side. "Put your arm around my shoulders," Jessie said. "I can take your weight."

With Jessie's help, Ruth managed to get up, placing all her weight on her one good leg.

"Victor, please," Ruth said. "What you've done is wrong. But I'm your wife. Let me help you find a good lawyer, get a fair trial. You need help. I know there is good inside you. I know that you love me and the kids."

"Over there! Now!" Victor yelled.

Jessie felt Ruth recoil from him. She guided Ruth to the precipice. They stopped a couple of feet from the edge where the wall of water would surely crush them. *He's going to shoot us here. Our bodies will drop fifty feet and get sucked beneath the underwater ledge. We will never be found. Victor will get away with murder again, despite Cuffy's dying declaration. He'll blame me for everything.*

Victor was pacing. "Why didn't you listen, Ruth?" His face was blotchy with anger. "I said stay away from her. I could have handled everything. I could have made it all go away." He waved the gun about recklessly.

"Why, Victor?" Ruth asked. "We have a good life. We have beautiful children. We came to Eagle Falls because you wanted to be here. Why kill those poor people?"

"Because they deserved it!" he shouted.

Ruth's face was white, as if she had been drained of blood. A beat passed before Ruth responded. "Why did they deserve it, Victor?"

Was Ruth buying them time? For what? Victor would shoot them if they bolted, and with Ruth's injured ankle, she couldn't run even if she tried. Jessie had no weapon. She looked around the cave for inspiration and saw nothing useful.

"Paul laughed at me when I confronted him about his brat bullying David," Victor said, kicking a pebble across the floor. "He said David was a wimp, just like me. He said I wasn't a real man. Don't you see, Ruth? Eric bullied David, just like Paul bullied me. I couldn't let that go on." He stopped moving and stared at Ruth. "Paul had a name for me when we were kids. You want to know what it was?"

"Tell me," Ruth said.

"Lard ass. I was a fat kid and he did everything he could to humiliate me. He took my glasses and stomped on them. When Mom told the principal about the bullying, it just got worse. That's when I set the school alight. My first fire." Victor smiled, as if he were watching a beautiful sunrise. "It was amazing. For the first time in my young life, I was powerful. I will never forget that moment. How good it made me feel."

"I thought Marty Spaan did that," Ruth said.

"That jerk? No. It was me." There was pride in his voice that made Jessie feel queasy.

"And Rob and Pat?" Ruth asked.

"I worked for them, back when they had the number one real estate business in the area. I was their star agent and Rob's favorite. One day he invited me to join a business venture. That's what he called it. Told me how the foreclosure fraud worked, not that he called it that. Said he'd give me fifteen percent of the profit if I did the scamming. Said I could make hundreds of thousands of dollars. I was hungry for money back then. So I did it. And finding the targets was too easy. I knew who was behind with their mortgage payments. In a small town everybody knows everybody's business."

"Bill lost everything because of you," Jessie said. "How could you do that?"

Victor shrugged. "I don't care. It's that simple."

"So why kill them?" Ruth asked.

"Rob got soft in his old age. He told the sheriff he wanted to give Bill money. You know, to make up for what he'd done. I couldn't let that happen. If Bill had ever worked out where the money came from, Rob might have implicated me." He grinned.

"What a fire that was! The adrenaline rush! There's nothing else like it."

Ruth made a choking noise. Listening to her husband say such hideous things must have made her feel sick to her core.

"And me?" Ruth asked in a strangled voice. "Why marry a cop?"

While they were talking, Jessie looked around her, desperate to find a way out. Could she grab Victor's gun before he shot her?

"Enough talk," Victor said. "Take a step back! Both of you."

Jessie glanced behind her. They were a couple of feet from the edge of the cave floor. If they stepped back any farther, the force of the water would knock them off balance and they would fall to their deaths. Jessie couldn't survive the fall a second time and Ruth was too weak to fight the currents.

"Please, Victor," Ruth pleaded. "David, Noah, think of them. They need a mom *and* a dad. I'll stand by you. I love you."

Victor shook his head. "Too late for that. Move back!"

"Not again," Jessie said, vehemently shaking her head. "I don't want to drown. Just shoot me and get it over and done with."

"No!" shouted Ruth. "Leave her alone. Talk to me, Victor. If you're going to kill me, at least tell me why you married me. Did you ever love me?"

"Why couldn't you let me have my moment of glory? It always had to be you, didn't it? Did you ever think about me? My life as the invisible husband. The loser without a career. My buddies stopped calling me, my life was nothing but bake sales and mothers' groups. *You* did this to me! *You!* Do you know what kept me going, *Ruth-ie*?" He injected such malice into the name that Jessie shivered. "The killing! The planning. Watching their houses burn. Hearing the screams. It was sublime." He looked up, as if he were communing with God.

A tear trickled down Ruth's cheek. "Why did you marry me then?"

"I married you *because* you were a cop. No one would ever suspect a cop's husband of murder. Marrying you meant I could keep doing what gave me the greatest pleasure."

Ruth doubled over. She gasped for air. Jessie put a protective arm around her.

"Where's your inhaler?" Jessie asked.

Ruth managed to gasp, "Pocket."

Jessie looked at Victor. "Can I get her inhaler?"

"No point."

Ruth made sucking noises as she tried to get enough air. "You tried to sabotage"—inhale—"my FBI application."

"What do you know!" he said sarcastically. "You finally worked it out. The FBI job meant you were never home. You had babies and then expected me to stay home and play mom."

"I don't understand, we discussed…"

"Let me spell it out for you. I hated every minute at home playing mom. It was demeaning." He yelled at her. "You emasculated me!"

Suddenly he lunged at Ruth. Jessie thought he was going to shove Ruth over the precipice, and she instinctively gripped Ruth's arm to prevent her fall. Instead, he came up behind his wife, wrapped an arm around her throat and jerked her head back, forcing her torso upward so that her feet couldn't touch the ground.

"No!" Jessie screamed.

Victor tightened his grip around Ruth's throat. "You choked the life out of me. Now it's your turn."

"Let her go!"

Jessie grabbed Victor's gun hand, trying to wrench the pistol from his grip. But Victor was stronger than he appeared. He broke free from her grasp and used the gun like brass knuckles and hit her in the throat with it. Suddenly Jessie couldn't breathe either.

L.A. Larkin

She staggered back, slipped and fell. For one terrifying moment she thought she had fallen through the curtain of water and into nothing but air. She landed with a thud on her butt, water pounding her head and shoulders.

A glint of light reflected off metal. To her right was her Glock. It hadn't fallen over the ledge as she had thought. She reached out, her fingers cold and trembling. She felt the gun's solidity. It was so wet, would it even fire? No time. Jessie swung it around and gripped it with both hands.

"Let Ruth go!" she shouted.

Ruth's face was red and swollen. Saliva dribbled from her purple lips. Her feet dangled above the floor. Victor was smiling. His eyes glistened. He looked elated.

"You'll miss," Victor said. "You're a lousy shot."

Hair glued to her sodden face, water lashing her head, her grip on the trigger slipping, Jessie fired. *Boom!*

Blood spattered outward. Jessie watched it turn the cave's ceiling and puddles red. Ruth and Victor dropped together, like felled trees. Jessie was momentarily deafened. Even the roar of the water seemed to stop. What had she done? She stared at the two bodies. Ruth lay on top of Victor. Neither person moved.

I've killed both of them!

Jessie's gun fell from her palm and she crawled up to the bodies. They were lying in a growing pool of blood. Whose blood? Jessie heard a keening sound and realized it was from her own lips. *Get the gun. He might be alive.* She tore it from Victor's fingers. He didn't resist. She watched his fingers retract in a creepy, lifeless way. She couldn't bear to touch him. Not even to check for a pulse. Tucking the Smith & Wesson in the back of her waistband, Jessie turned her attention to Ruth. Ruth's blond hair was covered in blood. Her eyes were closed.

"Ruth! Say something! Oh no, please, God! No!"

Jessie leaned her face close to Ruth's lips, hoping to feel warm breath. When that didn't work, she placed her index and middle fingers on Ruth's neck to one side of her windpipe. Jessie couldn't find a pulse.

She whimpered, "Breathe!"

There was something like a beat, or so she thought, but her hand was shaking so much she wasn't certain. She shifted her fingers a little and pressed harder. Then she felt a pulse clearly, like a minuscule punch.

Jessie laughed with joy.

Ruth was alive, but she wasn't responsive.

Who took the bullet? Did it pass through Ruth and into Victor?

Victor's head lay at an angle away from her. She had no choice: she had to touch the monster. She crawled close to his head and reached out to turn his face so she could look at it. The touch of his warm, damp skin made her gag. That's when she saw the dark red hole in his forehead, just above his left eyebrow. Victor's glasses were cracked and covered in blood spatter. She took them off him, wanting to see his eyes. He stared back at her. No, not at her. At nothing. There was no life in them.

Relieved, Jessie turned her attention back to Ruth. She needed urgent help. Who would come? The town was Armageddon. If there were any emergency response teams left, they would have their hands full.

"Don't die, Ruth! Please don't die!"

Jessie pulled out her phone and dialed 911. The signal was weak, but an operator answered. Jessie explained her location, and that one, possibly two adults had been shot. The operator told her that the ambulance service would not be able to reach her. Jessie hung up. She dialed the sheriff's office landline, knowing it would be diverted to one of the deputies' cell phones. Kinsley answered. He listened to her. He asked about the fire situation around the falls. Jessie stepped outside the cave and looked into the smoke-filled air. She couldn't see the orange glow of fire nearby. Kinsley told her that he and Deputy Wang were the only people left in the town, except for firefighters. They would attempt to come to her aid.

"But if we can't get to you, stay where you are. Wait it out."

Jessie sat next to Ruth and held her limp hand. She spoke to the unconscious woman who was her only friend.

"We'll be okay, I promise. I won't let you down."

CHAPTER SIXTY-SEVEN

It was Christmas Day and raining hard, as it had been for weeks. Nobody cared. In fact, many said it was what the town needed. To be washed clean so it could start anew.

It was three months since a third of the town and twenty thousand hectares of forest were consumed by the worst wildfire in Washington State's history. The residents still reeled at the death toll: nine men, five women, four of whom were firefighters. And that figure didn't include the Troyers, the Wilmots, Bill Moran, Marcus Harstad, or "Big John" Cuffy. Those deaths were investigated by Special Agent Samson and his team at the FBI. Samson confirmed that Victor Sullivan, deceased, was a serial arsonist responsible for twelve fires and thirty-one deaths, spanning the Eagle Falls and Seattle areas. He also confirmed that Cuffy was complicit in concealing acts of foreclosure fraud, murder, and arson committed by Victor, as well as failing to protect Jessie Lewis from domestic violence. Soon after this announcement, Cuffy's wife and son left town, bound for Montreal. Money and volunteers poured into Eagle Falls and the job of rebuilding the town began.

But the rain still tasted like ash. Whole streets were charred wastelands, and the "black mountains," as the kids now called them, were bereft of trees and wildlife. There would be no new, green shoots until spring.

Instead of crushing the folks who lived there, the tragedy brought them closer together.

"Thanks for inviting us," Ruth said, looking at Jessie, who was seated next to her at the table. "Noah and David are struggling to come to terms with what happened. Having Christmas lunch with you… Well, I haven't seen them this happy in a long time." Ruth looked at the smiling faces around a rectangular table laid for eight in the fire station's kitchen-cum-dining-room. Noah and David had just sat down after a tour of the fire trucks. The boys were grinning, their eyes popping with excitement.

Jessie's new family was the crew of the fire station where she now worked full-time. Bartie had become the station's mascot. He had his own coat with the station's insignia on it and when the firefighters returned from an incident, Bartie would always greet them with tail wags. Her dog sat next to her chair, his eyes focused on the big bird that had just been taken out of the oven.

"I'm glad you came," Jessie said. "You guys mean a lot to me."

Blake Jones, who had recently transferred from Seattle Fire Station 36, carried a huge roasting pan to the table. He wore a black apron with the words FIREFIGHTERS ARE ALWAYS HOT on the front.

"Hope you're hungry!" he said, laying the turkey on a couple of mats. Everyone leaned in to take a look. In the roasting pan was a golden turkey; cocktail sausages wrapped in bacon; pork, chestnut, and fruit meatballs; roasted potatoes; carrots and parsnips cut lengthways; and Brussels sprouts. "Traditional English Christmas lunch with all the trimmings." His parents were British. "I need a volunteer to help me serve." His eyes came to rest on Noah. "I could do with a hand, my friend."

Noah blushed, then rushed to Jones's side to assist.

"I'll carve and you hand out the plates, okay? Then everyone helps themselves to the trimmings."

Noah nodded eagerly.

Lloyd Mattias, the newly appointed station captain, who was as strong as an ox and as wide as he was tall, carried a jug of gravy to the table. "David, my friend," he said to Ruth's youngest, who looked dejected because he hadn't been picked, "Can you go get the creamy mashed potato and the serving spoons? Over there, on the countertop." He pointed.

David leapt up.

"Everyone's been so kind," Ruth said to Jessie. "I thought… well, I thought we wouldn't be welcome. After Victor… you know."

"They know it wasn't your fault. You were a victim, just as much as I was. He fooled everybody." Jessie glanced at Ruth. "Are you still thinking of going back to Seattle?"

"I don't know. I thought it would be best for the kids. A new start." Ruth's gaze came to rest on Noah, busy handing out plates laden with succulent turkey. "Noah has been the hardest hit. I think David's too young to fully understand."

"You must do what's best for your family, but I would really miss you if you decided to go," Jessie said.

Ruth took Jessie's hand and squeezed it. "I've been offered a job at the Bureau. A desk job. My lungs aren't up to much else. We need the money, and my mom can help with the kids." Jessie's smile faded. Ruth must have noticed. "You would be welcome to visit any time."

"I'd like that." Jessie paused to look at Noah and David who were busy assisting Jones and Mattias. They were far enough away not to overhear their conversation. "How are you holding up, Ruth?"

"I have good days and bad days. You know the worst of it? I feel so angry all the time. My kids will have to live with what Victor did for the rest of their lives. They'll always be the serial killer's kids. I'm considering changing my surname and theirs. Back to my maiden name. Jackson."

"Ruth Jackson. I like it."

Noah came up to them and gave them each a plate, then disappeared. Ruth started to help herself to some roast potatoes. "Like some?"

"Yes, please."

Ruth dropped two roast potatoes on Jessie's plate, then served herself. "I've been meaning to tell you," Ruth said, serving them both some baked Brussels sprouts. "You found Victor's pen on Pat and Rob's driveway, remember? Although you didn't know at the time that it was Victor's." She paused. Put down the serving spoon. "God! Even saying his name makes me feel sick."

"Tell me another time," Jessie said, stabbing a bacon-wrapped sausage and dropping it on Ruth's plate. "Enjoy your lunch."

Ruth shook her head. "I want to tell you. The pen was from the Commerce Bank of Washington. It turns out that there were four people in Eagle Falls with a Commerce bank account. Cuffy, Susie, Ford, and Victor. Victor opened his account in 2002. That's where he kept his share of the money he fraudulently obtained from the scams. I had no idea it existed. We banked with Bank of America." She turned her head and looked Jessie in the eye. "He used that money as a deposit for our first house. I didn't think to question where the money came from. He said it was from a savings account, which he then shut down. If I'd known…" Her voice trailed away.

"You didn't know, Ruth. Stop blaming yourself." Jessie looked down at her plate of hot food. She had been meaning to tell Ruth something and this was as good a time as any. "I've been meaning to say that I never meant to kill him. I'm sorry."

"You saved my life, Jessie. There's nothing to apologize for."

Lloyd stood at the head of the table and tapped a knife against a water glass. "I'd like to say a few words." There were groans. "Okay, okay. I'll keep it short." Everybody laughed. Lloyd was known for his long speeches. "We've been through one hell of a year. We lost four brave firefighters to Black Sunday and I'd like to remember them for a moment: Clyde Hudson, Maria Ramirez, Sammy Bloomberg, Ernie Borlaug. They, and you, saved this town and we honor them." There was a moment's silence. "And now I'd like to welcome rookie Solomon Dale." Everybody cheered and the young man in question shifted in his seat with embarrassment. "And I want to say, Jessie Lewis, welcome back." Cheers went up. "Now tuck in, everybody, and Merry Christmas!"

It was fair to say that the firefighters ate quickly. At any time they might be called out and bolting food had become a routine. Jessie gave Bartie some turkey when nobody was looking. She had just finished her meal when her phone vibrated in her pants pocket. It was Sheriff Kinsley. His message said that he was outside and wanted to have a quick word. It was Kinsley's day off and Deputy Wang was on duty. Jessie showed the message to Ruth.

"What do you think that's about?" Jessie said.

"I think I know. It's a good thing. Go let the poor guy in. He must be soaked."

"What have you been up to, Ruth?" Jessie gave her friend a playful nudge in the shoulder and went to the fire station's main door with Bartie close at heel. Kinsley stepped inside quickly, his rain jacket dripping wet. He wasn't in uniform, so this was an informal visit. Jessie found it hard to believe that only twelve weeks ago she was being hunted by Kinsley as a murder suspect.

"Happy holiday!" he said. He had under his arm a huge box of chocolates and two milk chocolate peanut-butter-filled candy canes. "The box is for everyone. The candy canes are for Noah and David."

"The boys will love them. Thank you. Come through. There's plenty of food left. Why don't you join us?"

Kinsley undid his sodden coat and peeled it off, hanging it on a rack near the door. "I'll say a quick hi, but I've got my wife and kids waiting at home. I'm here because I wanted to talk to you."

Jessie felt a twinge of nervousness. Her relationship with the sheriff's department had improved since Kinsley was appointed sheriff. Ruth had made a statement that Jessie shot Victor to save Ruth's life. Also, Jude Deleon had confirmed that Marcus Harstad was a violent man who had beaten and nearly killed Jessie and Jude. This, and forensic evidence, had confirmed that Jessie killed Marcus because she feared for her life. She was cleared of all charges.

"Okay, shoot." Jessie rested her hand on her dog's head. She found it comforting.

"I wouldn't blame you if you have a very poor view of the sheriff's office. But I'm in charge now and I'm determined to weed out any bad apples. I need people I can trust. Brave people, who will do the right thing when it really matters. I'm one person down and I'd like you to apply for a deputy's position."

Jessie laughed. "You're kidding, right?"

He stared back at her with a serious expression. "You have a degree in criminal justice. Don't let it go to waste. I want you to help me rebuild trust in the sheriff's office. Will you at least think about it?"

If Jessie knew one thing, it was that once someone had betrayed your trust, it was really hard to believe in them again. But she had trusted Ruth in a life-or-death situation, and it had worked out. So she understood Kinsley's problem. Would the community ever trust Kinsley and his deputies again?

"Sure, I'll think about it. But I've got a job here. I like being a firefighter."

Kinsley followed Jessie along a corridor, past the equipment room, then the bathrooms and into the communal area and kitchen. Heads turned as Kinsley entered the room. Lloyd welcomed him. Kinsley held up the box of chocolates and the two candy canes and said, "I come bearing gifts."

While Noah and David tore the wrapping off their candy canes, Kinsley went around the table wishing everyone a great Christmas, then he left to join his family.

Jessie sat down next to Ruth and gave her a knowing grin. "You knew, didn't you?"

"Yes. He asked me what I thought about the idea and I said that I would support you all the way. I hope you said yes."

"I said I would think on it."

Ruth pulled from her bag a present wrapped in festive red and green paper. "Happy Christmas," Ruth said, handing Jessie the box.

"I was going to drop around with my gifts when my shift's done."

"That would be lovely but open yours now."

Jessie tore off the paper. Inside the box was her father's antique pistol, which she had pawned in Marymere.

"But how did you find it?"

"It doesn't matter."

"Thank you," Jessie said, her eyes welling up with tears of happiness.

CHAPTER SIXTY-EIGHT

It was New Year's Day and Jude Deleon gave Jessie a hug.

"Thanks for stopping by," Jude said.

"Are you sure you don't want help with the packing?" Jessie asked.

"It's almost done," Jude said, clinging to Jessie. "Thank you for freeing me from Marcus."

The two victims of Marcus's sadistic abuse stood in the hallway of their abuser's lakeside house and held each other a moment longer. The floor around them was littered with packing paper, tape, bubble wrap, and boxes. Jude was moving to a new house tomorrow; she couldn't wait to get out of there.

"Thank you for speaking up," Jessie said in Jude's ear. "That took some courage."

The women separated. Jude studied Jessie's face. Gone were the furtive glances and the hunched shoulders of a woman who had been scorned by the folks she loved. Jessie's skin glowed, her movements were relaxed and best of all, she smiled.

"I was a total bitch to you. I'm so sorry," Jude said in a stammering voice. "Fear makes you do terrible things." She corrected herself. "*I* did terrible things. I'll never forgive myself for the lies I spread about you."

"All water under the bridge. He's gone and we can start again without being afraid." Jessie's eyes wandered up the stairs to the living area. "Don't you think it's kind of ironic that his house survived the fire?"

"I thought that too. His sister is selling it and hoping for a lot of money. I say, good luck with that. I mean, who wants to buy a killer's house?"

"I hear Marcus didn't make a will?" Jessie said.

"That's right. I wouldn't want anything of his anyway. I'm just glad it's all over. Marcus, Victor, and Cuffy are gone for good, and you've been exonerated."

Jessie turned to look at Jude, her boots squeaking on the damp porch floor. "There's one puzzle the sheriff's office hasn't solved. How could Victor have shot at Cuffy and me at his shooting range, when Ruth swears he was with her at the time?"

Jude shrugged. "Didn't someone also fire at you at Cathedral Cove? Must be the same guy."

"Turns out a rookie deputy fired by mistake at the beach. But nobody knows who tried to kill Cuffy at his rifle range."

"Who cares? They're gone and good riddance."

"I guess we'll never know," said Jessie. "See you around."

Jessie got into her pickup and drove away.

Jude shut the door and gazed at the empty boxes that she still had to pack. She checked her sewing room to make sure she hadn't left anything behind, then wandered into Marcus's weight room. His punching bag still hung from the ceiling and his dumbbells were neatly stacked on a rack. A towel he used to wipe the sweat from his face and neck was draped over the rack, just as he had left it. The smell of him made her gag. There was still a hole in the plaster where Marcus had punched a fist through it during one of his fits of temper. Jude would clear out all her possessions and leave everything else for his sister to sort out.

In the corner was a bench press. She shoved it to one side and knelt. Using a fingernail, she scratched at the corner tip of the carpet. When she had enough to grip, she tugged it up. Beneath the carpet, the floorboards had been cut to form a trap door with a circular metal ring recessed into it. She slid two fingers under that metal ring and pulled. The rectangular door came away, revealing a shallow recess approximately three feet long. In it was a black, waterproof bag. Jude pulled it out and unzipped it. She took out the telescopic hunting rifle, leaving the stand and ammunition boxes inside. The rifle was a beauty and so easy to use. Marcus had spent a fortune on the state-of-the-art scope, which basically meant he couldn't miss. She ran a finger along the barrel. Should she chuck it in the lake or keep it, she wondered? Marcus was dead, so he wouldn't miss it. Victor was dead so he couldn't deny causing the Devil Mountain fire with a stray bullet. And Cuffy? Well, Victor had done her a favor killing him, although it was a pity that it hadn't been her bullet that had put an end to the misogynist bastard's life.

Her finger now ran the length of the scope. Jude was a good shot. Marcus had taken her deer hunting often enough. Jude should have managed to kill Cuffy at his shooting range. But because of Jessie turning up unexpectedly, Jude had had to fire her first shot wide. Missing her target like that had made Jude angry with herself and she found it hard to concentrate. She'd been impatient with her second shot and fired before Cuffy was in the center of her crosshairs, and by the third, he was in deep cover. She reckoned it was that third bullet striking granite that caused the spark. Just one spark and Devil Mountain went up in flames.

The night before, Cuffy had dropped by to tell her that he was going to delete her complaint against her abuser. She was making him look incompetent, he had said, because it was now obvious that he had failed to adequately investigate Jessie's claims of domestic violence. Jude couldn't allow Cuffy to do that. Marcus was dead, but the whole town had to know the truth about the monster they had idolized for so long. She had reasoned, rightly, that with Cuffy out of the picture, their claims against Marcus would be taken seriously. She had meant to kill Cuffy. She had never imagined that her bullet would cause a wildfire.

Jude put the rifle back in the bag and carried it upstairs, where she buried it beneath some clothes she had packed into a suitcase. That suitcase would come with her in the car. Who knew when the hunting rifle might come in handy someday?

A LETTER FROM L.A. LARKIN

I am delighted that you chose my novel *The Safe Place*. Of all the central characters I have created, I think that Jessie Lewis is the one I love most. If you enjoyed her story and would like to keep up to date with my latest releases, just sign up at the following link. Your email address will never be shared, and you can unsubscribe at any time.

www.bookouture.com/la-larkin

The Safe Place is not just about the terrifying threat of a killer who uses fire to cover up his murders. It's also about a domestic abuse victim who isn't believed, and an unlikely friendship that blossoms between her and Ruth Sullivan, a retired FBI agent. The story is set in a small town that is brimming with secrets and lies. I hope you cheered on Jessie and Ruth as they got closer and closer to the truth and that you enjoyed the plot twists.

I'd love to hear what you think about *The Safe Place*. What was your favorite part of the book? What was the biggest surprise? Which was the scariest moment? Would you like to read more novels with Jessie in them? Please give me your feedback on my social media and through book reviews. Authors like me need reviews, especially on Amazon, so if you loved *The Safe Place* please, please take a minute or two to write a review.

Thank you so much for your support!
L.A. Larkin

LALarkinAuthor

@la_larkin_author

@lalarkinauthor

4174398.L_A_Larkin

www.lalarkin.com

ACKNOWLEDGMENTS

Writing a novel when most of the world is still in lockdown has been a challenging experience. It inevitably restricted my ability to travel and to interview people face to face. But the isolation kept me focused and the key event in this book—wildfire—is based on friends' firsthand experiences. I live in a city and even here the wildfires had an impact. One day I woke up to find the sky was the color of a bruised peach and ash was raining down on my house. The air was so smoky I couldn't go outside without a face mask and even then I couldn't stop coughing. Wildfires are terrifying and the toll on people, wildlife and forests is devastating. People I know lost their homes and almost lost their lives. I salute the incredible courage of firefighters everywhere and I dedicate this novel to them.

I want to thank my publisher, Helen Jenner, and all the wonderful editors, designers, proofreaders, and publicity and digital marketing experts at Bookouture, including Noelle Holten, Kim Nash, Peta Nightingale, Melanie Price, Alex Crow, Alexandra Holmes, Anne O'Brien, and Kelsie Marsden. I also wish to thank my editor Ian Hodder and my friend Selina Power for her invaluable advice on my social media and website. I would be lost without her cheery voice at the other end of the phone.

This book may not have been written if I hadn't received a grant from the Society of Authors and the Authors' Foundation. I thank them from the bottom of my heart for their support and encouragement. I also thank my literary agent, Phil Patterson, who never seems to sleep, and we somehow manage to have the best conversations when he's out walking his dog in the dead of night.

Thank you to my first readers, my husband, Michael Larkin, and my friend, David Gaylor, and to my brother, Nic Young for his support and love, and to my friends and family for cheering me on.

Congratulations to Penny Gilkes, who signed up to receive my newsletter and in so doing won a competition to have her name as a character in this book. And lastly, a huge thank you to you, my readers. Your feedback on my books on social media and in reviews means the world to me. Please keep them coming and happy reading!